Widow's Fire

Widow's Fire

A Widows & Shadows Mystery

Michelle Bennington

Author Photo Credit: Michelle Bennington

First edition

ISBN: 978-1-68512-766-4

Cover art by Level Best Designs

This book was professionally typeset on Reedsy.
Find out more at reedsy.com

Chapter One

U gh. *Franklin Smithwaite, Lord Thornley. Despicable man.* Ravenna Gordon, Lady Birchfield, couldn't stand the thought of being in his presence again. She hadn't dealt with him in years, since she'd worked at the Drury Lane theater, where he had enjoyed taking advantage of the actresses and chorus girls. He wasn't alone in such behavior; powerful and wealthy men often predated upon women who were too poor and powerless to say no, fend them off, or hold them to account. She had first encountered him in her chorus girl days. She and her colleagues giggled and sneered behind his back, labeling him The Great Fondler. While he had worked his way through most of the chorus line and primary actresses, she'd made it her sole mission to avoid him.

Even her lady's maid, Charlotte Hart, had said earlier that morning, her Scottish accent thickening in her enmity, "I can't believe you're having dealings with that man or his family. I detest the sight of him." She shuddered and screwed up her face as though she'd stepped in muck. "The very thought of him." She unwittingly tightened the wrap of Ravenna's plaits.

"I don't have a choice, Hart. The Thornleys have donated an enormous amount of money to the charity, and Lady Thornley insisted on hosting the event. Reverend Howarth accepted the offer before I knew anything about it. And he knows nothing of these inner politics. He saw only a benefactor."

1

Yet, as Ravenna stood in the receiving line, her scalp aching from the tight braids, she realized this was the way of the world: the rich and powerful balanced and eased their consciences with philanthropy in equal measure to their dark secrets. And those dedicated to true charity were often put in uncomfortable positions of having to accept such wicked, double-edged philanthropy—or, in their ignorance, were used as philanthropic shields. Which explained why Ravenna now stood in Thornley Hall, wedged between Lord Thornley and his mother as co-hostess for the opening of The Spitalfields Penitent House for Prostitutes, commonly known as The Penitent House. It was a charity Ravenna, and her women's club, *Les Roses Noires*, had been deeply involved in establishing for the past year. However, in spite of Thornley's artful though generous donations, Ravenna would endure much in order to help the women of The Penitent House succeed in reclaiming their lives.

As part of their philanthropy, Dowager Lady Mildreth Thornley insisted on hosting the celebration at Thornley Hall. Further, her son, Lord Franklin, who had recently returned from New South Wales, wanted to astonish the women with a talk of his travels and an exhibition of an artifact he'd recovered.

So here Ravenna stood with the Thornleys, smiling though her skin crawled and resolving to focus on the charity, the women who would be helped, and the work she and her women's club had accomplished. Ravenna and the Thornleys received about twenty former prostitutes of every age and disposition, along with several charitable aristocrats and clergy, as they filed into the ballroom at Thornley Hall.

White velvet drapes in the ballroom hung parted to allow the sunlight to pour in through long windows and drench the walls lined with grand mirrors, crystal chandeliers, and gold wall sconces. The furniture had been pushed back against the walls and a buffet banquet had been set in honor of the occasion. Roast suckling and goose, fish, vegetables, bread, cheese, fruits, and tall floral centerpieces from the Thornley greenhouse loaded the table.

The Penitent House women were outfitted in cast-off dresses and slippers donated by the charitable society doyennes. Many of them had likely never seen such fine furnishings and bountiful food.

Ravenna knew too well the wonder, the awkwardness, ache, and desperation many of these women likely felt. She, too, had come from poor, immigrant stock, forced to seek shelter with family in London to escape the massacres in her homeland of Ireland. She watched some of the girls, thin and gaunt, hover over the food table like stray cats around fish stalls. Her mind rolled back to the emptiness and desperate hunger that once lived under her own ribs as she'd searched for work when she'd first arrived in London. Her Aunt Brendae had provided only a breakfast of porridge or toast with a glass of small ale, which was all she could afford. Ravenna had been thankful for even that, knowing any other food she received would come from her work or kind strangers. There were many nights she went to bed hungry and dreamed of food.

Another group of women passed in front of her, pointing, whispering, and staring at the room décor with awe and admiration. Often, their shoulders slumped as they shrank into themselves. She remembered that shrinking feeling, too. How small she'd felt among the tall and mighty buildings of London. Coming from a village and expansive fields, the city buildings made her feel tiny and closed in like a bug squeezing through the cracks in her Aunt Brendae's floors. Her hunger, paired with the crush of people, carriages, animals, noise, and filth, resulted in a yawning desperation.

Though she'd married well and had enjoyed the comforts of nobility these six years, the memory of seeing prostitutes for the first time lived just under the surface of her mind. She had just come from the servant registry offices looking for work when she noticed the women like scarecrows lingering in doorways and alleys. They'd both frightened and saddened her in their garish makeup, pox-marked skin, and slovenly half-dress. A madam tried to lure her to a brothel with the promise of more money than she'd ever seen. She pulled from the woman's grip and ran to the nearby Drury Theatre to hide. Ravenna never imagined that one day she would be shaking hands with street women and smiling into their faces with true happiness and an offer of hope for a future.

The room echoed with laughter from a group of girls making faces with each other over their reflections in the mirrors. They resembled little delicate pastries in a confectioner's window in their pastel yellows, blues, pinks, whites, and greens. The laughter snapped Ravenna from her dark reverie. She shuddered and relaxed into her gratitude. Her heart filled with hope that this would be one of the most memorable days of their lives, motivating them to continue working on their reformation and aim for a better life.

Reverend Howarth arrived with the mistress of The Penitent House, Mariah Vincent, and a younger pastor unfamiliar to Ravenna. The younger pastor had a black eye patch over his left eye.

In the past year that Ravenna had been working to help establish The Penitent House, she'd grown fond of Mariah's steady, quiet nature and apparent good humor and had taken a special interest in her case. At only twenty, Mariah had come from the streets to live at The Penitent House, earning a small stipend as housemistress and seamstress with hopes of returning home one day to provide for her parents and siblings.

Ravenna's own cast-off rose gown with ivory lace, once her favorite, draped Mariah's slender form. She'd given it to Mariah because she didn't know if she had the heart to wear it again. Ravenna's husband had died eleven months ago, and though she could begin coming out of her black widow's weeds, she wasn't quite ready—in spite of her late husband's behavior. When she had discovered he'd ordered the attack on her village in County Wexford, she briefly entertained the notion of dressing in bright red and burning her widow's weeds—and the life-sized portrait of him hanging over the fireplace. But her heart warred against her. She still loved him. And he had always been an exceptional husband to her. He had been following directives from the prime minister and the rest of the cabinet. Then, when her stepson died, she couldn't cast off her weeds. He deserved at least six months of mourning time and remembrance. Besides, her black widow's garb had become a sort of armor, a defense against a world she wasn't ready to fully re-embrace.

Taking Mariah's hands, Ravenna beamed, pleased in the joy the dress had given another. "You look lovely. The dress is beautiful on you." Mariah's creamy skin glowed against the rose muslin like blooms in the snow. "And your hair is beautiful. I must know your secrets." Ravenna admired Mariah's chestnut hair fashioned into intricate braids surrounding a chignon.

"Thank you." Mariah's amber eyes gleamed as she ran her fingers over a braid. "One of the women at The House did it." She glanced around the ballroom. "This room is incredible. Two years ago, I could've never imagined being in a place such as this. As a guest. I've never seen anything so…splendid." Mariah continued down the receiving line, then rushed on tiptoes to speak with a cluster of women.

Reverend Howarth shook Ravenna's hand. He was a gentle, kind man with auburn hair, coffee-brown eyes, and ruddy cheeks just beginning to show the wear of his fifty-some years. His smile exaggerated his pointed chin. He was one of her favorite people, though his talkative nature sometimes fatigued her more introspective one. When she'd first met him a year ago, she'd been surprised to find he was a reverend when his physique was better suited for working the docks. He puffed his barrel chest. "Dear Lady Birchfield, thank you for making all this possible." His deep voice, perfect for making his Sunday sermons, carried through the room. "These women have had few kindnesses and advantages in their lives, but I assure you that your friendship, patronage, and beneficence have already compensated a great many of their sufferings."

"You flatter me, Reverend. I've only fulfilled my Christian duty and am happy to be of service." What she did not express was that through working with the prostitutes, she might find her own sister, who was rumored to now be a woman of the streets. She smiled at the younger preacher beside him as a hint to Revered Haworth to curb his usual long-windedness. The rules of propriety required she wait to be introduced.

"You're too humble," Reverend Howarth continued. "When you suggested this luncheon idea, I thought it would be too difficult, but you and the other ladies have done a fine job. A fine job, indeed. And then when I'd heard about Lord Franklin's return, I knew his lecture about New South Wales would be most entertaining for the women. And for myself, of course. But

I think the education—"

Ravenna interrupted. "Thank you, Reverend. You're too kind." She smiled.

He nodded enthusiastically. "Not at all. You've established a charity that…"

He lifted a finger and inhaled deeply as if to continue, but Ravenna, conscious of the line, broke with all propriety and nodded at the younger preacher. "I've not met your friend, Reverend. Is he to work at The Penitent House, too?"

The Reverend turned and clapped the young man on the shoulder. "Pray, forgive me. This is Mr. Evan McKirk. He's most eager to establish a career in the church and secure a parish of his own. In the meantime, he's come to us by way of Bristol to learn about The Penitent House and to assist me. He thinks of creating a similar institution in Bristol."

"How good of him." Ravenna bobbed a slight curtsey as McKirk bowed.

Mr. McKirk said, "You're very kind, milady."

The Reverend's attention fell on someone across the room. "Oh, pardon me, milady, but there is a man I must speak with just now. Please excuse me." He moved quickly down the receiving line, then toward his target.

She had difficulty not focusing on the eye patch. Her natural curiosity wanted to know how a man so young ended up with only one eye, but she dared not ask. Instead, she distracted herself with conversation. "What happy news that you seek to assist poor women to get them off the streets. How far have you come in your endeavor?"

McKirk was in his late twenties with dark, short hair parted down the middle, a hard-edged square, freckled face that appeared weathered in spite of his youth. He had a heavy-lidded gray eye and lips so thin as to appear embroidered upon his face. He said, "Not far at all. We're only now searching for locations and developing ways to raise the funds. I was hoping to get some insight from Reverend Howarth. He's done such a fine job."

"Indeed, he has. He will absolutely be the perfect mentor for you. If I or my women's club may be of any help, please do let me know. I feel secure in speaking for all of us when I say we are happy to help in any way possible."

"You're too kind, ma'am."

Ravenna tipped her head. She wasn't certain, but she thought his voice contained hints of an Irish accent. She wanted to talk to him longer, to find out more about him, but she needed to keep the reception line moving. "Welcome, Mr. McKirk. I'm sure you're quite a blessing to our good Reverend Howarth and the women of The Penitent House."

"I do what I can, milady. Thank you for welcoming us. I look forward to my time here." His eye drifted toward Mariah, and he moved down the line.

A man with an arrogant air sauntered toward the receiving line. He kissed Dowager Mildreth Thornley's sharp cheekbone.

"Good afternoon, Percy," she said. She turned to Ravenna and said, "Lady Birchfield, have you met my youngest son, Percy Smithwaite?"

Just the look of the man—the mask of boredom, his swagger—annoyed Ravenna as though she'd scraped her teeth on a fork. His character oozed from him like mud from under a shoe. She forced a smile. "I have not had the pleasure."

"Percy, this is Lord Philip Birchfield's widow, Lady Ravenna. Do you remember him?"

The family resemblance among the mother and her sons materialized in the high cheekbones, patrician noses, and large round eyes. The younger brother differed in his pale skin, honey-gold hair, and arrogant demeanor, whereas Lord Franklin's adventures in New South Wales had bronzed and reddened his skin to match his hair. And though Lord Franklin's true character was as slimy as his brother's, he hid his under a genial nature— which made him easier to stomach, though it also rendered him, in some ways, more dangerous.

Ravenna forced a smile at Percy. An affected ennui, all the rage among younger people, weighed his features into a dull gaze. He bowed and offered only a "Good day, milady" before his eyes roved over the crowd in the room.

He moved away to shake his brother's hand as Ravenna shot daggers at his back. The brothers greeted each other coolly like a couple of stray cats.

"You're back sooner than I expected," Percy said, offering his hand for a shake.

Thornley took the offered hand and said, "Yes. And just in time, from what mother tells me."

One corner of Percy's mouth eased upward. "Mother has a penchant for the theatrical." Before Thornley could speak, Percy said, "But I suppose I must thank you for bringing so many pretties into our home. It'll save me from having to hunt them on my own."

Thornley gripped his brother's hand tighter and pulled him close. "These are not for you. Do not ruin this."

Percy chuckled and moved away as Ravenna's best friend, Catherine, Lady Adair, fluttered into the room, wrapped in a pale blue sarsenet dress embroidered with gold flowers.

Catherine approached Lord Thornley, her eyes shining with anger. "Lord Thornley. So glad you've returned," she said through a tight smile. "I would love an opportunity to speak with you."

Thornley blushed. "I-I-I, uh. Certainly, if there is time. There's much to do today." Then he added quickly. "Thank you for coming. Excuse me. I need to speak to—" He abruptly walked away.

Catherine glared at his back, then she turned to Ravenna, infusing her smile with genuine warmth, though a hint of tension remained. "Hello, darling. I'm glad I'm not late," she breathed. Bright pink roses bloomed on her cheeks. "I couldn't break away from Lady Corliss." She linked her arm with Ravenna's as the greeting line broke.

Ravenna said, "Thornley offered you a strange greeting. What do you suppose is the matter?"

"Oh, a little something I'll need to tell you about later." She popped open her fan, causing her frosty blonde hair to fly in the breeze. She was a petite doll of a woman who appeared far younger than her forty-two years. She smelled of orange blossoms and sunshine.

Dearest Catherine. Perhaps it was the nature of this event and the culmination of much hard work to benefit the prostitutes, but Ravenna's gratitude surged warm and bright like the sun slipping from behind a cloud when she saw her best friend. Catherine had been in the Drury Theatre on that fateful day when Ravenna had escaped the clutches of the brothel

8

madam. Were it not for Catherine, Ravenna's life might've ended up much differently. She might've ended up in the streets herself—or worse. Though she'd applied for servant's jobs, many people didn't want the Irish in their homes, accusing them of being untrustworthy and prone to thievery.

For whatever reason, Catherine took an instant liking to Ravenna and swept her under wing. She helped Ravenna land a position selling oranges, then in the chorus line, and eventually helped her find minor acting parts until she climbed her way into leading roles. They'd become fast and lasting friends.

Catherine's cornflower blue eyes scanned the space. "Aren't they all lovely? Though I'm sorry for the...circumstances." She gave Ravenna a pointed look and cut her eyes at Lord Thornley, then rolled her eyes. She sighed, "I do wish Braedon were here, though. He'd be so thrilled to see how his donations have been used."

William Finleigh, Lord Braedon. The mere mention of Braedon's name barbed under Ravenna's ribs. She missed his blue wolfish eyes, perpetually filled with mischief, his mellow baritone stroking her name, the gentle touch of his fingertips at her elbow. She even missed his insistent pestering. Memories of him flooded her mind, grasping for purchase. No. She closed the shut the door, closing him out of her thoughts. For now.

They migrated to stand beside Reverend Howarth, who had claimed a central position in the room. She said, "You must tell me what Braedon is up to these days."

"I couldn't tell you for certain."

"Nonsense. I know he writes you far more often than he's writing me, the rascal. But I suppose I don't hold the same attractions..." She waggled her brows. "I fear you've supplanted me in his attentions. You shall now be his closest confidante and I his cast aside doll."

"Oh, stop it." Ravenna nudged her. "You know you are his best friend."

Reverend Howarth clapped his hands, collecting everyone around him for a lengthy speech expressing gratitude to the donors and the *Les Roses Noires* club. He finished his address expounding on his fatherly pride in the women of The Penitent House.

After the Reverend's speech, everyone gathered at the long dining table to eat. Ravenna sat on needles between Lord Thornley at the head of the table to her left, Mr. Samuel Gibson, Lord Thornley's travel companion, to her right, and Lady Mildreth across from her.

Mr. Gibson's stringy brown hair swept over his wide forehead. His round face consisted of pink pock-marked skin and quick russet eyes.

Forced to be polite and compatible for the next few hours, Ravenna played at conversation. "Lord Thornley, I hear you have a special treat for the women today."

His thick bronze brows arched. "Yes, yes. When I was in New South Wales, I discovered a magnificent stone."

Mr. Gibson cut his meat with hard strokes. "To be precise, I discovered the stone while excavating at the site of what we believe was once an ancient temple." He held up his hand like a claw, and a lusty glimmer filled his eyes. "I plucked it from the earth myself. With this very hand."

Lord Thornley's tight smile didn't reach into his eyes. "That is true. Yes." He paused. "Nevertheless. The stone is nearly as large as a goose egg and contains what can only be described as a fire like a rainbow within."

"A truly spectacular gem. A pity it should sit in a royal vault where no one should see it." A hint of disdain edged Mr. Gibson's voice.

Lord Thornley stabbed a potato. "The king could decide to bust it into a powder for his wig for all I care. It's not for us to say. I recovered the stone on behalf of the crown."

Mr. Gibson spoke with affected cordiality. "Rather, you decided it should go to the king, though I discovered it. And since you have commandeered it and will be the one to present it to him, *you'll* be rewarded handsomely, I wager."

"Tell me more about the gem." Ravenna shifted the course of the uncomfortable conversation. "What sort of stone is it?"

Lord Thornley answered. "An opal. Though the strangeness of its color is a shock to the senses. For where every opal I've ever seen has been white, this one is black as the night, which renders its fire more brilliant. That alone, I wager, increases its value much above the typical white opals."

"Never mind that we were warned to leave the jewel in New South Wales," Mr. Gibson said, chewing his food.

Ravenna lifted a brow, studying the man. "Warned? How dramatic. By whom?"

Lord Thornley's face hardened, and his nostrils flared as he struggled to remain calm. "You wouldn't have left it there either. We both wanted to bring the opal home."

Mr. Gibson, looking down at the meat he cut, added nonchalantly, "The indigenous people issued the warning. The village shaman specifically—"

Lord Thornley interrupted. "You see, Mr. Gibson disagrees with gifting our sovereign with a stone equaling his own majesty."

Lady Thornley cut in and, with the subtlety of an experienced hostess, changed the subject entirely. "I hear there are fine Arabians at Tattersall's this year. At least sixteen hands."

Ravenna picked up the cue. "Sixteen hands? That's monstrously big for an Arabian. The largest I've ever seen stood fourteen hands."

"Yes. I hear there's a new breeder from the American colonies." With that, the subject changed from opals to horses, which eased some of the tension sparking in the air around Thornley and Gibson.

After a luncheon full of excited chatter and laughter among The Penitent House women, everyone gathered in the formal parlor, which had been transformed into a lecture and music room. While the accomplished aristocratic women displayed their musical talents, The Penitent House guests squirmed and wiggled in their seats, ogling gilt-framed portraits, the marble fireplace, and the shelves of trinkets and books. They ran their slippers over the ornate Turkish carpet. A few even removed their shoes to scrub their stockinged feet over the lush carpet and giggled and whispered with each other.

Mariah intervened with a tap on their shoulders and a sharp whisper to pay attention to the musicians and singers.

Ravenna smiled to herself. In many ways, these women were still quite childlike in their behavior as they explored a domain unfamiliar to them. Though it was sometimes easy to forget they had seen and experienced indescribable suffering and wickedness.

When the music section of the entertainment had ended, Lord Thornley stood with a japanned box. He cleared his throat to quiet the room. "To complete our little gathering today, I have a special treat to share with you all. As some of you know, I have returned recently from New South Wales, many thousands of miles across the sea to the east, where we get our most exotic spices and silks. There are creatures and fauna there, the likes of which you've never seen. In fact, there are spiders as large as my hand." He held up his splayed fingers. The women gasped and muffled shrieks as they huddled closer together and shuddered in their seats.

One of the girls said, "Cor' a spider that size is the stuff of nightmares, idn't it?"

Another added, "I'd like to put it in my sister's bed and see how she'd jump and scream."

The women fell into laughter.

Mariah shushed them.

The group settled, and Lord Thornley pulled over a globe on a pedestal. He pointed to a small slice of land. "Here is England…" He spun the globe, allowing his finger to trace a trail. "And way over here is New South Wales."

The women craned their necks and twittered at the thought of such a long journey. One woman said, "God's nightgown! I'd vomit up ma stockings to spend so long on a ship."

The women laughed. Mariah flushed and tapped the woman's shoulder, though the woman seemed unaffected by the correction to her behavior. She shared a mischievous smile with the woman beside her.

Unfazed, Lord Thornley continued. "What I have in this box is unlike anything else in the world. I dug for months, surrounded by myriad dangers in the hills of New South Wales, under the blistering sun…"

Ravenna cast a glance at the red-faced and scowling Mr. Gibson, who crossed his arms over his chest. He glared at Thornley with his lips pinched together until they disappeared. Thornley wasn't shy about stealing all the credit and accolades for himself, and Mr. Gibson wasn't shy about displaying his ire.

Thornley continued. "I discovered many artifacts from the ruins of an ancient city. In one building, which appeared to have once been a temple of sorts, I uncovered a most stunning stone. I've brought it back to give to our King George and Queen Charlotte to add to the bounty and treasures of the British realm. But…" He lifted a finger, then lowered his voice as if sharing a great secret. "There's something else. The king and queen haven't yet seen this glorious stone. *You* are the *first*. You will lay eyes upon a wonder before even Queen Charlotte herself! Now, what do you think of that?"

The women gaped at each other as a low, unified susurration of excited voices went around the room.

He held up a hand. "Wait, wait. There's more wonder to this gem. The day I found the stone, we sat around the campfire with the natives of the region. The elder said this stone is the stuff of legend. He said, in fact, it is *cursed*." He lunged a little, causing the captivated women to jump in their seats.

Reverend Howarth said, "Oh, my. How dreadful."

Mr. Gibson interrupted. "Which is why the elder said we shouldn't take it out of their village. It had been buried—"

Lord Thornley held up his hand and glared at him with warning. He returned to his audience. "But what they call a curse, we can call a blessing. The elder said whoever holds the stone will hold great powers and defeat all his enemies."

Mr. Gibson stood. "With all due respect, sir, what the elder actually said was that the keeper of the stone becomes so drunk with power he views everyone as an enemy until he's driven mad and seeks to conquer all. The owner of the stone will turn his enemies' wives into widows. Thus, because of the power and the brilliant fire in the center of the stone, the shaman called it the Widow's Fire."

A low rumble of whispers went up around him, which seemed to please Gibson.

Lord Thornley smiled smugly. "Yes, thank you, Gibson." And he stared him down until Mr. Gibson resumed his seat. "I don't put much value in such fairy tales. But whatever power this stone contains will be safest in the

13

hands of our king, who will wield power with wisdom and responsibility."

"If it does have that sort of power, maybe we'll defeat Napoleon once and for all," one of the women said.

"Hear, hear!" shouted Percy, slapping his chair arm, his eyes lit with mocking humor. "And we can fill our war coffers from the gold at the end of rainbows."

Irritation scratched at Ravenna's rib. He shouldn't mock these poor women who had never had the advantages of education.

Reverend Howarth interjected. "I think we might be better served relying on Providence to open our path to victory rather than pagan charms and superstitions, milord."

"Yes, of course," Lord Thornley mumbled. "Of course." He opened the box. "At any rate, I'm going to pass around the stone so you all may behold its beauty."

An excited gasp went up as he removed the egg-shaped opal and placed it in the first woman's hand. She and the woman beside her giggled and whispered over the opal, testing its weight while other girls near them perched on the edges of their seats and craned their necks to see the wondrous stone.

Lord Thornley's chest puffed, and he looked proudly down his nose as the women chattered and barraged him with questions about how the stone got its powers, were there any other stones, the climate in New South Wales, and scores of other inquiries. Lord Thornley lapped up the attention while Mr. Gibson sat sullen, arms crossed over his chest. He suddenly stood, jerked the bottom of his waistcoat into place, and marched from the room.

Catherine leaned over and whispered behind her fan, "He's in a high dudgeon. Though I can't say I blame him."

Ravenna opened her own fan, covered her face to whisper. "He's jealous and bitter. He clearly had more to do with the discovery of the stone than what Lord Thornley will allow."

"It is unkind of Thornley. But I've never known Thornley to be generous without a purpose."

The stone landed in Mariah's hands. She turned it back and forth to see the fire.

Ravenna said, "It's a beautiful stone, is it not?"

Mariah sat awestruck. "It's the most beautiful thing I've ever seen. I wonder how much something like this would be worth?"

"It's difficult to say." Ravenna shrugged.

"Certainly a kingly amount," Catherine said.

"Do you think the legend is true? About the powers it holds?"

Ravenna smiled. "Doubtful. But it's a diverting story."

Mariah stared at the rainbow fire flinting and sparking inside the black stone. "It *must* hold great magic. How else could such brilliance be captured inside this stone?"

"Nature is often quite fantastical and works in inexplicable ways," Catherine said.

"Here." Mariah handed the stone to Ravenna.

The opal was cool and smooth to the touch, about the size of a goose egg. "It must weigh at least two pounds or more," Ravenna said, bouncing her hand.

Mariah watched the stone, entranced. "The beauty is overwhelming."

Chapter Two

After Lord Thornley's presentation, the women milled around, talking and sipping punch while Thornley removed himself to his study to squirrel away the opal to safety. His brother Percy walked with him. The brothers whispered intensely to each other as they passed through the door. Thornley's high shoulders pinched lips and lowered chin conveyed sheer annoyance with his brother, Percy.

Ravenna stood with Catherine, Lady Thornley, Reverends Howarth and McKirk, and Mariah in the light pouring in from a tall window. They chatted about the progress of the women and toyed with different ideas for educating them in sewing, reading, writing, and other necessary instruction.

At the other end of the room, a few young women fell into uproarious laughter. Mariah excused herself and crossed the floor to rein in the group.

Ravenna said to Reverend Howarth, "Mariah is a boon to The Penitent House, I think. You're lucky to have her."

"Oh, yes, indeed." He nodded. "The other women have great respect for her. She's come from terrible circumstances. She has three children, you know. All placed with a baby farmer."

"Three children!" Catherine's brows shot up. "So many for one so young?" She put her hand to her chest.

"Indeed. But it's the price of the profession. She might, as so many others, have gone the route of..." He stopped and flushed a deep red. "Pardon me, miladies. I think this is a rather indelicate subject. Sometimes I forget myself."

Ravenna understood his meaning well enough. She'd known many actresses who'd landed in trouble and resorted to "fixing" their situation in dim, dirty rooms with butchers or via vials of strong herbs with unpredictable results that sometimes led to grave illness or death. She shuddered and shifted closer to the window, soaking in the hot sun.

Reverend McKirk approached. "I beg your pardon for the interruption, but Reverend Howarth, I have some business in Foster Lane in regards to The Penitent House."

Reverend Howarth nodded. "Very well. Mariah and I will return directly with the women."

Reverend McKirk nodded his head in acquiescence and walked away. Reverend Howarth leaned in to whisper to Ravenna, "He's off to see our banker, I wager. We had to take out a bit of a loan to pay for some of the pianoforte. But I reckon one more fundraiser should set us up nicely and quickly erase all our debts."

"They'll have a pianoforte?" Ravenna failed to keep the surprise from her voice.

"Of course. How else are they to receive music instruction?"

"I rather think sewing or reading would be more useful."

"Certainly, they shall learn those things. But I believe music uplifts the soul, and these women need a great deal of uplifting."

"I suppose your logic is sound, but do you not think such instruction might give the women false hopes and cause them to reach for a station in life they can likely never attain?"

Catherine scoffed and laughed. "Good thing I never believed that about you when we met at the theater. The women need some entertainment, too, Ravenna."

Ravenna flushed. Perhaps Catherine was right. Ravenna couldn't help herself. A lifetime of trauma had pulled a veil over her spirits. She'd long ago lost the ability to give way to bouts of joy, laughter, and frivolity for its own sake. 1798 had changed her. She'd learned how serious life can be. And with the recent deaths of family and friends, she'd turned to hard practicalities as an anchor to something secure and stable to hold on to. Would she ever know the carefree joy she'd once known? Was it possible to reclaim it after so much suffering? And it would be wrong to stand in the way of a ray of happiness and hope for a group of women who had suffered deeply. After all, didn't they also deserve a chance to reclaim what they had lost? She smiled and shook her head. "I apologize. Lady Catherine is right. I am too serious at times. I trust your judgment in these matters, Reverend, so I leave it to you. If you think the women's spirits will be lifted with music instruction, then I will not quibble. Of course, the women should have entertainment."

Reverend Howarth laughed and engulfed her hands between his meaty palms. "Dear Lady Birchfield, I don't hold it against you. I know you mean well, and your heart for the charity is all goodness. It's clear you want only what is best for them."

Catherine winked at her, then turned the conversation to a list of exceptionally accomplished women who might be interested in volunteering their time to teach music at The Penitent House.

Ravenna scanned the room, noticing that Reverend McKirk hadn't yet left. He'd stopped to talk to a small group near the door. He stood close to Mariah, unusually close. Ravenna wasn't certain, but she thought she detected a lingering look from Mariah toward the young pastor. And, though it was quick and obscured by his robe and her dress, it appeared as if he pressed Mariah's hand as he said goodbye and left the room.

When the clock in the foyer struck three, Reverend Howarth stepped forward to the center of the room and clapped his hands together. "Dear friends, we don't want to overstay our welcome. So, it is time we bid *adieu* to our kind host and hostesses."

The guests applauded for Lady Mildreth Thornley, who flushed and looked around, her hazel eyes glittering with pride. She said, "So sorry. Please don't leave until Lord Franklin can bid fare-thee-wells to you all. He will return directly, I'm certain."

Reverend Howarth nodded with a warm smile. "Thank you, milady, but please don't bother him. I'm sure he's a busy man. We will write letters to Lord Franklin since we are deprived of the privilege of expressing our gratitude in person. We don't want to overstay our welcome, and we must return home. We have supper to prepare, and we don't want to miss our evening chapel service and prayers." He spoke to the women. "Come, my dears, shall we line up here to give our thanks and fare-thee-wells?"

Mariah corralled the ladies near her and drew strays in like an expert sheepdog, herding them all toward the door. They bobbed awkward and unbalanced curtsies as they passed by Lady Thornley and then Percy, who smirked furtively at the women.

When all The Penitent House guests had left, Ravenna and Catherine ordered their carriages to be brought around and praised Lady Mildreth's great success.

Percy yawned, crossing the floor toward the window. "At last, the tedium is ended." He sat in the window and looked down at the street. "Though a couple of them were pretty enough, I suppose." He chuckled. "Pretty enough for their purpose, at any rate."

Lady Mildreth rebuked him. "Percy! How dare you speak so. Such vulgarity in the presence of ladies. Shame on you!"

Ravenna glared at him. She didn't know him well, but he was certainly proving himself to be an utter cad. Her stomach turned upon the kernel of anger he'd planted. She didn't want to argue—especially in someone else's home on what had been a successful day. Yet, her tongue raced ahead of her. "How unkind of you. Those women are working hard to make a better life. They didn't want to live on the streets, or trade their flesh, or live in abject poverty, but fate had other ideas. It's horrid to treat them as if they are unworthy of any kindness."

He put a hand to his chest with mock sincerity. "I'm deeply touched by your pretty sermon, Lady Birchfield, and I beg your forgiveness."

Repulsive man! Her hand itched with the desire to slap the smarmy smile off his face. She clutched her folded lace fan, which held a thin dagger in its guard. A gift from her late husband, she carried it with her everywhere.

"Percy…" Lady Mildreth warned. "That is quite enough, thank you. Perhaps you can go find your brother. I would speak to him. He should have come back to say goodbye to the women instead of hiding away in his study. Though he failed his duties once, he can at least pay his respects to our more esteemed guests." She cast an apologetic glance at Ravenna and Catherine.

He leaned against the casement. "Am I my brother's keeper?"

"Percy…" Exasperation filled Lady Mildreth's voice.

He pushed himself to his feet with a heavy sigh. "Very well." He pulled his paisley waistcoat into place.

Before he reached the door, a woman's scream echoed through the house.

Ravenna, Catherine, Lady Mildreth, and Percy exchanged quizzical glances.

Ravenna rushed toward the door. "Heavens, whatever is the matter…" The door flew open, and she jumped back.

A petite maid stood there, crying and holding herself. "He's dead, milady! Lord Thornley is dead."

Chapter Three

The unfortunate Lord Thornley lay face down on a lush, red Turkish rug soaked with the poor man's blood. A jewel-encrusted knife jutted from his back. Ravenna gasped, but her curiosity soon overrode her initial fright. She squatted beside him, the coppery scent of blood assailing her nose, as the maid squealed again and ran off. Lady Thornley burst into wailing and fell into Catherine's arms. Catherine whispered consolation against the weeping mother's temple. Percy held a fist to his mouth, fighting against his own emotions.

The hair at the back of Thornley's head jutted messily like a bird's nest. It hadn't been that way before. Ravenna tipped her head to the side. Thornley laid on his hands, which were covered in blood. It appeared his throat had been cut. Bile rose in her throat at the sight of the gore. She shut her eyes and swallowed hard, gathering inside herself.

Ravenna blew out a breath to steady herself and looked again. Lord Thornley's eyes were glazed, his mouth slack and his skin had begun to take on a grayish, waxy texture. If she had to guess, he'd been surprised, ambushed. But how did he land in this peculiar position with his hands tucked under him and his hair mussed? Perhaps the killer set upon him from behind. Grabbed by the back of the head, throat cut to silence him so he couldn't scream out and alert the house for help. Thornley must've grabbed his throat reflexively, then dropped to his knees. Perhaps the killer stabbed him in the back to finish him once he had fallen to his face.

The metallic scent of blood hung heavy in Ravenna's lungs, making it difficult to breathe. Nausea and emotion overcame her. Though she'd disliked the man, she never wished him dead and didn't relish his murder. She wouldn't wish this horrid death on her worst enemy. He was a man who had behaved poorly, yet there was always room for redemption while he lived. He might've been convinced to be a better man. Now, however, he was out of reach of such an opportunity. Lady Thornley's cries plucked at chords of sorrow and mourning she carried from her own recent losses. She swallowed down the lump of sadness rising in her throat. Tears pricked her eyes as she removed her handkerchief from her bodice and lay it over his face. "Poor Thornley. Bless him."

Ravenna stood and moved back from him. Searching the faces of Thornley's family, she whispered, "I'm so very sorry."

Ravenna surveyed the room. With the exception of the corpse and blood, the study was an otherwise comfortable room with cherry wood paneled walls. A white marble fireplace flanked by two green leather wingback chairs held the wall across from the desk. A drink table sat between the chairs. To the right were a few tall windows clothed in dark olive velvet curtains. Behind the desk and along the wall by the door were shelves lined with books and a host of artifacts from nations around the world. Nothing seemed out of place.

She said, "There doesn't seem to have been a struggle." Which supported her notion that he'd been ambushed. "I think whatever happened, it was quick, unexpected."

Percy cleared his throat and sniffed, fighting his grief. "How can you tell?"

"The room is in order." One window stood open, allowing in the summer heat—and maybe a killer.

Ravenna wanted out of this house, away from death. She was sick of death and certain she'd seen more than her fair share of it. But she couldn't leave the family so soon after this terrible shock. It would be unkind. Their eyes fixed upon her with great intensity, as though they expected her to have all the answers.

The compulsion to talk, to distract them and herself from the horror at hand, overcame her. "It's likely he was taken by surprise." Ravenna stepped across the floor to the open window and glanced outside. The scent of freshly cut grass and flowers hung in the humid summer air. Two columnar shrubs flanked the window, the yard and garden were empty, and the gate at the back of the yard was closed. No sign of a disturbance outside either. She turned to face the wide-eyed stares. Did someone from inside the house kill Lord Thornley? And worse, the killer might still be in the house with them.

She looked again at Lord Thornley. Who would've wanted him dead? And for what purpose? Mr. Gibson sprang immediately to her mind. He was openly jealous of and angry with Thornley, and he left early in a fit of pique. Maybe he slipped into the study and lay in wait instead of leaving the house. Then, when Thornley entered the room, Gibson jumped out and killed him, leaving by the window. She turned her face again to the open window, taking in the rustling trees, the fall of lemon-yellow light on the flowers and shrubs. She pulled her glance down to inspect the wall just under the window. A smear of blood about an inch wide and three inches long. Could've been caused by a remnant of blood on the killer's hands, shoes, or clothes as he dropped from the window.

"What do we do?" Lady Thornley said, startling Ravenna from her reverie.

Ravenna turned to face the grieving mother, who dabbed her tears with a lace handkerchief. A man such as Thornley was still loved by his mother. *What an odd thought and at such a time, Ravenna,* she chided herself. Yet, she couldn't shake the completeness, the wholeness of a mother's love when there were an untold number of people who might've wanted Thornley dead. Her throat tightened, and tears filled her eyes. Not so much for Thornley, but for his mother and *her* loss.

Ravenna knew what needed to be done. Yet…She closed her eyes and rubbed the aching spot in the center of her forehead. *Another dead body.* Was she always to be surrounded by death? Fear and dread sank against her heart. Only a few months ago, she'd found the dead body of the foreign secretary in her own drawing room. The discovery had opened her to suspicion from Bow Street Runner, Mr. Chadwick. Shrewd, sharp, persistent—she feared Mr. Chadwick more than any man in London. If anyone were capable of sniffing out her secret past, it was him. Yet, she knew she needed to tell him and let him investigate to find the killer.

But how would she explain to Mr. Chadwick yet another dead man in her presence? Her neck tightened as she stared into Lord Thornley's glassy gaze. She dropped her hand to her collarbone and pressed against the tension deepening there. Not an hour ago, he was laughing, talking, sharing his knowledge and findings with his guests, and now...her bottom lip quivered, and she wiped at the few tears that slipped over her cheeks. How fragile life was. How unpredictable.

She couldn't worry about Chadwick's reaction. This wasn't about her. Lady Thornley's expectant eyes bore into her. Ravenna had to do something. The *right* thing. In spite of her fear of Mr. Chadwick, in spite of the risk to herself and the secrets she wished to keep, she knew what must be done. She sighed into her regrets. "I think I know someone who can help. I need a pen and paper. And someone who can deliver a message."

Within thirty minutes, a knock sounded at the front door, and the butler announced Mr. Chadwick. Lean and of middling height, he was an older gentleman with a prominent forehead crowned with receding gray hair slicked back with pomade. Sharp intelligence shone from his dark blue, almost black, heavy-lidded eyes.

He removed his round wool hat and bowed. "Lady Birchfield. I might consider myself glad to see you were it not for the fact you're once again in the presence of a dead man. They seem to follow you like a murder of crows, milady."

She flushed and straightened her back. "Yes. It would seem so, I fear. I'd rather they find someone else to follow."

He held her in a steady gaze.

She grew rigid, gripping her closed fan. Seeing Mr. Chadwick again recalled the people she'd lost only four months ago. He'd investigated the death of Foreign Secretary Lord Hawkestone—a death which had upended her entire world, ultimately revealing her late husband had also been murdered. Further, her determination to keep her past as a spy secret, likely made her a focus of suspicion under his penetrating gaze. She was certain Chadwick could sense her secrets—which, no doubt, created in him little trust and regard for her. All he needed was a single thread to pull on to unravel everything. Yet, he was the only Bow Street Runner she knew and the only one who seemed to operate with integrity, discretion, and thoroughness.

He said, "Please inform me as to what happened."

Lady Thornley sat in a chair by the dead fireplace, sobbing loudly as Percy and Catherine comforted her.

Ravenna took charge of the situation. She motioned to the body. "This is Lord Franklin Thornley. He's been killed. Obviously." She nodded in the direction of the others. "That's his mother, Lady Mildreth, and his younger brother, Percy. Lord Thornley had recently returned from New South Wales. We had just finished a small charity luncheon for The Penitent House when we discovered him here." The tight spot in the center of her forehead now marched through the rest of her skull until her entire head throbbed.

He said to the grieving mother and living son. "I'm sorry for your loss, Lady Thornley. Sir." Lady Mildreth sobbed harder, and Percy nodded, his face marked with somberness.

Mr. Chadwick turned back to the dead man. He tipped his head and walked around him, taking in all angles, then squatted near the body, scrutinizing it.

"What's happening?" A man's voice said from behind the crowd of servants in the doorway. The servants parted to allow his entrance.

Mr. Gibson froze. "Wh–wh–what…" He leaned against the door jamb and ran a finger under his black ascot. "What happened?"

Ravenna had seen far better actors than Mr. Gibson in her years as an actress. He didn't seem surprised enough. He seemed rather like the recipient of a gift who already knew what was inside the box. A dark gleam entered his russet eyes before he squeezed them shut.

"What are you doing here?" She blurted.

Chadwick looked up at her, then to Mr. Gibson.

Ravenna continued. "I thought you had left."

25

"I had. I needed to collect myself and regain my composure."

Mr. Chadwick said, "Why? Were you discomposed?"

"I was. Lord Franklin and I didn't get on well. Things soured dramatically after our recent return from New South Wales. I'm the archaeologist. Were it not for me, he would've never gone on any expeditions. Yet, he acts... acted...as though I was merely a servant to him. It made me angry."

"Then why did you come today?" Ravenna asked.

He sighed. "If I may speak plainly?"

Chadwick said, "Please do."

"While I am the one with the archaeological knowledge and expertise..." He inhaled deeply. "He was the one with the funding. I need his patronage to continue my work."

Lady Thornley shouted, her tear-streaked face growing red with fury. "You vile, vicious little man. How dare you—"

Percy said, "Mother, this is the way of the world. You know that. Our kind exists to assist his kind so the kingdom's sciences, art, and knowledge can improve and expand."

Lady Thornley sniffed. "True enough. Though I suppose the little scavenger will now have to find someone else's bones to pick clean, won't he?" She broke into fresh sobs.

Mr. Gibson glowered, then blew out a cleansing breath. He shook his head, and his eyes filled with tears. "I'll grant you, milady, Thornley and I had our differences. Our bond was a contentious one. Yet, I never wanted him dead." His eyes darted around the room. "Do you know who did this?"

Mr. Chadwick squinted, then drew his gaze to the area surrounding the body. He stroked his chin as he thought. He sighed and stood, his boot leather creaking. He spoke to Mr. Gibson. "Do you know what sort of knife this is?"

"It's a 16th-century Mughal knife. A rare beauty." Mr. Gibson said.

"Do you know where it came from? Since you're an archaeologist... " His voice trailed off as he directed his dark, piercing eyes at Mr. Gibson.

The short man puffed. "I do hope you aren't implicating me...."

"Sir, I merely asked a question. Where did this knife come from?"

"Lord Thornley was a collector. He came with me on a few excursions. He and I dined with Sultan Selim III on one of our trips where the Sultan gifted us with this knife. The knife was meant to go to the crown. At least, that's what Thornley had promised would happen. It appears he kept it, however."

Chadwick turned his gaze on Thornley's relatives. "Lady Thornley? Sir? Do either of you happen to know why this knife never made it to the king?"

Lady Thornley wiped her eyes and nose. "I don't know." Her bottom lip quivered. "I never inserted myself into his affairs. I didn't even know he possessed such an item."

Percy shrugged. "I never concerned myself with his treasure-hunting activities."

Chadwick turned back to Mr. Gibson. "And he never informed you as to why he never gave it to the king?"

"He never said anything to me about it. I had trusted him to manage it." Mr. Gibson opened his hands and shrugged. "He should've turned it in, but I suppose he thought it too pretty and valuable to give away."

"Shouldn't it have been in your hands, sir? As, according to you, you are the expert and Lord Thornley a mere aficionado?"

Mr. Gibson's eyes darted. "Erm, uh…"

Lady Mildreth snapped. "Mis-ter Gibson. I don't like your implications, sir. My son was no thief."

He stammered. "Of course not. I hadn't meant—"

Chadwick interrupted. "Notwithstanding…" He lifted a hand. "Does anyone know where he kept the knife?"

Lady Mildreth waved toward the desk with her handkerchief. "I'm not certain. I think it may have been kept on the shelf behind his desk."

Chadwick inspected the empty space where the knife had laid in a little rack. "Was there a sheath?"

Mr. Gibson paused, thinking. "Yes. It had come in a gold jewel-encrusted sheath."

Chadwick turned around in a slow circle, scanning the room. "I don't see it anywhere."

"I suspect the killer kept it," Mr. Gibson offered. "It would've been quite valuable."

The servants whispered among each other.

Ravenna searched the stacks of papers and books. There were several ink drawings, some building plans, and books of languages and cultures. "The primary question is…." She lifted a stack of books. "Why was he killed? What did the killer hope to gain from it?" She looked at Lady Mildreth. "Do you know if he kept money in this room?"

Lady Mildreth fingered the coral cameo resting on her chest. "I'm not sure. I rarely came in here. But don't all gentlemen keep money in their studies?"

"He had no money in here." Percy flopped into a nearby chair, crossing his arms and legs.

"How do you know?" Ravenna said, opening one of the desk drawers, peeking inside.

"Trust me. I know."

Chadwick said, "But *how* do you know, sir?" Chadwick sidled Ravenna and pushed the drawer shut, locking her eyes with a look of warning.

Ravenna lifted a brow and turned away.

Percy answered, "Because I was trying to borrow money from him. He told me he no longer kept money in the study since the last time I discovered his hiding spot and took all his money."

"How could you do that to your brother?" Lady Mildreth gasped.

Mr. Chadwick's gray brows knitted into a frown. "You stole from your own brother?"

Percy shrugged. "If I hadn't, some very bad men were going to put a bullet in my head for some debts I owed them. They had quite run out of patience, and I had run out of time. I did what was necessary. Once I explained my situation to Franklin, he forgave me."

Ravenna stared at him. Was everyone in this family deranged and execrable? She shook her head and circled the desk as Mr. Chadwick pelted him with questions. She had stopped listening as she focused on the desk. Her eyes roved over the papers, the pen and inkstand, the penknife, and other accoutrements typical to a gentleman's desk. "Wait. It appears something is missing." She pointed at the left corner of the desk near the inkstand. A round bit of polished wood surrounded by a light coating of dust, indicating an item once rested in the spot. "What was there?"

"One of his precious ancient trinkets." Percy rolled his wrist and turned away. "A figurine of sorts that looked barely human."

"What did it look like?"

Percy looked up at the ceiling to pull down the memory. "Ah, white stone. Heavy. A feminine figure, shaped similar to a heart, tiny head with broad bosom and hips. With thin legs. A strange-shaped creature."

"Was it valuable?" Ravenna asked.

"I have no idea."

Mr. Chadwick cleared his throat and spoke to Percy. "And you're quite certain there was no money in this room?"

"Quite. I checked. Thoroughly."

Ravenna studied Percy's profile, recalling their earlier intense conversation. She said, "I saw you and Thornley earlier. You were having a conversation. It seemed quite...heated."

Chadwick looked between them. "Interesting. What were you discussing?"

"I asked to borrow money. He refused. We argued."

Ravenna's brows shot up. What if the conversation had then descended into murder? Once they were closed in the study, Percy could've easily ambushed his brother as he stored the opal. *The opal!* She'd nearly forgotten about it. She spun around. "Where's the opal?"

A unified gasp and low grumble went up among the servants who had gathered at the door.

Catherine stood from her spot on the sofa where she was consoling Lady Thornley. "Do you think it's gone?"

Everyone looked around, confused, as Ravenna searched the room for the opal encased in the japanned box. Perhaps the killer had taken the box and opal with him. Though the box wasn't large, surely it was too large to secret in a pocket and remove it from the house without someone seeing it.

He might've wrapped it in a cloak or coat.

Ravenna called out to the crowd at the door. "Has anyone seen someone carrying a suspicious package? Or perhaps something tucked under a coat?"

The staff murmured, shook their heads, and answered, "No."

Chadwick stepped forward and added, "Has anyone seen or heard anything out of the ordinary?"

Again, the answer was "No."

Ravenna pushed her thumb against her front teeth, her mind spinning through possible scenarios. "Perhaps a bandit sneaked into the room through the open window. Lord Thornley caught him, and a fight ensued. Then the bandit killed him and absconded with the opal and the bejeweled sheath?"

He stared at her, something like puzzlement and suspicion in his hard onyx eyes. "Perhaps. It seems possible." He turned to Percy. "But you said you were conversing with your brother about money. Did you see anyone or hear anything?"

Percy winced and shook his head. "Nothing. He refused to give me money. We exchanged hard words. Then I left the room to collect myself while he closed himself in the study."

"Where did you go?" Chadwick said.

"The billiard room. I imbibed a bit of brandy, then returned to the gala."

Ravenna paced the room, absentmindedly making her way to the empty fireplace. She stared at the blackened grate to gather her thoughts. Rubbing her temples, she wanted all this to be over so she could go home, and curl up with a book and a glass of port. Her gaze trailed downward over the marble hearthstones. At the edge of one of the stones was a wood plank on the floor that didn't fit as it should. She twisted the gold medallion at the base of her black lace fan and released a knife from the shaft.

Lady Thornley gasped. "Oh, my. What a trick!"

Ravenna dropped to her knees and stuck the tip of the knife between the lips of the planks, lifting the jutting plank.

There it was. Shock pulsed through her body as she sat back on her feet. The japanned box was set down in a space about three times its size.

"What is it?" Chadwick asked. He and Catherine surrounded her.

"A hiding spot." She reached down and lifted the box out of the space. "Apparently, Lord Thornley was set upon as he stowed the gem."

Ravenna flipped the gold latch and lifted the shiny black lid. The Widow's Fire opal, a gem purported to wield great power for its owner, was gone.

Chapter Four

Mr. Chadwick turned on the small gathering of family and servants. "No one leaves until I've spoken with each and every one of you. I need a pen and paper to send for the coroner to inspect and register the death. In the meantime, we must leave this room." He said to Lady Thornley, "Milady, I require the use of another room where I might interview individuals in privacy."

Lady Mildreth called to the butler who stood among the servants. "Torrance, show Mr. Chadwick to the ballroom."

Chadwick said to the crowd. "I need everyone to come into the ballroom, please."

He passed through the parting bodies as Lady Thornley addressed the group. "You all will wait your turn in the ballroom. Once you've met with Mr. Chadwick, you may proceed with your work. Smith, Perkins, prepare the drawing room for Lord Franklin's display. We will need ice from the ice house, flowers, linens, vinegar water, and a clean suit."

"*After* the coroner has seen him. He shouldn't be moved or touched until then," Mr. Chadwick added.

Lady Thornley nodded. "Of course." Her voice broke. "We'll prepare his body when the coroner leaves."

The servants hesitated, glancing at each other. "Go. Now. Everyone." Lady Mildreth said, rubbing her brow.

Chadwick spoke as he led the group, "I'll start speaking with people now until the coroner arrives. Please notify me as soon as he appears." His voice trailed off down the hall.

Lady Mildreth turned to Ravenna. "I'd like to speak with you, please."

Ravenna followed Lady Mildreth into the billiard room. Lady Mildreth closed the door and said in a quiet voice, "I've heard things about you. Impressive things."

Ravenna fidgeted with her closed fan. "I can't imagine what you mean."

A sharp light filled the dowager's eyes. "Don't play sheepish with me, Lady Birchfield. It doesn't become a woman of your age and distinction. And it insults me."

Ravenna rolled back her shoulders and steeled herself. "Very well. What have you heard?"

Lady Mildreth sat in a nearby chair, smoothing her lavender organza skirts. "I've heard you have a talent for finding murderers."

This wasn't good news. Ravenna had hoped her involvement in discovering Lord Hawkestone's murderer could've been kept quiet. If so, she was fairly certain her past as a spy could remain a secret. However, if her name was too much connected to the investigation among the *ton*, it might uncover the lurid past she wanted to bury forever—a past she certainly didn't want Mr. Chadwick to catch wind of. "How did you hear of such a thing?"

"You're not stupid, dear. You know how people talk."

"I'd like to know who told you." Ravenna crossed her arms.

She spoke quickly. "If you must know, I heard it from Lady Violette Hawkestone. I'd mentioned seeing Mr. Norris from Angelo's school leaving your house and how I thought it was curious." She motioned with her hand as she spoke. "She told me you take fencing lessons. Of course, I thought it was quite strange, and asked how she could associate with someone so eccentric."

Ravenna frowned. She was not eccentric.

Lady Mildreth continued. "She defended you, of course. She said she owed you a debt of fealty few could claim from her. I pressed her, and she refused to tell me. Later, one of my maids spoke with one of her footmen who revealed that you were responsible for helping to bring Lord Hawkestone's murderer to justice."

Blasted servants! Could none of them be trusted? It was nearly impossible to maintain discretion in sensitive situations. She strained to keep from rolling her eyes. "I see," she said through gritted teeth.

So..." Lady Mildreth pressed her hands together. "Since I trust Violette's judgment, I'm asking you, no..." She interlaced her fingers. "I'm begging you. Will you please help me find out who killed my son?"

"Why me? Mr. Chadwick is a very capable man. It's his job—"

Lady Mildreth leaned forward and whispered, "I do not trust Bow Street Runners. He is not one of us, if you catch my meaning."

"*I* am not one of us, if you recall." Ravenna was an Irish immigrant, of common stock, and a former actress as well. Her marriage to Philip, her friendship with Catherine, and sheer will had been her saving grace and the only reason she was now even marginally accepted among the nobility.

Mildreth waved her hand. "You understand my meaning well enough. These Runners and constables still have one foot in the rookery and deal with all sorts of criminal elements. They are not to be trusted. And I require the utmost...discretion. I don't want my family's business strewn all over town for every fishwife to gossip over. That man in there..." She pointed at the door, indicating Mr. Chadwick. "All but called my son a *thief.* I think he's less interested in catching his killer and more interested in destroying my family's name and reputation."

Ravenna frowned with incredulity. Her raucous sons certainly needed no help in bringing the family name and reputation to ruin. "What would be Chadwick's purpose in destroying your family, Lady Mildreth?"

"Jealousy. It's known such men are jealous of the aristocracy and will do anything to tear it down. Is that not what France's Terror was all about?" She flourished her hand.

Ravenna shook her head. The terror was a decade ago. Granted, there was still a great deal of mistrust and tension between the poor and the wealthy, with pockets of rebellion and violence from the poor directed toward the rich. Yet, life had, for the most part, moved on, and a balance—albeit a delicate one—had been restored. "I cannot involve myself in this. I hope you understand it's not my place, Lady Thornley. This is Mr. Chadwick's vocation. I believe he is capable and trustworthy."

"You would do it for Violette, but not me?" She narrowed her hazel eyes. "Why should that be? Has my family not been kind and generous to you and your charity? We have given your charity a great deal of money. We have opened our house to your gala. Which, I might add, Franklin might still be alive if we had *not* been so generous."

Ravenna felt wedged between two stones. If she didn't investigate on behalf of Lady Mildreth, it could hurt her reputation among the wealthier nobility, which could have repercussions for The Penitent House, her heart's work. Ravenna's stomach twisted. If she angered the society doyennes, the reformed prostitutes might suffer from lack of funding and be cast back into the streets. Yet, she wanted nothing more than to avoid Mr. Chadwick. He wouldn't take kindly to her investigating as well, and the last thing she wanted to do was cross him.

"Well?" Lady Mildreth said.

"Please understand. I-I didn't do it for Lady Violette. I became involved on behalf of Lord Hawkestone because he and I had been friends and because I believed my family was being threatened. Which, as it turns out, was true."

Lady Mildreth puffed up and stood. Lady Mildreth was not a woman to make an enemy of. She was responsible for the Younger Pitt's resignation because she'd convinced King George III to keep the restrictions against the Irish Catholics in place. She was a formidable ally and an equally formidable enemy. Further, if Ravenna agreed to do the investigation, Lady Mildreth might be of a mind to help Ravenna's remaining stepson, Harrison, secure many important connections in Parliament who were out of even Catherine's reach. Yet, she didn't really want to get involved in this. Ravenna eased into her reply.

Before she could answer, a servant knocked on the door and announced the coroner.

Lady Mildreth swept past Ravenna. "We will discuss this later."

Ravenna stepped into the hall and headed toward the foyer to ask for her carriage. She stopped short to find a silver-haired, gangly man waiting.

It was Mr. Peterson, the coroner. Ravenna had met him once before during Lord Hawkestone's inquiry. The footman dashed off to retrieve Mr. Chadwick.

She wanted out of this house and away from Lady Thornley's pressure. She looked around for another footman to assist, but they were scurrying about on the butler's orders. She'd have to wait a moment. A couple of somber servant women and footmen entered the drawing room across the hall. The younger of the women carried a sheet and the other a bucket with water and vinegar. Other servants milled about in the foyer, arms crossed, whispering somberly. There weren't too many tears being shed. Thornley must not have been widely loved by the staff. When her own husband, Philip, had died last year, the staff wept openly, some for days. The butler entered the foyer and began passing out black armbands to the staff, who then busied themselves with their mourning accoutrement.

Mr. Chadwick met Mr. Peterson in the hall, and they shook hands. They turned toward the study. Mr. Peterson greeted Ravenna as he and Mr. Chadwick passed through to investigate the murder scene.

"Young woman," said Mr. Peterson to someone inside the study. "We need privacy, please."

A wiry, young servant exited the room and pressed her back against the wall with a heavy sigh. She set her bucket down beside her and swiped wisps of dark auburn hair out of her face. She seemed agitated. She was pretty with pouty lips and porcelain skin. Her mob cap sat back and slightly askew, signaling a rebellious nature.

Mr. Chadwick glanced at the girl, locked his gaze with Ravenna, then shut the door.

Though Ravenna wasn't actually investigating, her curiosity overcame her. She said to the girl. "You seem upset. You must've been quite fond of Lord Thornley." The acrid sting of vinegar from the bucket assailed Ravenna's nostrils.

The girl snorted and spoke with a thick Yorkshire accent. "I don't like being around the dead. Their ghosts are still hanging about and can get into your body if you're not careful. But good riddance to him, I say." She flashed angry olive-green eyes at Ravenna and pushed her rolled sleeves over her elbows.

"That seems unkind."

"Lord Thornley liked to chase me into corners and closed rooms…" She lifted her eyebrows pointedly. "If you catch my meaning, milady."

"Oh," Ravenna demurred. "I'm so sorry. I had no idea." It was an unfortunate hazard for young women in service. They were often taken advantage of by their wealthier and more powerful employers. Apparently, Lord Thornley didn't only accost theater girls. "I hope he didn't force you to…"

The girl scoffed and shook her head. "Nah. I was faster than him. I soon learned to avoid him and to lock my door at night. When he rang in the middle of the night, I sent Ruth." She jerked her thumb at the door to indicate the chubby, older woman who'd been present earlier. "He had no interest in her." She laughed.

Ravenna couldn't help but smile at the girl's spunk and ingenuity. "What's your name?"

"Evie, milady."

She seemed annoyed. "If you don't mind me saying so, you seem angry."

She leveled a steady, calculating gaze at Ravenna. "Why should I mind what you say, milady? Nothing the likes of me can do about it, is there?"

"Are you angry?" Ravenna pressed, watching the other servants mill about the foyer, whispering, concerned.

"I confess I am. He'd promised to speak to Lady Mildreth on my behalf for higher wages, a chambermaid position, and to hire my brother as a footman."

"Why would he promise all that? Especially if he wasn't getting what he'd hoped for from you."

The girl tipped her head and looked at Ravenna as if she were a simpleton. Her countenance dripped with wit and a sharp, if not bitter, intelligence. "Men always promise things to women when they hope to enjoy their charms."

"Are you in the habit of wagering your charms?"

"Promising my charms ain't the same as doling them out, is it?" She lifted a brow. She crossed her arms over her thin chest.

"You have a sharp tongue."

"Sometimes, it's all a girl has to defend herself, ain't it?"

Ravenna narrowed her eyes. "What's your position here, Evie?"

"Lower Housemaid."

Ravenna dropped the pieces into a place: a bitter, saucy, but intelligent maid, dangling the promise of sexual favors in exchange for better pay and positions for herself and her brother. Whether by accident or on purpose, Lord Thornley had failed to follow through, which angered the woman. All these pieces formed the larger part of a motive for murder.

"Where were you when Lord Thornley died?"

Evie wiped her forehead with the back of her wrist. "I was cleaning his study since he was in the ballroom. I blacked the fireplace grill, removed the ashes and such. I was dusting when Lord Thornley came in with that shiftless brother of his. They was saying something about money."

"You were cleaning, yet, I noticed there had been dust on his desk."

"Yeah, I hadn't finished my tasks. They interrupted me."

"I see. Were Lord Thornley and his brother angry? Or fighting?"

Her eyes lit with humor. "They was spitting at each other like a couple of fishwives."

"Did you happen to hear any of the conversation?"

Evie scratched her head under her mobcap. "When Lord Thornley opened the door, he said, 'I'm not made of money, you proffingate libertine.'"

"Proffingate? You mean profligate?"

"That's it."

"Profligate libertine." Ravenna's brows shot up. "Those are strong words from one brother to another."

"Ain't they? But I've noticed they was always fighting about something. I'd die to think if my brother and I hated each other like that. Best I could tell, they was always more enemies than brothers."

"I see. What else did they argue about?"

"Everything," she snorted. "Money, women, occupation, inheritance, horses, cards." She rolled her eyes. "It might be easier to answer what they ain't argued about."

That all certainly sounded like grounds for murder, too. "Did you hear any more of what they said when they entered the room?"

"Nah, I didn't hear nothing else. They stopped when they saw me and I ran out before Lord Thornley could even dismiss me." She pressed her red, chapped hands into the small of her back and leaned back to stretch. "But it weren't for trying." A sly smile crept over her lips. "I lingered for a spell outside the door to listen, but they lowered their voices, and it was all a muddle." She lifted the bucket. "And don't you know, just as I was about to press my ear to the door, the butler put me to work in the kitchen." Evie huffed out a breath. "Well, I reckon they're going to be in there for some time. I guess I'll do my other work and come back to this room later." She started to walk away.

"Thank you for talking with me, Evie."

Evie lifted her chin by way of acknowledgement. And, not waiting to be dismissed, she trudged away, leaning, with her bucket in hand.

Ravenna stopped a rushing footman to ask for her carriage. She wasn't going to wait for Lady Thornley or Mr. Chadwick. She sat on the foyer bench, bouncing her knee, watching the servants talking in low voices, waiting their turn to be interrogated.

As she waited, she processed what she'd learned. There were already at least three people who might've wanted Lord Thornley dead: Mr. Gibson, Percy, and Evie. Lord Thornley had reneged on his promises to the maid, Evie. And she struck Ravenna as the sort of woman who wouldn't easily accept someone coming between her and her money—and would do something about it.

Mr. Chadwick and Mr. Peterson exited the study, interrupting her thoughts. They whispered to each other as they crossed the hall.

Mr. Peterson said, "I'll get a jury together and bring them for an inquest." They shook hands, and Mr. Peterson exited the house. Mr. Chadwick turned to Percy. "Lord Percy, I would like to speak with you next, if you please, sir."

She watched Chadwick stride away with determination. *Where was the carriage? What was taking so long?* She bit the inside of her lip as she watched Percy stroll down the hall toward the ballroom.

Percy. She picked up where she'd left off in her list of suspects. Like so many younger brothers, he was dissolute, far too liberal with his money, and far too deep in debt to extract himself without aid. He was the new Lord Thornley now. How happy and eager was Percy for the change in station? She stared up at the portrait of Lord Franklin Thornley hanging over the staircase. He wore Ottoman garb: a golden wrap on his head like a sultan with a tassel hanging down the side, a red velvet coat patterned with paisleys and a golden sash around his waist. Thornley seemed to be more enamored with countries other than his own. A curious and strange man.

Percy was most likely the last one to see Lord Thornley alive. However, an embittered Evie might've come back to the room for a final reckoning when Percy had left. She would've had to work quickly. And then rush to change bloody clothes. Then there was the matter of whether she would've had the strength to overpower Lord Thornley—even if she'd ambushed him with a surprise attack. Perhaps, if Ravenna could talk to Percy to discover the true timeline, she could better narrow down the order of events. Not that she was investigating. She was just curious.

Finally, there was Mr. Gibson. Jealous, envious, angry. He wanted accolades and attention. He wanted acknowledgement and gratitude for his work. He wanted to impress people, especially powerful ones. And he needed money to perform his work. Lots of it. Of course, he had admitted that Thornley had funded many of his excursions. It would be stupid to kill his funding source. Unless he'd found another one, one who might treat him more fairly. But then, why kill Thornley? Why not just leave and break off with him? Unless…Ravenna bit her lip…unless he killed Thornley to steal the Widow's Fire opal. Perhaps he planned to take it to the king himself in hopes of attaining a great reward or to sell it to a collector to fund future excursions. Though there were others who might've wanted Thornley dead, Mr. Gibson seemed to be the clearest choice, so far.

She had to tell Mr. Chadwick, though, didn't she? He was the one with the authority to investigate crimes. She was merely a widow. She wanted nothing more than to lead a quiet life, work on charitable causes, indulge in a few fencing lessons, and avoid the Irish Unity who had, fortunately, been quiet these last couple of months. She didn't want to get involved in this.

Chapter Five

The footman announced Ravenna's carriage.

Finally. She stood and moved toward the front door as Catherine rushed down the hall toward her.

"I've come to tell you Mr. Chadwick would like to speak to you next."

"But my carriage is here."

"He's expecting you, dear." She lowered her voice to a whisper. "It might be best to not annoy him."

Ravenna's shoulders fell limp with her sigh. "You're right. I suppose it can wait."

"At least you and I have the honor of being questioned early. I insisted we could not possibly stay here waiting for him to interview all the staff. I told him we know nothing about the murder, but…" She rolled her eyes. "He will have his way in the matter." Sadness pitched her brows, and she shook her head. "It's tragic for poor Mildreth, however."

"Absolutely." Ravenna started toward the hall.

"You'll write or visit soon to tell me everything she said to you? You know I can't forgo even boring gossip." She smiled.

"Of course."

"Good. I'm leaving. I don't want to be here another minute."

Ravenna glanced longingly at the front door as she inched down the hall. With a goodbye wave to Catherine, she entered the ballroom. It seemed colder than it had before when it was filled with the giggling and chatty women of The Penitent House. Servants sat somberly in chairs at the far end of the room, waiting their turn.

Mr. Chadwick stood in front of the fireplace, staring into the cold, empty maw with his hands clasped behind his back. He had pulled a couple of chairs over and sat them facing each other.

Ravenna stood in the doorway. "You needed to speak with me, Mr. Chadwick?"

He glanced at her. "Yes. Please…" He motioned to a nearby chair. She sat, pressing her knees together, clutching her folded fan. "I wanted to ask you a few questions about the incident here today."

Ravenna lifted her chin and smoothed her palms over the raised texture of her Swiss-dotted muslin skirt. His cold, calculating stare bespoke a man who could be cunning and therefore not likely to be fully trusted—in spite of what she'd told Lady Thornley about his integrity.

"I was here in the ballroom for the gala. I didn't see or hear anything. That is, until the maid screamed."

He stared at the tip of his boot, leaning his chin against his fist. "Do you know what I find interesting?" He continued to look at his boot.

She paused. "I imagine any number of things."

His hard stare shot through her, and a chill trickled down her spine. "I find it interesting how death seems to surround you."

She blinked and clasped her hands in front of her. "Yes. It's quite unfortunate. Though purely coincidental, I assure you."

"Is it?"

Ravenna tipped her head, a slow heat rising through her center. "Exactly what are you implying, Mr. Chadwick?" Her finger toyed with the gold medallion at the base of her black lace fan, where a dagger hid within.

"Please show me your arms."

She frowned and blinked. "Whatever for."

He held his arms out and held his palms face up. "Like this."

She mimicked his movement. He leaned close and inspected her hands and arms through her sheer sleeves.

He released a sigh and sat back in his chair. "You're innocent. At least of committing the murder."

"Of course, I'm innocent."

"Though you still might've coerced or paid someone to commit a deed you couldn't stomach."

"I did no such thing. Why would I?"

"That's the question, isn't it? What motive would you have for killing Lord Thornley?" He removed a snuff-box from his inner pocket, lifted a pinch to his nostril, and sniffed. His eyes watered as he shut the lid with a click. "There's no blood on you. There would be if you'd stabbed him." Sniffing, he wiped his nose and returned the box to its hiding spot. "Though you might've hired someone to do your dirty work. A servant of this house, perhaps?"

Ravenna stood. "I'm not going to listen to these baseless accusations."

"Lady Catherine said some interesting things..."

Ravenna slowly lowered into her chair. What on earth could Catherine have said to lead him to suspect her? Catherine was her best friend. Ravenna didn't believe for one moment Catherine would've accused her of anything. "What do you mean?"

"She said Lord Thornley used to spend time at the theater where you and Lady Adair once worked. Is that true?"

"Yes."

"She said he also enjoyed accosting the women there."

"Also true. He was known among the girls there as The Great Fondler."

Amusement flashed in his eyes. "I'm thinking perhaps he had become aggressive with you and—"

She held up her hand. "Stop there. I haven't been in the theater for nearly six years. Further, I never had interactions with him. When I learned of his behavior, I worked diligently to avoid him. So, I had no desire or need to kill him. But even if he had done something to me, why would I wait so long?"

"Hm." He studied her face. "I see. Lady Catherine said much the same thing." He sighed and thought for a moment. "Whoever killed Lord Thornley had a connection to this house. A servant, a friend, or a family member. It was someone who knew about his collections, what was valuable, what wasn't."

"Yes. I think so, too. In fact, I have a few ideas about who might've done it."

He lifted his brows. "Go on."

"I think you should focus on the servant, Evie, Thornley's brother, or Mr. Gibson. They all stand out to me as having more reason than any to kill Thornley."

He narrowed his eyes and nodded.

She added, "But whoever is responsible, I believe the killer may well be among us. In this very house."

Chapter Six

When Mr. Chadwick released Ravenna, he warned her that he might visit if he had additional questions. Ravenna left Thornley Hall and returned to Gordon House. Her anxiety melted as she neared home, and dreamed of a good book, a glass of port, and a nap.

The butler, Mr. Banks, greeted her. He was a tall, burly man with thick gray hair and a haunted look in his gray eyes resulting from his experiences as a veteran in the American Rebellion. He'd allied with her from the day she'd married her late husband, Philip. Since Philip's death, Mr. Banks had been her most stalwart support in her grief and in managing the household. "You have a guest in the drawing room, ma'am."

Ravenna sighed, her spirits flagging as the door closed on her anticipated book, wine, and nap. She removed her black bonnet and gloves, then set about undoing the buttons on her black linen spencer as her mind picked through a variety of excuses.

He said, "I told them you were away, but they insisted upon waiting. They've been here for at least an hour. So, we sent in a repast."

The events of the day had drained her. "I truly don't feel up to visiting anyone."

"I fear you can't avoid the meeting, ma'am." He helped her out of her spencer.

"Very well," she sighed. She flicked through the names of her acquaintances, any number of who would never have waited so long to see her—unless there was an urgent matter. "Who is it?"

"A woman claiming to be your Aunt Brendae and a young lady named Miss Georgiana."

Brendae's name rattled Ravenna. She hadn't spoken to her Aunt since the terrible row they'd had before Ravenna married Philip five years ago. "Heavens," she breathed, steadying herself against the foyer table. "What was her...demeanor when you last spoke with her?"

Creases formed in the corners of his eyes. "I think agitated is a fair description."

Ravenna checked her face in the hall mirror. She'd grown quite pale with the events of the afternoon, and dark circles had formed under her eyes. With no time to freshen up, she checked her hair in the hall mirror and pinched color into her cheeks. She put a hand to the doorknob, the brass delightfully cold against her sweaty palm. "Banks, do send in some very strong tea. Directly, please."

Ravenna blew out a breath and entered the room. Seeing the rigid, bony form of her Aunt Brendae again pulled her immediately back to that night, where she stood at Aunt Brendae's door in Whitechapel with her sister and her crying child. The night was chilly with a drizzle in the air and the street more crowded and noisier than anything she'd known in County Wexford. She shuddered in a thin, damp dress, ripped, covered in blood, and stinking of the smoke from the village fires. She recalled the desperate hunger wracking her ribs as she prayed silently that they were at the right house. The memory was so powerful that though she now stood in her sunlit drawing room full of flowers, she looked down at her dress to ensure her dress was clean and intact.

"Stop slouching," Aunt Brendae snapped at a young girl beside her fresh and pink as peonies. She pinched the girl under the arm. The girl cried out and pouted, adjusting her posture and rubbing the spot. That must be Helen's daughter. The last time she'd seen her, she was a gawky, thin wisp of a girl.

The ghost pain of that pinch bloomed under Ravenna's arm. She remembered too well the biting pain. Even though she had been a grown young woman when she'd entered Aunt Brendae's cramped little tenement, it didn't prevent the nip of those sharp fingers.

Aunt Brendae was a flat-faced, dark-eyed woman with a long, pointed nose. Her short, delicate form wrapped in black bombazine somehow held together against the force of her formidable character. When she noticed Ravenna, she stood erect, a spine of steel. Silver wove through Aunt Brendae's once-dark hair, and the skin around her neck, eyes, and jaw had turned crepey, showing the advance of her years.

"Lady Birchfield." She pinched out the words as though they were sour on her tongue. She tapped the shoulder of the girl, who bounced to her feet and gaped at Ravenna.

Perhaps Ravenna should've rolled her shoulders back and lifted her chin to radiate the stateliness of her current title and circumstance. But Aunt Brendae's presence reduced her immediately to her condition six years ago, when she was a terrified, homeless woman fleeing violence in Ireland, broken under the loss of her family, friends, and village.

Ravenna's knees weakened, and her insides wilted. Afraid her voice would quaver and betray her, she cleared her throat. "Aunt Brendae, it's been a long time. It's good to see you." That was a lie. It wasn't good to see her aunt, but perhaps after several years' distance, Ravenna could put the past behind her, and they could start all over. She didn't like the way things had been left between them. She didn't like fighting with family.

Aunt Brendae's eyes flashed with contempt and disbelief. A corner of her mouth ticked upward. "Indeed, it has been a long time. I suppose you haven't heard from your brother?"

The mention of Niall recalled the last time she'd seen Aunt Brendae. Ravenna's face flushed under the memory of Aunt Brendae's vicious words—words that often scratched at Ravenna's thoughts in her darkest hours.

Ravenna's forehead tightened all the way down into her neck, and a deep throb pulsed against her skull as the bitter memories threatened to pull her under. She took a cleansing breath and tried to shove the anger, fear, hurt, and betrayal from that horrible night out of her mind. Maybe she and Aunt Brendae could repair what had been broken. Maybe Aunt Brendae had heard something from Helen. Ravenna would go find her sister, and they could reclaim their lost years and piece family back together.

Aunt Brendae's voice broke her dark reverie. "Well? Have you heard from Niall? Or has he utterly abandoned the family and his obligations to us?"

"I haven't heard from him in many years," Ravenna said.

Aunt Brendae scoffed. "Not surprising. And your sister? Have you managed to find her?"

"I haven't. In fact, I was hoping to ask you if you'd heard from her." Her sister, Helen, was a few years older than Ravenna when they landed in London. She had tried to stay with Aunt Brendae with her thirteen-year-old-daughter, Georgiana. But Helen had been unable to tolerate Aunt Brendae's authoritarian grip. So, Helen, unable to support herself and her child, abandoned Georgianna with Aunt Brendae.

"I've heard nothing from Helen. Nor do I expect to. It's probably best if she remained absent. Her presence would probably only corrupt the girl." She turned to the girl at her side and nudged her forward. "This is your niece, Georgiana. Helen's daughter. Surely, you remember her?"

"I do," Ravenna smiled through the guilt and shame snaking through her core. She had tried to get along with Aunt Brendae for Georgiana's sake. But on that fateful night, when Aunt Brendae had kicked her out, she knew she couldn't take Georgiana with her and put her through an unpredictable amount of suffering in a life on the streets. So, she too had abandoned the girl.

"You have a strange way of showing it, since you've never visited her."

Ravenna didn't want to argue with Aunt Brendae. But she wasn't wrong. Ravenna should've done more, especially once she'd married into comfort and security. She should've gone immediately to reclaim Georgiana and give her a home. But the first years of her marriage were overwhelming: a new husband, a new home with new staff and new stepsons who were slow to warm to her, and a new circle of friends, acquaintances, and her husband's political allies to try to impress—all while trying to learn how to navigate the aristocracy.

She looked down at the carpet. "You're right. I could've done better about visiting." She lifted her gaze to Georgiana. "I apologize to you, Georgiana.

I'm so very sorry for neglecting you. I'd always meant to come back for you."

Shock pushed like ocean waves through Ravenna as she stared at this beautiful young woman. It was like seeing a ghost of her eldest sister, Helen, the ash-blonde hair and kind blue eyes set in a heart-shaped face. She was taller than Aunt Brendae, nearly as tall as Ravenna, and well-formed enough to draw a great deal of attention. Tears of guilt, joy, and regret flooded Ravenna's eyes. She hadn't been able to help her family, to pull them together as she'd hoped. But above the guilt, shame, and regret crested an enormous wave of joy. Seeing her niece again filled Ravenna with elation and hope that she might also one day be reunited with her sister and brother.

The dewy-faced girl wore a dark green spencer over a matching sprigged muslin dress. She smiled shyly and shrugged a shoulder. "I forgive you. I understand."

Aunt Brendae continued, her dark eyes glittering with barely suppressed malice. "I've had the care of her ever since you and Helen abandoned us."

"But I did send money and write letters. Did you not receive them?" Ravenna asked Georgiana.

Georgiana glanced at Aunt Brendae and shook her head. "No. Never."

Ravenna lifted her brows at Aunt Brendae to indicate the silent questions *Oh, really? Why not?*

"The money was used for her needs. I couldn't trust her to manage it on her own."

"And the letters?"

Aunt Brendae ignored the question and nudged Georgiana's arm with her sharp elbow. "Do what I showed you."

Georgiana curled her lips and rubbed her arm as she performed an awkward curtsey. "A pleasure to see you again, milady."

Ravenna smiled warmly and opened her arms. "Family doesn't greet each other with curtsies. Come here."

Georgiana approached her shyly, and Ravenna hugged her tightly, kissing her cheek. She pulled back, holding Georgiana's cheeks. "You're so pretty. Just like your mother. And I promise you, from this moment forward, it will be my sole focus to bring us all together again."

Georgiana smiled and nodded. "Yes, ma'am."

Ravenna squeezed her hand. "And I can't wait to hear all about you."

A maid entered with a tray of tea and ginger biscuits. "Please..." Ravenna said, motioning to the sofa. "Sit. Join me."

Ravenna poured a cup of tea for everyone. She drank her tea, drawing strength from the stout brew. "Please forgive me. I don't know where to begin with conversation. I'm quite taken by surprise, though I'm very pleased you're both here." She drank again.

Aunt Brendae lifted her chin and said to Ravenna, "I *do* know where to begin. It's quite simple. What will you do to help us now?"

Ravenna blinked. "Pardon?" It's not that Ravenna had any qualms about assisting her family, but the rude presumption, the sheer vulgarity of Aunt Brendae's direct manner was too much to be borne.

Aunt Brendae rolled her eyes. "Don't play stupid, girl. Georgiana's eighteen. She's of an age now where she should have a husband and start a family. You're in a position to ensure she secures a good mate who can provide a stable life and a future for her. Perhaps even one who has a pretty title like you landed for yourself. Then you both will be in a position to recompense me for all the trouble you've caused me over the years."

A flare of anger shot through Ravenna. The night of their vicious row crashed down on her, and she grew hot under the anger and hurt firing in her chest. "I haven't even spoken to you for several years. You kicked me out of your house because I wouldn't give you all the money I'd earned at the theater. I gave you most of it, bought our food, and was nothing short of a servant in your home, though I worked at the theater as well. I worked hard—"

Aunt Brendae interrupted her. "You impudent—"

But Ravenna talked over her. "As I told you the last night I saw you, you blamed me and Niall for getting Colin killed. Colin was himself to blame. How many times did I try to explain the role Colin played in The Unity? Yet you would not hear it. *Colin* recruited my brother and put us all in danger. It was *Colin* who helped to establish The Unity." Memories of the sights and

51

sounds of the massacre in her village stormed her mind. "Stupid, foolish Colin." There was much more she wanted to say, but she didn't want to unleash her anger on Aunt Brendae in front of Georgiana. "I'm happy to help Georgiana, but I owe *you* nothing." She clutched her folded fan.

Aunt Brendae's face reddened. Suppressed rage coursed through her, shaking the fake curls at her temples. She clutched the chair arms. "I took you, your sister, and this child in when you had no one because that criminal brother of yours begged me to. He said he'd be back for you soon. But I never saw him again. Why didn't *he* go to work and support his family? I'll tell you why. He was always a shiftless ne'er-do-well. *He* should have provided a roof for your heads. Instead, he ran away." She pointed a crooked finger at Ravenna. "I worked my fingers to the bone doing extra laundry and sewing to provide food and to put a roof over your thankless heads. And hers." She jabbed her finger in Georgiana's direction.

Georgiana sat wide-eyed and baffled.

Aunt Brendae continued, holding up her knotted hands. "My hands hurt constantly from my years of toil. My eyes are nearly blind. I'm unable to do the work I did in my youth, so I can't make the money I once did." She dropped her hands and gripped her skirts. "Had it not been for me, you would've ended up a syphilitic prostitute, like your wastrel sister, who's probably dying of disease this very moment in some lice-ridden brothel." Georgiana blushed and looked down at her lap as Aunt Brendae continued. "Niall's to blame for my Colin's death. So, as I see it, you owe me." Her eyes were dry and hard, flinting with rage. "You and your whole rotten family. Why my brother married your—"

Ravenna scooted to the edge of her seat. "Don't you *dare* disparage my mother, old woman." Her fingers instinctively fell to the medallion on her black lace fan. The flick of a finger would release the blade. "In fact, I'll thank you to shut your venomous mouth. My mother left behind a good life in Italy, a successful life in the opera to marry Pa." Furious tears cracked her voice. "But Ireland broke her. The things she endured just to stay with Pa…" She shook her head, seething. "Then *your* Colin. Your stupid, stupid son became involved with The Irish Unity. They colluded with the French to invade England, hoping to free Ireland. He approached Niall with all his pretty words, speaking of freedom and bravery and revolt. And my foolish brother, trying to prove his mettle, fell for it like Eve taking the forbidden fruit."

Aunt Brendae scoffed and averted her face to stare at the door. Her hands clasped and unclasped over her black velvet reticule. She tapped her foot.

Ravenna continued. "I know you don't want to hear that, but it's true."

Aunt Brendae shot daggers at Ravenna. "How *dare* you speak ill of the dead." Deep lines formed around her thin lips. "Would you have me believe my son is a traitor to our family? To the Crown? To England?"

"Yes! You, uncle, and my parents may have been proud Loyalists to King George, but your son and my brother..." She lowered her voice in case someone in the foyer might overhear. "They were not. They were traitors. They believed the coercions of the radicals who were colluding with the French. A painful truth, I confess. But the truth nonetheless."

Aunt Brendae's nostrils flared. "I will not listen to one more word of this–this...*slander*." She stood, clutching her reticule. "I wash my hands of all of this." She looked down her nose at Ravenna. "And of *you*!" She stormed toward the door, surprisingly agile for a woman of her near seventy years.

Ravenna and Georgiana shot to their feet. Georgiana ran to catch up. Aunt Brendae turned and pointed. "Stay. She can be your caretaker now." She swiped her hand through the air, motioning around the room. "With all her apparent grand fortune."

"Aunt Brendae," Ravenna moved forward. "You can't abandon her here."

She scoffed. "And why not? You live in more comfort and wealth than I've ever known. You're far more equipped to manage her needs." She opened the door and, without looking back, walked out.

Georgiana chased after her. "Auntie, wait..." Georgiana's trunk sat in the foyer by the staircase. Aunt Brendae continued out of the house and down the street, ignoring Georgiana's shouts.

Ravenna put a hand on the girl's arm. "Let her go." She led the girl inside and closed the front door. Georgiana flew back to the drawing room, crying.

Banks asked, "What shall I do with the young lady's trunk?"

"Banks, the young lady is Miss Georgiana Sullivan. My niece. Please take her trunk to the pink room and have the room prepared for her." She rubbed her forehead. "And, uh, please have a bath prepared for her. I'm sure she shall want to refresh before dinner."

Ravenna returned to the drawing room. Georgiana was slumped face down in the corner of the sofa, sobbing. Ravenna knelt beside her, pulled a handkerchief from her bodice, and offered it to Georgiana. "Here. Please don't cry." She held her hand and rubbed circles on her back.

Georgiana accepted the handkerchief and sat up. "Why shouldn't I cry? What shall I do now? I have no home, and no one wants me. Not Aunt Brendae. Not you. Not my mother. And I don't know anyone else." She wiped her face and blew her nose. It turned a bright pink. She broke into fresh tears.

"All will be well. I promise. I never said I don't want you here. In fact, I'm having a room and bath prepared for you now. She sat beside Georgiana, holding her and drawing her head to rest on her shoulder. That seemed to placate the girl, who sniffled and seemed content to be held. It might be interesting, even fun, to have a young lady in the house. And, best of all, it was one step closer to bringing together her fractured family.

Having a young woman around would certainly be a diversion. Georgiana would no doubt want to attend every ball and function, as she should if she expected to find a husband. However, she needed some refinement. Finding a man of any consequence might be too difficult since youth and beauty carried a woman only so far. She might, however, find a second son or a wealthy merchant. Either way, Georgiana would need education of both books and comportment.

When Georgiana had calmed down, Ravenna gave her shoulders a squeeze, patted her arm, and said, "Come, I'll show you to your room. You can have a bath, and lie down for a nap, if you like. After you're settled in, I'll show you around the house." She stood and drew the girl to her feet.

At the top of the stairs, she pointed to the right. "My bedchamber is down that hall, the last door on the left, should you need anything. Your room is this way." She led her down the opposite hall and selected the first door on the right. She opened the door.

"Oh, my," Georgiana gasped. "It's lovely. This is all mine?" She stepped into the room and took in the pink walls, white bed hangings and window treatments, the sage green Turkish rug on the floor, the gray marble fireplace, and the small sitting area. She ran her hand over the washstand in the corner and let it trail over to the vanity. She bent to glance at herself in the mirror. "This room is almost as big as the whole of Aunt Brendae's home!"

That much was true. Though Ravenna was angry with Aunt Brendae, she carried a soft spot for the woman's rough life. If Ravenna could manage to swallow her bitter pride, she might send Aunt Brendae some money in the future. Though the spiteful old crone didn't deserve it. Ravenna would need to wait for a cooler head, however.

Georgiana spun around in wonder. "This is too much for one person." She stopped to open the doors of the wardrobe. "So much space and too many fine things."

Ravenna leaned against the door jamb, recalling when she had first moved into Birchfield Manor as a newlywed to Lord Philip Birchfield, the late foreign secretary of England. Everything seemed so grand and large, so clean and fine. She felt dirty and small and indelicate in comparison. She'd lived in constant fear of breaking something. "It certainly seems that way now." Ravenna smiled, then broke into a chuckle. "I promise you'll get accustomed to it soon enough."

Amused, Ravenna watched Georgiana flutter around the room, opening all the drawers and doors and touching everything. She was already warming to the idea of having this vibrant youth in the house. "Perhaps we can go shopping tomorrow." She lifted a brow and said conspiratorially, "After all, you will need new dresses for husband-hunting this season."

Chapter Seven

Ravenna and Georgiana, both having had a long, emotional day, retired to their respective bedchambers. The strain of the day peeled away with the black muslin dress Ravenna laid over the chest at the end of the bed. She slipped into a lavender silk dressing gown with frothy lace at the sleeves and poured a glass of port. She melted into the chair by the fire, eager to read the letters she'd received from her stepson, Harrison, and Lord Braedon. Saving Braedon's for last, she opened Harrison's.

She hadn't seen or heard from her youngest stepson since he'd been in town for his elder brother, Thomas's, funeral a few months ago. She was looking forward to seeing him. Since he'd been younger when she married into the family, she was able to develop a bond with Harrison that she'd struggled to build with Thomas.

He was a bit of a rogue, constantly asking for money, which ran through his hands like water. His letter was little more than a brief note to inform her of his arrival within the next few days and his intention to stay for the next few weeks at Gordon House until it was time to retire to Birchfield Manor for sporting season. Of course, in closing the letter, he hinted at a need for money when he arrived.

She sighed and rolled her eyes, dropping the note on the occasional table beside her. With more eagerness than was prudent, she picked up Braedon's letter.

Taking a deep breath, she studied the smooth garland of his writing in the address and pressed down on the spirits lifting inside her. He was handsome, intriguing, but an incurable flirt. Further, he was also engaged in a complicated entanglement with another woman—the same woman he was in Italy with now. A war waged in Ravenna's heart. Braedon swore he no longer wanted a relationship with Dianthe, yet he had escorted her and her mother to Italy to help Dianthe overcome her reliance on laudanum. Ravenna typically kept jealousy in check, but lately, it had picked away at her confidence.

Did Braedon go to Italy based on gentlemanly duty and compassion? Or was this trip rooted in his desires? She had witnessed how Dianthe continued to throw herself at him. Was Dianthe disoriented in her beliefs? Entirely possible in her opium haze. Or had Braedon encouraged Dianthe's expectations? Did it even matter now? He left. With Dianthe.

Yet, thoughts of him rushed into Ravenna's mind at the worst times— mostly when she tried to sleep: his tall, muscular physique; the dark, wavy lock of hair that fell over his frosty blue, wolfish eyes; the sensuous lips. And thoughts of him always left her both stirred up and hollow. She pushed back her own desire. Briefly, she considered not opening the letter. It was no good thinking of him since he was so far away. Yet, she truly enjoyed Braedon's presence, his conversation, his friendship, his wit and charm. The letters were one of the few bright spots in her life. They cast a light spell, allowing her to believe, for just a moment, he was once again with her. That, for a moment, she was visible to someone in the world.

She flipped the letter and ran her thumb over the red wax seal, feeling the impression of two stallions flanking a shield with a raven in the center, wings outspread, a sword and arrow in its claws. Heat expanded in her chest, blood thrummed in her ears, and her skin felt electric. She popped the seal, anticipation tingling in her fingertips, and she drank in the words like a fine, crisp champagne.

June 20, 1803
   My dearest little Raven,
   I've just returned from a moonlight sailing excursion on the Po. I confess, in spite of the wine and the ribaldry of my companions, I could

think only of your eyes so much like the dark water with the glint of moonlight reflected there. How could I bear to sleep now? With you ever on my mind it would be impossible. So, I take up my pen to string together these words to link a chain across the countries and waters between us. If only these frail words could tether us together forever! But alas, I awake each day, and the distance remains....

"Well, that is your fault," she muttered, turning the page.

Even now, I can see your lifted chin and the stubborn spirit in your eyes as you proclaim the fault is all mine and you would be correct....

Ravenna hid her face in the letter and giggled. She hadn't realized she was so predictable or that he had become so well-versed in reading her in such a short time. She sniffed the paper. It smelled of him, his sandalwood cologne. She sighed, pushing against the longing, attempting to unfurl inside her. She returned to the letter.

These last few months have been restless. Life is warmer and brighter under the Italian sun and moves at a slower pace, but the clime, the wine, the food, the atmosphere soaks into the blood, sets it on fire, and drives an inescapable longing deep into my bones for you. Only you. Peace evades me at every turn, and any attempt at diversion is fruitless....

She paused. She couldn't help but wonder what entertainments he had devised. Even if he'd lost his interest in Dianthe, there were certainly a great many Italian beauties around him. "Stop it, Ravenna!" She hissed. She shut her eyes. She could not, would not, allow herself to descend into jealousy for a man who had not promised himself to her. She blew out a breath and continued reading.

Italy is much like London with all the mundanities of fetes, balls, dinners, operas, and other such things. Yet, these trivial distractions are pointless. Italy is missing something London has—you. It's always your face I wish to see at dinner or across a ballroom, and I ache to bring you here, if only to hear you scold me for annoying you. Would you come if I asked you?

Ravenna scoffed and rolled her eyes. No. She would not carry herself all the way to Italy, while a war wages, to put herself between Braedon and his perceived duty to Dianthe. He would have to manage on his own.

I ask in vain. I know you would not come. And I do not blame you.

Dianthe struggles to break the hold laudanum has over her. Sometimes I wonder if the relapses into her love affair with her demon is intentional to keep us here, to keep me ever chained to her. Sometimes, I wish I were the sort of unprincipled man the rumor mill reports me to be. What liberty it would be to abandon my loyalties and chase only my desires, throwing all caution and care aside! Alas, I am no innocent. Yet, I am not such a man to abandon someone in need. But I swear, the moment she is well, I will fly to you.

Siren sleep calls me away for now, and I'm happy to go, for there, in the depths of my dreams, I often find you. How cruel and lovely my dreams are to bring me so close to you only to find when I wake it was all a vapor. Tomorrow I will write you a longer letter telling you all about Lido, an island in the Venetian Lagoon. I've heard tales of the Crusaders encamped there before setting out on their mission in the 11th century.

June 21, 1803

I've just returned from Dianthe's villa. Her mother applied for my assistance as the Wild One is missing and her mother bids me help. My visit to Lido is delayed. I don't know when I might write again. I search for her, but my thoughts remain with you. Though it pains me—adieu, sweetling.

Ever yrs.

B

Bittersweet nostalgia kissed with loneliness swept through Ravenna. She sighed, folding the papers. She laid the missive aside and sipped her wine. Ravenna missed Braedon more than she wanted to. Perhaps more than was acceptable for a woman in her situation. Yet, a certain light went out of her days in his absence. His energy, attention, and charm breathed life into her. In the last eleven months, she'd almost forgotten what living life felt like. She'd nearly disappeared from the world inside her black widow's weeds. In his presence, she felt *seen* again.

She wiped her eyes. Now that the war had resumed with France and he was in Italy with Dianthe, he had no reason to return. Further, the war might render travel too dangerous. Honestly, she was surprised he'd made it to Italy at all. In fact, she might never see him again. A chill skittered over her skin. She definitely didn't want to entertain those thoughts.

She turned herself instead to bed. The day had taken its toll, and sleep would not be denied. She crawled under the covers, pulling the counterpane up to her chin. In order to force Braedon from her mind, she turned her mind to Lord Thornley. Sometimes, it was easier to ponder murders than console an aching heart.

Mr. Gibson seemed to be the most bitter, angered that Lord Thornley had supplanted him and claimed the credit, fame, and fortune Mr. Gibson coveted. And he'd made no attempts to hide his ire at the gala. Lord Thornley's own brother seemed a likely suspect as well, since he was so deeply in debt. While Percy was a smug, self-satisfied man, was he so displeased with his brother as to commit fratricide? Then there was Evie, sharp and dangerous as a knife. And entangled in the center of this web of darkness and deceit was Lady Thornley. Was she in danger too? Perhaps Ravenna was wrong to decline Lady Thornley's request for help. A part of her wanted to investigate anyway. This was an interesting puzzle and her curiosity had been piqued. It was rather exciting to ferret out a killer as she'd done a few months ago. But such intrigue brought danger and terror with it. No, it was probably best to leave it alone.

Ravenna had just finished dressing and sat down to dash off a letter to

Reverend Howarth at The Penitent House when her stepson Harrison was announced. She jogged downstairs to meet him in the parlor. He stood at the window, hands clasped behind his back, staring down at the street. The sunlight glowed around him, casting fire in his dark auburn hair. He wore an olive coat, buff pantaloons, and shiny Hessian boots. A black mourning band remained on his upper arm in honor of his elder brother. He turned and bowed when she entered.

"Good morning, Amma," he said, using the pet name he and his brother had adopted in place of calling her mother. Where his brother had resembled his father, Harrison looked most like his late mother, according to portraits Ravenna had seen at Birchfield Manor. Harrison had large round eyes, dark and liquid as coffee, a round face, and light freckles spread over his nose and cheeks. Dark circles ringed his eyes. Grief shadowed him.

"It's good to see you, Harrison." Ravenna kissed his cheek and hugged him. "I trust you had uneventful travels?"

"I did, thank you."

They sat on the sofa together. She held his hand, as if afraid he'd escape her. The family ring that had belonged to his brother and his father, winked on his pinky. He was now Lord Birchfield. The final one unless he could provide an heir.

"How have you been? I've written to you a few times, yet you haven't responded to my many letters."

He sank into a corner of the sofa. "I haven't felt like writing back. I've been swamped with duties at Birchfield Manor. I don't know how I'll complete my final year of studies at university with so much on my shoulders."

"I'm sure the steward can manage while you're away. Or, if necessary, I can move back to Birchfield and take care of things until you complete your studies."

"Wiggins is a good sort, and he's performed well enough. It's only a couple more semesters. I'm probably over-anxious now that I'm lord of the manor." He flashed a fragile smile. "Besides, you seem to be enjoying yourself a great deal here in London. I wouldn't pull you away from your life here unnecessarily. Has Lord Braedon returned?"

There was a hint of accusation in his inquiry, which she chose to ignore. Better to keep the peace. "I'm not enjoying myself so much that I wouldn't move back to Birchfield if my assistance were needed. In fact, I'm quite looking forward to returning to the country."

He chuckled. "You cannot be satisfied can you, Amma? You left the country because you were bored and now you want to leave London. Why?"

She didn't want to admit she'd been wrong about returning to London. While she enjoyed her charity work, fencing lessons, and seeing Catherine more often, the last few months had been peaks of danger flanked by valleys of loneliness. Harrison was right. She couldn't be satisfied. Georgiana's entry saved Ravenna from having to answer.

Georgiana bounded into the room, lighting it with her brilliant smile. "I'm ready for our shop—" She stopped short. "Oh, I'm sorry. I didn't mean to interrupt." She was already dressed for their shopping trip, wearing a white muslin dress, mauve spencer, and a matching straw bonnet.

Harrison jumped to his feet. He flushed and bowed.

Ravenna pinched back a smile. "Harrison, meet my niece, Georgiana Sullivan. She just arrived yesterday afternoon. Georgiana, this is my stepson, Lord Harrison Birchfield."

"How strange that sounds," he laughed. "*Lord* Harrison Birchfield. I don't know if I'll ever grow accustomed to hearing it."

"You will. Sooner than you think," Ravenna said.

Georgiana dropped an unbalanced curtsey. "A pleasure to meet you, milord."

His tone smoothed. "I assure you the pleasure is entirely mine, Miss Sullivan."

Her eyes glittered with joy. "Are you going shopping with us?"

Flustered, Harrison glanced at Ravenna. "I—"

She intervened. "I'm sure the footmen would like having another strong man around to help carry packages." Ravenna winked at Harrison.

Harrison smiled and puffed a little. "I'd be most delighted."

Chapter Eight

"I'll get my things, and we'll go," Ravenna said as she left the drawing room with Harrison and Georgiana trailing behind. When the bell rang, Ravenna paused in the foyer to wait for Banks to announce the visitor.

Banks stepped aside to let in Lady Catherine Adair.

Catherine rushed forward in her sapphire blue muslin and white cape. "Ravenna..." She clutched Ravenna's hands with a surprising amount of strength in her bird-like hands. Her cornflower blue eyes were filled with fear. "I need your help."

Ravenna had never seen Catherine so frightened. "Of course, what's the matter? You look as though a demon chases you."

Catherine whispered. "I think one does."

"Please, go to the drawing room. I'll be in directly." When Catherine disappeared into the drawing room, Ravenna turned to Harrison and Georgiana. "Pray, forgive me. I have a bit of business to attend to first. Harrison, perhaps you can show Georgiana the garden? I'll send for you when I'm ready."

Concerned, Harrison cut his eyes between Ravenna and the drawing room. "Absolutely." He offered his arm to Georgiana who sheepishly hooked her arm in his and allowed him to lead her away.

Ravenna returned to the drawing room.

Catherine's cast-off cape dripped from the sofa like melting snow. She paced the floor, wringing her hands.

Ravenna locked the door and rushed to her friend. "Catherine, you must tell me what troubles you." She grabbed Catherine's hands and led her to the sofa.

"It's Mr. Chadwick."

"What about him?"

"He's been to the house this morning questioning Yarford and me."

"Why?"

"He thinks we've had something to do with Thornley's death."

Ravenna's eyes popped wide. "What! How—what..." She shook her head to stop her spinning thoughts. "That's unconscionable. Impossible."

"I don't know how he found out about the money and such, but..."

Ravenna drew back. "Wait..." She didn't want to think ill of Oliver Dorset, Lord Yarford, Catherine's long-term co-habitant lover. "Did Yarford do something?"

"No! Of course not! How could you ask such a thing?"

"I don't know. I'm confused. Start from the beginning and explain what's going on and why Chadwick would think you or Yarford had anything to do with Thornley's murder."

Catherine inhaled and huffed out a breath. "Yarford had given a great deal of money to Thornley to fund an excursion he wanted to make to Greece and Egypt. In order to collect the funding needed, Yarford sold one of the family mines. It had been in the family for generations, but was no longer producing well. Even still, Yarford fretted over the sale of it. However, Thornley had promised that Yarford would be named the founder of any artifacts and relics. Further, Thornley suggested he was working with the British Museum to open a new wing, which would be called the Yarford wing. So, you see, Yarford had hoped to leave a legacy for future generations to enjoy and to memorialize his family name."

Ravenna nodded. "I understand. Go on..."

"Well," Catherine breathed. "Thornley took the money and never built the ship, took the trip, or contacted the British Museum. It was all a lie!"

Ravenna's mouth dropped open as she processed the information. "You mean he stole your money?"

"Yes. He did."

"When did this happen?"

Catherine scratched her forehead. "Directly before he went to New South Wales. When Yarford found out Thornley had stolen the money, he tried to track him down to get the money back. Thornley evaded him. Finally, Yarford lost all his patience and, in his anger, challenged Thornley to a duel. The next day, Thornley forced himself into the New South Wales expedition and fled the country."

"Wait. I'm confused. Why wouldn't he make plans for New South Wales and get Yarford's money for that instead? Then he wouldn't be lying."

"I don't know. According to Yarford, Thornley had intended to proceed with his original plans for Greece and Egypt. However, after he'd paid a large sum of money to the shipbuilders, he was told it was going to cost far more than originally estimated."

"Do you think that was legitimate? Or were the shipbuilders simply hoping to cheat him?"

Catherine shook her head, her sapphire earrings winking. "I don't know. All I know is he told Yarford the building of the ship had to be suspended. Naturally, everything else fell through, too."

"And he didn't pay Yarford back?"

"No. By that time, he'd spent most of the money. He still had a sizable amount, of course, but had spent or lost nearly all the rest."

"Why on earth would Yarford get in business with a man like Lord Thornley?"

Catherine threw her hands up. "It baffles me! He runs in the same circles. He should know Thornley's reputation better than I do. I suppose Yarford knew about Thornley's philandering, but had never had an indication of him being dishonest with money. According to Yarford, Thornley had always paid his gambling debts."

"So that's why Thornley had behaved so strangely toward you yesterday."

"Yes. And he spent the entire gala avoiding me. I had gone to the event, in part, to confront him and ask him to do the right thing before Yarford took the matter into his own hands."

"Into his own hands?"

"To force him to duel or give his money back, but not *murder*!"

"Dueling isn't legal either, Catherine. And some would argue it's murder just the same."

Catherine waved away the response. "Oh, posh!

While Ravenna didn't favor dueling, it was a popular method for men, and a few women, to settle their disputes. Some politicians tried to argue death by duel was the same as murder, while others favored a manslaughter charge. In spite of the law, few duelists were ever punished. Once the reasons behind the duels came out, sympathy for the scorned individual typically reigned. Ravenna sighed. "So, Chadwick thinks Yarford killed Thornley because of the stolen money?"

"Yes. I didn't know what else to do, so I came here."

Ravenna tipped her head, puzzled.

"After all," Catherine continued. "You helped find Hawkestone's killer. I think you could find Thornley's. For Yarford's sake. I don't know what I'd do if he goes to prison. Or is… executed." Tears filled her eyes, which rattled Ravenna. Catherine rarely cried.

"I thought you trusted Chadwick. Don't you think he'll be fair in his investigation?"

"I trust you and your fairness more. Mr. Chadwick and other Bow Street Runners only want to get *someone*. Sometimes it matters little if it's the *right* one. You know Yarford. You know he wouldn't do something like this." She scooted closer. "You have to help me, Ravenna. Please."

"Heavens, Catherine. What a mess!" Ravenna stood, one hand to her back the other to her head. She paced a few small circles before crossing her arms over her chest and staring down at the flowers in front of the fireplace. She didn't want to be involved in another investigation. Yet, Catherine was her best friend. She couldn't let her go through this alone. Though Ravenna didn't think Chadwick was a dishonest man, she couldn't be certain he wouldn't make mistakes or take shortcuts just to have the case solved out of impatience so he could move on to another case. Perhaps it would be best to have a second person looking at the situation, someone who had Catherine and Yarford's best interests in mind—just to ensure everything came out fairly.

Ravenna turned and searched Catherine's hopeful face.

Catherine rarely cried, but she was on the verge of tears. "Please, Ravenna. I know you don't want to be involved. I know you want—"

Ravenna lifted a hand. "You're right. I don't really want to do this. I'd much rather hole away in my quiet little life. However, I will help you. I couldn't live with myself if I didn't."

Chapter Nine

Georgiana pressed her face to the carriage window to watch the buildings roll by. "Mayfair is much grander than anything I've ever seen in Whitechapel."

Harrison added, "Indeed. If you like, I'd be happy to show you around more."

She flashed him a smile. "I'd like that very much, Lord Birchfield."

Ravenna sat quietly, thinking about Catherine and Yarford, about their horrible situation, and about how she could even begin to help them. Her head began to throb.

"You've been very quiet since Lady Adair's visit, Amma," Harrison said.

"I apologize. I have a bit of a headache."

He nodded. "Hm. And is Lady Catherine well? She seemed upset this morning."

"Thank you for your concern, Harrison. I'm not at liberty to divulge the particulars. Let's just say she's going through a bit of trouble, but she's well."

They stopped first at La Belle's, a small dress shop tucked in a row of merchants on Bond Street.

Harrison jumped from the carriage and handed down Ravenna and Georgiana to the warm stones. The summer heat was oppressive, and the horse dung in the streets nearly closed off Ravenna's ability to breathe.

Harrison smiled. "I think my presence will not be wanted at the mantua maker's, so I'll step down the street to the Spotted Pig coffeehouse."

Coffee sounded delicious, and preferable to shopping, but Ravenna had more important things to address. "Very well. We will find you there directly. We'll try to be brief, but…"

He chuckled. "With two ladies shopping for dresses, I can hardly expect to wait less than an hour. I'll be patient enough, Amma. I'm sure good conversation among the locals and a newspaper or two shall keep me occupied." He touched the brim of his hat. "Happy hunting, ladies." He walked toward the Spotted Pig as Ravenna and Georgiana stepped inside La Belle's.

Large arched windows flooded the spacious store with light. The pale pink walls and white wainscotting wrapped around at least six counters all filled with women chattering, exploring dress designs, and talking with shop assistants. Along the walls were bolts of fabric of all types, shades, and patterns, as well as cabinets containing laces, buttons, ribbons, and other ornaments to embellish dresses.

Ravenna and Georgiana sat on chairs at a counter to look at a booklet of dress designs while they waited for Mrs. Roberts, the mantua maker, or one of her assistants. "Mrs. Roberts is the best mantua maker. She's made all my things and has enough staff to fulfill our order speedily. There's a ball next week at Carlton House in honor of the prince's birthday. So, you'll need at least one ball gown, which must be done first. You'll also need a walking dress, a couple of day dresses, and undergarments."

Georgiana blushed at the mention of underclothes.

Ravenna continued, "I have some things you can borrow until those items arrive. Of course, you'll need slippers and gloves for the ball gown. I can loan you ornaments, fans, and reticules in the meantime."

Mrs. Roberts approached the counter. She was a lithe, statuesque woman with a finely carved jawline and sculpted nose. Her dark brows arched over intense green eyes. Her dark hair was plaited neatly under a lace mob cap, and her silk puce and mauve striped dress fit her form perfectly. Her smile revealed high, rounded cheekbones. She spoke with a French accent. "Lady Birchfield, what a delight to see you today." She curtsied. "How shall we serve you?" She snapped her long, delicate fingers, and a short, red-faced girl with amber eyes and fawn hair stepped up beside her. Mrs. Roberts's gaze ran over Georgiana. "This is not your daughter? You don't look old enough to have a grown woman such as this."

"You flatter me. In fact, I am old enough," Ravenna chuckled. "But Georgiana is my niece. And she needs a new wardrobe."

Mrs. Roberts smiled slyly. "Ah. You need a husband-hunting kit, I wager."

Georgiana blushed and shrugged shyly. "I'm not certain."

"You would be correct, Mrs. Roberts," Ravenna laughed. "I knew only your capable hands could outfit her beautifully and quickly. " She listed the girl's needs then added, "We need the ball gown for next week. The rest can take longer."

"Let's start with the ball gown then." Mrs. Roberts studied Georgiana. "Yes. I know exactly the thing. Hannah, get her measurements while I find the fashion plate."

The short girl stepped up. "Come with me, miss." She led Georgiana to the back of the store. Georgiana looked back at Ravenna with concern.

Ravenna smiled. "Don't worry. It won't take but a moment."

Mrs. Roberts returned with a plate showing a pink silk dress with a low cut, rounded bodice, puffed sleeves, and a gold overdress. "We'll put spangles here and here." She ran her finger along the bottom of the bodice and the hem of the dress. "And perhaps a few sprinkled like dew along the skirt. With this gold overdress, she'll look like the dawn."

Ravenna said, "I think it's perfect. I'll ask her opinion when she returns. The poor girl doesn't have much."

"Very good," Mrs. Roberts said. "I'll show you the fabrics. Come with me." Ravenna followed her to the polished cherry wood tables across the store. Mrs. Roberts added, "You know Lady Thornley, do you not?"

"I do."

"She was in here earlier, the poor dear. She came to order some mourning accoutrement. To lose her son in such a horrible manner. And in his own home." She shook her head. "Dreadful."

"Yes. I was there," Ravenna said. "It happened during a gala."

"I understand it was…" She looked around and whispered, "Murder."

Ravenna didn't want to indulge the rumor mill. Normally, she wouldn't want to confirm or deny the rumors. However, now that she was going to investigate in earnest on Catherine's behalf, there might be some benefit to engaging with the rumor mill. Mrs. Roberts, however, didn't give her an opportunity to speak.

"If you ask me"—Mrs. Roberts selected a bolt of pink shot silk—"it was likely that brother of his. He's a despicable rogue." Her face twisted as though she ate something bitter.

"What makes you say so?"

"I've heard he's so deeply in debt that collectors have come to take back all the furniture they've rented to Thornley Hall. Apparently, he was going to flee to France, like so many debtors do, but the war prevented his escape. I've also heard he's been delving into..." She whispered again, "Smuggling." She laid the cloth on a table for Ravenna for inspection.

Ravenna lifted her brows in surprise. "Really?" Smuggling was common enough. Lord Percy Thornley wouldn't be the first, or last, penniless nobleman to engage in such business to make money.

"I also heard when his brother found out, he was furious. Something about reputation or credibility or something." Mrs. Roberts pulled down a sheer gold fabric, laying it on the table too.

Now, that was a bit of interesting information. Ravenna examined the fabrics as she turned the gossip over in her mind. Perhaps Lord Franklin had discovered something else about his brother, something dangerous or damning that would have necessitated Lord Percy killing his elder brother in order to silence him. Mr. Gibson was still the most likely suspect with the most to gain or lose. But it wouldn't hurt to talk to Lord Percy as soon as possible. He might be able to provide some insight—even if he was innocent. "These are beautiful fabrics and they'll look marvelous on her. You have a fantastic eye, Mrs. Robertson."

After Georgiana's approval for her dresses and fabrics, Ravenna and Georgiana exited the dress shop and continued on to other shops for the other necessities: fans, gloves, stockings, and shoes.

Footmen trailed along behind them carrying boxes as they exited their last shop. Ravenna said, "I think we've satisfied even your hunger for shopping today. Let's go meet Harrison at the Spotted Pig for a bit of coffee."

Georgiana was bubbling about her new dresses and purchases as she walked backward in front of Ravenna. She spun around to run smack into the firm-chested Lord Edmund Donovan. His blue-green eyes gleamed from under the brim of his beaver hat, and his longish hair, brushing his shoulders, caught the sunlight like spun gold.

Georgiana breathed. "So...sorry."

He touched the brim of his hat. "Pardon me, miss. I believe the fault was all mine." He glanced at Ravenna. "Lady Birchfield. How good to see you." He accepted the hand she offered. He wore a tobacco superfine coat and buff pantaloons. He was slightly shorter and leaner than Braedon, but well-cut by the expression of his attire.

"Lord Donovan. It's good to see you as well. This is my niece, Miss Georgiana Sullivan. My sister's child. Georgiana, this is my friend, Lord Donovan."

He bowed to Georgiana's clumsy curtsey. "I'm delighted to make your acquaintance, miss."

"A pleasure, sir."

He turned to Ravenna. "May I escort you ladies somewhere?"

"Oh, no, thank you. We were on our way to the Spotted Pig to retrieve Harrison."

Lord Donovan beamed. "Is Harrison here?"

"He just arrived this morning."

"Delightful. I saw him but briefly at Thomas' funeral but, prior to that, I hadn't seen him in ages. How is he handling everything?"

"As well as could be expected, I think. He has a big task before him in learning to manage the estate and his other duties as the new Lord Birchfield."

"As I myself know all too well."

"Why don't you come with us to say hello to him?"

Georgiana gasped. "Ah! Auntie, may we go there?" She pointed to a confectioner's shop with a pale blue door.

Ravenna nudged Georgiana's arm downward and whispered, "Don't point. It isn't polite." Then she said to Donovan, "My apologies for Georgiana's exuberance. This is her first shopping trip. We've just come from buying a ball gown, so she's quite carried away."

Donovan chuckled. "I can well imagine."

Ravenna said to her niece. "We're going to the Spotted Pig first."

Donovan wedged between the women and offered each an arm. "I'd be delighted to escort you to the coffeehouse."

They started toward the Spotted Pig sign down the street. The street was a crush of people and animals. The population of London had exploded in recent years. Carriage wheels rattled, horses' tack jingled, hammers pounded rhythmically on new construction projects, and vendors shouted about their goods. The scent of dung, earth, baked bread, and animals hung in the air, mingling with the perfumes, colognes, and tobacco of passersby.

With hesitation, Donovan said, "Have you heard from Braedon? I wonder how he's managing things in Italy."

"I had a letter from him yesterday, in fact, written a month ago. I think he has his hands quite full."

"No doubt he does. I've heard some of the rumors circulating about a particular woman in Italy. I hope she's able to recover to a balanced mind." His eyes flashed. "But I've heard very little of Braedon. I suspect he's guarding his own scandalous behavior."

No doubt Braedon had hoped he and Dianthe might withdraw from London and maintain a measure of privacy. However, at various balls and dinners, Ravenna had heard from more than one person about Dianthe's escapades. Braedon's letters were far more discreet than the gossip mill, which certainly cast his character in a positive light. She'd heard of Dianthe dancing publicly in the rain in the thinnest of muslin, of showing up at the homes of bachelor men in the wee hours of night, of presenting herself as a dish on a dinner table one evening, and other such irascible behaviors designed to forever mar her dignity. Yet, she'd heard nothing of Braedon. It seemed if bad reports found their way across the ocean about Dianthe, the same would be true of Braedon were he behaving scandalously.

"What do you mean Braedon is behaving scandalously?"

"I suspect he's tucking himself away in the Italian countryside to avoid the war. While taking advantage of an unstable woman as well."

"That's an unfair view of things."

"Ah." He lifted his chin. "Of course, you defend him. I'd forgotten he's a favorite of yours."

Ravenna chuckled. "I wager he'd say the same about you."

His gaze lingered on her. He seemed to be working something out in his mind.

Georgiana interrupted. "Lord Donovan, will you be at the prince's ball next week?"

"Yes. I think so." He said to Ravenna, "I hardly think Catherine would allow me to escape my *cavalier servente* duties." He winked.

"What does that mean?" Georgiana tipped her head and batted her eyes. Her pale blonde curls cascaded against the shoulder of her mauve spencer.

It was to Aunt Brendae's credit Georgiana remained so sheltered. Ravenna said, "I'll explain later."

Georgiana shrugged and turned her wide-eyed innocence to Lord Donovan. "Do you like to dance, Lord Donovan?"

"Sometimes."

Ravenna laughed. "Lord Donovan is not an avid dancer, I fear."

"Now, who is being unfair!" He joked.

"I have rarely seen you dance, sir. Don't deny it, or you'll make me a liar to my own niece." She laughed.

"I wouldn't dare call you a liar, madam." He said to Georgiana. "Do you see how I am unfairly persecuted?"

Georgiana smiled up at him. "Aye. It is unfair." Georgiana continued. "I've learned many dances. One of my friends taught me all the ones she knew, but I've never had an opportunity to actually use them at a ball. I think I might be too nervous."

He smiled warmly at her. "Nonsense. You need only an experienced partner, and you'll dance like the most accomplished lady."

"What if I forget the steps? Everyone will laugh at me."

He leaned over and whispered, "Then you'll have only your negligent partner to blame. For I shall dance the first dance with you. And I dare anyone to laugh."

Chapter Ten

After a cup of coffee and conversation at the Spotted Pig, Catherine's troubles still plagued Ravenna. Though she wanted to spend more time with Harrison and Georgiana, she would have to wait until after she questioned her main suspect. The happy party left the Spotted Pig and returned to Ravenna's carriage.

Ravenna shouted up to the driver, "Please take us to Mr. Gibson's in Ludgate Hill."

Donovan handed Ravenna into the carriage, concern marking his voice. "You're going to Ludgate?"

"Yes." She settled against the blue kid leather seat. "It shouldn't take long."

He frowned. "Perhaps I should come with you. There are cutpurses and all sorts of unsavory folk there."

She smoothed her skirts. "I thank you, no. Our footman is armed. As am I."

Humor lit his sea-eyes like the sun on the waters. "You carry a pistol?"

"A blade." She tipped her head. "Though I might someday consider carrying a pistol, too. But they're rather cumbersome and tricky to load. A blade is much better when one must act quickly."

Harrison added with a smirk. "Do not worry, Lord Donovan. I'm here to watch after the ladies. I do have my pistol, if needed."

Donovan nodded. "Yes, of course. Forgive me. Lady Birchfield, I shan't detain you any longer. Miss Georgiana…" He offered his hand to assist her into the carriage. "It was a pleasure to meet you."

She claimed a spot in the carriage and arranged her skirts, smiling at him under her lashes. "You won't forget about the dance you promised me at the prince's ball? Otherwise, I shall be crushed for the rest of the evening."

"I hope to grow two hooves and a tail if I do forget."

She giggled bashfully.

Harrison glanced between them, a line cutting between his brows.

She beamed, her beauty blooming to full effect. "That would make the dancing more difficult, Lord Donovan."

Ravenna said, "Thank you for the coffees, Lord Donovan." She glanced knowingly at Georgiana. "I'm sure we'll be counting the days until we meet again at the ball."

"I know I shall." He bowed and stepped away from the carriage as the footman shut the women and Harrison inside and climbed onto the back.

The carriage pulled away from the curb, and Georgiana practically pressed her nose against the glass to stare at Donovan. She turned, melted into the seat, and gushed, "He's so handsome! I'll be the envy of every woman at the ball when I have the first dance."

Harrison snapped, "He's requested the first dance? You only met him today."

The women ignored him.

Ravenna said, "Indeed, you shall be the target of many jealous women for he seldom dances, though many women have desired the favor." Donovan came from a good family, a solid fortune, and he was an honorable and distinguished politician in parliament with potential for a stellar career. Georgiana could do worse than land Lord Donovan as a husband, though the chances were slim. Yet, she didn't want Georgiana to lose all hope. After all, with some education and comportment lessons, she could be greatly improved. "I can count on one hand the number of times I've seen him dance. Everyone will wonder about you, the charming stranger who secured Lord Donovan for the first dance of the evening."

The carriage rocked as the wheels clattered toward Ludgate Hill. Soon, the carriage slowed to a near stop as the density of the traffic made it impossible to travel beyond a snail's pace.

"Amma," Harrison said. "Do you not think Georgiana would be better advised to stand up with me at the ball?" He hedged. "For her safety and protection. There are many rakes and unsavory sorts lingering around London's ballrooms."

"I'm sure Georgiana will make room for you among her bevy of potential suitors."

"Of course. We shall dance as much as we please," Georgiana said. "And I'm sure you can help me make many introductions." She gushed and squirmed. "This is my first ball *ever!* I'm so excited. I'm certain I won't be able to sleep for days."

"Besides, Harrison"—Ravenna tugged at her sleeves and wiped the lint from them— "you know Donovan. He's certainly no threat to her. And while there are many fast people among our acquaintances, you and I can ensure Georgiana's safety well enough between the two of us."

Harrison opened his mouth to respond, but Georgiana interrupted him.

"I can't believe Lord Donovan could possibly be interested in the likes of me." She clapped her hand over her heart, her eyes beaming with joy. "He's so dashing and handsome. Like a hero from a novel. Is he not, Auntie?"

This was dangerous territory. While Ravenna would love to make such a match for her niece, Donovan presented a special challenge. He was a serious politician and thought of little else. It would take a woman stunning of mind, body, connections, and accomplishments to turn his head. For a girl like Georgiana who had little experience of the world, no connections or accomplishments, touching a heart like his would be difficult, if not impossible. Yet, Ravenna didn't have the heart to dash the girl's hopes and dreams so quickly after having them lifted. She eased close to the truth to temper the girl's hopes. "Be careful, Georgiana. You're about to enter a new realm. You're quite young and shouldn't be in a hurry to make a husband of the first man you meet. I would absolutely recommend you to Donovan. However, it wouldn't be wise to set your cap at him simply because he's handsome and the first man to show you attention. There will be many men at the ball to dance with. You might find one of them far more attractive than Donovan upon closer acquaintance."

Harrison, who had been scowling and staring out the window, jumped in.

"Yes. That's right. Many other men."

Georgiana said, "Not likely. Lord Donovan is the handsomest man I've ever seen."

Harrison said, "There's more to a good husband than handsomeness."

The carriage stopped in Ludgate Hill in front of a row house with a flat facade. The white stucco lacked the character of brick or stone. A window trimmed in blue flanked the door of the same color, and the upper level had only three small windows, two of which were boarded up, likely to evade the window tax.

Ravenna sent her footman to knock on the door. Mr. Gibson answered, peeking around the footman's broad shoulders. The footman returned to Ravenna and helped her from the carriage. Before closing the door, she said to Georgiana and Harrison, "Wait here. I'll return directly. I need only to speak with Mr. Gibson for a few moments."

The sun burned bright and hot against her black widows' weeds. She wished for colder days where the coal smoke blanked out the sun, and her layers provided welcome warmth instead of beads of sweat springing up in the most uncomfortable places. The footman held open the gate for her and she stepped through toward the door where Mr. Gibson awaited her.

"Good afternoon, Lady Birchfield." He bowed. "I wish I'd known you were coming; I might've prepared some refreshment for you."

"Oh, thank you, but don't trouble yourself. I won't be long." She glanced around the bare foyer of navy and white-striped wallpaper and white wainscotting. The house was small, at least a third the size of Gordon House or smaller. Stairs trailed along the right-hand wall with a dining room on the same side. A small sitting room appeared to double as a study on her left.

"Please, this way." He led her into the study and closed the door. The room was paneled in stained pine with a simple fireplace at one end of the room near the desk and drink table. The other half of the room held shelves and tables loaded with various artifacts. There were only a few places to sit, which bespoke a home with few visitors. A shame, since there were so many interesting artifacts to enjoy.

"I hope I'm not interrupting."

His rumpled coat hung loosely on his form, his black ascot sat slightly askew, and a button hung loose on his wine-stained waistcoat.

"Oh, not at all. I was doing a bit of writing."

"You have an interesting room." She ran her eyes over the various vases, rocks, spear pieces, and a whole host of other what-nots.

"Thank you. It's been my life's work."

"Your wife and children must be quite understanding." She sat in the worn chair he offered her.

"I'm not married and don't have a family to speak of, so this is how I occupy my time. Can I at least offer you a sherry or a cordial? I'm sure it's not as fine as what you're accustomed to, but I think you'll find it refreshing."

"No, thank you."

"Very well. May I?"

"Of course, please."

He poured sherry into a small crystal glass for himself. "How may I help you?"

"I was hoping to speak with you about Lord Thornley."

The crystal plug clattered as he stoppered the decanter. His face flushed. "I see," he said quietly. He downed his drink. "I'm not sure what there is to discuss on the matter." He poured another drink. "Seems a perverse sort of curiosity would bring a lady here for such a discussion."

Ravenna smiled politely. "Yes, perhaps." Let him think what he wanted. She had a duty and an obligation to her friends.

He pulled his desk chair over and sat across from her, crossing his ankle on his knee. "What would you like to know?"

She decided to begin with the information Mrs. Roberts, the dressmaker, had shared. "Why did Lord Thornley go to New South Wales with you?"

"He told me because he had an interest in travel and expeditions. He claimed to be something of an aficionado and collector. He offered me a great deal of money to take him."

Money that, according to Catherine, had likely belonged to Yarford. *Despicable man.* She tried to tamp down her disgust with Thornley. "I

80

see." She thought for a moment. "How did you meet Lord Thornley?"

"I met him at The Spotted Pig. I had been there meeting other investors for the New South Wales trip. He was there, reading a newspaper and listening in. He then approached me and expressed interest. He said he had money to give me for the trip."

"You didn't ask where the money came from?"

He shook his head. "Why would I? He's a lord. His money and how he came about it was his concern, not mine. And when you're in a position like mine, you need all the money you can get. Every quid provides more food, more ship crew, more ale, and more time at the dig site. So, I certainly wouldn't turn away the additional funding. Besides, when he joined the expedition, it helped convince the other investors. His titles added more legitimacy to my cause."

Ravenna nodded. "I see."

"The problems arose *after* we set sail. He sought to rule us all, and his presence threatened the success of the trip."

"I'm curious; what were the particular reasons you had to be upset with Lord Thornley?"

He sipped his drink and set the glass aside. He leaned his elbows on his chair arms and interlaced his ink-stained fingers. Hate glimmered darkly in his eye. "And why should I discuss any more of this matter with you? Who *are* you to demand answers of me?"

Naturally, she couldn't tell him that a friend had requested her to investigate the matter like some female Bow Street Runner—as if such a creature could ever exist. She edged as close to the truth as she could. "I'm not making demands. I simply want a conversation. I have friends with an interest in this matter and I'm concerned about the effects this will have on them. Surely, you can appreciate that the family deserves to know who killed her son. And…" In hopes of appealing to his masculine nature, she added, "Perhaps his brother might have the satisfaction of knowing who the killer is so he can redeem the family's honor."

He snorted. "Mr. Percy Smithwaite? Wait, it's *Lord* Percy now, isn't it? He is the last to redeem the family's honor." He broke into a belly laugh that shook his whole body and slapped his knee. "He's been the primary cause of the family's dishonor."

"Why do you say so?" She changed tactics. She might have more luck appealing to his self-important, supercilious nature. "I'd always thought Lord Percy was an upstanding, honorable sort of man."

He looked down his short nose at her. "A so-called friend of the family ought to know better, milady. But allow me to disillusion you." He picked up his drink and sipped, careful to stick out the pinky and flash his ring. He smiled imperiously. "Lord Percy, like many men and women of the *ton*, has a debilitating gambling problem. He is also guilty of seducing a tavern keeper's daughter under the guise of marrying her. He bedded her before marriage, of course, then wagered her in a game of loo and lost her to a scoundrel who did unspeakable things to the girl. She was later found floating in the Thames."

She swallowed the knot of disgust rising in her throat. Horrific. She knew enough of Lord Percy's reputation to believe this story, and much worse, was true of him. Mr. Gibson regarded her with a twisted delight, as if he'd been hoping to repulse her. She blanked her face, unwilling to give him the satisfaction. "That's awful. Did he…" She didn't want to finish the sentence.

He shrugged. "No one knows if she killed herself in desperation or if he killed her because she was an inconvenience. Or if the other man killed her. If that's what you're asking" He lifted the glass to his lips again. "At any rate, he's not a man of honor. He is, in fact, just the sort of man who would kill his own brother for a quid if he thought it was the only way to get it."

"And you think he's responsible for Lord Thornley's death?"

"Of course, he is." He stretched his legs out, crossing them at the ankles.

"Do you happen to have any proof?"

"I witnessed him going into the study myself as I was coming out."

"You were in the study with Lord Thornley?"

"Yes. We were having a conversation about the opal."

"May I ask what the conversation entailed?"

He snorted. "Such impertinence. Milady, I will not be intimidated by your titles and noble lineage. I'm not one of your servants to be ordered about, and I will not be compelled to answer your questions."

She smiled, clamping down on the anger blooming hot in her chest. "Then you are in luck, for I have no noble lineage. My title comes to me only by way of marriage. I'm nothing more than an Irish immigrant who escaped the terrors of Wexford and landed at the theater to sell oranges and later take to the stage."

He lifted his brows and flushed in response. "Well, I..."

Clearly, he was unpracticed in apologies. She clutched her folded fan tightly in her lap, her index finger lingering near the medallion. With one flick of her finger, she could release the blade and launch herself at him. If necessary. And since he was provoking her ire and dislike, a part of her hoped he would give her a reason. Instead, for the moment, she would rely on her sharp tongue. "So, I should reciprocate and inform you that your repugnant lack of breeding and ill-mannered, ungentlemanly behavior does not shock or intimidate me, sir. I want to know what you spoke of regarding the opal because what I witnessed at the gala was a jealous little man, desperate for the attention Lord Thornley was taking from you." This wasn't exactly going to her plan of stroking his ego.

His face turned scarlet, and his beady, rodent-like eyes grew bloodshot.

She continued. "And you hated him for it. Hated him for daring to take credit for the opal and get in the way of the windfall you'd hoped to claim for yourself." She leaned forward and hissed. "Which means I think *you're* the sort of man who would kill Lord Thornley." As soon as the words left her lips, she knew she shouldn't have revealed her true thoughts. She was a better gambler than this. But he had rankled her.

He shook with barely suppressed rage. She could see in his eyes that he'd delight in wringing her neck. He licked his lips and sniffed. "Yes, I was angry with him. And I hated him for using his position, his titles, connections, and wealth to overtake the dig, to claim the findings as his alone without offering any of the credit to me." His voice choked with suppressed emotion. "All he had to do was mention my name, and my fortune would've been made. That's all. I would've been able to publish pamphlets and books, do lecture circuits, and attend important functions. I might've even been invited to court to…"

His voice broke. "So yes, I hated him, hated what he did to me. And when I asked him to just extend a hand of kindness…" He extended his own hand, shaking. "To help lift my status and fortunes in the world, he denied me." He clenched his hand into a fist, and tears pooled in his eyes. "It would've been so little effort on his part." He dropped his hand and scooted to the edge of his seat, sitting with his legs spread apart. "Oh, I *wanted* to kill him. Yes, I did. I thought of half a dozen plants I could grind into a poison and deliver into his dinner plate…" He sniffed and pulled a handkerchief from his pocket to wipe his nose. "I hated him. Yes, I did. In fact, I hope he's burning in the pits of hell right now." He poked his knee for emphasis. "But I'm a scholar, not a killer. Ultimately, I'm not made of such stuff. So, if you want to ruin me, madam, you're too late."

He stood, marched to the door, and opened it. "This conversation is over. I'd thank you to leave now. You've inconvenienced me long enough, and I need to return to my work."

Though she had detected no lies on his part, he had certainly made clear his growing vexation. She didn't want to provoke him any longer. "Very well." As she turned to leave, Ravenna caught a glimpse of an item tucked in with a mass of other relics. White stone, heart-shaped. It was a small feminine figurine, round with long, thin legs, very like the one Lord Percy had described was missing from Lord Franklin's desk. She opened her mouth to ask him about it when he rudely pushed her out the door and pulled it shut behind him. He clutched her elbow, fingers digging into her arm, and practically dragged her to the front door.

She fought to twist free. "Unhand me, you vile creature." But his grip only tightened as she fumbled to try to release the blade from her fan. He opened the door and gave her an ungentle shove out. She had barely cleared the threshold before he slammed the door in her face and locked it.

That could've ended better.

Angry and insulted, she huffed, straightened her back, and strode away. Her arm ached. She kept her chin high, glancing around to ascertain if anyone had witnessed the embarrassing scene. As she exited the iron gate,

Mr. Chadwick approached. He was dressed neatly in a navy blue coat of fine worsted wool, a red waistcoat over a coarse linen shirt with a black cravat loosely tied. Black pantaloons, polished boots, and a top hat completed his attire. His dark blue eyes grabbed her in their hard gaze. If he was surprised to see her at Mr. Gibson's house, his face didn't betray it. He was probably a fabulous Faro player. He stopped at the gate, bowed his head, and touched the brim of his hat. "Lady Birchfield. How…interesting to see you here."

She pinched off a brief smile. "I think the feeling is mutual."

He glanced at Mr. Gibson's house, then back at her. "I must say I'm surprised to discover you and Mr. Gibson run in the same circle. And that you would visit him alone is"—he lifted his brows—"most peculiar."

She shrugged. "I'm not alone. My stepson and my niece are just there in the carriage. I needed to speak with Mr. Gibson for only a few moments. But I'm not sure why my social calls would be of any concern to you."

He clasped his hands behind his back and rocked onto his heels. "I wonder what you would have to discuss with him."

She clamped down on her patience. "Is it your habit to interfere in the private matters of women unrelated to you, Mr. Chadwick?"

"Only when I'm investigating a heinous crime that said women might be involved in."

Ravenna arched a brow and looked down her nose at him, a cold anger hardening in her veins. "I hope you aren't accusing me of Lord Thornley's murder or of being a participant in such a vile act, sir."

The corners of his eyes wrinkled. "Madam, until I've discovered who has committed the crime, I presume everyone surrounding the victim is guilty. As I'm currently investigating a murder, I would very much like to know why you would be visiting Mr. Gibson." He ran his eyes over her form, an act which made her feel exposed. "You seem rather out of his reach and far too discerning to allow him to use you as his social ladder."

She may be in her thirties and a widow, but she understood her charms well enough to know her bloom was not yet entirely off the rose. She also needed to keep Chadwick out of her way. Perhaps if she kept him focused on Mr. Gibson, she would be freed to pursue other suspects. She popped her fan open and batted her eyes. "If you must know, Mr. Chadwick, and as you might recall, there was a figurine missing from Lord Thornley's desk. I suspected Mr. Gibson had taken it from Lord Thornley in a fit of jealous pique over the opal."

"Why?"

"Because Mr. Gibson had been quite aggravated with Lord Thornley during the gala. So, I came here in search of it and noticed the statue in his study, but he removed me from the house before I could reclaim it."

A light of intense interest shone in his eyes, but the rest of his demeanor remained stoic. "Interesting. And what were you hoping to do with the statue had you captured it?"

"Return it to the family, of course."

He puckered his lips, then said, "I spoke with your friends Lady Adair and Lord Yarford today."

Was he setting a trap? Perhaps it was best to pretend ignorance. "Is that so?"

"They have an interesting...situation, don't you think?"

"What do you mean?"

"They live together, but aren't married."

"Is that a crime now?"

Humor marked his features. "No, of course not. But I think it speaks to a certain lack of character."

"You seem to be saying something, but the meaning escapes me."

He smiled knowingly. "Ah, I think you know exactly what I mean. You may choose to play the daft coquette if it amuses you, but you will find I will not play such games. What do you know of the disagreement between your friends and Lord Thornley?"

She didn't have to answer his questions and she would rather burn at the stake than say a word to this man about Catherine. A slow smile spread over her lips as she cast a coquettish side glance up at him. "Mr. Chadwick, I must bid you *adieu*. You should know it's rude to keep a lady standing in the street for a chat." She brushed past him. "Good day, sir. Best of luck in your investigation."

Chapter Eleven

Ravenna, Georgiana, and Harrison returned to Gordon House. Ravenna left the young folks to entertain themselves while she retired to her bedchamber. She needed to think about Mr. Gibson and what he'd related to her. She poured a glass of port, kicked off her slippers and stretched out on the sofa. She sipped the dark magic, pulling it into her veins. It spread a relaxing warmth through her body. She rested her head in the corner of the sofa and closed her eyes.

Mr. Gibson had tried to push the murder onto Lord Percy, but she couldn't be certain Mr. Gibson was innocent. His anger, both at the gala and in his home earlier, suggested he was temperamental and likely capable of murdering someone—especially if his reputation and career were at stake. He had wanted the credit and the accolades for the discovery of the opal. That much was clear. And, no doubt, he wanted the opportunity to not only meet the king and queen but to enjoy the substantial rewards. After all, for such a treasure, the king was likely to grant money, lands, titles—all which would attract any number of connections and marital prospects among the nobility and wealthy merchants. The fact that he'd stolen Thornley's figurine indicated he might've stolen the opal as well. The temptation to have the opal and the access to society it would grant may have been too much for Mr. Gibson to resist.

Her lady's maid, Charlotte Hart, entered the room with a dress folded over her arm. "I have your dinner dress." Her fawn hair was twisted into a simple chignon at the nape of her neck, and her dove gray calico dress was topped with a lace fichu. A gray velvet cameo choker covered the scar,

87

necklacing her throat.

"Should I select a dress of yours for Miss Georgiana? She claims she has nothing appropriate for dinner."

"Let me see what I have." Ravenna moved from the sofa and stood over Hart's shoulder. She pointed at a blue satin dress. "This one."

"Yes, that'll be lovely on her." Hart extracted the dress. "I'll have it prepared immediately." Her top lip pouted over the bottom like a rabbit as she spoke. "You know, I think Miss Georgiana is completely oblivious to the fact that Lord Harrison is utterly smitten with her."

Ravenna chuckled and lifted her hands over her head to stretch out her back. "Indeed. I expect a spectacular scene before we depart for Birchfield Manor for the Great Twelfth in August."

Hart lifted a thin brow. "Really? Why?"

"It was such a sight to see," Ravenna said. "We met Lord Donovan while we were out shopping, and Harrison could hardly contain himself." Touched with compassion, she added, "Of course, Georgiana fell heels over head for Donovan, who barely noticed her."

"Oh, the poor dears. Let's hope it's mere calf love on her part."

"I'm sure it is. And let's hope the prince invites a great many handsome beaux to the Carlton House ball to tempt Georgiana's attention away from Donovan. For both of their sakes." She laughed, flopping down on the sofa and reaching for the newspaper on the table.

"What about Lord Harrison? He would be a good match for her, I think."

Ravenna shook her head. "I'm not sure. He's most irresponsible, but he's improving. Perhaps with time."

"I think with his new lordship responsibilities, he'll settle more. And adding a wife might be the thing to steady him and bring him around."

Harrison as a husband for Georgiana wasn't the worst idea. "We'll see. It all depends on Georgiana, really. I'm not sure she likes him enough. At least not yet. I certainly won't discourage the match, were it to bloom." Ravenna sat up. "Which reminds me. Please have a seat. I have need of your…special skills."

Intrigued, Hart sat on a nearby chair.

"I went to see one Mr. Gibson today in Ludgate Hill. He's an archaeologist. He and Lord Thornley had been in New South Wales until recently, digging up artifacts. I believe he might've had something to do with Lord Thornley's death."

"Oh…" Hart lifted a brow. "What makes you think so?"

"I was at his house earlier today, and I noticed a figurine I believe to have belonged to Lord Thornley. Thornley's brother, Lord Percy, described a statue identical to the one I saw at Mr. Gibson's, but he threw me out of his house before I was able to ascertain if it was the same one." She described the statue.

"And you were hoping I might find a way into his house to discover the statue?"

Ravenna smiled. "You read my mind."

A smile crept onto Hart's lips. "I think I can stop by to see his cook for a cup of sugar and talk my way into getting a peek around his study."

"Thank you." Ravenna opened the newspaper. A letter fell out. When she picked it up, she noticed there was no address. Dread filling her heart, she flipped the envelope to discover a black seal. Her breath caught. She'd seen letters like this before.

A chill covered her, and she held up the letter. "Do you happen to know how it came to be inside the paper?"

"No. I don't. Who is it from?"

"Guess." She flipped the letter around so Hart could see the blank front and black seal on the back.

"The Unity." Hart moved to the edge of her chair. "What does it say?"

Ravenna opened the seal. There were five words scrawled across the page in a jagged scrawl: *We will meet again. Soon.* She handed the letter to Hart, who read it with her lips pinched into a tight line.

"You haven't noticed any strangers hanging about?"

Hart shook her head. "No. I'm sorry, but I'll ask the staff." She stood. "I'll see if this dress will fit Miss Georgiana and then have it prepared. I'll return to assist you later, ma'am."

Chapter Twelve

Hart returned a few hours later to assist Ravenna. She buttoned the back of Ravenna's black satin dining gown and put her hair in simple plaits, ending in a spill of curls from the crown of her head. "Incidentally, I spoke with the staff. None of them have seen strangers around the house, nor do they know how the letter was put in your paper."

Ravenna selected her jet earrings and bracelet. "Thank you. I'd like you to keep your eyes open in this regard."

"Of course. I've already warned everyone to be vigilant."

Georgiana eased into the room, uncertain.

Ravenna turned, smiling at the girl. The sapphire blue fabric suited her perfectly. "You look beautiful. I think you should keep the dress."

"Oh, I couldn't take it from you."

"Yes, you can. The dress is far prettier on you than it ever was on me, at any rate."

"Oh…" Georgiana hesitated. "I-I don't know. It's far too fine for the likes of me, I think."

"Nonsense. You'll take it and be beautiful in it." Ravenna searched the girl's face. Not a trace of guile or malice or cunning. All of which meant there was likely no wisdom, either. She'd have to watch her carefully. She was nothing like her mother.

Ravenna's sister, Helen, was bold, direct, active, with a tendency to rebellion, and spoke her mind—which was the primary reason she couldn't get on well under Aunt Brendae's roof. Helen was also sharp, intelligent, and understood the world. It was nearly impossible to manipulate her or

90

take advantage of her. Georgiana was cowed, shy, passive. No doubt, living with Aunt Brendae's bullying misshaped the girl's character. However, there was a good-natured spark in Georgiana, a quality of unbreakable happiness that Ravenna admired.

She took Georgiana's hand and drew her to the nearby sofa. "Let's talk for a moment."

Georgiana sat on the edge of the cushion, running her hands over and over her skirt. "What did you want to discuss?" She tipped her head, her curls touching her clavicle.

"What do you want from life?"

Georgiana smirked, and her eyes darted. She stifled a laugh. "I don't know what you mean. I can either marry or maybe become a governess, if I'm lucky."

"Granted, we women don't have the same positions in the world as the men do. However…" Ravenna lifted a finger. "By marrying well, you might have much of the world at your disposal. But you must also be accomplished to marry well. Most of the time." She thought of herself and Philip's marriage. She hadn't been particularly accomplished. She had merely her beauty, charm, and verve to recommend her. Yet, she'd managed to marry an earl. She'd been fortunate. She folded her hands in her lap. "My primary point is you should have an idea in mind of the sort of man you'd like to marry, the sort of woman you'd like to be, and the sort of life you'd like to lead."

Georgiana rolled her eyes, sighed, and slumped. "I have no idea. I'd like to be married and have lots of children. I really like children."

"What sort of man would you like to marry?"

"A man like…" She blushed a deep crimson and looked down at her toes. "Like Lord Donovan. He's so very dashing. And a member of parliament. So, he must be rich and important."

Ravenna laughed. "That isn't always the situation. Many lords are profligate and wastrels and end up running from their debtors."

The girl blinked. "Oh. Is Lord Donovan like that?"

"I don't think so. He seems quite buttoned up. Whatever his personal life is like, I do know he's deeply dedicated to his career and is a very serious sort of man. I was married to a man like that."

Ravenna shoulders tightened. It hurt to think of Philip these days. She had loved him, respected him, and had thought him kind and generous, which was true in every aspect of his character she'd known. Yet, she'd recently learned he could be ruthless in his career. Only a few months ago, she'd discovered that before he'd ever met her, Philip had ordered the attack on her village. Sadness weighed cold and heavy in her as if she were made of marble. She'd told him of the carnage in her village. But he'd never let on that he knew anything about it. He'd kept the secret until he died. Did she really even know him? But she couldn't go into such things with Georgiana. It would be best to keep it simple and sweet.

Ravenna rubbed at the heaviness in her head. "He was very good to me. Generous, kind, wise. In many ways, he was a wonderful husband and he was well-suited for my temperament since I have more of a serious and reserved bent. But you..." Ravenna bit her lip and studied the girl, who looked at her apprehensively. "You are a very different sort of girl. You strike me as a sensitive and gentle girl. Therefore, you might need more attention than a man like Donovan could provide."

"You want to persuade me from him." Georgiana lifted her chin and pinched her lips together.

"Not necessarily. If Donovan finds himself in love with you at some point, I wouldn't deny you the match. I only wish you to keep your options open, to think about the woman you want to be, the sort of man you want to be married to, the life you want to live, and then decide which man might best provide those things. Some men like a wife who is active in charity. Some men prefer a wife to remain at home. Some men like an artistic wife. Some men prefer a more philosophical wife. A man like Donovan, I suspect, would expect *much* of his wife. Education, refinement, and a sort of political and intellectual savvy to play hostess to a wide range of politicians, intellectuals, and artists. A woman who could entertain such high-minded guests without putting his career or reputation at risk. And many hostesses will shrewdly cultivate particular friendships to help their husbands and their careers. That's a heavy responsibility."

Georgiana scoffed. "I should think there are only three such women in all of England."

Ravenna chuckled. "There are many celebrated hostesses in London, just as I described. Lady Jersey, Lady Adair, Lady Melbourne, Lady Devonshire, to name a few. However, they've had advantages you haven't had. They have grown up in households where the men have all been powerful and important, and their mothers have been canny managers of the society their families keep. So these women learned from a very young age how to manage their social circles to the best advantage."

"That sounds difficult. And perhaps deceitful."

Ravenna smiled at the girl's astuteness. "It can be both. It can be daunting. And one misplaced word can destroy a husband's career and reputation. It comes with great reward, but also with great responsibility., and a lot of work."

Worry marred Georgiana's face. "I could never do it," she whispered. "I wouldn't know where to begin."

"What sort of education have you had?"

Georgiana slid her arms around her middle. "I've not had any except reading, writing, and basic arithmetic. My Aunt Brendae didn't think it necessary for a ninny like me to be educated beyond those things."

"She said that to you?"

Georgiana nodded, looking at the floor.

"I see." Anger pulsed in Ravenna's veins. Aunt Brendae had said the same things to Ravenna, too. The difference was that Ravenna had been too spirited and stubborn to care much about the opinions of a dour old harridan like Aunt Brendae. However, to speak to Georgiana in such a way was unconscionable. Clearly, the girl wasn't as sturdy in mind and spirit as Ravenna or Helen had been. "Well, that will change when you're in this house."

Ravenna wrapped her arm around Georgiana and continued, speaking to her in encouraging tones. "I have a library full of books on every subject. You will read them all. You will learn dancing, singing, French, and drawing and so much more. You won't learn all these things before the end of the season, but we will get you started immediately. You will learn how to manage a household and run the accounts as any good wife would. You're as worthy of an education as any of the fine ladies of the royal court."

Georgiana squinted. "Must I do all of that to catch a husband?"

Ravenna laughed. "Absolutely. If you're going to catch one worth having." She looked down her nose. "I hope you're not lazy."

"Aunt Brendae said I am."

Ravenna stood with a sigh. "Well, we won't pay any mind to what she said. She's not here. I say you are *not* lazy. Your lessons will begin tomorrow. Between myself and my ladies' maid, Hart, you will learn a great deal. And I will hire a tutor as well."

Georgiana stood, her face a mixture of nervousness and excitement. "It sounds so difficult and formidable. What if I can't do it?"

Ravenna squeezed her shoulders. "You can, my darling, and you will. It's important and serious business to secure a proper husband if you are to create a content and prosperous future. It's not something to approach with a half-mind or frivolity." She hugged her. "Don't fret. All will be well. I promise."

There was a knock at the door. Keene, a maid she'd rescued from Pelham House only a few months ago, entered with a dress across her arms. She was a pretty, dewy lass with brunette hair, green eyes, and light freckles over her nose and round cheeks.

"I have your—" She stopped short and flushed. "Sorry, ma'am. I have the chemise Miss Hart repaired."

"Very good. Place it on the bed."

Georgiana stood, mouth agape. "Sarah Keene? Is that you?"

Keene placed the chemise on the bed and smiled bashfully. "'Tis."

Ravenna looked between them. "You two know each other?"

"Aye," Sarah said. "We do, ma'am. Though only in passing."

"How is your family?" Georgiana asked.

"Very well. Though my mom is in bad condition with the grippe. She's very sickly, as you know. Always down with one thing or another."

"Yes."

"How do you know each other?" Ravenna asked.

"Keene's family lives near Aunt Brendae's house."

Ravenna blinked. "Astonishing! I had no idea. Why did you never tell me?"

Keene shrugged, and a twinkle rose in her green eyes. "You never asked what street my family lived on, ma'am."

Smiling, Ravenna nodded. "True. I learned you lived in Whitechapel and left it there probably because of my own past in that part of town. I apologize."

Keene flinched, taken aback. "You shouldn't be apologizing to the likes of me, ma'am."

"So, why did I never see you when I lived in Montague Street?"

"My family only moved there a few years ago after my father's business…" She shifted and looked down at the ground. "We wasn't always poor."

Ravenna bit the inside of her lip. "I'm sorry, Keene. I didn't mean to bring up uncomfortable memories."

Georgiana interjected. "Keene and I often crossed paths."

"How lucky you should be under the same roof now." She turned to her niece. "Georgiana, Keene is learning to be a ladies' maid and is coming along quite nicely in her education. Soon, she'll be among the best of them, I'm certain. She'll likely be stolen away by some duchess or even one of Queen Charlotte's daughters."

Georgiana beamed. "I have no doubt. Keene is so clever. I'll begin studies myself tomorrow."

Keene smiled. "Good for you, miss. I hope you'll enjoy your studies as much as I enjoy my own."

"I just had an idea, Keene." Ravenna clapped her hands together. "You can attend Miss Georgiana. Instead of only assisting Hart and learning from observation and instruction, you can practice everything you learn on Georgiana. Your skills will grow much faster, and it would be a wonderful match since you are of similar age. I'm certain Hart would welcome the help. What do you think of that?"

Both girls seemed pleased with the suggestion.

Keene nodded. "I think it's a grand idea, ma'am."

"Me too!" Georgiana gushed.

"I'll make Hart aware of the change. Georgiana, go finish getting dressed for dinner. We will need to leave soon."

"Come, Keene, let's see if anything can be done with my hair." The girls rushed from the room.

As Ravenna, Georgiana, and Harrison gathered in the foyer to prepare to leave for dinner at Adair House, the doorbell rang.

Mr. Banks, the butler, opened the door to allow entrance to Mr. McKirk. It was an odd time to visit, as hours for social calls had passed.

In spite of this, Ravenna stepped forward, smiling and offering her hand. "Good evening, Mr. McKirk."

"Good evening." He removed his flat cleric's hat. "I apologize. It appears I've caught you at a bad time."

"Not at all. We are on our way out to dine with good friends this evening, but we can spare a few moments. Allow me to introduce you. This is my stepson, Harrison, Lord Birchfield, and my niece, Miss Georgiana Sullivan."

McKirk bowed to them. "Good evening."

Ravenna said, "This is Mr. McKirk. He is working with Reverend Howarth at The Penitent House."

"A worthy charity, sir," Georgiana said.

"Yes, miss. I'm glad to be a part of it."

"Is the Penitent House helping to find my mother?" Georgiana asked.

Mr. McKirk and Ravenna exchanged uncomfortable glances while Harrison looked on in bafflement.

Harrison said, "Pardon. Do you mean to say—"

Ravenna cut him off. "So, Mr. McKirk. How may I assist you this evening?"

"I come on an errand for Reverend Howarth. He, Mariah, and I all met and discussed the recent gala at Lord Thornley's. The women had such a delightful time we were wondering if we might have a gratitude dinner at The Penitent House, inviting any of the donors who have been so beneficent, of course. We thought we might receive some assistance with the food for the dinner. A fine, fat goose and other items. We might need to borrow someone's cook for the evening to assist. And I thought we could give them a small gift. These women have seldom known the delight of a gift and they have so many needs. But they also are eager to feel the joy of giving back to those who have given so much. They have offered to make some handmade items to give to the donors."

Georgiana jumped in. "We could give them all a fan or a lace handkerchief."

Mr. McKirk smiled. "You have a generous spirit, miss. However, women in such reduced circumstances need items they can use on a daily basis. New dresses, shoes, even, uh—" He flushed. "Unmentionables."

Ravenna suppressed her smile. "Yes. But that can also come at a grievous cost. Especially now that we're at war again, and everything will eventually be rationed again. I think the dinner is a wonderful idea, and I think we can absolutely bring it to life." She thought for a moment. "I hope this won't sound too parsimonious, but what if we simply gave them gently worn dresses as part of the charity and then arranged to gift them with shoes and wool stockings for Christmas with some candies and oranges—if we can get the oranges by then."

"If not, we might substitute the oranges with something else," McKirk offered. He rocked back on his heels. "I think your idea is most generous, ma'am."

"And then we can arrange in a few months to provide them with their, uh, unmentionables."

"Thank you, ma'am. I can't wait to bring this news to Reverend Howarth." Creases formed at the corner of his good eye.

Ravenna chuckled. "I'll start working on the matter first thing in the morning."

After Mr. McKirk dashed from the house, Harrison turned to Georgiana. "Your mother is a prostitute?"

Georgiana blushed. "I'm not sure. We think so. She left my Aunt Brendae's after a row. She tried to visit me once a couple of years ago, but my aunt was so ashamed of her, she chased her from the doorstep before we could meet."

Harrison licked his lips and glanced with discomfort between the women. "I'm sorry to hear it. I apologize for prying."

Chapter Thirteen

Ravenna, Georgiana, and Harrison entered Adair House and were shown into the formal drawing room, which reflected its mistress well—vibrant coral walls trimmed in white and lined with gold-framed portraits and landscapes. The robin's egg blue-colored chairs and sofas had been pushed against the walls to allow for freer movement and for the card tables to be erected during dinner. Large vases of white lilacs filled the corners, their sweet scent entwined with the citrus, spice, herbal, and floral scents of various perfumes created a pleasant potpourri Ravenna had always associated with Adair House.

Lady Catherine greeted Ravenna with a kiss to the cheek. "I'm so glad you're here. I was dying of boredom, listening to Lady Clerkenwell's stories about her health. If I hear one more account of her dyspepsia, I shall faint completely away."

Catherine wore a white dress with a pale violet overlay, which lent a touch of lavender to Catherine's blue eyes. Catherine was such a good actress few would be able to see what Ravenna saw: the bit of tension in her smile, the too-bright laughter, the fear in her eyes, and the hint of franticness in her manner. She wore her hostessing like a brilliant crown and never let it slip. She gushed over Harrison, welcoming him warmly and asking how he had been since they last met at Thomas's funeral.

Ravenna introduced Georgiana. "This is Georgiana Sullivan. My sister's child."

"Oh, my dear." Catherine embraced her, then pulled back. "Welcome. I saw you earlier at Gordon House, but I didn't have the chance to meet you properly. I do apologize for my rudeness."

"Don't fret over it, Catherine," Ravenna said. "You were in some distress. I didn't think introductions were important at the moment."

"Well, we're meeting now, aren't we? That's all that matters," Catherine said.

Georgiana nodded, smiling. "Yes, milady."

Catherine didn't give her an opportunity to speak. "Aren't you a beauty? We shall have no trouble finding a perfect husband for you. You leave it to me. I can already think of three men who would fall over themselves for your hand, and they are witty, intelligent, wealthy and, as a man should be if he can, very good dancers. We shall have a great deal of fun with what's left of the season."

Ravenna laughed. "Careful, Catherine. I think you might be frightening her. We don't need to rush to get her married this season."

Catherine winked at Georgiana. "I'll manage it."

Ravenna held up a finger. "No rogues."

Catherine laughed and shrugged, her diamonds pooling in her clavicle. "But, darling, those are the best sorts of men. It's a bit of a fight to get them to the altar, but they make entertaining and adventurous husbands." She clapped her hands together, and she said to Georgiana. "Oh, we shall have so much fun, you and I."

"With all this talk of husbands," Harrison said, "I feel neglected for want of a wife."

"Oh, bother." Catherine touched his arm. "Of course, we shall snag you a wife, but it's much easier to pair a fine, eligible man such as yourself with a young woman panting to be married. We shall find someone for you as well. In fact, a few girls' names have already entered my mind."

"Will any of them be here tonight?" Harrison asked.

"Unfortunately, no. I didn't know you would be in town this soon, or I would've arranged it. However, I'm sure they will be at the various balls before the Great Twelfth when everyone retires to the countryside."

Lord Donovan approached their group with a dashing man at his side of a shorter, thicker build. He had straight hair, close-cropped in the back with a shock of dark hair swept across his forehead, no doubt meant to signal an adventurous spirit, as if he stood at the bow of a ship, looking into the wind and the future. His nose was a bit too long and sharp and his lips too thin, but his dark, sparking eyes spoke of a vigorous, determined mind and character that could easily erase his less attractive features.

Georgiana whispered. "I didn't know Lord Donovan would be here this evening."

"Of course," Catherine said. "Since Braedon abandoned us, Donovan proves a worthy, though temporary replacement. I delight in Braedon's impishness and find Donovan far too serious sometimes, but he can be diverting enough. I'm certain he's holding on to some exciting secrets, and I aim to get at them."

"Do you think so?" Ravenna said.

"Oh yes. Still waters run deep." She nudged Ravenna with her elbow. "As *you* well know, my dear." She waggled her brows.

"Good evening, friends," Lord Donovan said. "I'd like to present to you all Mr. Josiah Emmett. He's a barrister-artist I met at Tattersall's." He then introduced Catherine, Harrison, Ravenna, and Georgiana in their turn.

Ravenna lifted a brow. "A barrister-artist? That's quite a combination."

"One is my career of choice. The other provides the paints." He smiled. "And often, I find myself tutoring young lords and ladies in art so I might eat."

"Oh, a painter then? Intriguing. I've always admired painters and how they interpret the world around them," Ravenna said.

Georgiana tipped her head. "What do you paint, sir?"

"Landscapes mostly. But occasionally, I like to paint portraits if I can get someone to sit still long enough." His gaze lingered over Georgiana, who suppressed a smile.

"I think I should like to learn to paint someday," Ravenna said.

"Not me," Catherine added. "I haven't the patience for it. Though I like to look at them and collect them. As you see." She swept her hand around the room to indicate the paintings on the wall.

"Yes. I was just admiring the Turner landscape in the foyer," Emmett said.

"A gift from the artist himself. It's of Dolbadarn Castle in Wales. I visited the castle once with friends and fell in love with the place. So, when I saw it, I had to have it."

"You've met Turner?" Emmett brightened. "I've heard he's quite reclusive and wary of strangers."

"Oh yes, quite. An eccentric, strange sort of fellow. Intensely private."

"How ever did you come by the painting then?"

"Through a mutual acquaintance who worked as an architectural draftsman with him. He managed to acquire an invitation to Turner's home. We had a brief visit that was all at once pleasant, annoying, and frightening."

Lord Donovan said, "Lady Catherine knows everyone and grabs hold of their secrets as soon as possible."

"Don't tell stories. I don't have any of your secrets, Donovan." She narrowed her eyes playfully. "Yet."

He laughed. "I haven't any."

"I don't believe you, sir. Everyone has secrets."

Ravenna said, "Do you live here in London, Mr. Emmett?"

"I do. For now."

"And do I detect Irish in your voice?"

"Not quite, ma'am. I'm Welsh."

"Oh." She frowned. She knew the difference between Irish and Welsh. Surely, he was lying. But why would he lie about such a thing? Granted, many in England didn't like the Irish, so perhaps he was afraid of people's prejudice. That wasn't an issue in Catherine's house. Of course, as a newcomer, he wouldn't know that. Perhaps Ravenna was mistaken. She shook her head and smiled. Maybe if she revealed her heritage, it would put him more at ease. "Forgive me. I'm Irish. I was certain I detected the tones of my homeland."

"Ah. I see. Perhaps you're homesick."

"Aye. I've been homesick for many years."

"Why haven't you returned?"

She didn't want to ruin the happy spirit of the dinner party by dredging up painful memories, so she shrugged. "I married and found my family

102

here."

Georgiana asked Emmett, "But why would you wish to cover your true accent?"

"I find it's sometimes best to blend in with your surroundings when you're unsure of who your friends are."

Georgiana smiled. "I think you'll find we're all friends here."

He lifted his brows. "Indeed. I think you're right. I've certainly found no enemies."

The dinner bell rang, and the crowd of thirty people meandered toward the dining room.

After the men enjoyed their cigars and brandy in the billiard room, they rejoined the ladies for cards and conversation. Lord Yarford, Catherine's lover, approached Ravenna as she stood talking with Georgiana and Donovan.

Yarford was in his fifties, swarthy as a high seas adventurer with short salt and pepper hair and a strong physique. Deep smile lines pleated the corners of his hazel eyes. He said, "Lady Birchfield. May I have a moment?"

She stepped away from her friends and walked alongside Yarford to the far end of the room. They stood under a large landscape painting, sipping their champagne punch. He pointed up at the painting. "That's my ancestral home in Scotland, near Aberdeen. It no longer exists, unfortunately."

"It's lovely. What happened to it?"

"Bad business decisions. My father was eventually forced to sell it. The new owner eventually razed it because it was too dilapidated to restore. It was once an abbey. Built in 1495. The new owner built a new house on the land."

"Incredible history. I'm sorry to hear of its demise. It's always a shame to see something beautiful with such deep history be destroyed."

"Indeed. But it seems bad business decisions run in my family's blood." He drank from his glass. "I understand Catherine told you our troubles."

"She did. And I'm so sorry to hear you're dealing with such a base accusation."

He nodded. "I wish I'd never entered into business with Thornley. But I wanted to thank you for attempting to assist in the matter. I did not kill him." He looked down at her. "I wanted to. But I didn't."

"Why would you involve yourself with Thornley? Surely you knew what he was?"

"I let my pride get in the way. I don't know if I can explain it properly, but as a young lad, I'd always wanted to sail the seas, have adventures, travel to distant lands and I had my heart set on the navy or privateering. Or both. But my father died early, and I was cast into the responsibility of running the estate before I even left university."

"But you have money now, don't you? Catherine said you'd sold a valuable mine."

"Yes. Admittedly, one of the mines I own came through wagers at the card table. With the money from that mine, I managed to buy others and extend my business reach to overseas ventures and such. But I'm certainly not as wealthy as the Devonshires. My coffers aren't infinite. And now, with another war waging, I'm certain the few investments I have overseas will suffer. While the mine I sold wasn't producing much, it was producing enough that it would bring in some money were the overseas ventures to suffer."

"I understand. Why would you take such a risk with Thornley?"

"I had no reason to doubt him. There have been numerous times when he had lost sizable amounts in cards and always paid the debt. I knew he was a scoundrel with women, but that didn't mean he was a cheat with money." He sighed. "And, I admit, I was flattered by the idea of a ship named after me. *The Yarford*. And the expedition would be in my name; the artifacts given to the crown would be given in my name. Don't you see?" He smiled at her. "It was the stuff of all my boyhood fantasies."

Ravenna nodded. "I see. Thornley could flatter when it suited him." She turned the crystal glass in her hands. Yarford seemed genuine. She'd known him for as long as she'd known Catherine, and she had no reason to suspect him. Yet, she wondered if there was more to his story. "When you discovered his fraud, what did you do? How did you act?"

"I was furious, of course. I asked him what happened, why the expedition fell through. He said building the ship and hiring the crew would prove far more expensive than he'd initially estimated. When I asked to have the money back, he said he'd already spent most of it. I confronted him at his home one day and challenged him to repay or fight a duel. He swore he would get the money and pay me back. We arranged to meet a week later because he said he would need to sell some properties in order to get the money. When I'd returned to collect what was owed me, I was told he'd left for New South Wales. And the family didn't know when he would return."

"Disgraceful."

He nodded, disgust twisting his mouth. "Indeed. And now, I'm being accused of murdering him. I only learned of his return about a week ago when Catherine told me of The Penitent House gala. I hadn't yet had the opportunity to confront him, though I was certainly going to. He died before I could."

"And you told all this to Mr. Chadwick?"

"Of course. I suspect he doesn't believe me, however."

"He doesn't."

"At any rate, I hope the killer, the actual killer, will be found and brought to justice."

"I will do my best."

Deep lines formed along his mouth and cheeks. "It's good to have friends like you, Lady Birchfield."

Ravenna returned to where Harrison and Mr. Emmett stood along the wall, engaged in conversation. Harrison watched Georgiana and Donovan talking with others across the room.

After some conversation about Mr. Emmett's adventures in tutoring two wild twin boys in Wales, Ravenna turned to him. "Mr. Emmett, you may not realize it, but your being here tonight is quite fortuitous."

"Oh, how so?" He smiled at her.

"Georgiana has recently come to stay with me and I now find myself in charge of her education. Unfortunately, she has none. And as you are a tutor, I wonder if you might be willing to tutor her in drawing and painting?

At least to start. We might add other subjects later as she improves."

"Only if she isn't as wild as the Kenner Twins," he teased.

She returned the playfulness. "I think I can promise she may only be half as wild."

He said, "Then I'd be happy to tutor her. She strikes me as a bright and capable young lady. And I'm always searching for a reason to paint."

"Would tomorrow at two be too early to start?"

"Of course not! However, I'm also a solicitor. I could also teach her geography, Latin, Greek…any number of subjects."

"That would be wonderful. But let's see how she takes to art first."

Catherine called across the room. "Yoo-hoo! Mr. Emmett, you must come here. Lady Corliss would ask you a question."

He said, "Please excuse me, Lady Birchfield. I look forward to lessons with Miss Sullivan. I'll be at Gordon House at two." He walked away to join Catherine.

Harrison said, "I could tutor Georgiana in Latin, French, or any of the sciences, you know."

"Yes, but in your recent note you said you planned to stay for only a few weeks."

He hemmed. "I could extend my stay if necessary. And, I assume you'll bring her with you to Birchfield when we retire to the country on the Great Twelfth. We could resume studies there. After all, I doubt I'll be sporting all day, every day."

She sipped her punch. "I'm sorry, Harrison, it never occurred to me. If you want to offer your services to Georgiana, I won't stop you. I thought, however, you weren't as successful in Latin as you now claim to be."

"How many women need Latin, at any rate? I can teach her other subjects," he said defensively.

Ravenna's own defenses rose. "Harrison, tutor her, if it makes you happy. Or split the job with Mr. Emmett since you're terrible at art. Or do nothing at all. It's of no consequence to me as long as you're both happy and she is educated well enough to be a proper wife and mother fully capable of running a successful household."

Harrison said to Ravenna, "Do you think it's wise to invite him to tutor Georgiana, though?"

"What would be the problem?"

He hemmed. "I don't know, exactly. I just…"

Ravenna linked her arm with his and pulled him close. "Oh, Harrison. I'm no fool. I see the way you look at her. But you don't really want her, do you? She has nothing to recommend her. She's beautiful, to be sure, but a pretty face and a fine figure are not the only things to consider in marriage. You must think of your position now. You need a woman with connections, money, and accomplishments. Beauty, I fear, is the last thing to consider. You need a woman who can be a valuable hostess. Once you take your seat in parliament, you'll need to learn to navigate the often precarious political waters. And you'll need a woman at your side who can help build your career with the right connections. If you're being honest, do you truly believe Georgiana can fulfill that role? Besides…" She nodded toward Donovan and Georgiana, who were walking across the room arm in arm. "At the moment, I think her sights are elsewhere."

"Yes, but shouldn't you be more careful? We don't know this Mr. Emmett."

"By the end of this evening, we will know plenty. Catherine will ferret out a great deal of information. As she usually does. And when he comes to Gordon House tomorrow, I will learn more about him and ask for his references. I'll set Banks and Hart to look into his referrals."

Harrison said, "I shall try to find out something about him too. Pardon me." He stepped away.

Ravenna sighed, watching Harrison. *Poor smitten man.* She drank her punch and thought about how she could best help this situation between Harrison and Georgiana. If there was any help to offer. As she turned the puzzle over in her mind, she caught a bit of a conversation nearby between Lady Montgomery and Lady Corliss.

Lady Montgomery, a dumpy woman with fake blonde curls peeking from beneath a gold and pink striped turban, said, "I think his brother killed him."

Lady Corliss, a tall woman with coppery hair, said, "I believe so, too. It's my understanding Lord Franklin had quit giving his brother money because of his outrageous gambling debts."

Ravenna looked down at the floor and inched closer to hear better.

"I hadn't heard that," Lady Montgomery said. "How do you know?"

"Oh, yes. I have it from Lady Thornley herself. She said they've had to sell off some of their furniture and business interests to pay off his debts."

Ravenna bit the inside of her lip.

"I can't believe it!" Lady Montgomery gasped.

"It's true. Lady Thornley told me that between the money Thornley spent on his archaeological adventures and Lord Percy's gambling, the family is very nearly broke. She has great fears of being rendered utterly destitute."

"Oh!" Lady Montgomery covered her wrinkled mouth. "I hadn't realized she was in such dire circumstances."

"Indeed, she is."

Ravenna bit down harder on her lip to keep from showing her shock at this news. She'd gathered from Evie, the maid at Thornley Hall, that the younger son was a spendthrift, but she hadn't realized the Thornley family was in such disarray and desperation. Maybe, given the circumstances, Lord Percy was just desperate enough to remove the obstacle to his gambling habit and money by murdering his own brother.

Chapter Fourteen

The dinner party ended as it always did at Adair House parties—with cards. Cards, losing and winning big at faro, whist, loo, picquet, or quadrille were among Catherine's favorite delights, and she sought such opportunities at every chance possible.

Georgiana beelined to sit beside Donovan, and Harrison, close on her heels, took the chair beside her. Ravenna sat at a nearby table to keep a watchful eye and ear on Georgiana's table. Her own table was filled with Catherine, Mr. Emmett, and Lady Montgomery. Ravenna found herself longing to share the card table with Braedon. She pushed back the memory of the last time they'd played cards together. His blue eyes and mischievous smile. She fanned her cards to focus on them.

Georgiana said, "I've never played loo before. Lord Donovan, will you show me?"

"Of course," he said, with an edge in his voice. He was clearly only being polite.

Lady Corliss said, "Perhaps you shouldn't have taken a seat to play, if you don't understand the game."

"Or you might mind your own cards, ma'am. If Lord Donovan doesn't mind teaching me, it can be nothing to you."

Both shocked and amused at Georgiana's sharpness, Ravenna's brows shot up, and she sat guarded, listening, ready to intervene if necessary. She didn't know the girl had such pluck.

"Aren't you a saucy one?" Lady Corliss said, picking through her cards.

Georgiana lifted her chin and opened her mouth to speak, but Harrison intervened. "I can show you." He moved his chair closer. Then, he addressed Donovan and Corliss. "Georgiana is bright. It should only take a round or so for her to catch on. Shall we proceed?" He softly explained the game as Lady Corliss dropped her first card.

Though Harrison attempted to explain, Georgiana leaned close to Donovan, showing him her cards. "Sir, which do you think I should play?"

Ravenna played her cards while watching the scene to her left unfold.

Lord Donovan smiled. "Miss, you shouldn't show me your hand, else I might use it against you."

Georgiana smiled and chuckled. "You're too much of a gentleman to do such a thing."

Lady Corliss scoffed, rolled her eyes, and downed her drink.

Georgiana said, "Is something the matter, Lady Corliss?"

"Only that your attempts are both transparent and juvenile. We all see what you're about, and you reach too high, little fox." She cast a side glance at Harrison. "Best to jump for the grapes lowest to the ground."

Georgiana flushed red. "And you should shut your mouth, or I shall be forced to do it for you."

Lady Corliss laughed. "Oh my, what a vulgar chit. Have you come directly from the streets?"

Ravenna jumped up. "Excuse me, Lady Catherine, Mr. Emmett, Lady Montgomery, I must leave for the evening. I do apologize, but I have a horrible headache." Of course, everyone knew the headache excuse was the most often employed to politely escape an uncomfortable situation. Ravenna stepped over to Georgiana's table and said, "Georgiana, it's time for us to go. Let's get our things. Harrison, call for our carriage immediately, please."

Harrison scooted out of his chair and rushed from the room.

Ravenna flashed a look of warning. "Georgiana, please see if Harrison needs assistance."

The room quieted down, and all eyes turned to the little tempest brewing.

"But—"

"Now."

Georgiana shot to her feet, strode from the room, and slammed the door, causing everyone to jump.

Ravenna grew hot, and buttoning down her anger, she said to the room, "I do apologize for the disturbance. Catherine, Yarford, thank you for an otherwise delightful evening. Enjoy your cards, everyone."

The unhappy trio stood in the foyer in tense silence until the carriage was brought around.

When they had settled into the carriage, Ravenna said to Georgiana, "I have never been so embarrassed. How dare you behave that way to someone entirely above you in rank, station, accomplishment, and age? If you're going to stay with me, you will learn how to conduct yourself. I will not bring you into public to act like a fishwife. Am I clear?"

Georgiana looked down at her hands. "Yes, ma'am."

Harrison watched the exchange.

"And another thing. I've tried to coax you away from Lord Donovan because I know he would never be interested in you. I'm trying to save you from the heartbreak I know awaits you. I have tried to persuade you gently from him and appeal to your logic, but now I see you have your mother's stubbornness and will not be easily swayed. So, I must speak plainly. You do not have the money, connections, education, refinement, or accomplishments to turn Lord Donovan's head, and it's likely you never will. He sees you as a child fresh from the nursery. He will only ever treat you as he would a sister or a niece."

Georgiana broke into tears. "Why should it be so?"

Ravenna softened. "Sweet, darling, Georgiana, because that is the way of the world. I don't know him closely, but I'm familiar enough with him to know he likes older women. Women who have seen something of the world and life. Women who are educated and refined." She slipped her arm around the crying girl and placed a kiss on her temple. "I'm sorry Georgiana. I don't want to hurt you, but it's necessary to tell you the truth. The truth is precious, and it's the most loving thing I can do for you so you can focus on someone better suited to you."

Georgiana seethed. "You mean he likes women like *you*."

111

"Don't be silly."

"I've seen the way he looks at you. He played cards with Lady Corliss, because she didn't give him a choice. But I saw the way he looked at you the rest of the evening and the way he hung around you like a lamb."

"Donovan does seem partial to you, Amma," Harrison said.

Ravenna scoffed. "Nonsense. He's good friends with Catherine, and I was with Catherine most of the evening. At any rate, if I'm to take you into society again, I must know you will be better behaved. Can I even take you to the upcoming ball?"

Georgiana sniffled and spoke with panic through tears. "Oh, yes. Please don't keep me from the ball. I will behave better. I promise. It's just…that Lady Corliss…aggravated me."

"I know. She can be aggravating. You will often encounter aggravating people, especially among this lot. But it doesn't benefit you to ruin your character in the eyes of others. When you sass her openly, you think you're showing people who *she* is, but, in fact, you're proving who *you* are. Do you understand?"

Georgiana nodded. "Yes."

"You simply cannot act like that. A woman of her station and disposition will ruin you and all your chances."

"I understand. Please let me go to the ball. Lord Donovan promised to dance with me."

Ravenna sighed. Her words had not even entered the solid clay of Georgiana's mind. "Of course, you can go to the ball."

As the carriage slowed to a stop in front of Gordon House, Georgiana asked, "Auntie, do you want him for yourself? Is he your beau?"

"How could you ask such a thing? Do you really think I would hurt your feelings to dissuade you from a man because I have designs on him?"

"I don't know…I suppose not."

"I think you should be quiet now and go straight to your bedchamber once we're inside."

A footman carrying a torch approached the carriage to light the way. Harrison opened the door and jumped to the ground to assist Georgiana.

Her face was swollen and blotchy with tears.

Harrison snapped his head around. "What was that?"

"What is it?" Ravenna stepped forward, preparing her fan.

"I heard something. Stay here." He held out his hand to the footman. "Give me the torch." He walked in the direction of the noise.

Georgiana gaped, wide-eyed. Ravenna shoved her toward the door. "Go inside, this instant." Georgiana entered the house, pausing at the door to look back.

"Go," Ravenna said, moving to follow Harrison.

"Stop!" Harrison shouted and ran into the shadows and fog.

"No, wait." Ravenna pulled up her skirts and gave chase. "Harrison!"

They ran down the street, pushing through the few people peppering the pavement. Puddles soaked through Ravenna's thin slippers, and the arches of her feet ached as they slammed against the stones. Her shoes certainly were not meant for running. "Harrison!" She shouted again, breathless. They ran for what seemed an eternity all the way down Curzon Street, where they rounded the corner onto South Audley Street and ran down that street as hard and fast as their legs would carry them. They finally stopped where South Audley intersected with Mount Street.

Harrison slowed his pace and stopped running, doubling over at the street corner under the gas lamp. He leaned against the post, holding his knees.

Ravenna caught up to him. "Are you hurt?" She asked.

He said through panting breaths. "I lost him. I lost him." He dropped the snuffed torch.

"Who was it?" Ravenna searched the darkness.

"I don't know. I caught him by the shoulder, and he punched me in the stomach." He coughed. "I tried to hold him, but he slipped away across the street between the carriages." He motioned at the carriages barreling down the cobblestone street. He began to catch his breath. "I think he came out of that alley by our house."

She searched the darkness, fear crawling over her skin like thousands of spiders. "Let's go home. And please don't chase anyone like that again." They turned back toward Curzon Street.

"Why shouldn't I chase some dirty ruffian from our door?"

"Things aren't as they seem." Ravenna looked over her shoulder. If people were lurking around her house in the dead of night, it likely meant The Unity. Especially since she'd just received a threatening letter from them.

"What do you mean?"

She couldn't tell him everything. It would ultimately reveal too much about the past she wanted to keep secret. All she could say at the moment was, "It's complicated."

"And what does that mean?"

"Harrison, there are some things I'm not at liberty to discuss. But I ask you to trust me, please. And don't chase strangers into the night again. Please."

"Sorry, Amma. I cannot make such a promise. I will protect my home and my family whatever the cost."

They walked in silence the rest of the way. Ravenna had never been so happy to enter Gordon House. Her shins, ankles, and feet hurt, and her slippers were destroyed.

They found Georgiana kneeling in a foyer chair, peeking through the curtains. "There you both are! I was getting worried. What happened? Who was it?"

"Some vagrant hanging about the house, no doubt," Harrison said. "I suspect he won't return."

Ravenna picked up the stack of letters and invitations from the table.

"Did you fight?" Georgiana gasped.

"No." Harrison smiled. "He got away from me in the fog, but I came very close to catching him."

Georgiana looked up at him with admiration. "You're so brave. He might've hurt you. Weren't you scared?"

Harrison puffed a little. "Not really. I was too concerned with catching the miscreant."

"Georgiana," Ravenna said. "It's time for you to go to bed. We'll begin your lessons after breakfast tomorrow."

The girl flashed a look of anger, hurt, and distrust at Ravenna and jogged up the stairs.

Ravenna blew out a breath. "She is not happy with me."

Harrison watched Georgiana. "I think you were too hard on her this evening."

"Trust me, I was not. She is stubborn, foolish, and uneducated. She's flirting with trouble and will ruin her reputation if I don't rein her in. Donovan will break her heart to pieces, if I allow this to continue. Not on purpose, of course, but unwittingly."

Harrison said, "No worries. I'll catch the pieces as they fall."

Chapter Fifteen

Ravenna limped up the stairs, aching all over as the excitement of the evening drained from her body. She kicked off her shoes and tossed them by the fireplace. They were unsalvageable. She would need to get another pair.

She wiped off the sweat and dirt then changed into a lavender nightgown and wrapped herself in a shawl. She poured a glass of port and settled on the sofa to read her mail. She opened an invitation to a picnic and another to a dinner party. One letter was from Catherine, who wrote though they saw each other a few times a week. Another letter was from Niall, her brother, whom she hadn't heard from in about a year. She rushed to open the letter and quickly read it. In the letter, he let her know he had recently married a Creole woman from New Orleans, and they were expecting their first child.

Ravenna gasped. "Married?" She lamented the distance between them. Disappointment weighed between her shoulders. She wished she could've been there to meet her new sister-in-law. Niall was all the way in America. She might never meet his new wife or her new niece or nephew. She hated this fragmentation of her family. There might be hope for him to return home if The Unity weren't around. Or, she could go to America herself. To escape The Unity, and start afresh. After a few moments of playing out that fantasy, she concluded she didn't have the heart to make another big move. And from everything she'd heard about living in America, life was considerably harder. Her life was here now in England. The letter ended with Niall's desire to see her again. And to return, if he could, so Ravenna could meet his wife—a teacher at a girls' school.

That alarmed her. Niall should not return to London just now–especially with a new wife and a baby on the way. She would write to him tomorrow, warning him not to come. Though, if he did intend to sail, the letter likely wouldn't reach him in time. This letter was dated June 29. But she had to try.

She put aside the letter and opened one from Reverend Howarth. He was excited by the news Reverend McKirk had shared and asked if she would come to a meeting the next morning at ten o'clock. Her day was already getting quite full. She needed to write letters before breakfast, visit Reverend Howarth by ten, and be back at Gordon House for Georgiana's lessons with Mr. Emmett by two and for her own fencing lessons with Mr. Norris from Angelo's School.

Already, it was approaching midnight. She'd finish reading her mail, then go to bed.

She put Reverend Howarth's letter aside and moved to the last one. It was from Lady Thornley. She was disappointed for two reasons. First, Lady Thornley was likely to be put out with her. Second, the letter wasn't from Braedon. She found herself eagerly looking for post deliveries every day, hoping for another letter from him. When there wasn't one, she dropped into disappointment.

She steeled herself to face the letter from Lady Thornley with a cleansing sigh. She opened the letter.

> *Dear Lady Birchfield,*
>
> *I'm disappointed you will not help me. I write in hopes you've changed your mind. It is your Christian duty to help where you can. Please visit soon to tell me you will, in fact, help in my time of need. I don't trust these Bow Street men.*
>
> *Sincerely,*
> *Mildreth*

Ravenna rolled her eyes. It annoyed her when people used religion as a thrashing rod to guilt people into doing something against their will. She sighed and folded the letter. She sipped her port and stared into the fire. She had, however, unbeknownst to Lady Thornley, changed her mind. Yet, she didn't want to meet with Lady Thornley. It wasn't likely to be pleasant. Ravenna had no idea who had killed Lord Thornley and, so far, had few suspicions. Mr. Gibson was certainly her primary suspect. His jealousy could easily have driven him to kill the man in the way of his fortune and fame.

Yet, Lord Percy was a serious consideration. Though he and Lord Thornley were brothers, Lord Percy had pushed the family to a point of desperation yet would want to ensure the money remained entirely in his control. Lady Thornley would most certainly not want to hear one son might've killed the other. She also wouldn't want to hear that one of the maids living in her house, Evie, might be a killer.

But was the solution so obvious and simple? Possibly. Or there was a chance someone else had been involved. Since the opal was stolen, she needed to consider who else would've known about it and why they would want it. Mr. Gibson would've coveted the opal to build his reputation, connections, and wealth while pleasing The Crown. Lord Percy would've wanted it to sell for money to gamble or pay debts. Who would have such wealth to pay for it? Prince George? The Devonshires? Or he might've gambled it and lost it to an opponent. Evie, too, might have a motive to steal it and sell it. It wasn't likely she had connections with the sort of people who would have enough money to purchase it for its value? Of course, she might've sold it for an amount painfully below its value for whatever money she could get. In any case, the stone could now be in anyone's hands.

Ravenna woke early the next morning, washed her face in rose water, and rang for her breakfast. While she waited for her food, she sat at her writing desk to address last night's letters. She wrote to her brother, excited for the happy news, but concerned about his desire to return to England. She cautioned him against such foolishness, warning him of The Unity's determination to hunt him down. Yet, she assured him he and his wife would have a place to stay at Birchfield Manor. She signed the letter, hoping it would reach Niall before he attempted to set sail.

As a maid brought in breakfast and sat it on a nearby table, she dashed off quick notes to Reverend Howarth and Lady Thornley, assuring them she would visit as soon as possible today. She didn't want to visit Lady Thornley, but it was best to do it and be done with it. She peppered sand over the ink to dry it, sealed the letters with a wax seal, and asked the maid to send a footman to deliver them immediately. Yet, as she sat down to her caraway buns and tea, her motivation to visit Lady Thornley sank further.

Hart entered with Ravenna's dress, followed by a couple of maids with buckets of warm water for a bath. Ravenna slipped behind a screen to unclothe as she asked Hart to prepare Georgiana, Keene, and herself for running errands. "I'd like you all to go with me today. I want to take a basket of bread, cheese, and tea to The Penitent House, and there are other places we will visit this morning. "Also Mr. Emmett will be here to tutor Georgiana at two o'clock, so we must make haste."

"Very well. I'll see everything is prepared." Hart rushed out.

Ravenna eased into the warm water, her legs and feet aching from running the night before, and quickly bathed.

After dressing, Ravenna met Georgiana, Keene, and Hart in the foyer.

Harrison trotted down the stairs, riding crop in hand. "Can I interest anyone with a ride in the park? The groom is preparing my horse now. I could have a curricle prepared as well."

Georgiana looked at him wistfully as Ravenna spoke. "Sorry, we're off to run our errands. But we'll gladly join you another day. Perhaps tomorrow."

"Very well." Harrison mounted his horse and ambled toward Hyde Park as the ladies climbed into the carriage with their baskets of sundries for The Penitent House.

Spitalfields was a distinct contrast to Ravenna's life in Mayfair. Though all of London suffered the coal smoke, muck, traffic, and street bustle, the poverty was rampant, palpable, in Spitalfields. The area had been largely developed by the Irish immigrants who had come for the silk trade when the linen trade declined in Ireland. But the importation of French silk and calico combined with economic crises destroyed the silk industry and impoverished the citizens, sometimes leading to riots. The houses were smaller, dingier, in some instances, dilapidated. Animals roamed the streets, being corralled toward the slaughterhouses. The streets were filled with working men and women, dirty, thin, and ragged. Rookeries where crime and dissolution prevailed were around every corner.

The Christ Church, built by the Huguenots, with its tall white spire, jutted against the gray sky and shone like a beacon of light among the destitute. Nearby on Wood Street, a narrow street to the left of the church, stood a three-story gray stone structure with an oak door. This was The Penitent House.

The women descended from the carriage and entered through the iron gate to the front door.

Mariah answered the door, dressed severely in a gray dress with her hair pulled into a tight bun. Her face was pale, with dark circles under her eyes. "Good morning, Lady Birchfield." She stepped aside to allow entry. "I see you brought friends." She pushed a smile onto her face.

Ravenna made introductions. "We bring gifts as well." She held up her basket.

"How generous of you. Please, set them here on the bench, and I'll have them carried to the kitchen. I know the women will be grateful and excited to have this for tea this afternoon." She showed them into the parlor, which was decorated sparsely with worn, handed down furniture. "Please wait here. I'll hunt down Reverend Howarth."

The ladies sat around the room wherever a place could be found. The parlor rug was worn and covered creaky, scuffed wood floors. The sofa and chair cushions were lumpy, the curtains faded, and the paint peeled on the window casements. The floral and striped paper was yellowed in places, especially around the fireplace and ceiling, where spots had formed from fireplace and candle use over the years. Yet for all this, there was a sort of pride and care in the maintenance and cleanliness of the room that warmed Ravenna's heart.

Reverend McKirk entered the room and stopped short. "Oh. Pardon me, ladies." He removed his flat black hat and bowed. "I was searching for

Reverend Howarth."

Ravenna answered, "Mariah has gone to find him."

"Ah." He stepped further into the room. He was dressed all in black, as was customary for men of the cloth. Where he had appeared somber on their first meeting, he now seemed full of youth and vigor, which had improved his looks. "Then you won't mind if I keep you company?"

"Not at all," Ravenna said. She introduced the other women to Mr. McKirk. "We stopped by for only a brief visit and brought some gifts for the household."

"Oh, I suppose these baskets in the hall are from you?"

"Yes."

"How kind." He paused, his gaze lingering over Keene.

Reverend Howarth entered the room with Mariah on his heels. She caught the lingering looks between McKirk and Keene. She set her jaw, her mouth forming a tight line.

Reverend Howarth seemed out of breath and agitated. "Forgive me for making you wait. But I've just now been extricating the young Lord Percy Thornley from the house."

Ravenna blinked. "Whatever do you mean?"

"Apparently, he had met one of the ladies at the gala and has been coming to seduce her into her old ways. Miss Mariah, who oversees the women and inspects their rooms, found letters, gifts, and coin from the man. She uncovered the indiscretion before the woman returned to habits that would surely pull her back into the streets and endanger the salvation she is working for."

"Good heavens!" Ravenna gasped. "I can't believe...I mean, I knew Lord Percy was a cad a-a-a rake, but I never imagined he would stoop so low as to compromise a young woman in this very house. And to destroy her while she is working diligently to clean up her life and advance herself! Despicable, horrid man." The longer Ravenna spoke of the matter, the higher the anger climbed. "I assure you, I will have a word with him." She blew out a breath and reined in her temper. She said to Mariah, "Thank you, Mariah, for your honesty, conscientiousness, and integrity. I don't yet know how I will reward you, but I will ensure you will be rewarded."

She smiled. "Thank you, milady. Truly, my work is reward enough. I'm only thankful I was able to call attention to it before the woman was lost forever. I had managed to stop her on the cusp of sneaking off with that man, Lord Thornley."

Ravenna wasn't sure, but she thought she detected a sneer as Mariah said, "That man." Which was understandable. She'd caught the man behaving despicably. Yet, the manner in which she said "Lord Thornley" seemed specific to him, as if the particular man and the particular name disgusted her. She made a mental note to ask her about him before she left.

Hart and Keene exchanged a glance.

"What will happen to her?" Georgiana asked.

Reverend Howarth puffed and sat in a nearby chair. "I assure you, she will take on the scullery duties for a time. It's the most suitable punishment."

"That seems harsh," Georgiana said.

Ravenna grabbed her hand and squeezed it until the girl winced.

Reverend Howarth lifted a brow and studied her with his beady, chestnut-colored eyes. "You give a decided opinion for someone so young and, I daresay, likely unacquainted with the ways of the world—especially the sort of world these women come from. They have lived in squalor, crime, licentiousness, and every dirty and gruesome thing. Most are forced into such a life, but some choose it of their own free will. I assure you, miss, in this case, the punishment fits the moral crime."

"I don't understand. It seems you would exhibit more charity—"

Mr. McKirk interrupted, speaking with tenderness. "Dear Miss Georgiana, your innocence is admirable. You have clearly lived with people who have had a care for your welfare. So, it must be difficult for you to comprehend the level of...misfortune these women have had to endure. Punishment for misbehavior *is* an act of kindness and love, though I know it must be difficult for you to see it at the moment." His gaze lingered on her.

Georgiana shook her head, confused.

Mariah's eyes glittered darkly. "Mr. McKirk," she said. "I've just been reminded. There was a passage in 1 Peter I do not understand. I came across it this morning and meant to ask you about it, but was distracted. Will you explain it to me before our Bible study this afternoon?"

He smiled. "Yes, of course. I'm happy to help." He turned to the visitors. "Please excuse us, ladies. This is a matter of import. We can't have the leader of the ladies fall behind in her studies."

Mariah smiled. "That's right. I'll be teased mercilessly. Thank you again for the sundries, Lady Birchfield."

"Thank you for your dedication, Mariah. I will see you happily rewarded. I promise."

She flashed a smile of acquiescence and left the room with Mr. McKirk on her heels.

Reverend Howarth was not to be pushed off the lesson at hand. He continued, speaking to Georgiana. "Young lady, we have blessed the women here with a bounty of time, money, food, and board. They want for nothing. All we ask is they repent of their former lives as prostitutes and turn toward a brighter, safer, more robust future. They understand the rules when they come here, and they understand the consequences if they break the rules. Without rules and consequences, there is chaos, and nothing good comes of chaos. So, misbehavior of the sort we discovered today shall not be tolerated."

In time, Ravenna turned the discussion to the donor dinner. The dinner would be held at The Penitent House. It was decided that the Penitent women would prepare most of the food under the guidance of Ravenna's cook. Ravenna would also loan out the service of some of her maids and footmen, paying them extra for the additional service. The Penitent women would make small gifts and write letters of gratitude to the donors and they would all sit together over a fat goose, and several side dishes and dessert.

When everything had been decided, Ravenna, Georgiana, Keene, and Hart all stood and said their goodbyes. Reverend Howarth said, "At the risk of being rude, I must leave immediately for an engagement." He patted his chest and sides. "But I need my spectacles and my Bible." He said to a girl passing in the hall, "Annie, come here. Be a dear and see the ladies to their carriage." He bid the visitors adieu and rushed away.

Annie walked them to the door and held it open for them. They walked toward the carriage. Ravenna stopped. "I almost forgot. I need to speak with Mariah about something." She turned to her companions. "Please get in the carriage. I'll return directly." She re-entered The Penitent House. "Excuse me, Annie. Where can I find Miss Mariah? I need to speak with her."

Annie was not a trained maid who understood proper etiquette. A proper maid would've asked her to wait and left to retrieve Mariah. Instead, Annie, a rough and ready girl plucked from the streets, swiped her nose on her hand and pointed down the hall. She spoke with a thick, almost unintelligible Cockney. "She were in the study last I saw. Go to the end of the hall, turn left. The study's the first door on the left." Then she flounced away with the baskets before Ravenna could ask for an escort.

"Very well," Ravenna muttered. She found her way to the study. The door was cracked open. Ravenna lifted her hand to knock, but heard sharp whispering voices. She paused.

A female voice sounding much like Mariah said, "This is like the time you…" Her voice dipped too low to hear. Ravenna strained to hear.

"I can't believe you're still angry about such a silly thing."

Ravenna's eyes widened. That was Mr. McKirk. *Oh, my!* This sounded much like a lover's quarrel unfolding.

"You made promises to me, and if you don't keep them…." Mariah said.

"I will. I am."

"*All* the promises."

"Yes. I haven't forgotten. I would think you'd express more gratitude for what I've already accomplished. It's been no easy task. Name another who would've—"

She cut him off with a hiss. "I want my children here with me. That's all I know. They are all I have left of…" her voice broke. "A life and a man I loved."

How was Mr. McKirk going to help her with them? Perhaps this wasn't a lover's quarrel, after all. Perhaps she was merely a disappointed woman who had depended on the clergy to help her with a sensitive issue.

Ravenna heard giggling. A couple of girls strolled down the hall toward her. She didn't want to appear to be eavesdropping, so she shot into motion and passed the study. She looked around as if lost. "Pardon me, where is the study?"

One of the girls said in a low, mocking voice, "Pardon me..." Then they fell against each other in giggles.

Irritation scratched at Ravenna's ribs for a moment before she remembered these girls weren't taught how to behave properly.

The other girl said, "It's behind you. Right there." She pointed.

Mariah and Mr. McKirk must've heard because he stepped into the hall and said, "Lady Birchfield? Are you looking for us? Mariah and I are studying in here."

It did not escape Ravenna's notice that he used Mariah's given name instead of her surname, which was far too familiar.

"Yes. I needed to speak with her for a moment."

"Of course. Come in." He stepped aside and allowed Ravenna to enter. "Excuse me. I'll let you have your privacy." He bowed, pinned Mariah with a steady look, and then closed the door.

The study was a small room with a wall of bookshelves on one side. The remaining walls were covered with green jacquard paper. A few watercolor paintings and drawings hung on the wall around the fireplace and a large desk with several chairs occupied the center of the room.

Mariah had clearly been crying. Her eyes were red and puffy, and she sniffled, dabbing her nose with a handkerchief. She sat at the table, the window to her back. Ravenna noticed there was no Bible on the table. "How may I help you, Lady Birchfield?"

Ravenna sat across from her. "I won't keep you. I'm sure you're busy. But I was wondering what you know of the Thornley family."

"Not much. Only what little I learned at the gala. And then the recent business with the younger son, who has been sniffing around here like a fox around a chicken coop. Why do you ask?"

"Earlier, when you mentioned Lord Thornley, there seemed to be a certain anger or resentment in your voice toward him or his family."

Mariah straightened and looked down at the table. "No. I have no particular resentment toward him or the family. The Thornleys were very kind to host the gala for us. I am angry with the new Lord Thornley, perhaps, but I think you can understand why." She lifted her light brown eyes to gaze steadily at Ravenna. Clasped her hands, her knuckles turning white.

She was lying. Ravenna wasn't sure about what or why, but she could feel it in her bones. She didn't want to openly call Mariah a liar. If she did, it might lock up her willingness to talk. Ravenna tipped her head. "Are you sure you don't know something you could share with me?"

Mariah set her jaw. "I'm sure. Why do you want to know?"

Ravenna's mind raced. She needed to come up with a satisfactory answer quickly, but she fell flat. "I'm curious if the elder brother was as much a cad as the younger. I've heard rumors...." She let her voice trail away.

A malicious light filled Mariah's eyes at the mention of the elder Lord Thornley. "I wouldn't know."

Ravenna wasn't going to get any answers from Mariah at the moment. She stood. "Very well. Thank you for your time." She started toward the door and paused. "If there's anything at all I can help you with, don't hesitate to ask."

Mariah straightened her back, looking every bit the serious governess. "I'll remember that, ma'am. Thank you for your many kindnesses to us."

Chapter Sixteen

Ravenna's carriage stopped in front of Thornley Hall, a grand, buff stone manor of nearly a hundred yards. She said to the rest of her party, "I need to stop here for a brief visit." They climbed out of the carriage. "Georgiana, please say nothing."

"Yes, ma'am."

Ravenna turned to Hart. "You and Keene please go sit in the kitchen. See what you can discover about the Thornley sons and what the life of this house is like."

Hart nodded, her soft brown eyes taking in the grandeur of the house. "Will do." She absentmindedly touched the scar on her neck. "I know too well how many secrets these grand houses hold." She cut her eyes at Ravenna.

"Indeed."

Several men came out of the house carrying chairs and tables, led by a short, round, sweaty man in pantaloons, a green and white striped waistcoat, and a green jacket. Lady Mildreth trailed behind them, in a black silk dressing gown and mob cap, waving her handkerchief. "Just one more month. I swear that's all I need. Please wait. Just...." She stopped and stomped with each word. "Please! One. More. Month!"

The portly perspirer turned. "We have been more than patient, milady. We cannot wait another month. Should I go entirely out of business because you insist on living in arrears?"

Ravenna and her party froze like scared rabbits. Lady Mildreth caught sight of them. "Oh, hang it all, you cruel wretch. Leave me, an old lady, sitting on the floor then. The devil take you for all I care!"

Georgiana gasped. Keene tucked her chin and bit down on her lower lip to stifle a giggle.

Lady Mildreth shouted at Ravenna and her companions, her curls shaking and the lines in her face growing deeper. "Well, come on inside and be witness to my utter shame!" She spun around and stormed into the house. Her voice echoed from within as she shouted something indiscernible, likely at the servants.

Ravenna muttered to the others, "This should be interesting."

Hart and Keene were directed to follow a footman to the kitchen while the butler showed Ravenna and Georgiana into the parlor, where Lady Mildreth lay in a heap on the sofa wailing.

"I'm so sorry to come at this horrible time. I had no idea..." Ravenna and Georgiana sat in chairs, flanking the sofa. Ravenna looked around. Apparently, the furniture man hadn't cleaned out this room. "We won't inopportune you long."

"All is lost," Lady Mildreth said into the sofa cushion. "I will be destitute. Cast out into the street to fend for myself. And how shall I?"

Ravenna slid from her seat to kneel beside Lady Mildreth and placed a comforting hand on her arm. The dowager smelled of violets and camphor. "Oh, don't say that, milady. All will be well. This matter will work itself out somehow." She wasn't sure she believed that. Oftentimes, things did not, in fact, work out well. But it was too painful to watch a woman as proud, strong, and dignified as Lady Mildreth reduced into a pile of tears. "As painful as it may be, perhaps there are some jewels you can sell?"

Lady Mildreth wailed louder. "I sold some today! And it wasn't enough. I'm losing everything. All at once." She sat up and held a handkerchief over her face. "My eldest, most rational son is dead. My youngest son, the profligate, is destroying our fortune and cares nothing for what will become of us. My jewels, which have been in my family since Henry II. My furniture. Next will be my very home!" She pounded her chest with her fist. "Maybe even the clothes on my very back!" She turned her blotchy face to Ravenna. "And you won't help me with finding out who killed my son. What am I to do?"

Ravenna eased herself up to sit on the sofa beside Lady Mildreth and took her hands, bare of the rings she once wore. "I'm so sorry this is happening to you, and I came to speak to you about how I might help. But first, let's discuss the more immediate concern. Your furniture and jewels. There must be a relative. Someone who can help."

Lady Mildreth sniffled and blew her nose. "I suppose my sister and brother-in-law could help, but they're all the way in India."

"You should write to them."

"Yes. Nothing matters but the jewelry. I must have that back. I think I can purchase the items back from the pawnbroker."

"I understand. What did you sell?"

"My diamond earbobs and my rings. A ruby, a diamond, and a sapphire."

"And to whom did you sell them?"

"Mr. Shervey in Bride's Lane, Snow Hill."

"Okay. I will try to get them back for you."

Her bottom lip quivered, and she whispered through her tears. "No, pet. I can't ask you to do that. It's too much like…charity because I don't when or if I can ever repay you."

Ravenna tried not to smile. "We all need a little charity from time to time. You will get through this difficult time, and I will help you."

Lady Mildreth blew out a breath and dabbed her eyes. "I'm quite glad for you, Lady Birchfield. You've brought me much relief." She noticed Georgiana for the first time. "Oh, dear." She patted her face with her knotted hands. "I'm so sorry you witnessed my shame. So sorry." Her hazel eyes pleaded with Ravenna.

"I'm sorry, too, under the circumstances. This is my niece, Georgiana Sullivan. She's staying with me now. Georgiana, come meet Lady Mildreth Thornley."

Georgiana rose to deliver an unbalanced curtsey. "A pleasure to meet you, ma'am. Though I'm sorry for the circumstances."

"Yes, thank you. Aren't you a dear?" She turned to Ravenna as Georgiana resumed her seat. "I had no idea you had a niece. And such a pretty one."

She studied Georgiana. "I don't suppose she has fortune or connections?"

Ravenna smiled. "I'm afraid not."

"A pity. Of course, my profligate son would never deserve one such as you, even if I could convince him to take a wife. It would be reprehensible to wed you to him at any rate. Though, I confess, the temptation would be much greater to do so, if you had any money or connections." She blew out a ragged breath. "At least you're pretty, dear. It might help you secure a decent future and I hope for your sake he's a wealthy man with stellar connections."

Georgiana looked between Lady Mildreth and Ravenna, then resumed her seat. "Yes, ma'am."

"And if you are wise…" Lady Mildreth held up a finger. "You will not throw away your charms on some idle wastrel like my son Percy." She clasped her hands in her lap, her nails digging into her knuckles. "I should not wish him on my worst enemy. I don't know what to do about him." She turned to Ravenna. "Please tell me you will help me discover what happened to Franklin?"

Ravenna turned to her baffled niece. "Georgiana, will you please wait in the foyer?"

They waited for Georgiana to leave, then Ravenna said, "I am looking into it." She didn't have the heart to tell her it was for Catherine and Yarford's sake.

"Oh!" Lady Mildreth fell back in her seat, clapping her hand over her heart. "Thank the heavens. You must tell me the moment you see or hear anything important."

"Of course. So far, I've managed to speak only to Mr. Gibson. At first, I thought he was the most likely suspect since he was clearly jealous of Lord Franklin. He wanted the attention and accolades, and he couldn't bear being overshadowed by Lord Franklin. He's a jealous and angry sort. And a thief. I'm convinced he stole a statue from Lord Thornley's desk. However, I'm not certain he's the sort to murder."

"I need to know who killed my son!"

"I understand. But no one is presenting himself as a viable option. That's why I'm here. I thought if I could look around in Lord Franklin's study again, maybe talk to Evie again—"

"Evie? What has she to do with it?"

"I spoke with her on the day of the murder. She gave me some information about Percy and Franklin's relationship. I thought maybe she might remember more."

Lady Mildreth scoffed. "How can you put any faith in the idle gossip of servants? If you wanted to know about my sons, I could've told you."

"At the time, you were busy."

"Well…" She sniffed. "Do whatever you need to do." She stood and marched to the bellpull and rang it. "I'll have Evie summoned to meet you in the study. In the meantime, I'll have you escorted there now."

A footman appeared.

"Perkins, take Lady Birchfield to Lord Franklin's study."

"Thank you," Ravenna said as she followed the footman.

When Ravenna passed out of the room, Georgiana stood. "Shall I come too?"

"No, stay there. I promise we won't be here much longer."

Ravenna entered the study. The room looked much as it had a few days ago: cherry wood-paneled walls, marble fireplace, a tall window clothed in dark velvet curtains, artifacts, and trinkets from around the world. Yet, a certain spirit or life had been completely sucked from the room, as if the space grieved its former occupant, and a faint stain marred the carpet where Lord Franklin had been killed. Blood was almost impossible to completely remove from fabrics.

Ravenna knelt down and inspected the carpet, running her hands over the tuft. She felt a prick. A pin. Easy enough to explain away. It could've fallen out of the dress of any woman who had been in the study since pins were commonly used to secure dresses into place.

To the left was the empty rack that had once held the Mughal knife found in Lord Franklin's back. She stood and studied the shelf. Nothing was there. Just the empty holders. Then she saw a single hair. Not very long. Dark. This was brown and shorter like a man's. Could be a footman's. Could be anyone's. There were scores of people in these finer homes. That wasn't helpful. She walked the perimeter of the room, looking for anything that might hint at the murder.

She traveled around to the other side of the room and looked out the window. The ground was only a few feet below. There had been a muddy footprint on the day of the murder, indicating the murderer had sneaked in from outside and had probably escaped the same way. There was no damage to the window, so the killer didn't break in. She opened the window and hung out, looking left and right. There were doors on either side of the courtyard. The killer might have entered and exited through either side. She sighed. Nothing.

In an impulsive moment, she straddled the casement, left her fan and reticule sitting on the sill, then dropped to the ground. She searched directly under the window. There was a patch of dry dirt there. She looked up. A rain spout hung from the roof above. That explained how mud had formed in this spot. And it had rained off and on for a couple days prior to the gala. She walked to the entry gate on the left. She tugged on it. The hinges and fixtures were so rusted she couldn't even open it; this door clearly hadn't been used for some time. She ran to the other end of the yard to the entry gate on the right. The hinges and fixtures were newer. Trying it, she opened it with a creak and found a host of prints on the ground. Not unusual. They likely belonged to the gardeners and staff. At the bottom of the door, hung in the metal corner trim, was a small piece of rose cloth.

Ravenna squatted and pulled the material from the door. She ran it between her fingers. Taffeta. That was unusual. This was not a cloth likely to belong to a servant or landscaper. She closed the door and studied the cloth as she returned to the window. It could belong to Lady Mildreth. She'd ask before leaving the house.

She tucked the bit of cloth into the bodice of her dress and returned to the window. Grabbing hold of the sill, she launched herself into the window. Ravenna hung there a moment, balancing on her abdomen, flailing her legs. She hoped no one bore witness to this spectacle, because they were sure to get a flash of her unmentionables, a thought that seized her in a brief chuckle. She managed to get one leg up on the window sill and then pulled herself up. After catching her breath, she spun on her rear and dropped to her feet inside the study. She dusted off her dress and hands and wiped wisps of hair out of her face.

Ravenna scanned the room. The clock in the foyer struck noon. She needed to return to Gordon House by two for Georgiana's studies with Mr. Emmett and Ravenna's fencing lesson.

The wind swept around her, lifting corners of the papers on the desk to her left and billowing the tapestry on the wall, revealing an opening rather than a wall. She rushed to the tapestry and pushed it aside. There, she found an alcove—completely empty—but big enough for a person to hide. She stepped inside the space and ran her hands along the wood paneling, searching for a trigger to a secret door. Such things existed in real life, not just in Gothic novels.

She found nothing.

However, the murderer might have known about this area and hid here, lying in wait for Lord Franklin. Turning to leave the alcove, something pushed under the sole of her thin kid leather slipper. Ravenna bent down and felt around, her fingers falling on something flat and small, shaped like a half-moon. She picked it up and stepped out of the nook into the light.

Her breath caught. It was a portion of a black wax seal with a harp in the center surrounded by writing, though only a few of the letters were visible: *bás nó saoirse.* Liberty or death. Her fingers touched the base of her throat as if to still her drumming heart. An Irish Unity seal. This was worse than she'd imagined.

When a knock sounded on the door, Ravenna stepped from behind the wall to see Evie peeking over the threshold.

"Come in," Ravenna said.

Evie froze. "Must I come inside?" She looked around the room with frightened eyes.

"Is there a reason why you don't want to?"

"This room gives me the chills since Lord Thornley died here. It's haunted."

Ravenna lifted her brows. "You don't really believe in ghosts?"

"Aye, I do. And if you were wise, you wouldn't be in there either, milady." That was bold talk for a servant.

She continued, "Else the spirit might enter you and make you do all manner of wicked things. You need to drink a cup of rowan tea as soon as possible, ma'am."

Ravenna didn't want to upset the girl any more than necessary or it might hinder her desire to be open. "I understand. I'll take the tea as soon as I get home." She had no intention of drinking such a bitter potion. "But first, I'd like to speak with you. I'll come out there." She grabbed her fan and reticule from the window sill, pulled the windows closed, and joined Evie in the hall.

"I only have a few moments before the housemistress hunts me down."

"I understand," Ravenna said. "I won't keep you long. I'm curious to know if you remember seeing or hearing anything unusual or strange the day Lord Franklin Thornley died."

The girl shrugged. "Nothing more than I already told you."

"You're certain there were no strangers lurking about?"

"None I saw..." She crossed her arms. "But then the house was full of strangers that day, weren't it?"

"Granted." Ravenna couldn't help but smile at the sharp woman.

"Do you know anything about a group called The Irish Unity?"

She screwed up her mouth. "Ain't never heard of them."

"Do you know if Lord Franklin had any enemies?"

Evie snorted. "I imagine a great many lords have enemies. Especially this family."

Aha! Ravenna tipped her head. "What do you mean? What's wrong with this family?"

Evie eyed her suspiciously. "I ain't losing my job."

"I promise everything you tell me will remain between us. And if for some reason you lose your job because you talked to me, I'll give you a job in my own house. Or find you a job in a house as fine as this one."

Evie studied Ravenna, taking the measure of her. She glanced around.

"There are, or were, people in this house who aren't sad that Lord Franklin is dead."

"Like his brother, Lord Percy?"

"He's one to be sure. But there was a footman..." She leaned in and whispered, "I've heard him threaten the life of milord on more than one occasion."

It had to be serious for a servant to threaten the life of the man paying him. "Why?"

"Mi'lord was not a good man."

"Why do you say so?"

"Evie," a sharp voice snapped. The housemistress appeared, cutting cold glances between Ravenna and Evie. "You're needed upstairs."

Evie said, "Excuse me, ma'am." She curtsied.

Ravenna said, "One moment." She rummaged through her reticule, fished out a few shillings, and pressed them into Evie's chapped hand. "Thank you for your time. And if you ever want to speak to me, come see me at Gordon House in Curzon Street."

Evie dropped the coins in her pocket with a glimmer in her eyes. "Thank'ee, ma'am." She popped a curtsey and jogged toward the housemistress, who shot a final glare of distrust at Ravenna.

Ravenna returned to Lady Mildreth in the drawing room.

Lady Mildreth lowered her embroidery, hope in her looks. "Did you discover anything?"

"Not much. However, I did find this." She showed the black wax seal to Lady Mildreth.

Lady Mildreth inspected the partial disc. "What a strange seal." She handed it back to Ravenna. "I've never seen anything like it."

"Never?"

"No."

In that case, it was likely Lady Mildreth had never heard of The Irish Unity, but Ravenna was going to ask anyway. "Have you ever heard of The Irish Unity?"

Lady Mildreth frowned. "Should I have?"

"No. I was curious if your sons might've had interactions with them."

"I have no idea. Who are The Irish Unity?"

"They're a rebellious group allied with the French against Great Britain."

Lady Mildreth's face melted into a blend of fear and concern, but her voice was angry. "You think *my* sons would conspire with that lot against our own country? Are you insinuating my sons are *traitors*? My family has been loyal to the crown since Henry II."

Ravenna lifted her hand. "I had to ask because I found this in Lord Franklin's study."

"It probably belongs to whoever killed him."

"I believe so, too, but I had to ensure there were no other explanations for its presence. I'm in no way trying to impugn your sons' integrity." Though she was seriously beginning to doubt the integrity and honor of the Thornley men. However, since Lady Mildreth was defensive and sensitive on the heels of her rough morning, this wasn't the best time to broach the subject of her sons' potential wickedness. The younger son carried his dishonor like a banner flag, but Evie had hinted at dishonor in the elder son, which would be difficult for Lady Mildreth to bear, considering her partiality to him. She wouldn't force the woman to confront her favorite's lack of honor until she had more evidence.

"Then you should get to work finding the owner of that seal."

"I will." She removed the cloth from her bodice. "I have one more question." She held up the rose-colored scrap. "Do you have a dress this color?"

"No. I haven't worn a color like that since long before my husband died. It's all drab colors for me now. Such a color is for a younger woman. Though I've seen older women wear such vibrant colors, you must grant they are prettier on a younger woman."

Having gathered a few bits of additional information, Ravenna had reached a temporary impasse. It was time to leave Thornley Hall before she and the other ladies had overstayed their welcome. Ravenna, Georgiana, Hart, and Keene all bid *adieu* to Lady Mildreth.

Lady Mildreth clutched Ravenna's hand and said in a hoarse whisper. "I hope you discover my son's killer soon."

Though her confidence in her abilities wavered, Ravenna assured the dowager, "I'll do my best."

Upon arrival at Gordon House, Ravenna turned to Georgiana and Keene. "Please, go inside. I need a private word with Hart."

The girls climbed out of the carriage and shut the door.

"What did you discover at Thornley Hall?" Ravenna asked.

"Much more than I'd bargained for." Hart, in her copper brown cape and matching bonnet, folded her hands in her lap. "It seems Lord Franklin liked to press himself on the servant girls at Thornley Hall."

"Yes, I'd heard as much from Evie, a housemaid, the day of the murder."

Hart lifted a brow. "Seems to be a family trait, milady. And Evie the housemaid wasn't the only girl."

"Tell me what you learned."

"The cook told me a story about a girl named Iris Cossard who no longer works there. Her brother, Adam Cossard, was a footman in the house as well. Something happened to Iris; it roused Adam's anger, and he threatened Lord Thornley's life. At first behind his back."

Interesting. Evie had mentioned a servant who threatened Lord Franklin. Perhaps she was speaking of this Cossard fellow.

Hart continued. "Though he was angry with Lord Franklin and was threatening him behind his back, he didn't act rashly. He bided his time because he still needed money to help his sister and family."

"Did the cook say what happened to Iris?"

"Supposedly, she didn't end well. She fell into gin and then madness. Lord Franklin had turned her away with no references, so it became difficult to find quality work. Seeing his sister in decline only angered Cossard more. According to the cook, one night, he'd gone so far as to hold a knife to Lord Franklin's neck while he slept."

"Whatever happened to Iris must've been horrific to make her brother behave in such a manner."

"It would seem so, though I can't confirm it with details. The cook said after this event, Cossard left the house. Though the Thornley's claimed Iris and Cossard were dismissed for stealing silver, the servants all knew better. Apparently, Lord Franklin's abuses were common knowledge among the staff. They soon discovered that Lord Franklin had dismissed Cossard in the middle of the night in order to silence him."

"Horrible."

"There's more."

Ravenna sighed and steeled herself for the news. "Iris became habituated to gin and became a beggar and pickpocket to make money for her drink. One evening, while out begging for money, she was dragged into an alley and…" Charlotte paused and touched the scar on her neck, and a line formed between her brows. "Uh, was taken advantage of and…there is no pretty way to put it." She rushed on. "She was gutted like a fish and left to die."

Ravenna squeezed her eyes shut and bowed her head. "Oh, heavens, how awful." She couldn't help but imagine the young woman lying in the alley, bleeding to death, no one bothering to help her because she'd been mistaken for a drunken prostitute.

Hart said, "According to the cook, Cossard returned a week after his sister's death. He sneaked into Lord Franklin's room, held a knife to his throat, and threatened to do to him what had been done to his sister. Of course, in Cossard's mind, his sister's death might've never happened had Lord Franklin not abused her."

"Probably true," Ravenna said.

Hart continued. "Interestingly, this was on the same day Lord Franklin died. Adam Cossard was seen leaving Thornley Hall in the wee hours that morning."

"Now, that *is* interesting." She thought about the ease of access to the courtyard and the mud print on the window. He would know the layout of the house. And likely knew about the alcove where he could hide to attack Lord Franklin. But it didn't explain the wax seal. Unless Adam was a member of The Unity. "I suppose I can write to Lady Mildreth to see if she knows where Adam lives."

"Not necessary." Hart smiled, her brown eyes full of warmth. "I took the liberty of asking where he lives."

Ravenna smiled. "What a clever girl you are!"

"The cook didn't know exactly where he lived, but she did know he liked to drink at the Crook and Ivy tavern in Shelton Street."

Ravenna reached across and grabbed Hart's folded hands. "Thank you so much, Hart. You are absolutely invaluable to me."

Hart looked down at her lap, a faint smile tickling her lips. "I'm happy to do it. If I may speak plainly, I'm tired of men like Lord Franklin." She locked her eyes with Ravenna's.

Usually, Hart's eyes exuded softness and tenderness, but now they sparked with a quiet fury that shocked Ravenna.

"I'm glad Cossard confronted Lord Franklin. I'm only sorry for his sake that the honor of his family remains unsatisfied. Though news of his death will bring some relief, I'm sure Cossard will regret not being the deliverer of justice."

Ravenna lifted her brows, surprised. She'd never heard Hart speak like this.

Hart said, "I know when such a thing happened to my family, I didn't rest until..." She stopped. She searched Ravenna's face, then flicked her tongue over her lips. She smiled. "Well, listen to me chattering away..." She smoothed her skirts. "I'm sure you don't want to hear...Uh...At any rate..." She grabbed the door handle. "I need to get some sewing done." She moved to open the door.

Ravenna touched her arm to stay her. "Hart?"

Hart sat down, looking at the floor.

"I'm not naive. I have a past myself. Should you ever want to confide in me, I will not judge you or think ill of you. And I'd take your secrets to my grave. You can be assured of that. I give you my word."

Hart lifted her gaze, scrutinizing Ravenna. "I have no doubt, milady. I know I can trust you implicitly. That's why I stay in your employ. Perhaps someday I'll tell you. But I don't like to think of it."

"Nightmares?"

Hart nodded.

"Me, too," Ravenna whispered. "I think that's the hardest part. The inability to forget."

Hart nodded. "Yes, milady. It is."

After a moment of silence where each woman sat trapped in her own dark thoughts, Hart shifted in her seat and reached for the door. "Well, the sewing awaits." She opened the carriage door and stepped to the ground. She turned. "Are you coming, milady?"

"Hart, I'm going to Shelton Street. Tell Mr. Norris I need to reschedule our lesson and give him my sincerest apologies. Also give my apologies to Mr. Emmett for my absence and failure to greet him today. Though I do hope to return before he leaves."

Fear filled Hart's eyes. "Milady, you can't go alone to Shelton Street. At least let me go with you."

"You can't come, Hart. I need you to represent me here today."

She handed Ravenna her reticule. "Then take this. Use it if you must."

Ravenna accepted the brown reticule and weighed it in her hand. "Why is it so heavy? What do you have here, Hart?" She opened the drawstring pouch, peered inside. She reached in and pulled out a small pistol no bigger than her hand. "You continually surprise me, Hart. Who would think a delicate thing like you could use it?"

Hart arched her thin brow. "I have before and will again. If necessary. There's only one shot, so aim well."

Ravenna nodded, returning the pistol to its hiding spot.

"Be safe," Hart said, her face marked with distress, before closing the door.

Chapter Seventeen

Shelton Street was as dark and dreary a rookery as any St. Giles had to offer. The dilapidated tenements of rotted wood, covered in soot and peeling paint, leaned against each other like wounded soldiers. The windows were all boarded over to evade the window taxes. Several families squashed themselves into the smallest spaces like rats. Muck and filth slicked the streets, and a stench of rotten cabbage and feces hung in the air. How anyone lived in such dire circumstances baffled Ravenna and cut her to her core. She had known poverty in Ireland, but poverty in the country was a different sort of thing compared to city poverty. In the country, at least, there were open spaces and fresh air, something to remind one of their humanity. But in the city, people had no fresh air, no grass or open spaces, and sometimes, when the fog or coal smoke was thick, they didn't even have the sun. City folk lived among vermin and filth of every kind, stripping them of even their last shred of humanity. There was a desperation and hollowness in the eyes of these poor souls like she'd never encountered outside of the city. London was both beautiful and vile.

She needed to find The Crook and Ivy Tavern and get out of this slum as soon as possible. A child stood on the street corner, poking at a dead rat with a stick.

Ravenna called out to the child. "Yoo-hoo. Little boy."

The grimy lad with matted hair looked up from his entertainment. "Yeah?"

"Come here."

He approached the carriage and squinted up at her with a lazy eye and several missing teeth. "Wot ye want?"

"Where is The Crook and Ivy Tavern?"

"That way." He pointed to the left. "At the end of the street."

"On the left or the right?"

"Wot?"

"You don't know your left from your right?"

He grimaced at her.

She pointed to the left. "Is it on that side?" Then she pointed to the right. "Or that side of the street?"

He pointed to the right. "That side."

"Very well. Thank you." She pulled a few coins out of her reticule. "Here's something for your trouble. Be a good boy and keep it a secret so no one steals it from you. Use it for food. Understand?"

His face brightened. "Thank'ee, ma'am. I will."

The carriage picked through the street until the alley narrowed to an impossible width. The footman climbed down and opened the door. "Ma'am. We can go no further." The footman, a hulking Englishman from York named Miller. Most footmen weren't quite as brawny, but Ravenna felt the added protection couldn't hurt.

"Miller, can you see how far the tavern is from here?"

He craned his neck. "I daresay not fifty feet, milady."

Ravenna scanned the destitution and potential danger around her and blew out a breath. "Very well. We shall attempt it."

Miller assisted her from the carriage. She shaded her eyes with her hand and looked down the alley. Ravenna turned to the driver. "It would seem the distance from the tavern to the other side of the alley is shorter. Drive around and meet us there." Though she knew he was armed as one must be these days, she bade him, "Make haste. And do be careful."

"Aye, ma'am." He flicked the reins and turned the carriage around.

Ravenna said, "Miller, give me your arm so I don't slip on these streets."

He hesitated, a little shocked by the breach of etiquette, yet he offered his arm.

Ravenna hung Hart's reticule from her wrist, the weight of the pistol causing the strings to dig into her glove. With her other arm, she clung to Miller as they picked their way around the dung and rubbish, careful to avoid bodies passed out from too much drink, prostitutes beckoning or fighting, rats, dogs, and cats scavenging for food alongside the hungry children.

Miller's pale blue eyes darted along the street, constantly surveying for threats.

Relief washed over Ravenna when they finally reached their destination. That is, until she stepped inside the tavern. It was a dark hole of a place with low ceilings filled with dirty, grizzled men hovering over their tankards. Many of these men labored in mines, or on the docks or ships, as evidenced by the grime on their faces and hands. The scent of sweat and brine mingled with the animal scent of the tallow candles.

Ravenna took a table beside the tiny, dirt-smeared window. A slovenly woman with barely enough dress to cover her bosom slammed two tankards on the wooden table, sloshing the ale.

The woman ran her eyes over Ravenna. "Can't say, as I've seen the likes of you around here before, ma'am." She was missing no less than four teeth. "I think'ee've lost yer way." She snorted through her laughter.

"Yes, it would seem so," Ravenna said. "However, I'm looking for a Mr. Adam Cossard. Do you know where I can find him?"

The bar wench planted a dimpled, chapped hand in her beefy hip. "Now, what would a lady be wanting with Cossie? I hope yer not aiming to bring 'im trouble. He ain't done nothing that wasn't deserved."

"Not at all. I'm hoping, in fact, to clear him from trouble. I've heard there was a bit of a strife with Lord Thornley over his sister, Iris."

"If yer from the Thornley House—"

Ravenna raised her gloved hand. "No, I'm not. I only want to ask him about it."

"Are ye helping with that fancy boy Bow Street Runner? Mister Chardbick as'ee calls hisself."

"Mr. Chadwick? He's been here?"

"Oh yeah. More'n once. Looking for Cossie. To cart 'im off to Newgate, no doubt, when it ought to be that rich man who sits in prison for wot he did to poor Iris."

"That's the problem. Lord Thornley has been killed and—"

Her face brightened, and her thick lips formed an O. "Has he now? Mr. Chadwick did'na tell me tha." She turned around and shouted. "Hey. Guess what. That fancy lord wot hurt Iris is dead."

A few of the patrons raised their tankards and shouted and whistled their approval.

She turned back to Ravenna. "Could'na happened to a better one if'ee ask me." She snort-laughed again.

"Is Mr. Cossard here? I am not working with Mr. Chadwick at all. Rather, I'm working to discover the truth *before* he does."

The woman narrowed her eyes. "Why? Wot's your concern in the matter?"

A man in the corner stood. He was tall, lanky, with greasy blond hair. "Leave her alone, Cathy. I'll talk to her." He scuffed across the wood floor, tankard in hand. His linen shirt and dark brown jacket were rumpled as though he'd slept in them. He wore no cravat, so his shirt neck hung open, revealing a pale, bony chest. Stubble shadowed his long chin. His face was sallow and dark circles ringed his brown eyes. He pulled a chair from a nearby table and flopped down. "I'm Adam Cossard. Who wants to know?"

Miller perked and stepped forward. "Mind your manners."

Ravenna lifted her hand. "Never mind, Miller." She said to Adam, "I'm Lady Ravenna Birchfield. I'm an acquaintance of the Thornley family. I came to talk to you about Lord Thornley."

Adam snarled. "That dog." He downed his beer and placed the empty tankard on the table. "He's dead, is he?"

"Yes. He was stabbed with one of his relics. A gem-encrusted knife from the Ottoman Empire."

He chuckled. "I couldn't imagine a better fate for him. I only wish I'd had the courage to do it myself."

"You didn't do it? Because there are some rumors among the staff that you might've been behind the murder. I simply wanted to hear your side of things."

"Why?"

"Because I think there's more to the story."

"It's idle gossip. I didn't kill him. Though I wish I had. If I hadn't been overcome with cowardice, my sister might still be alive." He indicated one of the full tankards on the table. "May I?"

"Please do. Why do you wish to have killed Lord Thornley?"

He drew deeply from the cup and wiped the foam on his coat sleeve. "My sister and I served the Thornley's faithfully."

"I'd heard you and Iris stole silver from the family and were dismissed for it."

"Lies!" He slammed the tankard down on the table, drawing the attention of the few men sitting in the tavern. "I never did such a thing, and I'll fight anyone who says so."

Miller edged forward, his cold stare trained on the drunken Adam.

Adam leaned in close enough for Ravenna to see the gold flecks in his brown eyes. "That old blaggard forced himself on my sister and ruined her. Not only one time, but many times. He'd catch her cleaning in his study and lock the door so she couldn't escape him. Or he'd catch her in the hall and pull her into his room. Or he'd visit her in the dead of night."

"Is there any way Lord Thornley could've misinterpreted her intent… thought perhaps she was encouraging him? Sometimes, young women will…" She let her voice trail off.

"*No!*" He slammed his fist on the table, rattling the tankards. "Iris was a good girl. A steady, God-fearing girl. She prayed every morning and every night. She spent her Sunday half-day in church. She would never give herself away before marriage. Every time it happened, it was against her will." His sallow face reddened, and tears filled his eyes.

"I'm sorry. I didn't mean to insinuate anything. I didn't know your sister. It's, of course, all the more grievous to know she was taken advantage of and wasn't encouraging his advances."

He pressed his thumb and forefinger against his closed eyes. After a moment, he sniffed, sat up, and drank from his tankard.

Ravenna prodded gently. "I understand he forced her from the house?"

"Yes. His treatment of her broke her heart and her spirit. She couldn't work. She was frightened of everything. She was sick too often and missed more work days. Iris was afraid to say anything because she didn't want to lose her job. But he apparently became more depraved, expecting her to do things even a strumpet would blush to do. When she could take it no longer, she finally gathered enough courage to threaten him with telling Lady Thornley if he didn't leave her alone."

"That's why he dismissed her?"

"Yes. Without references. Work in a good home is hard enough to find for folks like us, Lady Birchfield. But when we have no references to speak for us, we're forced into worse circumstances, which pays much less and breaks the body. If only he'd given her proper references..." He ran his hand over his greasy hair. "She might still be alive."

"Yes, I understand." Ravenna thought for a moment, looking at the light filtering through the greasy windows. "What did Lady Thornley say when Iris was dismissed? Could she not have provided proper references?"

"She said nothing. I'm not even sure she noticed Iris was gone."

"That's unfortunate."

He poked the table. "Lord Thornley killed my sister the same as if he'd cut her himself."

"Could she find no work after her dismissal?"

He glared at her as if she's sprouted horns. "No. He had broken her spirit. She was terrified to work in a home around men, so she had fewer opportunities. She was left to do laundry and sewing, which paid almost nothing. She loved home service. It was dignified. Paid well. In her brokenness she turned to drink. Whatever money she made, she drank it up just to quiet the demons in her head. One evening, as she left a gin shop, she was set upon by ruffians. They used her in every vile manner possible and stole her money and gin. For an added flourish, they gutted her and left her to die in the street muck."

"Oh, heavens. How awful." Though she'd already heard this story from Hart, it still repulsed her to hear it.

"*That's* why I put a knife to his neck. Because of what he did to Iris. And to my whole family."

"Were there parents and siblings at home relying on you?"

"Yes. But that's not what I mean. I mean, his father helped to destroy my father and our whole family before Iris and I even went to work for him."

Ravenna frowned. "How so?"

"My great-grandfather was a master weaver and eventually worked his way into owning a silk mill. He was a Huguenot. Our family came here to escape the violent Catholic oppression from the dastardly Louis XIV. My great-grandfather passed the trade on to my grandfather, who taught my father. And my father taught me and my brothers and sisters. We were supposed to inherit the business. I was meant to be a weaver, a businessman, not a footman." He glanced at Miller standing over Ravenna's shoulder. He added through gritted teeth, "We had been a wealthy family. Our family's silk work was highly regarded by French and English nobility alike. But then the blasted Irish came."

Ravenna flinched. It wasn't the first time she'd heard her people spoken of with venom, but it never failed to sting. She fought the urge to come to the defense of the starving and oppressed Irish peasants who needed work and money and often immigrated to England and other places in search of provisions for their families. But it would do no good to argue the point with him—not if she wanted to get the rest of his story and solve the riddle of Thornley's murder. She bit down on the inside of her lip.

He continued. "The Thornley family also owned mills. They discovered the Irish would work for cheaper prices, which undercut master weavers like my family. Cheaper and cheaper, they worked until we cut our prices so deep we could no longer afford to pay workers or feed our family. Little by little, our business was destroyed. It broke my heart to see people we once employed, people we thought of as family, left to starve, driven out of a respectable trade they'd trained for, mastered, and performed for most of their lives. And then to watch their wives and daughters turn to scrubbing laundry and floors, or worse, turn to trade their flesh just to feed their families...." He balled his hand into a white-knuckled fist and shook his head. "It was heart-breaking. And my father, a once highly sought after merchant, was reduced to nothing. We lost everything." Fire glinted in his eyes. "Owing all to the Thornley's."

"If you hated the Thornleys so much, why did you go work for him? Had you always planned to harm him?"

He paused. "My mother, devout in her faith, asked me to do it for two reasons. First, we needed the money desperately. As my father had been ruined and given over to drink, it fell to me as the eldest son to provide for the family. Second, she believed service to our oppressor would be an act of forgiveness and, thereby, a blessing to our family. Like when Joseph served Pharaoh, though he'd been captured and sold as a slave into Pharaoh's command. Yet, he was blessed for serving faithfully and rose to become the second most powerful man in the Egyptian kingdom." He looked down at his hands. "I think my mother, rest her soul, expected I might also rise to greatness by serving a man who had taken everything from us." He lifted his gaze, glaring at Ravenna from under his lashes. "However, unknown to my mother, I went with hate in my heart. I went entirely for the purpose of somehow ruining him or harming him in some way. I wanted him to suffer."

"What stopped you? You had been with the Thornleys for some time, right?"

He worked his mouth, and his face grew red. "I'm ashamed to admit that I was soon won over by the money. The Thornleys paid well. Providing for my family brought me comfort and relief. It became too difficult to destroy such an opportunity. My desire to make money and serve my family soon overpowered my desire for revenge. And, due to my mother's constant letter-writing reminding me of my Christian duties, the fire of vengeance died out. Until..." He pinched his lips together, his nostrils flaring. His voice shook with emotion. "Until he put Iris in harm's way. That was the last straw to break the camel's back."

"Then you attacked him."

"I meant to. But as I put the blade against his flesh, something stopped me." He shook his head, and his voice broke. "God help me, I couldn't do it." He swiped his eyes and sniffed. "I wished I could, to avenge my sister's honor." His lip quivered. His voice broke. "But I couldn't complete the task.

All I could see and hear was my mother…" He swiped his eyes with the back of his hand and stared out the dirty window.

"What sort of knife did you use?"

"I stole one from the kitchen."

"Was there anything special about it?"

"No. Simply the sharpest I could find."

"I see. I know your desire for vengeance must've been great, indeed. But, it's for the best that you didn't avenge your sister. It might've gone much worse for you."

His dark eyes glimmered with malice. "You think I care if I rot in prison or hang on the scaffold? Especially after what he did to my sister?"

"You didn't retaliate against him at all?"

"No," he said emphatically.

Ravenna studied Adam's features as he drained the tankard. His temperament was unstable and violent, but he seemed entirely genuine in his denials about killing Lord Thornley.

"Where were you while Lord Thornley was being killed? Were you in or near Thornley Hall?"

"When he felt my blade against his throat, his eyes popped open. He became angry, grabbed my wrist, and twisted it until I dropped the knife. He rolled out of bed and snarled like a dog, cursing me and telling me I was to pack my bags and leave immediately. Then he grabbed a riding crop from a nearby chair and beat me about the head and back until I ran from his room." His cheeks grew red. "He told me if I was still in the house by dawn, he'd kill me himself and dump me in the Thames."

Ravenna tipped her head. "Mr. Cossard, this detail is very important. Are you saying you weren't in the house during the gala?"

"No, I wasn't. I left before dawn and never looked back."

"Is there anyone who can verify this?"

He shook his head and scoffed. "No. I ensured we were alone when I attacked him. Do you think I want someone seeing me trying to kill my employer?"

"Unfortunately, it also means no one can speak to your innocence."

Ravenna searched his face. Though Cossard was angry with Thornley, she couldn't believe he was, in fact, guilty. She couldn't dismiss it completely, but even if he had killed Thornley, she also could understand his motivation to do so. Not that the murder solved the problem or made anything right. But it was difficult to see Thornley in a sympathetic light.

She stood. "I think I've taken enough of your time, Mr. Cossard. I shan't keep you any longer. I'm very sorry for you and your family." She paused, removed a few shillings from her reticule, and laid them on the table. "I hope you can make peace with yourself someday. I think you'll find that your greatest challenge. Come along, Miller."

The chair scraped the floor as Adam stood. "Thank you, milady. If the Thornleys were half so kind as you I might not be in this position." His eyes watered, and he swallowed. "If you ever have need of a footman, I'll make you a fine one and serve you loyally."

She forced a smile against the sadness and sympathy twisting her heart. "Thank you. I'll keep you in mind should I or any of my friends have need of one."

Ravenna and Miller made their way through the shorter end of the narrow and dark alley to find the carriage waiting in the light-drenched and busy Drury Lane.

As she lifted her leg to step up into the carriage, she glanced over her arm and spotted Lord Percy Thornley exiting a building with a laughing woman on his arm. Just the man she wanted to see.

Ravenna said, "Miller, stay here. I'll return directly." She marched toward Lord Percy. "Lord Thornley."

He stopped and swayed in his boots, bleary-eyed. He studied her for a moment. "Do I know you?"

The brunette on his arm sniggered and leaned against him.

"I'm Lady Birchfield."

"Oooh. La-di-da," the brunette said. "A *lady*." She giggled again.

"Oh, yes, yes." He bowed his head and touched the brim of his hat by way of greeting. "How do you do?" He slurred.

"I'm very well." She was in no mood to be polite or civil after finding out about his abhorrent behavior at The Penitent House. "I'm *quite* put out with you, sir."

"Oh?" He had the audacity to feign surprise.

"I've recently learned about your clandestine visits to The Penitent House."

A sly smile crossed his lips as the brunette laid her head on his shoulder. "How did you find out about that?"

"Let's just say a little bird told me. How dare you take advantage of those poor women? They have been rescued from the streets, are working to make their lives better, and your behavior threatens to undo their every effort."

"Oh, it was a mere diversion."

Ravenna balled her fist. "Destroying the chances of vulnerable women is *not* a diversion, you letch!"

His brows shot up, and he laughed. "My, my, my. You're a spirited one, aren't you?" He turned to his strumpet. "Would you have thought this dowdy widow would've had such fire?"

Dowdy! Ravenna seethed. Slapping the smirk off this man's face would have given her the greatest pleasure. "You *will* stay away from those women. Or else."

He laughed harder. "Or else what? What can *you* do to me?" He stepped close, the stench of whisky assaulting her nose. "If I want to blaze through the women in that house like a fire, I will. And there's nothing you can do about it, Dowager Birchfield."

The brunette laughed. "Maybe she's jealous."

Ravenna's stomach twisted in revulsion. "I assure you there is nothing about this debauchee that appeals to me." She turned to Lord Percy. "And you would be surprised what I might do to keep you away from those women. They deserve protection, and I will protect them. At any cost."

In a flash, he gripped her arm. "Are you threatening me?"

There it was. The hatred. The violence. The viciousness. Just the sort of man who might kill his own brother if he dared to get in the way of Percy's amusements.

Refusing to be intimidated, her ire rose to meet his. She jerked her arm from his grip. "Unhand me, you jackal." The spot hurt, but she refused to rub her arm or show any fear or weakness to him.

He hissed. "You will find, madam, I will not be threatened by a mere slip of a woman."

In one motion, she flicked the gold medallion at the end of her fan, whipped out the blade, and put it under his chin.

The woman gasped and staggered back. He froze and looked down at the blade. "And you will find I will not be threatened by a lewd, inebriated fool."

He glared at her, his nostrils flaring. Wicked machinations unfolded behind his eyes. What was he thinking about doing to her? Would he slip up and reveal himself? She narrowed her eyes. "You killed your brother, didn't you?"

The brunette stood to the side, gaping, watching the scene unfold.

He worked his jaw, little knots pulsing. He wanted to kill her. The desire clouded his eyes like a storm. A faint, sneering smirk tugged at one corner of his mouth. He stepped back and touched the spot where the blade had been. He looked at his hand and showed it to her. A touch of blood. "You should watch your step lest you fall, milady." His eyes glinted darkly. "Dangers abound everywhere."

He stepped back a couple more paces and held out his hand to the brunette. "Come, my dear. We have a big evening ahead of us."

The brunette, eyes locked on Ravenna, rushed to Percy's side. He linked his arm with the brunette's, touched the tip of his hat at Ravenna. They slowly turned and walked away. The woman glanced back over her shoulder.

Ravenna didn't know if the woman was of the streets or not, but, just in case, she ran after her. "You don't have to live a life like this. You don't have to sell your flesh to men. You can find refuge at The Penitent House in Spitalfields, near St. Peter's Church."

The woman flashed a longing, doe-eyed gaze at Ravenna. Ten years dropped from her features. She was nothing more than a frightened and confused girl.

"Leave us, Lady Birchfield," Percy said coldly. "I've endured you long enough, and I won't allow you to ruin our fun."

The brunette looked back at her again.

Ravenna stopped in her tracks, watching Lord Percy's cocksure swagger as they crossed the street and disappeared into the crowd. Revulsion burned in her gut. She returned her blade to its home. Percy was a cad and a libertine and wouldn't stop molesting the women at The Penitent House. Though she didn't know him well, she knew his *type*. Her warning him off the women would now only encourage him to press forward. But how could she stop him?

Across the street, a group of soldiers in their redcoats marched by with their guns slung over their shoulders. One of the men stood on the corner and shouted to the civilian men passing by. "Come join us! Help us fight Old Boney before he invades England. We need sturdy, smart men like yourselves. You'll get paid and have the great honor of saving our country from the tyrant Napoleon!"

A few men stopped to listen and ask questions. How long before the soldiers would stop asking the men and begin forcing them? She'd seen the press gangs in action before, forcing men into military service, both in her village in County Wexford and in Whitechapel. It was always the same. At first, they would ask the men to join, luring them with pay they often never received. But, the longer the war went on, the more soldiers died or were irreparably injured, and the government became more desperate. That's when the asking stopped, and enforcement began. The press gangs roamed the streets, often going into poor villages, forcing men against their will into military service so they could go to foreign lands, thousands of miles from their homes and families, to fight, die, and lose limbs in wars they hadn't started or even understood. Her stomach twisted and knotted. It disgusted her. But…an idea began to form on the edge of her mind. A brilliant idea that would certainly put Lord Percy in his place. She would write to Lord Donovan about it when she arrived home.

Chapter Eighteen

"I don't like this Emmett fellow," Harrison said as he and Ravenna moved into the garden to the table sitting under a large oak. It was a fine and temperate summer day without a cloud in the sky, perfect for an outdoor afternoon tea.

Emmett and Georgiana sat on a bench under a willow tree across the garden, their heads bent over a book.

"I know you have a fancy for Georgiana, but you must allow she will choose whom she loves. And the man she chooses might not be you. Besides, Mr. Emmett is her tutor. In her mind, he's probably ten years shy of ancient." She chuckled, sitting at the clothed table near the small copse of linden trees.

Harrison flopped into the chair beside her. "At any rate, I think he's a climber and-and—"

"Nonsense." Ravenna poured them each a cup of tea. "Your jealousy is speaking. It's not a handsome quality."

He huffed and selected a few cucumber sandwiches and lemon biscuits. "At any rate, I'm not fond of him."

"Perhaps you'll change your mind when you know him better." She called out to Georgiana and Mr. Emmett to join them.

Georgiana ran, smiling, the sunlight shining through the thin muslin of her dress, highlighting her lithe form. Mr. Emmett strode, waving a greeting. Georgiana plopped into her seat. "Thank goodness! I'm half-starved."

"Georgiana…" Ravenna corrected her with a pointed glance as she poured cups of tea for her niece and Mr. Emmett.

Georgiana grabbed a few biscuits and sandwiches, munching happily as

Mr. Emmett sat beside her and accepted his tea with gratitude.

"Good afternoon, Mr. Emmett," Ravenna said. "I'm glad you're still here. I was afraid I might miss you. I apologize for being late. I'd hoped to greet you when you arrived, but I had some business to attend to."

He sipped his tea. "No apologies required, ma'am, I assure you."

"How go the lessons? Do I have a scholar on my hands? Shall she be condemned to be an unmarriageable bluestocking, do you think?" Ravenna teased, selecting a ginger biscuit.

Georgiana snorted through laughter. "Lor' no danger of that, I wager." She held her orange cake between her fingers and bit into it, crumbs littering her bodice.

Heavens, she eats like a milkmaid. Ravenna struggled against correcting and thereby embarrassing the girl. On the one hand, she didn't care for all the stuffy rules polite society demanded. Yet, if Georgiana was going to move in these circles and eventually land a good husband and a good future, she needed to learn some delicacy and refinement of manners. She would have to work with her alone. Soon.

Mr. Emmett selected an orange cake, placing it on his saucer. "I fear Miss Georgiana diminishes her natural abilities. She has a quick mind and wit. She is already wrestling with Edmund Burke in his *Reflections on Revolution in France,* and she very nearly has all the French alphabet and the planets in our solar system memorized." He cut a bite of cake with his fork.

"And I've already drawn my first sketch in charcoal. Of my own hand." She beamed.

"Already so much?" Ravenna smiled.

Georgiana lifted her teacup. "I put it down to Mr. Emmett's instruction. He makes it easy to learn."

He leaned over to Ravenna and said conspiratorially, "You see, she flatters me already in hopes I might go easy with her."

Georgiana protested. "That's not true!"

Ravenna chuckled. "He's teasing you, Georgiana. I have no doubt you're catching on quickly. You come from good stock. Your mother was exceptionally bright." She added a lump of sugar to her tea and stirred.

"We didn't have many books in our house, or even in our village for that matter, but Helen read every book she could touch. Your father was equally intelligent."

"And you read all the time, too, auntie."

"That's true."

"I very much like drawing," Georgiana beamed, sipping her tea.

"She has a talent for it, I believe."

Ravenna lifted her brows, marveling at Georgiana, who blushed and smiled demurely.

"Though I should warn you, art is our last priority," Emmett said. "The lessons will get much harder. I proceeded gently on our first day."

Georgiana slumped. "Harder? Ugh." She rolled her eyes. "How much harder? Will I be made to feel stupid?"

He smiled. "Not at all. But to learn, everyone must go through some feeling of stupidity."

Harrison's eyes glimmered. "And did you?"

"Of course! Sometimes, I'm still amazed by all the things I don't know. I consider myself similar to Chaucer's Clerk. 'Gladly would he learn and gladly teach.' Always eager to know more—"

"And then go about sharing the knowledge with others? Don't you think that speaks more to the Clerk's vaingloriousness?" Harrison glared at Emmett.

Emmett paused, measuring his next words. "I don't consider the desire to instill knowledge a vainglorious enterprise. Though, I suppose in the hands of the wrong teacher, it might be. I think Chaucer's clerk is one of the humblest of all his Canterbury Pilgrims. Anyone who values real learning will always be humble. For if we realize we don't know everything and remain eager to be taught, we must by that very nature be humble."

"I suppose." Harrison fell quiet and fumed into this teacup.

Georgiana gasped. "I almost forgot to tell you!" She leaned on the table. "Mr. Emmett might've saved me."

Ravenna tipped her head, puzzled. "What do you mean?"

"Oh," Emmett laughed and blushed. "It wasn't so dramatic, I assure you."

"Yes, it is!" Georgiana said. "You're being too modest. There was a man who came to the garden gate..." Georgiana finished off her cake.

Fear pulsed through Ravenna as she perked to listen intently. "What man?"

"I don't know who he was." She shrugged, wiping her mouth with her cloth napkin. "I've never seen him in my life."

Ravenna looked between Georgiana and Emmett, her fear increasing. "Who was he?"

"He didn't tell me his name," Georgiana said.

"What did he want?"

"He wanted to know who I was and wanted to know about you and Uncle Niall."

Ravenna's heart rabbited. "What did you tell him?"

Georgiana paused. "I told him I didn't know where Uncle Niall was and that I hadn't heard from him since I was a child."

Ravenna put her fist to her mouth. "What else did you tell him?"

"I intervened before she said much," Mr. Emmett said. "He looked like a scoundrel, so I chased him off."

Georgiana smiled at him. "It's true. Who knows what he might've done? He tried to convince me to unlock the gate and allow him inside."

"That's when I heard what was being said, and I intervened."

Ravenna closed her eyes and rubbed her forehead. "Thank heavens you were here, Mr. Emmett. What did he look like?"

"White hair, long thin face. A bit of Irish brogue."

The description sounded similar to the man who had attacked her at a house party a few months ago. She'd fought for her life and had stabbed him with the dagger hidden in her fan. He'd cut her face. She touched her cheek where the scar had long since healed, but the flesh rippled under her fingertips. She'd believed he was dead. He'd been with The Unity. Mr. Larson, as he was known. If that was his real name. Could he still be alive? Still be hunting her?

Mr. Emmett said, "Milady? Are you unwell? You've grown quite pale."

"Yes, thank you," she breathed. "But I need to know *exactly* what information you shared with him."

"I told you," Georgiana's voice tensed with defensiveness. "Only that I didn't know where Uncle Niall was."

"What did you tell him about me?"

"I told him you were away, but should return soon." She motioned to Emmett. "That's when Mr. Emmett intervened."

"What's the matter?" Harrison asked. "She's not hurt. She didn't let him in the gate."

Ravenna calmed some. "You're right. Thanks to Mr. Emmett's wisdom. Thank you, sir." She turned to Georgiana. "If the man returns, do *not* talk to him and never, *ever* allow him inside the house or gardens. Do you understand?"

"I understand." Georgiana eyed Ravenna as if she were a lunatic.

"I don't mean to be harsh, but I promise you, if that man is who I think he is, he is dangerous and should be avoided at all costs."

Georgiana nodded, her eyes wide with guilt.

"Do you think he was the man I chased?" Harrison asked.

"Possibly."

"What makes him dangerous? If I may ask," said Emmett.

Ravenna didn't want to pull Mr. Emmett too deeply into her personal affairs. One thread of information might unravel a host of information she'd rather not divulge—such as her past as a spy. "I don't want to go into particulars. I think it's the same man who once attacked me and left me this small prize." She pointed to the scar on her cheek. "He is seeking out my brother, who is nowhere near England. This stranger no doubt means equal or greater harm to him."

Emmett grew somber. "I see. Then, I am even happier to have been of service to you today. Should I see him again, I'll handle him with more severity."

"Thank you, though you shouldn't endanger yourself."

"Why should I care about harm to myself if I can be in service to you and Miss Georgiana?"

Georgiana studied him as if she were seeing a new, unusual flower or a beautiful new gown trimmed in the finest Parisian lace. When Emmett glanced at her, she blushed and looked away.

Harrison glowered at them, then turned to Ravenna. "But who is this man? Why won't you tell us? Aren't you potentially putting us in greater danger by keeping us ignorant of the particulars?"

Anger sparked in Ravenna. Though he wasn't wrong, if she told him about the Irish Unity chasing her, he would want to know why. It would release a torrent of questions. Questions she didn't want to answer. She couldn't expose her past as a spy. Though she'd participated in it to save herself and what remained of her family, she had committed treason nonetheless. Harrison was not likely to understand."Harrison, I have my reasons, and that must suffice."

Thinking about her past called up ghosts of the massacre of her village. It was strange how a stray thought could, in a blink, recall the smell of smoke as houses and churches burned, the stench of burning hair and flesh, the screams of women and children. The shouting of men. The sounds of death and destruction. She closed her eyes and pinched the bridge of her nose as she shoved the haunts from her mind.

"It doesn't suffice. I want to know—" He pressed.

She slammed her hand on the table, rattling the china. "It's enough!"

Everyone stared at her with wide eyes.

Harrison put a hand on her shoulder. "Amma?"

Ravenna licked her dry lips. "Pardon me." She forced a smile on her face. "I didn't mean to...I-I think I'm overtired. It's been a long day. Please excuse me. Enjoy your tea." She stood and rushed from the table.

Chapter Nineteen

Ravenna shut herself in her bedchamber, relieved to be alone in the quiet, dimly lit room. Approaching the drink table in the corner, she poured a glass of port and carried it to her favorite wingback chair near the fireplace. She stared into the empty fireplace, assuring herself she'd done her best to warn Georgiana, Harrison, and Mr. Emmett to avoid the strange man. That had to be good enough. She drew from her glass, allowing the wine's magic to work its charms. She couldn't be bullied into divulging the particulars. While the details were a curiosity to them, they were dangerous to herself. She'd worked too hard to put her past behind her to have it dragged into the open now.

She lay her head back against the chair and closed her eyes. Her greatest concern at the moment was finding Lord Thornley's killer and the missing opal. Lady Thornley wanted answers, and she was a powerful woman in society. It was best not to cross her. So far, there were three likely suspects: Mr. Gibson, Adam Cossard, or Lord Percy Thornley. Evie, the maid at Thornley house, might be a potential fourth suspect.

Mr. Gibson was jealous, craving for attention and accolades. He had said nothing to dispel her suspicions. In fact, his behavior had only compounded her distrust of him.

Adam Cossard was another story. When she'd first heard about Adam's story, she was disposed to believe he'd been involved in Lord Thornley's murder somehow. However, confusion reigned after meeting him. He had every reason to commit violence against Lord Franklin. If Adam was to be believed, Lord Franklin had destroyed everything: his living, his future, his family's fortune, and his sister. Yet, he claimed he stopped before hurting Lord Franklin. It was difficult to trust his story there. He had been furious, lusting for revenge. Could he stay his hand when he was so twisted up with rage and vengeance? He could be lying to her to avoid arrest and execution. Supposedly he had been kicked out of the house before Lord Franklin had been killed. However, even if true, it was likely the killer accessed the house through Lord Franklin's study window. Adam Cossard certainly possessed a good understanding of the house's layout and would've known how to easily access the house without being caught. So, even if he didn't kill Lord Franklin, could he have arranged for someone else to put an end to his enemy? His intimate knowledge of the house could've made this possible.

This familiarity with the house was a consideration for Lord Percy, as well. He not only possessed knowledge of the house, but also knew Lord Franklin's itinerary and habits. Further, he was a libertine. Most importantly, under the rules of primogeniture, upon Lord Franklin's death, Lord Percy was next in line to gain all the titles, lands, homes, businesses, stores of money, and family jewelry. Women could inherit in special circumstances, and it was possible a small sum had been left to Lady Mildreth, but the majority of the family's wealth would pass to the eldest male relative.

Given Percy's lavish spending and enormous debt, whatever remained of the Thornley fortune was likely running through his hands like water. In fact, based on what Ravenna had witnessed earlier, the family was in desperate straits if the furniture shop repossessed the Thornley's rented furniture. Furniture merchants were reluctant to repossess the furniture of the nobility. Because of the nobility's power and connections, merchants often extended credit until their own circumstances became unbearable. Repossession was an absolute last resort because the merchant feared retaliation or social repercussions—which made Lady Thornley's situation all the more pitiable and difficult. This consideration put Percy high on Ravenna's list of suspects.

Just the thought of him made her fume. He repulsed her to the core, especially in regards to his behavior with The Penitent House women.

Thinking of the charity reminded her of her little plan to separate Lord Percy from tempting the women. She moved to her writing desk and took out a quill pen and paper. She scratched out a note to Lord Donovan to invite him to supper. She needed to speak with him as soon as possible.

Lord Donovan arrived about thirty minutes before dinner. Georgiana fawned over him, and Harrison tried to be civil to him in spite of his jealousy. Ravenna found the trio in the formal drawing room enjoying a glass of cordial.

Ravenna entered in a black satin gown with short puffed sleeves. Her dark, glossy ringlets spilled from her crown, ornamented with a jet hair comb. "Good evening, Lord Donovan. I'm glad you were able to join our happy party."

A smile lit his eyes like the sun on the sea as he stood and bowed. Clean-shaven and polished to a shine, his blond hair and summer-blushed face gave him the appearance of coming out of the fields with his hunting dogs and horse. He was about the same height as Braedon, but thinner. And though he was handsome and likable, he was not Braedon. That recognition opened a hollow of longing inside her to see Braedon again or to even have another letter—anything to pluck the invisible chord tying them together through the miles. "Good evening, Lady Birchfield. It was a delightful surprise to receive your invitation. I trust you are well?"

She offered him her hand. "I am, thank you. And I trust you're well?"

"Much better now." He kissed her hand, glancing up at her through his lashes.

"I'm glad." She withdrew her hand. "May I see you for a moment on the promenade?" She motioned toward the back door of the drawing room. "I have a matter I would discuss with you."

They stepped outside, enveloped in the warm air. The sun melted pink and gold into the horizon, casting long shadows over the garden with intermittent lights of glow worms blinking from the pockets of darkness in the bushes and trees.

"I won't keep you long or tease you with superficial chatter," she said.

"I've asked you here this evening because I require your assistance, if you're willing to grant it."

"Absolutely. If it's in my power to do so."

"You know Lord Percy Thornley?"

"I do."

"You know he's a libertine?"

He chuckled. "I think all of London is aware of that fact, madam."

"Here is my issue. If he is going to patronize the women who are actively selling their flesh, there is little I can do about that. However, there is a group of women I am dedicated to helping leave the streets behind forever."

"Right. The Penitent House. I've contributed to it. I have high regard for the work you're doing there."

"Thank you. As you can imagine, those women are special to me. I am deeply invested in their reform and in helping them understand there are options other than prostitution. That they can have a future."

"I understand."

"Lord Percy seems to think the women of The Penitent House are his personal coterie."

Lord Donovan paused, surprised. "Oh, I see. That's unfortunate."

"Yes, it is. He is going to single-handedly undo all the efforts these women have invested in climbing out of their plight. He will undo all the work the good Reverend Haworth and the church have done. And I can't allow it." Her voice filled with a warning. "I *will* not allow it."

"How will you prevent it?" The songs of a nightingale in a nearby tree echoed across the garden.

"That's where I hope you can assist."

"How so?"

She took a deep breath of the sweet lilac and honeysuckle floating in the air. "Now that we are again at war with Napoleon, I'm sure the Crown needs all the soldiers it can get. I would like Lord Percy to be commissioned into the military. I understand an officer position would be suitable for his station and titles, but I think it's necessary for him to honor his family and our country with his service as so many other second and third sons do."

"I can talk to him, I suppose—"

She turned to him. "Rather, I was hoping you would have him conscripted."

He tipped his head, considering her. "That's not typically how nobility enter the military."

"But it's acceptable to send press gangs to force poor men into service? Like in Easton?"

"Well—" He turned to look out across the garden.

A faint smile crossed her lips. "Lord Donovan, I don't want to quarrel. I want to see what can be done to put the largest possible obstacle in his path to protect those women. I am determined."

He leaned on the railing and looked out across the garden, thinking. He sighed. "I know his debts are sizable…"

"Yes." She leaned her hip against the railing. "And his spending habits are so calamitous that debt collectors are taking away Lady Thornley's furniture."

He looked up at her with surprise. "Surely you jest."

"I do not. I witnessed it myself. It was a horrible spectacle. It's appalling to see a woman like her brought so low."

"Indeed." He rubbed his chin pensively. "It's likely her late husband is turning in his grave over the chaos his family and estate has fallen into."

"Apparently, some of her jewels have been pawned as well."

He turned to study her face. "Is it as bad as all that?"

"It is. So not only is he working upon the destruction of the poor women at The Penitent House, but he is destroying his own mother and the family's wealth and reputation. So, you see, his removal would be a boon to more than The Penitent House women."

"Yes." He faced the sunset again, deep in thought. The sun cast a deep honey-gold light on his face. "Then Percy is in great debt…"

"He is."

"Probably more than he can ever crawl out of on his own."

"Yes."

"So, if he were to receive a commission sizable enough to pay off his debts..."

She leaned on the railing, pressing her shoulder against his. "And a promise of plenty of jades and brandy on the battlefield..."

He gazed at her, his eyes trailing over her face and then downward. "And a threat of debtor's prison..."

"It's not unheard of for unpopular nobles to land there..." Her voice filled with mirth as she nudged his arm.

He returned her smile. "He might be induced to become an officer."

"What if he won't go willingly?"

In unison, they stood to face each other, each with a hand resting on the balustrade. He grew serious. "What do you want to happen?" He said in a quiet voice.

She leaned in and looked up into his face. "I want him to simply wake up one morning in France, or Spain, or wherever the Navy will carry him."

He flicked his tongue over his dry lips as he nodded. The corners of his eyes creased.

"Why are you smiling at me?"

"I simply am reminding myself to never cross you."

She chuckled. "Yes, yes. But will you press him if it comes to that?"

His eyes filled with something like tenderness and admiration. "If it will make you happy, I will do it."

"Just as I hoped." Ravenna squeezed his warm hand. "Thank you, Lord Donovan. I see we are of the same mind." She turned to leave. But Lord Donovan continued to hold her hand. He drew her gently back to himself.

"Are we?"

"Pardon?"

"Are we of the same mind?" He stepped closer, hope and desire mingled in his eyes.

Oh, dear. She hadn't intended to lead him on. "On the matter of Lord Percy, we are of one mind."

"In other matters?" He continued to hold her hand. "Dare I hope?"

She smiled. "No. You shouldn't hope in me. My affections are... elsewhere."

"Ah…" He dropped her hand and stepped away. "With Lord Braedon?"

"I'd rather not say. I'm a private person and don't feel comfortable—"

"You know he doesn't deserve you. He will break your heart."

"I appreciate your opinion, but you really overstep your place."

"Is it overstepping for a friend to warn a friend about a cad?"

"Let's not do this, Lord Donovan."

"Please, call me Edmund."

"Let's remain friends and go have dinner. Besides, even if my affections weren't reserved, it would be ill-advised to secure them with you."

"Why should that be? I would never hurt you."

"Not on my account, but on my niece's."

"Miss Georgiana? What of her?"

Ravenna tipped her head. "Oh, Donovan. You're not so obtuse. Surely you've noticed how Georgiana watches you with calf-eyes."

He looked down and chuckled. "I confess, I have."

"I know she's young, but—"

He lifted his hand. "No. It's not only a matter of her youth. Her lack of education and connections make her most assuredly an improper consideration. I couldn't possibly consider her as a suitable match."

"I expected you might feel that way." She sighed. "I am sorry for her. I hope I can throw another in her path to turn her head." She rubbed the back of her neck. "But she is stubborn."

"I suspect stubbornness is a family quality." He smiled.

Ravenna laughed. "Perhaps." After a moment, she said, "We should probably return to the others before rumors begin."

"Ah, yes," he sighed. "And leave the nightingales out here to sing of my lost hopes."

Chapter Twenty

As Hart buttoned the back of Ravenna's dress early the next morning, Ravenna said, "Please have the carriage brought round for me this morning. I need to visit Snow Hill."

"I assume you're going to Shervy's Pawnshop?"

"I am. And it's quite intimidating. I've never dealt with a pawn brokerman before. I don't know the process at all."

Hart paused and looked at Ravenna in the mirror. "I do. I've had many dealings with such establishments in the past. I should go with you to ensure they don't take advantage of you."

Ravenna lifted her brows. "You surprise me, Hart." She turned to face her lady's maid. "When did you ever have dealings with a pawn brokerman? And for what purpose?"

"It was in Edinburgh. Many years ago. My family was once wealthy, ma'am. We had to sell off many of our things in order to escape."

"Escape? Escape what?"

Hart said in a quiet voice, "Nothing I care to talk about at the moment, ma'am."

Ravenna studied her. The plain, dainty features, the limpid brown eyes, the scar on her neck. Hart had always been a quiet girl, but Ravenna had liked her instantly. There was something in her manner, in her quietness, that Ravenna knew she could trust. Which was why Ravenna practically begged her to be her ladies' maid when she'd married. For several years, Ravenna had never pressed Hart about her past. She'd allowed Hart as much privacy as she'd wanted. Lately, however, Ravenna's curiosity had been piqued about this quiet creature who seemed content to operate in the shadows and keep Ravenna's world in order. More than anything, Hart's steadfast loyalty had nurtured in Ravenna a desire to know Hart better. To transcend the boundaries of employer servant. To be friends.

Ravenna said, "You've seen some horrible things, haven't you?"

"Aye. I expect I've done some, too."

Ravenna's eyes widened in shock. She certainly hadn't expected *that* answer.

Hart added, "But there was none who didn't deserve it. Now, ma'am…" She released a light sigh. "May I continue getting you dressed? Or do you plan to go to the pawnbroker's half undone?"

Ravenna turned around to face the mirror again, her mind in a whirl. She watched Hart in the mirror. What could Hart have meant by what she'd said? What sort of things had she seen? What sort of things had she done? Would Ravenna ever really know this woman who was so close to her, yet so distant?

After a few moments, Hart said, "I understand Mr. Emmett will be here again today?"

"Yes."

Hart finished her task and turned away to collect the cast-off clothes. "I'll ensure Keene prepares Miss Georgiana for Mr. Emmett." She stopped at the door. "Shall I have a repast sent up since you won't be here for breakfast?"

"Buttered toast and tea will be sufficient. Thank you."

Hart bobbed a curtsey and left the room.

After a quick breakfast, Ravenna and Hart climbed in the carriage. The sky hung heavy with gray clouds, and a steady wind shook the trees. The scent of rain hung in the air. They headed out of Mayfair, past the British Museum, down Holborn to Snow Hill. They turned onto Bride's Lane, and the driver slowed the carriage to a crawl to better navigate through the traffic and the pedestrians.

Hart said, "There's Mr. Shervy's shop." She pointed out a shop with wide windows displaying a wide array of goods. Above the door hung an ornate wrought iron bar with three golden balls hanging from it to symbolize

St. Nicholas who, according to legend, had saved three young girls from destitution by loaning them each a bag of gold so they could get married.

"Yes." Ravenna knocked on the ceiling to signal the driver to pull the carriage over.

Ravenna and Hart entered the pawn shop. It was a small, dingy room lined with shelves and tables, stuffed with an array of shoes, toys, bonnets, canes, vases, scraps of ribbons, laces, fabrics, and sewing materials, paintings, tools, hats, luggage, and babies' clothes. The windows were so loaded with things that only fragments of light spilled into the shop. From the ceiling hung a cord upon which dresses, coats, capes, and other adult clothing hung to display. Items even filled the spaces beneath the tables. Ravenna had never seen so many objects in one area. She took a deep breath, feeling suffocated and closed-in. The place smelled of fusty roses, butter, and old paper, underpinned with old potatoes. The dust made Ravenna's nose itch.

Mr. Shervy was a short, thin man with a head of bushy black hair streaked with silver, dark, intelligent eyes and a thick beard. "Good day there, madams." He had an accent Ravenna couldn't discern. He wore a navy coat and a red waistcoat. His black ascot was neatly pinned into place. He leaned on the desk. "How may I help you?"

"I've heard some jewels were recently pawned here from the Thornley family. I would like to purchase them."

His thick black brows lifted. "Is that so?"

"Do you still have them?"

"Yes, yes." He held up a finger. "One moment, madam."

He disappeared into another room and momentarily brought out a wooden case. "I've kept these tucked away for fear someone would steal them. And…" He lifted a shoulder. "I had reasonable assurances that the seller would return to purchase them."

"Oh? Did he make such a promise? Because his mother doesn't seem to be aware of such an agreement."

"The young lord who sold me these said he would return by week's end. Though that was at least two weeks ago."

And at least two weeks before Lord Franklin Thornley's murder. Apparently, Lord Percy had been desperate for money for some time. Perhaps his desperation finally pushed him into killing his brother in order to inherit and control all the money.

Mr. Shervy said, "I cannot keep these jewels forever."

"I understand. May I see them?"

He opened the wooden box to reveal a diamond and emerald necklace with the diamond earbobs Lady Thornley was desperate to have returned. There was also a gold chain and a matching coral bracelet, necklace, and earbob set. An ivory brooch and a sapphire ring. The jewels were stunning.

Ravenna sank and clutched her reticule. She hoped she had enough money. She hated the thought of spending the money on behalf of Lady Thornley, but she also couldn't bear seeing the woman suffer—especially because of such a profligate son. She clung to the hope that Lady Thornley would be honorable enough to repay Ravenna for this sacrifice, though she wasn't sure how the money could be raised. Ravenna mentally calculated her personal funds. Though she'd married into the aristocracy, she'd retained the frugal habits from her impoverished past. So, she'd saved a great deal of her pin money from her marriage, and she spent only on necessities since her husband's Philip's death.

"How much for all of it?" Ravenna asked.

He pursed his lips and ran his eyes over her. "Seventy pounds."

Before Ravenna could speak, Hart stepped forward, her usually soft brown eyes flashing with ire. "Absolutely not!"

Ravenna looked at her, stunned. Hart had rarely asserted herself in such a manner. It was highly improper to step out of her place as lady's maid and companion to interrupt her lady's conversation.

"Pardon?" Mr. Shervy said.

"I cannot allow this. I know for a fact you have purchased these jewels for far less than they're worth, probably twenty or thirty pounds, and now you're trying to sell them for far higher than they are worth."

Mr. Shervy dithered. "Well, I-I-I...You must understand, this is a business. I must make money, too."

"You will still make plenty of money. If you bought them for twenty or thirty pounds and sell them now for, say, fifty pounds, you will still make twenty or thirty pounds profit."

Ravenna stared at the man. "And you want to sell them to me for seventy? It's outrageous to attempt to take advantage of me in such a manner."

"Madam, this is the usual way for pawnbrokers to make their money."

"You'll forgive me if I trust my friend's assessment of this situation."

He licked his lips. "Very well. I will take sixty pounds for the jewels."

Hart said, "Unacceptable. We will give you no more than fifty."

His face reddened. "I will not be coerced—"

"Then you'll take nothing," Hart said. She linked her arm with Ravenna's. "We should go."

"W-wait," Ravenna whispered. "What are you—"

"Trust me," Hart whispered as she nudged Ravenna to turn around, and they started for the door.

"Wait, wait, wait!" Mr. Shervy ran from behind his desk. "Fifty pounds! I'll sell the jewels to you for fifty pounds."

Hart looked at Ravenna. "Is that acceptable to you?"

It was nearly all the money Ravenna had brought with her. She turned to Mr. Shervy. "Fifty pounds."

He thought and looked back at the jewels.

Hart said, "You can sell them now, for a reasonable profit."

"Or I might sell them for a better price later."

"Or you might never sell them. The man who promised to come back two weeks ago still hasn't come back. Is he likely to?"

Mr. Shervy hesitated, rubbing his beard. "Very well. Fifty pounds."

Ravenna pulled the banknotes from her reticule and handed them to the pawnbroker. He put the jewelry in a sheet of brown paper and wrapped them, tying the bundle with twine.

On their way out the door, Ravenna said, "How surprising you are, Hart! I never knew you were such a deft and clever negotiator."

Hart smiled. "My family might not have survived if I hadn't learned early how to deal with them. They are a sneaky lot and will take more than their share if given a chance."

"Then I am happy you are my friend, and I daresay, Lady Thornley will be thrilled to call you friend as well."

Hart laughed. "I doubt Lady Thornley would be glad to call one such as me 'friend,' but I am most happy to be your friend, milady."

Chapter Twenty-One

Upon arriving at Thornley Hall, Ravenna asked Hart to wait in the carriage. "I shouldn't be long."

Ravenna found Lady Mildreth in the drawing room with Mr. Chadwick.

He stood and bowed, his blue eyes glinting with curiosity. "Lady Birchfield. What a surprise to see you here. I was just speaking with Lady Thornley about Lord Franklin's murder and who she thought might be responsible for his death."

Lady Mildreth stood and rushed toward Ravenna. "Lady Birchfield, I'm so glad you have come. I'm all in a flutter. I don't know how to answer these questions."

Ravenna took her hands and guided her toward her chair, taking the adjacent seat. Hart sat in a nearby chair. "Never fear, Lady Thornley. All will be well." She lowered her voice to a whisper and said with more mirth than she felt, "We can't allow Mr. Chadwick to frighten us with his serious looks." She faced Mr. Chadwick. "Surely Lady Thornley has told you everything she knows already?"

"She has answered many questions, but I've discovered more after speaking with other people. I would think Lady Thornley would have no qualms about assisting me in finding her son's murderer."

"But I am at my wit's end, sir," she whimpered. She turned to Ravenna. "Can you believe he has come to question me as though *I* am a suspect? Can you imagine such audacity to accuse a mother of murdering her own son?"

Ravenna gaped at Chadwick. "Are you accusing her of such a gruesome thing?"

"The human heart can devise and commit a thousand gruesome things before breakfast. You wouldn't comprehend some of the things I've witnessed in my time, madam."

This was a truth she was far too familiar with. She lifted her chin. "I suspect I would comprehend more than you think."

He lifted a brow. "How could that be?"

Careful. Any question could start a loose thread upon which he could pull and eventually unravel the truth about her past as a spy where, for a brief moment, she was forced to gather secrets from the English on behalf of the Franco-Irish alliance. Instead of answering his question, she folded her hands in her lap. "Why do you think Lady Thornley killed her son? What evidence has led you to such an assumption?"

"Lord Franklin Thornley kept a tight fist on the money. She had to fight him for every ha'penny of pin money due to her. Her younger son was not so frugal. Between the two of them, they planned to loosen his grip. The younger son would happily throw money his mother's way—"

"That's not true," Ravenna said. "As I understand the matter, he sold his mother's jewels. He's been so spendthrift they haven't been able to pay for their furniture rental. I, myself, witnessed the collectors retrieve her furniture yesterday morning."

Chadwick's hard gaze glinted. "Ah. And how did you come to this understanding of the matter, madam?" he said in a velvety voice.

Ravenna hemmed. "Well, of course, Lady Mildreth herself told me." She rushed to add, "But I have no reason to doubt her veracity."

A sly smile slipped over his mouth. "Is that so? And how can you be certain you were told the truth?"

"What do you mean?"

Chadwick looked at Lady Thornley, who studied the ring on her finger to avoid Ravenna's questioning eyes. "Lady Thornley?" Ravenna prodded.

Lady Mildreth tipped her head and pursed her lips. "Well..." She lifted a shoulder.

"Lady Thornley," Ravenna's voice issued a warning. "What does Mr.

Chadwick mean?"

"Oh?" Chadwick said. "Did milady mislead you?" He paused, looking between the women. "It appears she did. Allow me." He shifted in his seat and crossed his legs. "Lord Percy and Lady Thornley wanted to loosen Lord Franklin's tight grip on the money. They wanted more of it for themselves for whatever frivolous—"

"No!" Lady Mildreth shouted, holding up a knotted finger. "I will not allow you to sit here in my home on what little furniture I have left to besmirch my family's name and reputation, you ill-gotten ruffian."

Bemusement marked Chadwick's features.

She turned to Ravenna. "He's misleading you. I will tell you the truth." She cut daggers at Chadwick. "And put to rights Mr. Chadwick's deep misunderstanding." She exhaled a shaky breath. "My eldest son, Franklin, was an adventurer. He loved to travel to distant lands, explore, and dig for artifacts. He wanted nothing more than to bring glory to his king and nation by unearthing artifacts, claiming them in King George's name, and bringing them home to expand our treasure store. In fact, our own British Museum owes a large debt of gratitude to my son's findings." She sat straighter with mother's pride. "As you know, he had recently returned from such a trip with a grand black opal to give to the Crown."

"The Crown didn't recompense his trips or the artifacts he brought home?" Chadwick asked.

"They did not. We had hoped there would be something. The king gave him a few mines, but they were defunct or depleted. He was also given a couple of titles for impoverished hamlets. At any rate, my Franklin wasn't upset with such treatment. He enjoyed the adventure. He appealed to the king for funding for more trips, but he was denied. Nevertheless, he would not be gainsaid. He used our own funds. Occasionally, he would borrow money from friends who wanted to share in the adventure."

Ravenna asked. "So, most of the money funding his trips came from your own coffers?"

"Precisely."

"How could you afford such a thing?" Ravenna asked.

"There's the rub. He was neglecting our own debts. Cut down our staff to almost nothing. Selling off profitable lands and mills. Cutting back workers at the mills, causing them to lose their jobs, their ability to support their families, and causing them to starve and riot. I am not ignorant of the fact it is our obligation to provide work for the people in our territories so they may eat and provide for their families. He was neglecting them as well as important repairs for our country estate."

Chadwick said, "Could not your younger son have managed it?"

Lady Mildreth glared at him. "Clearly, sir, you do not understand our ways. He did his best, but since he is the second son, there was much out of his control and ability. He cannot sign bank notes and such when we need money." She took a cleansing breath. "At any rate, my eldest wanted only to travel and dig in remote lands, and it was all at our expense. And a great expense it has been. In regards to the last trip, he was no sooner home than he began planning and discussing a new trip."

"And how did you react?" Chadwick said.

"My younger son, Percy, and myself both approached him about leaving more money with us so we might better care for our debts and estate in his absence. He refused. He said he would need every penny possible at his disposal. In fact, he said he needed more money and was looking for ways to acquire more."

"Unconscionable," Ravenna said.

"It gets worse. When discussing these financial matters, Percy mentioned that once Franklin sold the opal to the king, he would have all the money he needed to complete his next adventure. Well…" She huffed. "Franklin said the king was not purchasing the opal. He was going to *gift* it to the king! He said it was enough to have the gratitude and acknowledgement of the Crown."

"Why would he make such a concession?" Chadwick said.

Lady Mildreth threw her hands up. "I don't know. It made absolutely no sense to me. I told him he should reap *some* reward for his efforts. But he said giving the opal to the Crown might ensure a bevy of future favors and rewards from the king. Then, in no time, my jewelry was sold to the pawnbroker to pay for his next trip."

"Wait…" Ravenna held up her hand. "One moment. You told me Lord Percy sold the jewelry."

"He did, too. They both did. But for different reasons. Franklin sold them to fund his trip. Percy sold some to fund his gambling and other such diversions."

Anger flared in Ravenna, and her voice shook. "Why did you mislead me?"

Flustered, Lady Thornley stuttered, "I-I-I didn't mislead you…exactly. I wanted to keep my family's troubles discreet. I didn't want my troubles bandied about, but it has all gone out of control."

Ravenna shook her head. "I do not understand why you would blame Percy for things Franklin has done."

Lady Mildreth shouted, her face red and her curls twitching with her energy. "I was grieving!" She pounded her fists on her chair arms. "I didn't want to speak ill of my dead son!" She stamped her slippered feet.

Ravenna sighed. Deflated, she stared at her lap, ripples of anger pulsing through her.

"So, in your frustration, did you and Percy collaborate to kill Franklin in order to remove his power over the money?" Chadwick asked.

"No!" Lady Mildreth shouted, her eyes filled with tears. "No matter our troubles and disagreements, we would never do such a thing. And if you are going to make such vile accusations, you can leave my house this instant!"

"Then who do you think killed him?" Chadwick said. "Who else would have a reason?"

"I don't know." She broke into tears. "I don't know. That's what *you* are supposed to discover, is it not?"

Chadwick studied her in intense silence.

She whined. "We have our problems, Mr. Chadwick. As any family does. But we never would do the wicked things you suggest."

Ravenna stood, angry. "I'm finished. I will not continue."

"No, please, you must!" Lady Thornley said. "I'm convinced the killer is among us, in our circle. I'm certain you can find him."

Mr. Chadwick frowned, confused. "What does Lady Birchfield have to do with the matter?"

Lady Mildreth said, "I heard Lady Birchfield has a talent for discovering killers since she assisted with the murder of Lord Hawkestone several months ago."

No. Ravenna shut her eyes and bowed her head, panic firing through her body. This was exactly what she did *not* want—Mr. Chadwick's attention. Nor did she want him to know she was in any way investigating the murder. She didn't want to give him any reason to look closer at her past. She glanced at Mr. Chadwick enough to catch his scowl.

Ravenna lifted her hand. "At any rate, I am finished with this. By the way." She tossed the package at Lady Thornley.

The package bounced off her chest and landed in her lap. Lady Thornley stared at it, then lifted it up. "What's this?"

"Your jewels. I felt pity for your predicament, so I purchased them back for you. Perhaps someday, pay me back the fifty pounds I paid."

"Oh," she gasped, her eyes filling with tears. "You're so very kind."

"Yes. And my kindness for this family is done, Lady Mildreth." What she did not tell Lady Mildreth or Chadwick was that she still fully intended to continue the investigation for Catherine and Yarford's benefit. They were her primary concern at any rate. She turned for the door.

Lady Mildreth jumped from her seat and cried out. "Oh, please do not abandon me in this matter, Lady Birchfield!"

Mr. Chadwick followed her out the door. "Wait, Lady Birchfield, please."

Ravenna stormed out of Thornley Hall. Lady Thornley's wailing could still be heard from inside as though she were a ghost haunting the house. The summer air was still and hot, and birds chirped and rustled in the trees. She turned to face Mr. Chadwick, squinting against the sun. "Yes, sir?"

"What does Lady Thornley mean when she says you have a talent for discovering killers? What gives you the ability?"

"I have no special ability, sir. She's half-lunatic." She motioned toward the house to indicate the continued wailing. "I'm sure she's referencing the *luck* I had in stumbling upon Lord Hawkestone's killer some months back.

That's all. Her imagination has carried her away. She's a desperate, grieving mother reaching out for any hope to cling to, sir."

"Have you been investigating her son's murder?" When she didn't answer, he said, "Have you discovered anything regarding Lord Franklin's murder?"

"I've discovered nothing." That wasn't a lie. She hadn't found any real answers, only a few interesting items. "I have found only a man who was deeply unlikeable and had apparently given more than one person a motive to kill him."

"Are you justifying his murder?"

"Absolutely not. You misunderstand me. Willfully, I might add. I'm simply saying there are at least a few people who might've wanted him dead."

"Like who?"

She tipped her head and smiled. "Shouldn't you know? It is your job, after all."

"I'm interested in hearing what you've uncovered."

She sighed and crossed her arms over her chest. "As I've told you before, I think Mr. Gibson and Lord Percy are likely suspects. As is Mr. Cossard. Possibly the maid here, Evie."

"I see." He studied her, picking apart her words. "It would seem your suspect list matches my own. Except for one name."

"Lord Yarford?"

"Exactly. I wonder why you would neglect to mention him?"

She shrugged. "Because he's innocent."

"How can you be certain?"

"I know him. He would never do such a thing, and it's likely Thornley was killed by someone who knew his schedule and had access to, and intimate knowledge of, this house. Lord Yarford had neither."

"He might've hired someone."

"Why would he? He had already threatened Thornley with a duel. He wasn't so craven to hire someone else to protect his honor."

He puckered his lips and nodded, thinking. "Fair enough."

She added, "We—" He snapped his gaze at her. "I mean, *you* would be better served to focus on those who had access to Lord Thornley's study where he was killed. It would've been quite easy for any one of them to hide in the alcove and spring on him unawares."

He perked. "Alcove? What alcove?"

She blinked back her surprise. "You don't know of it?"

"No."

Lady Mildreth opened the door. Her watery eyes popped open in surprise. "Oh! Here you both are." She dabbed her cheeks. "So, you haven't given up on me?" She pleaded with Ravenna.

Before Ravenna could answer, Mr. Chadwick said, "I would like to see your son's study, ma'am. May I?"

"Of course." She led them to Lord Franklin's study. She hovered in the doorway while Ravenna and Chadwick entered the room.

Chadwick turned to Ravenna. "Where is the alcove?"

Ravenna led him past the desk and lifted the tapestry. "Here."

Mr. Chadwick entered the space and looked around from the ceiling, down the walls, to the floor, in all the corners. Ravenna kept to herself the little tidbit of information about the Irish Unity seal she'd found. She didn't want any reason for him to begin investigating them for fear it would somehow lead back to herself.

"I imagine the killer could've come in that window." She pointed to the window. "Hid in here to wait for Lord Franklin." She pointed to the alcove. "Then escaped through the same window."

"Or the killer might've already been in the house. Hid in here, then fled out the window." He squatted and inspected the floor.

"Yes."

"This would've been good to know about in the beginning." He stood and stepped out of the alcove. He shot a look at Lady Mildreth, who dipped her head and inspected her nails as if chastised. He sighed. "At any rate, I know about it now."

"Yet, it doesn't change the essentials. Someone killed Lord Thornley, and I wager it was someone who knew him."

"Yes. But who?"

Lady Mildreth cleared her throat. "Perhaps this isn't the best time to bring up this matter, but the prince is having a birthday ball tomorrow. I would like very much to present the opal to him in my son's name. In doing so, maybe the prince will favor me in his stead. Can you appeal to Mr. Gibson to return the opal to me? If only he will do so, I will do everything I can to help him stay out of prison."

"How do you know Mr. Gibson has the opal?" Ravenna asked. "When I spoke to him, he was adamant that he didn't have it."

Mr. Chadwick said, "You cannot be sincere in such a request or promise. It will be impossible to recover the gem by tomorrow since we aren't sure Mr. Gibson has the stone."

"Surely he has it. Who else could it be?"

"Even if that's true, to promise to keep him out of prison when he may have murdered your son is incomprehensible. Why would you do such a thing? It truly baffles the mind, ma'am."

Lady Mildreth wrung her hands. "But think how kindly the prince will look upon me, what generous favors he might bestow, if I can give him such a unique and beautiful gift."

Chapter Twenty-Two

Ravenna stormed from the house, muttering to herself. "Absurd, cork-brained woman."

Hart stood by the carriage, fanning herself in the summer heat, waiting for Ravenna. "I'm sure Lady Thornley was thrilled to have her jewels returned to her?"

"Not as much as one would think." Ravenna rolled her eyes. "She's an impossible creature."

They turned to climb into the carriage when the footman, Miller, approached. "Lady Birchfield, a man asked me to give you this note."

She opened it.

It would be a shame if anything were to happen to the pretty young girl.

Her hand clapped over her chest, and her breath caught. Panic flurried through her. "Oh Lord," she whispered.

"What is it?" Hart said. "What's the matter?"

As Hart's eyes swept over the words, they widened. "Oh, dear. Surely this means Georgiana."

"I believe so." Ravenna turned to the footman. "Who handed you this?"

"I don't know who he was. Never saw him before."

"When was he here?" Hart asked. "I've been standing here the whole time."

"A few minutes ago."

Ravenna ran around the carriage and searched up and down the street. Hart and Miller followed.

Hart said, "I didn't see anyone hanging around the carriage." She turned to Miller. "Where were you when he handed it to you?"

"I was sitting by the driver. I had just climbed down to let Lady Birchfield into the carriage. He caught me as I stepped to the ground. He said, 'Give this to Lady Birchfield.' He shoved it in my hand and walked away. He barely stopped. Didn't even look up. He had his hat pulled down over his eyes and the collar of his greatcoat pulled up around his chin. He didn't give me a chance to respond or ask who he was."

"What did he look like?" Ravenna asked.

"I didn't get a good look. He was pale. Shorter than me. Very light hair, I think."

The description sounded very much like The Unity man, Mr. Larson, who had attacked her several months ago. "Did he walk with a limp?"

"I'm not certain. Maybe."

Ravenna locked eyes with Hart. "I think it's him."

"Who?" Hart frowned.

"Get inside." She nudged Hart toward the carriage.

Miller handed them inside.

When they settled into their seats, and Miller had closed them inside, Ravenna said, "I think it's Mr. Larson. From The Unity."

"How? I thought you killed him."

"I thought so, too. But the evening of the attack, when Lord Braedon had gone looking for me, he said he hadn't seen a body. He found only some blood and my fan."

"So somehow the man survived, and now he's come back?"

"And based on this letter, I'd wager, he's likely seeking revenge."

When Ravenna arrived home, she ran inside, shouting. "Georgiana! Georgiana!" She found Harrison and Mr. Emmett in the drawing room.

Harrison stood, concerned. "What's the matter, Amma? Are you unwell?"

"Where's Georgiana?"

Hart rushed in behind her.

"She's upstairs trying on her new ball gown," Harrison said. "It's just arrived."

183

Ravenna relaxed and put her hand to her chest. *Thank heavens!*

Mr. Emmett stood, bowed in greeting, and smiled. "Education is defeated by a ballgown. I knew she wouldn't be able to focus on her studies until she'd tried on the dress."

The door jerked open and Georgiana dashed into the room wearing a pink and gold silk gown like the dawn. Her ash blonde ringlets spilled from the back of her head and trailed over her creamy shoulders. "Isn't it beautiful?" She giggled and stepped side to side, and turned in the first steps of a country dance. "It's my first ever fancy dress. It's for the prince's ball tomorrow evening. I'm so excited, I know I shan't sleep at all. I'm going to dance until holes wear in my slippers." She hid her laughter behind her hands.

Emmett said, "I hope you will save a dance for me?"

Ravenna lifted a brow. "You're going to the prince's birthday ball?"

He chuckled. "I see I've shocked you that I, a lowly tutor, could gain a ticket to the ball."

Ravenna tried to backtrack. "Oh, no, I-I..."

"I take no offense. Lord Donovan assisted me with a ticket."

"How lucky! Then we shall dance," Georgiana said.

Harrison interrupted. "May I hope to secure the first two dances?"

Georgiana dithered. "I-I'm not...I don't know...Perhaps not *two.*"

It was a little bold for Harrison to request the first two dances. The first two dances indicated a serious relationship, or at least a man's serious interest in a lady. Yet, Ravenna felt sorry for Harrison. An almost desperate hope marked his features. "You should at least take the first dance with him, Georgiana."

"Certainly!" She beamed.

"The dress is lovely. It's perfect on you." Ravenna wouldn't say anything yet to warn Georgiana about the note she'd received. She would let the girl enjoy the thrill of a new dress and the exciting dreams of her first ball.

A maid entered with afternoon tea.

Ravenna said, "Georgiana, you should change out of your dress so you don't get it dirty before the ball. We'll wait for you."

Georgiana dashed out of the room.

Ravenna turned to Emmett, "How go her studies today?"

"Quite well. Until the dress arrived."

"And what has she been working on?"

"We are continuing with what we started yesterday. She's learning to introduce herself in French as well as her first verbs and their conjugates."

"Fantastic. Does she seem to enjoy her lessons?"

Harrison interrupted. "I'd say she enjoys them rather well." He glanced at Mr. Emmett. "But then I daresay I've never seen such an *attentive* tutor."

Emmett set his jaw and seemed to be measuring his next words. He said, "I am sorry for your lack of attentive tutors, Lord Birchfield. Yet, it's important to note Miss Georgiana's enthusiasm for learning. She has an eager and hungry mind." Mr. Emmett went on at some length about Georgiana's curiosity and fervor and how quickly she was learning until the girl in question returned.

Georgiana breezed into the room and changed the subject to the ball, where it remained until tea was over. Ravenna had forgotten how much matter a young girl could extract from the subject of a ball. Had Ravenna herself ever been so young and frivolous? Some days, it seemed as though she was born a widow in her thirties. With all the death and suffering she'd witnessed in her life, she wasn't sure she could ever fully give herself over to such lighthearted diversion.

Perhaps, then, it was a bit of providence for Georgiana to appear in her life at this time. It must surely be a good thing to have a youthful spirit to bring lightness and fun and a constant reminder to be less serious. Though sometimes Georgiana's constant chatter and fidgeting grew wearisome, Ravenna's heart buoyed to hear her laughter and be near the girl's natural vivacity. Every day, the girl reminded her more and more of Helen, serving a stew of bittersweet memories and deepening Ravenna's desire to find her sister, Helen, and be reunited.

When all the tiny sandwiches and biscuits and buns had been eaten, and the teapot was dry, Emmett stood. "Miss Georgiana, it's time for us to return to our books before they get dusty."

Georgiana swiped the crumbs from her hands and followed him to the table in the corner at the back of the room. The table looked out on the garden and sunlight poured over them as they tipped their heads together to look at the same book. They sat *very* close, so that their shoulders nearly touched. There certainly seemed to be an attraction growing between the pair. That thought brought a smile to Ravenna's lips. Emmett could do better, to be sure, but Georgiana could certainly do worse.

The closeness of the pair hadn't escaped Harrison's sharp gaze either.

"They've sat crammed together at such a tiny table all afternoon. I have no doubt he fancies her," Harrison whispered.

"They do seem to get on quite well."

"*Too* well, I wager. He is too attentive, I think. More like a suitor than a tutor."

Ravenna glanced over her shoulder. "I see. And would it be a terrible thing if they fancied each other? He seems to be a good sort of man. Learned, amiable, kind. She could do worse for a husband."

"I'm all those things, too, Amma. But she barely gives me a second glance."

"Harrison, my dear." She put her hand over his. "I'm sure she likes you very much, but you must come to terms with the fact that she may never love you the way you would like. Since she lives in this house with you, and you are my stepson, she may have already come to think of you much like a brother or cousin. Would that be such a horrible thing?"

He sighed. "Yes, it would. I don't want to be her brother. I want to be her…" He slumped back in his chair, sulking.

"There are so many attractive and accomplished girls, Harrison. Many will be at the ball tomorrow evening. You could find a girl ten times Georgiana's consequence." She squeezed his hand. "You cannot force love, my dear."

"Perhaps you're right, but I intend to keep hoping until she gives me a reason not to."

Ravenna sighed, twisting her cloth napkin around her fingers. "You do seem determined to have your heart broken. I cannot stop you, and I fear you won't be easy until the job is done. I just hope you'll heal quickly when you've had your way."

Chapter Twenty-Three

As Ravenna enjoyed a light breakfast over the morning paper, she received a letter from Braedon which lifted her heart like a kite on the wind. She also received a letter from Lady Thornley which promptly jerked the kite back to earth. She opened Lady Thornley's first, finding another letter tucked inside.

> *Dear Lady Birchfield,*
> *I'm certain this letter will find you quite vexed with me. I've behaved abhorrently, and I hope you will find it in your heart to forgive me.*

Ravenna rolled her eyes. The woman was certainly testing the limits of her patience.

> *But I do need your help. You are more resourceful than I and Lady Violette assures me you are the best person to find my son's killer and treat my family's troubles with discretion. Therefore, I hope you will continue to help me. In going through my son's papers this afternoon, I discovered this letter from Mr. Gibson to Franklin, which I hope will shed some light on the matter.*
> *Sincerely,*
> *Mildreth*

Curiosity outweighed her annoyance, so she opened the other letter.

Thornley,

You will not get away with stealing the opal from me. I will hunt you until your last days. You know you took the gem from my possession when we were still in New South Wales, and you shall rue the day you did it. Unless you return the gem to me, I will destroy you. Any hopes for your future endeavors with the Crown and the British Museum will be blown to bits. Your reputation will be like ashes on the wind, and they will never support your work or trust you again.

SG

Though she had witnessed Mr. Gibson's jealousy firsthand, this letter made the animosity and his determination clear. She rang the bell. When the maid entered the room, she asked to have the carriage brought around, and to have Hart come to help her prepare to go out.

She resumed her seat to read the letter from Braedon. She opened it eagerly.

July 10, 1803

My darling Raven,

I received your letter, dated nearly a month ago, and now have a moment to respond. I have just come from a dinner at Count Arnetti's casa where the food was good, the wine better, and the conversation tedious. In my relief, I'm now at my writing desk where I can look out the window and stare at the moon. Yet all I see is you, the sky as dark as your hair, the light as pale as your face the last time I saw you. Every night, my thoughts are carried away to you, and I think, 'She would like that music. She would find that woman boring, that man entertaining, that play diverting.'

My time here plays upon my nerves like a child slapping out a discordant tune on the pianoforte, so I spend my days boxing with my valet, shooting at targets, or riding along the Italian countryside— anything to spend as little time as possible with Dianthe and her mother. I can bear them no longer. I escorted them to this infernal place because no other escort could be found at the time, and, admittedly, I felt something of an obligation given that her parents blame me for Dianthe's troubles—though I tried more than once to extricate myself from her and they have done little to rein in their daughter's obstinate nature and egregious behavior.

But there is hope. This past week, Dianthe seems to be doing better and is more agreeable to everyone, so I'm already preparing for my return to England. Her mother is arranging for an uncle to come take my place where his business prevented him from chaperoning the women to begin with. Better yet, Dianthe has shown an interest in a young Italian count and, I confess, I am encouraging the match with great enthusiasm in hopes I can return to England, and you, as soon as possible.

Dearest, do not toy with me by denying me your letters. Write, dear Ravenna. Write daily. I live on your words like bread and wine. Even an angry word from you is a balm.

Ever Yours,

B.

She folded the letter. Lord Braedon. She sighed. She longed to see him again, even if to be provoked by him. This letter was written weeks ago. Much could've changed in that time. He might already be crossing the sea toward England even now. If she wrote to him now, would the letter even reach him?

Hart entered with her dress draped over her arms. "Here's your dress."

"Good. I want to leave as soon as possible." She stepped behind the screen and removed her dressing gown. Hart pulled the black sarsenet gown over Ravenna's head and buttoned up the back.

Within the half-hour, Ravenna and Hart were in the carriage, headed to Mr. Gibson's house in Ludgate Hill. The sky was gray and dull as a slate. Rain dripped from the leaves, and the streets were muddy and filled with mucky puddles. Humidity and the scent of moss and earth hung thick in the air.

The carriage stopped in front of Mr. Gibson's row house. Ravenna stepped out of the bounds of propriety to knock on the door herself. Hart stood close behind her, glancing up and down the street. Ravenna knocked again. "I suppose he's not home."

Hart stepped away to press her face against the front window. "I think I see him sitting in a chair. Knock louder."

Ravenna pounded on the door. Again. No answer. Nervous, she put her hand to the knob and turned it. It gave way. "It's not locked," she whispered to Hart.

They pressed the door open, and the unmistakable scent of death knocked them back. Ravenna pressed her gloved hand over her mouth and pinched her nose. "Heavens!"

"Smells like a rat has died," Hart said.

"Or someone." Ravenna tiptoed into the house, across the tiny foyer, and opened the door on the left to Mr. Gibson's study.

Ravenna jumped and gasped. As soon as she saw the body slumped in the chair, his chest covered with a blood-soaked newspaper, she slammed the door. Her stomach churning, she said, "He's dead." She nudged Hart toward the front door. "We need to send for Mr. Chadwick. He should know about this."

"I'll go."

Ravenna gave her directions to his office. "Take the carriage."

"No. I can probably move faster on foot. I'll return directly."

Ravenna sat in the carriage, waiting, biting her lip and bouncing her knee. Trying to shove the image of the dead Mr. Gibson from her mind. The scent of death still coated her nostrils. She pressed her rose-scented handkerchief to her nose, to little avail. Though the summer heat pressed all around her, she shivered. The hour crept by, each minute twisting her muscles into knots. Finally, Mr. Chadwick appeared, his great coat billowing in the breeze.

Ravenna jumped from the carriage. "Mr. Chadwick. Thank you for coming. He's in here." She opened the door and guided him to the study.

Hart hung back in the foyer. Ravenna rushed in behind Mr. Chadwick,

190

pressing her handkerchief to her nose to block the odor of decay. The messy room was full of a life now gone; it didn't seem out of the ordinary since it was cluttered the first time she visited. There appeared to have been a struggle, however. The rug was bunched up, and a chair and occasional table were overturned. Some papers lay scattered on the floor, along with a broken glass and a wine stain.

She turned to look at his desk while Chadwick studied the body. Papers comprising a portion of Mr. Gibson's life's work littered the desktop. The sign of an active mind and life. Most of them were letters from friends and associates. A few empty wine bottles stood on the desk or lay on the floor. Quill shavings, empty ink pots, broken pens, and wax bits sprinkled the papers. A candle burned to its end pooled in a nearby holder. A register book detailing his accounts lay open on the desk. Such a complex and rich life. Though Ravenna hadn't liked him, sorrow hung on her. Maybe she couldn't shed a tear for him, but she did feel sorry for him, for the way his busy life had ended, for the way his work and his hopes and dreams had been cut short. That alone was sad.

A leatherbound book occupied one corner. A journal. She opened it to the last few pages. One entry from a few days ago lashed out against Lord Thornley. Another entry written only yesterday discussed an unknown man and woman.

> *I don't know them. But I suspect they are connected to Lord Thornley's death. I think I saw them come out of the garden on the day of the gala. I am determined to find out who they are so that dastardly Bow Street Runner, Chadwick, will leave me in peace. He torments me day and night.*

Then, later, he wrote

> *The man I have been seeking has found me in my home, I think. I am almost certain the man I witnessed at Thornley Hall is the same man who has been following me. It's nearly dark outside, but I think I see*

him now outside my window.

Nothing else was written down.

Mr. Chadwick lifted the newspaper covering Mr. Gibson's torso. "He's been stabbed. Multiple times. I see no other harm." He looked at the newspaper. "Sometime yesterday, according to the date on this paper."

"I think you're right," Ravenna said. "Here's a journal entry from yesterday evening, and nothing has been written since."

He stood and approached. "A journal is most helpful." He took the journal and flipped through it.

"Apparently, he was being followed by the man who killed Lord Thornley, and he was trying to discover the identity of the man so he could direct your inquiry."

He turned to the last entry and read it. "Interesting. Yet..." He sighed and looked out the window. "He left no description of the man, unfortunately." He closed the journal and tapped it against his palm. "Perhaps I can talk to the neighbors to see if they've noticed a particular stranger in this area." He dropped the book into his pocket and stepped toward the door. He inspected the knob and the latch. "Strange..."

"What's that?"

"There's no forced entry as one might expect if he were afraid."

"Many people don't lock their doors."

He turned his steely blue gaze on her. "Wouldn't you bolt your door if you were being followed?"

"Granted." She paused and considered. "Then are we to believe the killer was someone he knew?"

"Yes. Or, at the very least, someone he didn't feel threatened by."

He turned and looked at the scene again, carefully running his eyes over every detail of the room. Then, his attention locked on something. "What's that?" He stepped toward the body and knelt to pick up an item from under the sofa. He pulled up a delicate gold chain.

"This looks very much like a lady's necklace, does it not?"

"It does."

CHAPTER TWENTY-THREE

He searched the area. "Yet, I don't see a locket or pendant of any kind."

Having had necklaces break herself, Ravenna knew it was possible the locket dropped down the lady's bodice, trapped by her bosom, while the chain slipped away to the ground or floor. She explained this to Mr. Chadwick.

"Yes. That's what I was thinking. Such a thing has happened to my wife and daughters a time or two."

Ravenna wondered what sort of woman would marry this hard, steely man with his penetrating, hawkish gaze. She couldn't imagine spending a lifetime with a man like him. And then to have children with him? She tried to imagine a domestic scene around a fire where he sat in a chair with children climbing on his knee, but the image faded before she could produce it.

He wrapped the chain in his handkerchief and stuffed the wad of cloth in his pocket. "I wonder if our Mr. Gibson had a lover?"

"I don't know. It's possible, I suppose." Though Ravenna couldn't imagine what woman would want to pair herself with a red-faced, angry little man like Mr. Gibson. "He might've entertained a strumpet."

"Perhaps." He gazed at her over his shoulder with hard, blue eyes. "Or perhaps our killer is female?"

She thought of telling Mr. Chadwick about the taffeta fabric she'd found in the Thornley garden gate, but she was afraid he would confiscate it from her. She wanted to keep it a while longer to see if she could find the match. Then she would turn it over. It wasn't that she mistrusted Chadwick or that she believed he wouldn't investigate with integrity. But she felt it was necessary to stay one step ahead of him in order to best protect Catherine and Yarford.

Ravenna returned home in a fog of overwhelm. She couldn't let go of the image of Mr. Gibson's corpse and what his death meant. She eased into a hot bath scented with rose water and let her mind roll over these mysteries while she bathed in preparation for the prince's birthday ball.

With Mr. Gibson dead the names on Ravenna's list dropped to only Adam Cossard or Lord Percy. But the gold necklace Mr. Chadwick discovered seemed to indicate the involvement of a woman, though Ravenna couldn't imagine who. Unless Mr. Gibson frequented a woman of the streets. Such women sometimes went home with a man and robbed him. It wasn't unheard of for such women or their pimps to also injure or kill their targets. Mr. Gibson's death might've been coincidence—a death at the hands of a stranger completely unconnected to Lord Thornley. However, such an occurrence seemed more than coincidental.

She stepped out of the bath and ran a towel over her skin. Who was she missing? Adam Cossard, though justifiably angry with the Thornleys, didn't seem to be the sort of man who could kill. He had stated how he'd held the knife to Lord Franklin Thornley's neck and couldn't proceed. However, she supposed he could've been lying about his squeamishness to deflect suspicion from himself. Then there was Lord Percy. He was as likely as any: jealous, covetous, greedy for the money. He was still the most likely suspect in her estimation.

Yet for all that, Mr. Gibson had mentioned a mysterious man in his journal. The man had been following him because Mr. Gibson had apparently witnessed something related to Thornley's death. And that was why Mr. Gibson died. But who was the man? Was it Adam Cossard, Lord Percy, or a stranger? If a stranger, then finding the killer became a nearly impossible task.

As she slipped into her jet-beaded black dress, she remembered she needed to warn Georgiana to be wary of pale men with white hair asking too many questions about her family—especially her uncle Niall.

Chapter Twenty-Four

Carlton House was the home of the Prince Regent George IV in Westminster. It faced the south side of the Pall Mall, and its gardens lay adjacent to St. James Park. The grand white stone structure was reminiscent of an ancient Greek temple, nestled like a jewel between Buckingham Palace, Westminster Abbey, the Thames, and Covent Garden—all of which were close to Gordon House in Curzon Street.

Georgiana's exuberance could hardly be contained in the carriage.

"You must remember what I told you, Georgiana," Ravenna said, hoping to use this final moment together to remind her niece of the threatening letter. Once they were inside, Ravenna knew she would see very little of her niece.

"Yes, yes." Georgiana pressed her face to the carriage window to look out, though there was little to see of the Pall Mall in the near darkness.

"Truly, I think someone means you and this family harm."

"Who do you think means us harm?" Harrison said. "And why?"

Ravenna didn't want to answer his questions. It would open up her past for inspection. She didn't want him to know how she'd once been a spy. She didn't want her stepson to think ill of her, if she could help it. And, she was certain, since his father and brother had been government officials, he wouldn't understand the role she played and why she played it. He would see her as a traitor to the Crown his father had once served. The same Crown he, too, would be called to serve. She said, "I can't go into particulars, but I have it on good authority."

He chuckled. "Yes, but *whose* authority?"

"I need you two to trust me."

"But why should someone want to hurt me?" Georgiana screwed up her face. "I haven't done anything to anyone."

"Sometimes, there is evil in the world without reason. I want you to be careful."

"I will." The exasperation loaded Georgiana's voice. "But I will not allow this pale man, whoever he is, to destroy my first-ever ball. And at Prince George's house, no less. Am I not the luckiest girl in the world? My friends back in Whitechapel would never believe me, but I must write to them. They'll all be absolutely green with envy. I have a new ball gown, which suits me nicely, I think. And I'm going to a ball at Carlton House, where I will meet the prince!"

Given Prinny's abhorrent and profligate behavior, Ravenna was less excited about her young, naive niece meeting him. "Yes. You are very lucky. And you are to avoid spending any amount of time with the prince. Especially alone. I'm more afraid for you on that account than I am over the pale man, if I'm being honest."

The carriage fell into line behind the carriages entering the estate through a stone gate of Greek columns, all lit with torches.

"Why should I be afraid of the prince?" Georgiana looked at her.

"Because he has a horrible reputation for seducing women and keeping mistresses. While there are many mothers and guardians who throw their daughters in his path, hoping to raise their fortunes, I am not one of them. You may meet him in my presence, but you must avoid him. And never be alone with him."

The carriage inched toward the portico and the main entrance.

"Yes, yes, yes. You worry far too much, Auntie, and you're driving me mad with it. I won't listen to any more of your warnings because I'm in no mood to be frightened." She clasped her hands and gushed. "I'm going to dance with all the handsome men and maybe even some of the ugly ones. I'm going to have the best night of my life tonight. And you shan't keep me from such joy."

Harrison added, "Though I'm concerned by Amma's secrecy, she seems to have reason to be afraid. Surely, you can enjoy the ball while being careful and conscientious."

"I'm worried. That's all. You are still very young and innocent. You don't understand as much of the world as you think you do, poppet. I want only to keep you safe."

"Don't worry, Amma. I'll help you keep an eye on things," Harrison smiled in the dim torchlight that crossed his face as they pulled up in front of their destination.

Large torches lined the drive leading to Carlton House and all along the front of the building. Footmen holding smaller torches stood ready in front of the entry steps to assist guests from their carriages and to light their way under the grand Grecian hexastyle portico into the house.

Georgiana gaped as they entered the two-story vestibule with its columns of yellow marble. The doors to the anterooms on the left were thrown open to reveal card tables where many gentlemen and ladies gathered in their finery to gamble away their inheritances. To the left, the anteroom opened to reveal a refreshment room with all sorts of punches, champagnes, wines, cakes, cold meats, biscuits, breads, fruits, ices, and cheeses. The musicians were established in this room as well so they wouldn't be in the way of the dancers.

They passed by the rollicking music into the Crimson Drawing Room, which had been specially prepared for the ball. Gold-plated scrollwork graced the white ceilings. One grand crystal chandelier flanked by two smaller ones glittered in the candlelight. Red curtains trimmed in gold fringe festooned the perimeter of the room and draped the windows. One wall was covered in red wallpaper with gold lattice, pinned with landscapes and portraits. The red velvet sofas and chairs, and the marble statues and other furniture that usually occupied the room had been moved out to accommodate the dancers. It was everything a young girl at her first ball could ever hope for.

At the far end of the room, the doughy, dandified prince sat on a dais with his illegitimate wife, Maria Fitzherbert, who, six years his senior, wore a white dress, her blonde hair like a cloud around her heart-shaped face and aquiline nose. The couple were surrounded by people who boasted of friendship or kinship or no relationship, but all hoping for royal favor. The Protestant prince, more in love than he had been with his legitimate wife, Caroline of Brunswick, held the hand of the twice-widowed and Catholic Mrs. Fitzherbert—who happened to also be the first cousin to the prince's cast-off wife. They smiled and whispered to each other as they watched the dancers skip down the line. The dancers turned in a circle on the perky violin notes, joined with other partners, wove around each other, formed separate circles, then broke into another line.

Harrison stopped to talk to friends as Ravenna and Georgiana made their way through the crowd to find someone they knew. Spotting Lord Donovan and Mr. Emmett across the room, they pushed through the crowd to join them.

Lord Donovan bowed and smiled warmly at them. "Lady Birchfield and Miss Georgiana. What a pleasure to see you here this evening."

Georgiana gazed up at Donovan. "I'm excited to be here." She glanced at the dancers. "And so eager to dance." The hint was clear, but Lord Donovan didn't pick up on it. Or rather, didn't act on it.

Mr. Emmett extended his hand. "Then we shall dance."

Ravenna said, "Georgiana, didn't you promise the first dance to Harrison?"

"Yes, but he's not here. He's over there with friends, and I want to dance now." She placed her hand in Mr. Emmett's and, giggling, swept him away to join the other dancers.

Lord Donovan's sea-green eyes lit up. "So, now that we have this moment alone, I'll take this opportunity to inform you that I have spoken with some...friends. They assure me Lord Percy will be commissioned into the Navy as an officer. It seems his debt was sizable, as such he was willing to allow it to be purchased for two years in the Navy as a lieutenant. That was all the time I could get for you. For now. But he seems happy enough to not only be put to sea to escape his debtors, but to be paid a lieutenant's salary."

She smiled. "I can't thank you enough. Two years will be sufficient, I think."

"Yes, and if all goes well, he will enjoy the sailor's life so much he'll never want to leave it."

She chuckled. "I have heard once some men get a taste for the sea, they can't separate themselves from it."

"And, if we are very lucky, he should be shipped out by Michaelmas."

"So soon? Even better!" Ravenna squeezed his arm. "I can't thank you enough, Donovan."

Harrison joined them, looking around. "Where is Georgiana? I was supposed to have the first dance with her."

"She is dancing with Mr. Emmett," Ravenna said.

The line of Harrison's mouth drew downward.

Donovan intervened, "But you may be able to snag her for the next dance, if you hurry."

Harrison dashed off.

Ravenna and Donovan exchanged a knowing look.

Ravenna said, "He likes her very much."

Donovan nodded toward Mr. Emmett and Georgiana standing across the room, looking out the window. Emmett pushed a curl out of Georgiana's face. "I think he has a rival."

Harrison approached the couple and spoke to Georgiana. She went to the dance floor with Harrison. They danced happily down the line, smiling at each other.

Mr. Emmett glanced at Ravenna and waved. He began walking toward them when a man approached him. Emmett smiled broadly, shook hands with the man, and patted him on the back as they exchanged words. Emmett then nodded in Ravenna's direction, and the two men moved in her direction.

Mr. Emmett bowed. "Good evening, Lady Birchfield. Miss Georgiana is an enthusiastic dancer. I'm glad there are plenty of men here to keep up with her zeal for the exercise." They laughed and he turned to the man at his side. "This is my brother Robert. He's visiting for a few months."

Robert Emmett was handsome enough. He looked similar to Mr. Emmett, except he was more muscular with a square jaw and a rounder nose, where Emmett's features were narrow and pointed.

Ravenna curtsied. "A pleasure to meet you."

Robert's dark eyes glittered. "Yes, I'm hoping to find work here in London to make the move permanent."

"And what do you do?"

He glanced at Emmett. "I'm a solicitor."

Donovan said, "I think London can never have enough solicitors." Everyone laughed.

Ravenna added, "Perhaps we need more of the *good* and *capable* variety?"

"Indeed," Donovan said. "The supply is short enough, I wager."

Mr. Emmett clasped his hands behind his back. "I have some exciting news of my own. I have been most fortunate to secure a position with the royal family."

Ravenna gaped. "Is that so? How lucky for you!"

"No luck at all." He clapped Donovan on his back. "Donovan recommended me for the position."

"I was happy to do it," Donovan beamed. "I couldn't think of a better man to teach an heir to the throne."

"An heir? Who will you tutor? All of the king's children are grown."

"The prince's daughter, Princess Charlotte. I understand she's third in line to the throne."

"Of course, yes. She will be different from teaching Georgiana, I wager, at only seven years of age." Ravenna laughed. "It will be quite a change for you."

"I confess, it will."

Ravenna said, "I would've thought the princess already had a tutor."

"She did until recently. An older gentleman. Uh, a Mr. Bealmouth, I believe is his name. He has been the tutor for all thirteen of King George's surviving children."

"He's apparently fallen ill," Mr. Emmett said.

"Oh, I hope it's not too serious." Ravenna fanned herself with her lace fan. The ballroom was growing warm with the press of bodies.

Sadness crossed Mr. Emmett's features. "I understand he's quite ill and has taken to bed. He's not expected to recover."

"Then I am sorry for Mr. Bealmouth," Ravenna said. "But what happy news for you. I imagine you will be leaving us then. I hope you can suggest someone else to tutor Georgiana?"

"Oh no, milady! I can do both."

She laughed. "Oh, Mr. Emmett, I think you'll find working for the royal family will be quite demanding of your time. But if you think you can do both..."

"I will do my best."

"I apologize for changing the subject from my brother's happy news," Robert said. "But I have it on good authority there has been some scandal in town these past several days. The murder of a lord? A missing rare gem?"

"Yes," Donovan said. "It's been quite the spectacle."

"Have the killer and the gem been found?"

"Not yet," said Ravenna. "But I understand the search for both is quite heated."

"What sort of gem was it? Does anyone know?" Robert's eyes gleamed with interest. He was a man of vibrant energy, where his brother was more subdued.

"It was a black opal from New South Wales," Ravenna said. "It's rare enough of its own accord, but there is a legend that it comes with special powers."

"Fascinating! What sort of powers could a gem possess?"

"Apparently, whoever possesses the gem will conquer their enemies and turn their enemies' wives into widows. Thus, the opal is called the Widow's Fire."

"What I wouldn't give to see such a gem." Robert's face lit with wonder.

"It's quite awe-inspiring," Ravenna said. All the men focused on her.

"You've seen it?" Donovan said, fascinated.

"I have. I had the honor of attending a gala where Lord Franklin Thornley, shortly before his murder, showed us all the opal and allowed us to hold it."

Robert chuckled. "You jest!"

"I do not. It was about the size of a goose egg, black as night with a rainbow in its center. The colors glowed, as if the stone was lit from within. It's a singular stone in all respects."

"Incredible. I hope it's recovered," Robert said.

Ravenna agreed. "And soon. Lord Thornley's intention was to gift the opal to King George, not for just its beauty but the legend surrounding it. He believed that if the gem contained special powers, it would be best kept in the responsible hands of our nation rather than fall into the power-mad hands of one like Napoleon. Further, if it's returned to the Crown, it might be placed in the British Museum so everyone can enjoy its wonders."

"Indeed, I know I would love to see it," Robert added. He crossed his arms over his chest, and his face took on a pensive quality. "But do you really believe in such curses or powers?"

She smiled. "There are more things in heaven and earth—"

"Than are dreamt of in your philosophies." Robert completed her thought, and they laughed together. "I see your point, but I think a rational mind cannot believe in such fantasies, Lady Birchfield."

"Granted, but I wager there are areas in our kingdom today where there exists a profound fear of and belief in ghosts and witches. Half of my staff still leave food for fairies to ward off their trickery."

The men chuckled.

She continued. "Does it not follow then that if those things are true, then this stone might, in fact, prove to have powers?"

Robert nodded, then lifted a finger. "Ah, but the belief of a thing and the actuality or reality of a thing are not always the same. One can *believe* in witches and ghosts, but that does not make them live."

"It also doesn't disprove their existence. I won't go so far as to say I actually believe the stone has powers, but I suppose I won't deny the claim unless and until it's been proven. It's interesting to think of, is it not?"

Donovan added, "The idea of a stone impacting the fate of nations? A curious notion, but I suppose entirely as silly as it sounds. After all, I have heard Napoleon believes he is guided by a lucky star and searches for it in the night sky."

The men sniffed with humor. Ravenna raised her brows. "It is curious. But think of it. If Napoleon has accomplished so much already, driven by a belief in the power of a single star in the sky, what more might he do if a stone with the opal's power were placed in his hands? I wonder if the power is not so much in the thing itself, but in the mind of its keeper."

"Spoken like a true philosopher." Donovan chuckled.

With that, the men fell into a deep political discussion about matters Ravenna could not find interest in, so she went in search of her friend, Lady Catherine. They whiled away the hours in gossip, discussing where good lace and muslin might be found with the French trade embargoes creating such a disaster and watching Georgiana dance and laugh to her heart's delight.

Chapter Twenty-Five

I n the wee hours of the morning, Ravenna, Harrison, and Georgiana climbed into the carriage. Harrison sulked in his corner as Georgiana flopped into her seat. "Heavens, what a grand time I've had! Every part of me hurts. I've never danced so much in my life!" She pushed the sweaty tendrils of hair off her forehead and neck. "But I've never been so happy." She fanned herself furiously. "I hope there will be another ball soon."

"I'm sure there shall be," Ravenna said. "There is certainly no shortage of balls during the season."

"Then I hope the season never ends."

They entered the house and all scattered to their respective bedchambers. Ravenna, exhausted, dragged upstairs, holding a candle. The flame cast long, dancing shadows along the walls and down the hall. She opened her door, the shadows pushing to the edges of the room. There, in the dim candlelight, she discovered a dark figure leaning over her writing desk.

She gasped, and the man stopped. He was dressed in a black cape with a black piece of fabric tied around his face. A wide-brimmed hat sat low over his head.

"Who are you? What are you doing here?" she demanded.

He looked at the window, then back at her.

It happened all at once. He charged her and knocked her down, the candle falling to the wood floor, just missing the carpet.

"Help!" she shouted. "Intruder! Intruder!"

Ravenna stretched and crawled toward the candle to blow it out before it caught the rug aflame as the man jumped over her and ran out the door.

"Stop! Thief!"

She grabbed her fan, fought to untangle her legs from the skirts of her ballgown, and scrambled to her feet. She ran after the man, drawing the thin blade from her fan, casting the fan itself aside.

Ravenna's dress fluttered around her legs as she tore down the hall after the intruder. He slid down the balustrade just ahead of her, the staircase too dark to reveal his identity.

Georgiana peeked out her door, still in her gown, her hair taken down.

Harrison came running, in his shirt sleeves, unarmed. Still in his evening wear, he was not prepared to take on the ruffian. "What's the matter?" Harrison said.

"Intruder!" She shouted, lifting her skirts to jog down the stairs. The thief was too far ahead of her. He had already reached the curve at the bottom of the stairs and slid off the railing to the ground, dashing for the front door.

Harrison ran past her, then jumped over the railing, chasing after the man. "Harrison, no! You're unarmed. Don't go out there."

But he was already gone.

Ravenna ran out into the darkness. The men were several yards ahead of her. She could only hear the echoes of Harrison's shouts at the intruder. She ran in the direction of the men, hoping to catch up with them, until her side stitched and made it impossible to catch her breath.

She slowed her pace and doubled over, bracing herself with a hand to the gas lamp at the street corner. When she could breathe well enough to speak, she called out to Harrison. At first, there was no answer. She walked briskly in the direction Harrison had run, stopping at the next lamp. "Harrison! Where are you?"

Soon, he limped out of the shadows and fog, gasping for air. "I'm here, Amma. I'm here."

Ravenna ran to him. "Were you able to catch him at all?"

"Only briefly." He showed her his right arm. "Until he cut my arm."

She inspected it under the dim light. A light spot of blood soaked through his left bicep. The scar on her face tingled. "It doesn't look too bad. A surface wound. Let's get you home and get your arm cleaned up. Why are you limping?"

"I don't know. I think I landed wrong on my foot when I jumped the balustrade. It hurts."

She put her arm around his waist. He smelled of sweat, and his body was hot from the exertion of the chase. "Lean on me if you need to." He put some of his weight against her, and they walked back to Gordon House. The servants stood in the foyer, milling about and whispering in a state of confusion, when Ravenna and Harrison entered the house.

Ravenna said to Keene and Hart, "Please bring a bowl of vinegar water, some linen, and my medicine chest to Harrison's bedchamber."

Georgiana stood in the gallery above, looking down on the foyer. As Ravenna and Harrison topped the stairs and turned toward his bedchamber, she said, "Harrison? Are you hurt badly?"

He shook his head. "Not too badly. I'll be well."

She wrung her hands. "Can I bring you a glass of wine or brandy?"

He smiled. "Please. That would be most welcome."

When Ravenna had led him back to his bedchamber, he flopped into a nearby wooden chair with a grunt of relief.

Ravenna knelt beside him. "Remove your arm from the shirt so I can see it clearly."

He tenderly pulled his arm out, and Ravenna held a candle close to the wound to inspect it. "It's not a deep cut. You're very fortunate. You shouldn't have chased him out into the street."

"You called for help. I helped."

"Granted, but I didn't mean for you to chase him unarmed into the London streets at night. You might've come to far more harm."

"All ended well, Amma. Don't fuss at me now."

"Were you able to identify him at all?"

"Not at all."

She sighed, sitting on a footstool to wait for the supplies she needed. "That's unfortunate."

"Something tells me, though, Amma, he might have something to do with the stranger you warned Georgiana against earlier this evening. Am I correct in my assumption?"

"I don't know."

"Don't you think it's unfair for you to keep us in the dark if we are in danger?"

She looked down at her hands. "You're right. But, I hope you'll understand that in telling you the particulars, I can put someone else in danger."

He frowned. "Are you in trouble?"

"No." She sighed and searched his face. She picked through her past and pulled out the safest bits. "What I can tell you is…" She chose her words carefully. "My brother, whom you never met, was involved with some bad people. They are looking for him. They've been pestering me to find out where he is." It wasn't a lie, but it wasn't the whole truth either. "That's all I feel comfortable telling you right now."

He nodded. "I understand. And one of the men is pale with white hair and a limp?"

"Yes. He's the only one I know of, but there could be others."

"I see. How can I protect you and Georgiana if I don't know these things?"

She smiled at him tenderly. Though he was twenty-one, she still saw him as the young sixteen-year-old lad she'd first met when she married his father. Yet, even at twenty-one, he was still so young to carry the burden of supporting and protecting a family and estate. "Sweet Harrison." She squeezed his hand. "Thank you. You're so serious and brave. Very much like your father." The portion of his father she still loved. Tears filled her eyes. "He would be so proud." She wanted to change the subject. She looked at his feet. "Which foot hurts?"

"The left."

"I'm going to remove your stocking and shoe so I can see if it's swollen." She pulled his foot into her lap, removing his black loafer. She reached under his knee breeches to untie the ribbon from the top of the white silk stocking and pulled the stocking down to reveal his pale leg covered in auburn hair.

Georgiana entered with a glass of wine and stopped short. "Oh." She blushed and looked away. "Pardon me. I brought you a glass of wine." She eased forward, glancing between him and the floor. "I didn't expect you in, uh, *dishabille*."

He sniffed a laugh. *"Dishabille?"*

"Yes. It's a French word I learned recently from Hart. I didn't know what it meant until Mr. Emmett explained it to me."

Ravenna and Harrison shared an amused glance.

"Thank you for the wine." He reached out with his good arm. Their fingers brushed when she handed him the wine.

As Hart and Keene entered with the supplies Ravenna required, Georgiana faded into the shadows against the wall.

Ravenna tore off a piece of linen and dipped it in the vinegar water. "Georgiana, come here. You will need to know how to do this. Someday, you will have a family, and you'll need to know how to care for them. My mother taught me, and I'll teach you."

Georgiana stepped forward shyly.

Ravenna said, "I'm using vinegar water. The vinegar is good for cleaning." She cleaned the wound, explaining how it wasn't deep enough for stitches. Harrison sucked in his breath. Ravenna smiled. "The vinegar does sting a bit. If you don't have vinegar on hand, whisky, gin, brandy, or turpentine will work."

With the blood cleaned off, she removed an ointment from her medicine chest. "This is chamomile ointment." She explained the ointment and its uses and its ingredients as she rubbed a bit of the ointment on the cut then ripped a clean strip of linen. "Now, I'll wrap this tight. Once the bleeding stops, he can take off the wrapping."

Ravenna moved to Harrison's foot. "The foot isn't sprained or broken."

"How do you know?"

"There's no swelling or unusual color or bruises. So I won't need a poultice. Instead, I will wash the foot, then wrap it to give it support. I wager by morning his foot will feel better." She tore off another strip of linen and wrapped his foot. "I'm wrapping it tightly to help keep the foot in place." Ravenna wrapped the foot and tied the bandage into place. "There."

"Thank you, Amma." Harrison sipped his wine and slipped his injured arm back into his shirt sleeve.

"That was amazing!" Georgiana gasped. "How do you know such things?"

Ravenna laughed. "Growing up with a house full of raucous brothers, cousins, and uncles kept my mother busy with healing practices. They provided her with plenty of opportunities to teach me."

"I want to learn it all!"

"I'll teach you everything I know, for certain. Especially if Harrison insists on chasing strange men through the streets," she teased. "But for now..." Ravenna stood, nudging the girl out the door. "It's late. We've had much excitement and adventure tonight."

Georgiana paused in the doorway. "Good night, Harrison. I'm glad you're safe." She cast a lingering look of admiration at him, then disappeared down the hall."

"Good night, Georgiana," Harrison said, dropping a self-satisfied smile into his wine glass as he lifted it to his lips.

Ravenna kissed the top of Harrison's head and stroked his hair. "Rest well. I'm grateful you're safe. I couldn't bear losing you, too." She touched his cheek tenderly and left the room.

When she stepped into the hallway, Mr. Banks lingered in the hallway. "Ma'am, may I have a word?"

"Yes, Banks, what's the matter?" He opened his palm to reveal bits of a broken seal stuck to a bit of paper. "While you tended to Lord Birchfield, I became curious about how the intruder entered the house. So, I took the liberty of checking all the lower-level windows and doors leading to the exterior. I found no forced entry anywhere except in one location. The kitchen. Someone stuck this in the door's strike plate, preventing the door from latching completely."

Dread pushing on her chest, she pushed the black wax seal pieces together in his palm to reveal the shape of a harp. *The Unity.* Her throat went dry. The Unity had been in her home. In her bedchamber. She cleared her throat. "I see." She removed the pieces from his hand. "Thank you, Banks, for bringing this to my attention."

Banks continued. "What I can't figure out is how the intruder managed this. Did he send someone in his stead to pose as a visitor, and he or she pushed it into place when the kitchen staff wasn't looking or..."

She shuddered at the other conclusion, one indicating a far more serious concern. She finished his thought. "Or was it someone inside Gordon House colluding with the intruder?"

His mouth pulled downward, and he grew more somber. He nodded. "A terrible thought, milady," he whispered.

"Yes. But one we mustn't ignore." She rolled the broken wax pieces in her hand. The clock in the hall chimed once. Half past two in the morning. "It's late, Mr. Banks. Please go to bed. We will discuss this with the staff in the morning. "Thank you, again, for finding this. Good night."

Ravenna returned to her bedchamber with the seal for evidence. She re-lit her candle and searched the area where the intruder had been. What had he been looking for? She pored over the desktop and her vanity. He wasn't there to steal money or jewels because there were coins in a cup on her desk and jewels on her vanity. He left all that behind. Her eyes roamed over the space. He must've been connected to The Unity. What was he looking for?

Niall. The man was probably looking for information about her brother's location. The Unity had been looking for him for years. *The letters.* Of course, the intruder would search the desk. Most people kept their letters in their desks. Yet, as a former spy, she wouldn't dare keep important information in such an obvious location. She opened the wardrobe, knelt down, and pushed her shoes aside. She felt for the little notch in the wood at the back and lifted the small wood panel. She dipped her hand inside and felt the twine string around the letters. Relief washed over her. She removed them. She just needed to see them. She pressed the bundle of papers to her forehead. *Thank heavens!* Of course, her brother understood the danger. He had never given away his location except in the broadest terms. He was in America. Somewhere in the south. That's all she knew, and that's all the letters described. He'd been very careful never to provide any details.

For a brief moment, she considered burning letters, but...she ran her hands over the papers bundled with twine. She couldn't bear to. He was one of the few people in her family still alive. She returned the letters to their hiding spot, finding comfort in the fact they hadn't been discovered. The Unity had been looking for Niall for years, but when they'd learned of her betrayal and her part in destroying their plans, they began coming after her, too. She sighed and put the cover back in place, replaced the shoes, and prepared for bed.

Ravenna lay among the down blankets, staring at the moonlight pouring in through the window. She could find neither ease nor comfort; it was as if she lay on a bed of broken glass. The thought of a strange man in her room twisted her gut. And his clever method for gaining entrance into her home was more frightening in its subtlety.

She'd betrayed The Crown by gathering information from her late friend, Lord Hawkestone. The Unity had threatened to kill her and what remained of her family if she didn't help. When Hawkestone caught her, he demanded she reveal everything or suffer the execution reserved for traitors. The thought of hanging in the public square and the blemish of treason on her name terrified her more than The Unity. So she divulged everything. Under the threat of reporting her crime, he then insisted she feed the rebels false information while finding out their plans. Once Hawkestone had discovered everything he needed, he sent soldiers to put a stop to the planned invasion of England from Ireland.

When she'd married her husband, Philip, his position offered her much-needed protection from The Unity, but since his death, they had ramped up their threats and attacks against her. She couldn't continue like this, just sitting and waiting for them to kill her. Once she discovered Thornley's killer, she needed to find a way to seek out The Unity, to destroy their network, and put a stop to their threats forever. She thought she'd accomplished that a few months ago when she'd discovered Lord Hawkestone's killer, but, apparently, she'd only destroyed a branch of their organization—and stirred up a hornet's nest.

Her mind buzzed, flitting from one thought to another. The clock downstairs chimed four. She needed rest. She slipped from bed and opened her medicine chest to find a bottle of laudanum. She put a couple of drops of the red-brown liquid on her tongue, just enough to help her sleep, to ease her mind, and release the knots in her muscles. She screwed up her mouth at the bitter taste and crawled back under the covers. She sat up, her head against the headboard, waiting for the opiate to do its work.

Thankfully, the intruder had entered the house while the family was out. Her mind turned to a vivid image of the stranger sneaking from room to room, invading her home, and invading her space. Everything suddenly felt dirty and dishonored. She shuddered. What if he had come in while she slept, vulnerable and unable to defend herself? Her head began to feel both heavy and airy, and her eyelids drooped.

She left the bed again, pulled the bedchamber key out of the drawer in the vanity, and locked her door. It would inconvenience the staff in the morning when they set about their chores, but she didn't want to chance the man possibly coming back. He likely wouldn't, but having the door locked gave her a small measure of protection.

She returned to bed. Even with the door locked, she didn't feel entirely safe. The sanctum of her bedchamber had been tainted. She lifted her black lace fan from the bedside table. Flipping the gold medallion at the base, she released the blade inside and extracted it. She tucked the blade under her pillow and lay down, staring at the moonlight slicing across her bed. Somehow, in spite of her busy mind, the laudanum finally overtook her.

Chapter Twenty-Six

After only a few hours of sleep, Ravenna woke with the dawn and dressed in a black muslin day dress. Her head felt heavy and dry as though stuffed with cotton. She wanted to speak with the kitchen staff before they became too embroiled in their day's work. Checking the mirror, her face was wan, so she put a little rouge on her cheeks to give her face some color. Unfortunately, she had nothing in her cosmetic drawer to treat the dark bags pleating the skin under her eyes.

She jogged down two flights of stairs to the kitchen with the seal Mr. Banks had given her last night.

When Ravenna entered the kitchen, the staff stood and glanced at each other.

"Good morning," Mr. Banks said. "Is something the matter, ma'am?"

"Good morning, Banks. I wanted a word with the staff. I apologize for interrupting your breakfast. Please be seated. I won't keep you long."

The staff resumed their seats.

Ravenna continued. "Last night, as you know, we had an intruder. I found him in my room when I arrived home from the ball." They all nodded. "Mr. Banks has discovered the stranger likely entered through the kitchen." She placed the seal on the kitchen table. "He discovered this seal lodged in the strike plate of that door..." She pointed to the servants' door on the right. "To prevent the door from closing completely. Meaning any attempt to lock the door wouldn't be successful. The stranger could then come back at any time and enter the house with ease. Apparently, he came back last night while the family was at the prince's ball."

The servants looked among each other.

"Do any of you recall a stranger coming to the kitchen door?"

The cook, Mrs. Lyle, a large-boned, broad-shouldered woman with doughy jowls and gray-streaked dark hair, said, "It could be anyone, milady. There are many who come to the door to deliver coal, milk, candles, and other such household items."

"Yes, but they're likely to be the same people. Was there anyone who wasn't the usual?"

The scullery maid, a mousy girl named Junie, said, "There was a man who delivered the flour a few days ago; he were different, milady."

"How?"

"Well, the usual man is an older gent with a white beard and a big nose. This were a short man with hair as orange as that fire." She pointed to the fireplace where a kettle of porridge cooked above low flames. "And it stuck out all around under his cap. When I asked him where old Mr. Ford was, he said he was under the weather like."

"Did you at any time take your eyes from him?"

Junie thought. "Yes, ma'am, I did. He took on a coughing fit and asked if he might have a bit to drink. I got him a cup of small ale."

Ravenna and Mr. Banks exchanged a knowing glance. Mr. Banks said, "He must've stuffed the seal in the door when Hannah's back was turned."

"I'm so sorry," Junie said, her eyes large, worried, and filled with tears. "I didn't mean—"

Ravenna lifted her hand. "Don't fret about it, Junie. You had no way of knowing." She paused, then asked, "Was the man Irish?"

"It was difficult to tell. Sometimes, he sounded Irish, but he also sounded English."

"Like he was trying to hide his accent?"

"Maybe," Junie wrung her chapped hands.

"What was his name, Junie?" Mr. Banks asked.

She shrugged, diffident. "I don't know, sir. I didn't ask, and he didn't say."

Ravenna turned to Mrs. Lyle. "Where do we get our flour?"

"Albishore's Mill in Southwark," she said.

"Thank you." Ravenna picked up the wax seal pieces. "I want to apologize to you all. I have been too discreet for fear of alarming you. But I think now, I have reached the time to tell you to be on guard." She paused. She needed to choose her words carefully. She didn't want to cause undue fear, but she also needed to instill a sense of urgency in the staff. Further, she didn't want to reveal anything about her past as a spy, which would not only feed the gossip mill, spread like wildfire through the *ton,* and destroy whatever respect the staff had for her.

The servants exchanged worried glances.

"I don't believe any of *you* are in any direct danger, but there are some wicked men who intend to do me and my family harm." Several of them gasped. "I cannot go into the particulars about *why* these men seek to harm me, and the particulars are irrelevant, at any rate. The primary issue is I need you to be wary of any strangers around the premises. You should be vigilant about finding out who they are, ensuring you don't leave them alone, and so forth." She closed her fingers around the seal. "I'm sorry to put you in this position where you must live in fear and be on guard, but I hope the duration will be short." She tried to offer a reassuring smile, but it fell short. "Thank you for your attention. Please resume your breakfast." She turned to the cook and Mr. Banks. "Mrs. Lyle, please have coffee and a piece of last night's honey cake sent up. Mr. Banks, please have the carriage prepared. I'm going out this morning." She already had several errands to run, but she'd just added another.

She would pay a visit to the mill to search for the red-haired man.

After Ravenna finished writing an important letter to Reverend Haworth at The Penitent House, she dressed to go out, including her black bonnet with a veil in case she needed anonymity when she went to the Albishore Mill. She hung her black lace fan containing her dagger from her wrist. By the time Ravenna was ready to leave the house, Mr. Emmett had arrived to tutor Georgiana.

Ravenna met him in the foyer. "Mr. Emmett. What a happy surprise! I hadn't expected to see you so early in the morning after our late evening last night."

He was clean and polished, without any indication of sleepiness or fatigue. "Good morning, Lady Birchfield." He bowed. "I am eager to get started with my day and teach Miss Georgiana as much as I can before I begin working with the young princess." He stepped closer and said in a quieter voice, "And Miss Georgiana tells me she has some expertise with small children. I hope she can give me some advice on how best to manage them."

Ravenna smiled, sliding her hands into black kid gloves. "I understand. It's wise to get her assistance. What will you two work on today?"

"Surgeoning!" Georgiana shouted from the gallery above. She jogged down the stairs, her flaxen ringlets bouncing.

Amusement glowed in Mr. Emmett's brown eyes. "Pardon?"

Ravenna said with humor, "She has determined to study to be a lady surgeon."

"Is that so?" He watched Georgiana descend the stairs with a mixture of admiration and curiosity.

Georgiana landed beside them. "Yes, indeed. My Aunt Ravenna showed me something of the healing arts last night and it was the most fascinating and wonderful thing I've ever seen."

Emmett tipped his head, speaking with hesitation to Ravenna. "You're a lady-surgeon?"

"Not exactly. I have some knowledge of healing passed down to me from my mother through generations of women in our family. It's a fairly common practice among women as we're called on to tend to our sick and injured family and friends."

"Of course," he nodded. "I see." Then he turned to Georgiana. "Yet, you want to be an actual surgeon?" His mouth tipped into a sideways grin. "I fear that tends to be a man's profession because it can be rather, uh, grotesque at times with blood and gore and such."

"I don't care. I want to learn it."

"Even if you'll never be able to actually practice it?"

"There might be some forward-thinking person who would allow me to practice."

CHAPTER TWENTY-SIX

"You won't be able to train in any of the universities."

"This is what I've tried to tell her," Ravenna said.

Exasperation gripped Georgiana. "Why does everyone insist on dissuading me? I'll worry about the strategy. I only need someone to teach me what I need to know. You can do that, can't you, Mr. Emmett?"

Emmett looked between Ravenna and Georgiana. "To a point. If your aunt doesn't mind."

Ravenna shrugged a shoulder. "She will not be gainsaid. Unfortunately, my family is of a profoundly stubborn nature, rendering us only able to learn from the harshest experiences rather than the easier path of sage advice."

Emmett laughed. "So I gather." He turned to Georgiana. "I should remind you, Miss, I'm not a surgeon, so my knowledge is lacking in many areas."

"I don't mind. Teach me all you know, and I'll find someone else to teach me the rest." She linked her arm in his. "Let's see if there are any anatomy books in the library."

Ravenna left the tutor and his student to their work and stepped outside. The slate gray sky pressed low against the rooftops, and the wind fluttered her bonnet ribbons. It would likely rain today. She climbed into the carriage, asking the driver to take her to The Penitent House first. She needed to discuss with Reverend Howarth and Mariah the arrangements for the donor dinner.

Reverend Haworth and Mariah met her in the foyer. Reverend Howarth clasped his hands together. "Lady Birchfield! So good of you to come in answer to my letter. Let's step into the library to discuss the donor dinner."

She followed them down the hall of cream and ivy wallpaper to the library. Light from the windows flanking the fireplace poured across the room. Two walls were lined floor to ceiling with near-empty bookshelves while the remaining walls covered in mauve wallpaper displayed landscape paintings and reading chairs. In the center of the room spread a large table topped with an inkstand and paper.

The Reverend indicated a seat. "Please, be seated."

He and Mariah sat across from her. He said, "Miss Mariah and I have been discussing the dinner. We would like to invite everyone here next week, if you think that will give us enough time?"

"Yes. I think that would be perfect. Most people will leave town for their country homes around The Great Twelfth. So, hosting the dinner before August tenth is ideal. How many guests were you thinking about?"

He handed her a piece of foolscap paper with a list of names. "We have twenty primary donors I've listed here."

Her eyes fell to Lord Braedon's name, and her stomach fluttered a bit as her mind fell back to the last time she saw him: his frosty blue, wolfish eyes, his full lips smiling at her as he teased her. The touch of his hand. She forced back the thought and continued reading the list. "There are at least twenty names here." She looked around. "Plus, you would need to invite their spouses and include the women from this house. That's about sixty people."

"Granted."

"Do you have enough space here?"

"I think so. Our dining hall accommodates up to fifty people at least and we could probably squeeze in a few extra if necessary. When we designed the house, I wanted a large dining hall and sleeping quarters, hoping to accommodate as many women as we could rescue." He lifted a finger and looked over his spectacles. "Furthermore, I predict many of these guests will not come. Either they will have previous engagements, or they wouldn't want to…" He templed his hands and pursed his lips. "Ah, associate with women formerly of the street. Yet, I feel compelled to send the invitations even to those who might decline."

"Yes, of course. I do know that at least three will not accept. Lord Braedon, Lady Dianthe, and her mother are all out of the country."

"I understand."

"I would also recommend taking these names off the list. I happen to know this one has a daughter getting married that day. This one is currently very ill. This one has already left for the country. And this one will be traveling soon." She scratched through the names on the list. "I cannot speak for the others."

"Oh. See!" He smiled. "My prediction is coming true already."

Since paper was expensive, in addition to the required printer's fees, Ravenna said, "Please allow me to issue the invitations to the remaining guests." Reverend Howarth made a gesture to object. She raised her hand and stopped him. "Please. I insist. Besides, based on this list, I will need to deliver the invitations and visit with each recipient."

"Dear Lady Birchfield," Reverend Howarth said. "I don't know how our little charity could exist without you."

"You are too kind, sir." She folded the list and put it in her reticule. "I'll take this with me."

They then discussed what foods should be prepared. It was decided that the vegetables and fruits needed would come from The Penitent House's garden and hothouse and that they would provide the fattened goose, bread, and desserts. Ravenna insisted that she and a few of the other committee ladies would provide wine, cheese, and a few meat dishes. Ravenna also offered to loan her cook, Mrs. Lyle, and wanted to offer her servants to serve the meal, but Mariah insisted The Penitent House women would provide the service.

When the meeting came to an end, Ravenna stood. "Once I've received acceptances from the invitees, we should meet again to establish the seating arrangements."

"Yes, of course." The Reverend and Mariah walked to the door with her. "Thank you for coming by and for taking so much upon yourself. We are so very proud of the work we have done here. It is our desire to keep the donations coming in for as long as possible, and I believe showing our gratitude will assist with that endeavor."

"It certainly won't hurt," Ravenna said. They all chuckled.

They stepped into the hall, and as they engaged in idle chatter about the dinner, different dishes, and the weather, a young woman approached holding a rose-colored dress.

Ravenna studied the dress. She'd seen that color and taffeta fabric before.

The girl was short and wiry, with frizzy brown curls tamed under a bandeau and a large gap between her two front teeth. "Mariah, I think you'll like what I've done." She held up the hem of the dress. "You see here. You can't even tell it was ripped, can you?"

Ripped? Ravenna perked. Only a couple days ago, she'd found a piece of fabric matching this dress and had asked Lady Thornley if it had belonged to her. Lady Thornley denied it, saying she was too old for that color. Ravenna frowned at Mariah.

"No! It's lovely work, Annie," Mariah said.

Annie flipped the hem around to show the underneath. "See here. Where it was ripped, I stitched it together, which left a bad patch. So, starting here..." She pointed to the repaired rip. "I sewed some ribbon all around, ending where I began. Then I put these little embroidery embellishments to further mask the repair."

"You've done remarkable work, Annie," Mariah gushed, running the hem through her hands, studying her friend's work. "This was my favorite dress. I was so sad when it ripped. I can't wait to wear it to the donor dinner."

Suspicions rose in Ravenna's mind. "The work is impeccable. You can't even tell it was damaged. You are lucky to have such a talented seamstress here." She pressed forward, hoping to get more information. "How did you tear it?"

Mariah said, still looking at the dress. "I'm not sure. I think it happened on the day of the gala at the Thornley House. I caught it on the entry door."

Ravenna blanked her face, though inside, she gasped. Why wouldn't Mariah look at her? She seemed to be purposely avoiding eye contact. Ravenna struggled to keep her voice steady and warm with empathy. "I understand. Such accidents happen all the time."

Ravenna said her goodbyes and left The Penitent House to visit the Albishore Mill.

She sat back and thought about Mariah and the rose-colored dress. When Ravenna had found the scrap of cloth, she'd verified it wasn't Lady Thornley's. But she was certain it was the same fabric and color as the scrap of cloth in her possession. The next time she came to The Penitent House, she needed to bring the scrap with her to compare it to Mariah's dress. Somehow. If the fabrics matched, it would mean Mariah had been in the garden at Thornley Hall. There were only two reasons for her to be in the garden behind the house. First, she might've had a genuine curiosity about the garden and a burning desire to sneak away from the gala to see it. Or…Ravenna cringed inwardly. She couldn't bear the thought, because she genuinely liked Mariah. She seemed to set a good example for the other women. She was steady, smart, well-behaved, and studious. But Ravenna couldn't escape the evidence that seemed to be pointing to a question she didn't want to consider: What if Mariah had something to do with Lord Thornley's murder?

Chapter Twenty-Seven

Ravenna stared out the carriage window, watching the multitude of carriages, horses, and people go by. The wind had picked up, billowing the coats and dresses of the pedestrians, forcing them to hold their hats and bonnets in place. Darker clouds rolled in. She'd hoped her errands would be completed and she'd be at home again before the rain came. It looked as though her luck was about to run out.

Before she had reached the Thames, however, the sight of flaming red hair caught Ravenna's attention. He was pale, short, and thin. Just as Hannah, her scullery maid, had described. But what were the chances she should see that very man out of the nearly million people in London? Another man came up behind him. They shook hands. This man had dark hair. He looked familiar. She couldn't be certain because his back was partially turned to her, but looked quite similar to Mr. Emmett's brother, Robert.

She knocked on the roof of the carriage, signaling the driver to stop; it slowed to rest across from the Dancing Fiddler tavern. The footman, Miller, helped her to the stones. She pulled her veil down over her face and clasped her folded black lace fan in her hand, taking a sense of safety from it.

Lifting her skirts to keep them out of the muck, she ran on tiptoes across the street and entered the Dancing Fiddler. Several people looked in her direction, curious to see a widow of some apparent refinement in the tavern. But they soon turned their attention back to their ales and conversations. Ravenna noticed the red-haired man and his friend go up the stairs. She quickly dug into her reticule for some coins. Typically, as a matter of propriety, she should've had her footman secure the room on her behalf, but she didn't have time for propriety. One thing she had learned in her life as a commoner was that a good deal of impropriety could be overlooked for the right price. Further, few people cared about a widow's comings and goings as long as she didn't cause much of a spectacle. Widows were invisible, moving like shadows in society.

She didn't really need a room. She just needed a reason to go upstairs without the landlord questioning her motives. "I need a room, please. For only a few hours."

The bald, beefy man narrowed his eyes. "I don't want trouble here…"

She tossed a shilling sterling on the countertop, three times the room's price. "I'll be no trouble. And you should forget you ever saw me."

He looked at the coin. Then at her. With a perturbed sneer, he grabbed up the coin and handed her a key. "Second door on the left. And I never saw you."

She grabbed the key and rushed up the stairs. She paused at the first door to listen. No one was there. She stepped to the door across the hall and heard a female voice, then moved to the next door and heard two male voices. She squatted in front of the door and peeked in the keyhole to find the red-haired man and the back of the dark-haired man who turned as he paced. *Robert Emmett!* Her fist tightened around her fan. Why was he here? And what did he have to do with this man who may have broken into her home last night?

Robert said, "Were you able to find anything?"

"No. I was interrupted. The woman came home and caught me at her desk."

Ravenna's mouth dropped open. *Vile miscreant.* Why would Robert Emmett want anything from her room?

"That's unfortunate. We'll figure out another way. Let's discuss the other matter."

Just then, Ravenna heard someone coming up the stairs, so she jumped up and turned to put the key in the door of her room. The man and a woman looked at her and smiled, then entered their room. She unlocked the door and pretended to go in. Once the couple's door closed, she stuck her head out her door and peeked around to ensure she was again alone. She returned to her position at Robert Emmett's door.

They had lowered their voices so she caught only snippets of their conversation.

The red-haired man said in a thick Irish brogue, "...a cart of muni..." The noise below in the tavern clouded her hearing. She strained to listen. "Midnight...then loading them...make their way east. I have a man there... across the channel to home. Can you get more men?"

"I think I can. There are many here, angry...their work taken...silk trade gone to the blasted Huguenots. Better yet, they're still communicating with family and friends back home. They can rouse more. I'm sure of it."

She heard footsteps on the stairs again. Aggravated, she rushed across the hall into her own room, anxious to know what information she might be missing. She peeked through the keyhole to watch a servant deliver a tray to the couple's room and then disappear back down the stairs.

Ravenna eased open the door and returned to her station. The two men had finished talking. The red-haired man handed a note to Robert.

"I'll let you know the moment I hear something, Fletcher." Robert tucked the note in the right-hand pocket of his great coat. They shook hands and headed toward the door.

Ravenna jumped to her feet and flew down the stairs. She slid the key on the bar counter on her way out of the tavern. Once outside, she stood on the pavement, waiting for Robert and Fletcher to come out. Rain began to patter against her bonnet and the stones. Soon, Robert came out of the tavern alone. Ravenna launched herself against him as if they had accidentally bumped into each other.

"Oh, mercy!" She put on her Irish brogue, in hopes it would soften his attitude toward her. She fell against him. "I'm so sorry. I wasn't watching where I was goin', sir." As he attempted to hold her up to keep her from falling, she dipped her hand into his right-side coat pocket. "Ach, ma ankle. I think I might've injured it."

By now, a light, steady rain began to fall. He was so focused on helping her stand, he didn't notice when she'd extracted the paper from his pocket.

She stood and slipped her fan off of her wrist to make it drop to the ground. As he bent to pick it up for her, she pushed the paper under her veil and under her bonnet.

Ravenna accepted the fan as he offered it to her. "Thank you, sir. I'm so very sorry for bumping into you." Though the veil hid her identity, she held her breath, hoping he wouldn't recognize her.

He didn't seem to remember her from their one meeting at the ball. "May I escort you somewhere?" He looked around, distracted.

"Oh, no, thank you." She scanned the street. She didn't want him to see her get in a carriage. He might recognize it as the Birchfield family carriage. She spotted a mantua maker across the street. "I'm going to be measured for a new dress. Thank you, kind sir."

He gave a quick nod and a touch to the brim of his hat and sped away.

She stepped into the street, remembering to limp, and headed toward the mantua maker. When she reached the street, she turned to watch him. He paid no attention to her. He had already rounded the street corner.

Ravenna ran in the opposite direction toward her carriage, darting between people. Miller opened the door, and she jumped inside. She sat back against the kid leather seat, panting—a little from the running and a little from her boldness to not only spy on a potentially dangerous man, but to pick his pocket. She pushed the veil away from her face, rolling it rest on the brim of her bonnet.

Miller asked, "Where would you like to go, milady?"

She considered taking what she'd learned to Mr. Chadwick, but she needed some time and quiet to think through everything first. More than anything, she just wanted to go home, have a big cup of tea and some of Mrs. Lyle's delicious ginger biscuits, and duck into a book. However, it would have to wait until she completed one more errand. "Please take me to Mr. Humphrey's Print Shop. Then we'll go home."

Chapter Twenty-Eight

There would be no peace at Gordon House. That much was evident as soon as Ravenna stepped inside the home. No sooner than she'd handed her gloves and bonnet to Mr. Banks, secreting the purloined note among the rest of the mail on the tray, she was accosted by Georgiana.

The girl was in hysterics. Her hair in disarray, her face red and tear-streaked. "He has challenged Mr. Emmett to a duel!"

Ravenna blinked at her. Then glanced at the butler. "Mr. Banks, will you excuse us for a moment?"

He dipped his head and stepped down the hall.

"Now, calm down…" She took Georgiana by the hands and led her to a bench in the foyer. She pushed the hair out of Georgiana's face and handed her a handkerchief. "Now, *calmly* tell me what the matter is. Who has challenged Mr. Emmett?"

Georgiana blew her nose and wiped her eyes with her hands. Her breath stuttered in shaking gasps. "Harrison. Harrison slapped him across the face and challenged him to a duel."

Ravenna knew Harrison was jealous of the attention Georgiana gave to other men, but this sounded out of character. "That doesn't sound like Harrison. Why would he do such a thing?"

Georgiana struggled with her words. "Something about honor. And protecting me." Her breath fluttered. "I don't need Harrison's protection. I need him to leave me alone. And leave Mr. Emmett alone." She doubled over, her face in her hands, and began crying anew.

Ravenna rubbed her back. "Sh, sh, sh. All is well. I will talk to Harrison. Is Mr. Emmett still here?"

"No." Her breath shuddered. "He left and said he might never return. What am I going to do? I need a tutor if I want to be a lady surgeon."

Ravenna gathered her patience. She hoped Georgiana would eventually drop this lady-surgeon notion, which was certain to lead to an unkind future full of suffering. She forced her voice into a soothing calmness. "Go to your bedchamber. Wash your face, take a nap, fix your hair, and regain your composure. I will talk to Harrison and try to fix this situation. You shall have a tutor, even if it's not Mr. Emmett."

Despair marked Georgiana's face. "Noooo," she whined. "I *like* Mr. Emmett. He explains things so well. He helps me understand. He—"

Ravenna squeezed her hand. "I won't hear more. I said I will speak to Harrison and do my best to fix this. Go on."

Scowling, Georgiana sniffled and stood. "Yes, ma'am." She slumped up the stairs.

"Mr. Banks," Ravenna called.

He stepped out from an alcove down the hall and approached. "Yes, milady."

"Sounds like we've had some excitement here today."

"It would seem so, ma'am." He struggled against a smile.

"Please send tea and biscuits to Miss Georgiana's bedchamber. And please send a small nuncheon to my room."

"Yes, ma'am."

"Is Lord Birchfield still home?"

"He is not, ma'am. He went out for a ride shortly after the, uh, event."

"When he arrives home, please tell him I *insist* on seeing him."

"Yes, ma'am."

Ravenna grabbed the mail from the tray and closed herself in her bedchamber. After she changed out of her damp clothes and poured herself a glass of port, she sat near the dead fireplace covered with a bough-pot bursting with white, pink, and purple lilac and sprigs of lavender, mint, and ivy. She covered herself with a shawl to break the chill and laid the stack of letters, visiting cards, and invitations in her lap.

She had much to think about. First, there was Mariah Vincent at The Penitent House. She had a rose-colored dress with a rip in it. The color of the dress was very much like the scrap of fabric she'd found. While that didn't secure her as a suspect, it didn't look good. There was a chance she had simply been wandering through the garden without permission. She would ask Mariah about it the next time they met. Also, Ravenna needed to take the fabric sample with her and compare it to the dress, just in case she was wrong. It was possible she had misjudged the color. She wanted to be certain before she accused Mariah of anything. It could destroy her reformation to be accused of something so vile.

Then there was the matter of Mr. Emmett's brother, Robert, and the red-haired man, Fletcher. She'd heard Fletcher say he'd been in her house. And he was Irish. He must be connected to The Unity. But he was meeting with Robert, and Robert seemed to know about Fletcher in her room. They were working together. But, were *both* Emmett brothers actually in The Unity or simply colluding with them? It was possible only Robert was involved, and Josiah was ignorant of it. She'd often seen such political divisions in families when she'd lived in Wexford as the rebellion against England grew in strength. In fact, even in her own family, she had witnessed her Loyalist parents argue with her anti-Loyalist brother, Niall.

Either way, she didn't like what Robert and Fletcher were up to. They had been discussing a cart of something at midnight and loading up. Were they merely smugglers? No. There would've been no reason to be snooping in her room if that was the case. Then they said something about going across the channel and gathering men. The pieces began clicking together to form the whole picture. *Rebellion.* But where? When?

She pulled the note she'd stolen from Robert's pocket out of the stack of mail and opened it. It looked like a poem.

At St. George of Clennam
There lies the ghost of Billy O'Brien
Who'd been shot with guns and a cannon

He lost a leg by powder kegs
And never saw his dear Éirinn again

But by the stroke of midnight he rises,
Full of holes and a leg of wood.
He dances a jig to the fiddler's tune
'Til meeting four men at Albishore docks
And he begs them to take him to his Éire.

Good Billy will sail from England
To search for his precious lass Éire
Waiting on the shores of the Bray
With a hug and kiss they're together again
And then they'll have their glorious day!

She frowned at the paper. At first glance, the poem was strange and nonsensical—and frankly, horrible. Had she not witnessed the note being passed and not heard the bits of conversation she'd heard, she would think this was nothing more than a silly and poor attempt at poetry. She read the poem again. There was something odd about this poem. Why would Fletcher give this awful poem to Robert? She read it again. There had to be more to it. She thought about it, playing with her bottom lip as she stared at the flowers in front of the fireplace. Then it hit her. What if there was a hidden message here? Julius Caesar often sent secret messages nearly two thousand years ago. So, it wasn't outlandish to think such messages were still in use—especially among rebels working in secret against the government.

She moved to her writing desk and picked up a pencil. She compared what she'd heard at the tavern to the information in the poem. She circled the word midnight. So they were going to meet at midnight, but where? She underlined all the places mentioned in the poem: St. George of Clennam, Albishore, Thames, Bray. St. George's of Clennam was a church down around the Southwark area. So maybe they were going to meet there. For

229

what? A cart of something. She thought for a moment. Fletcher had said something about 'loading up a cart of muni...'

Ravenna pressed her fingertips to her forehead and squeezed her eyes shut as if she could push out the answer. She mumbled. "Loading up a cart of muni...a cart of muni... muni... Munitions!" It was there in the poem: guns, powder kegs, a cannon. She scratched double lines under those words.

Some of the lines didn't quite make sense to her, but it seemed they, whoever *they* were, would meet at the Albishore docks. Probably to sail to Ireland. Fletcher had said something about crossing the channel to "home," and he was clearly Irish. Further, the poem mentioned Bray and Éire. The Celtic word for Ireland. Then she recalled Robert and Fletcher had discussed getting people together. They were, in fact, planning another rebellion. She sat back and looked at the paper. She needed to contact Mr. Chadwick. This was larger than what she could handle alone.

A knock sounded on her door. She folded the letter and squirreled it away. "Come in." She stood as Harrison opened the door and stepped in her room.

"Banks said you wanted to see me?"

"Yes, please come in. Close the door."

Harrison closed the door and sat in a chair across from her.

Ravenna sat with a sigh. "When I came home today, Georgiana informed me you slapped Mr. Emmett and challenged him to a duel. I would like to hear your side of the story."

He grew somber. "She's telling the truth."

"What provoked such rash behavior?"

"They were at their lessons, presumably. But when I walked into the drawing room, he was on top of her on the sofa, kissing her."

Ravenna's brows shot up. "Pardon?"

His chestnut brown eyes sparked. "It seems she neglected to tell you a critical part of the story."

"Oh, Georgiana." Ravenna groaned, rubbing her forehead. She shook her head. "I know you're jealous—"

"Forgive me. That's not the only reason. It is a part of it. But the larger part is that he has come into our home under the guise of a tutor only to take advantage of a girl inexperienced in the ways of men and the world. His behavior dishonors us all. Now that I'm Lord of the Birchfield estate and head of this family, I'll not stand for this."

"I see. Harrison, I appreciate your protectiveness, but dueling is illegal. And you're the last of your line. You can't do this. There are other ways. I'll dismiss him without a reference and tell people about what he's done. Soon, he won't be accepted in any respectable household in the *ton,* and he'll lose his position teaching the princess."

"Too late. The challenge has been issued. If I fail to go forward, I'll be branded a coward and my reputation ruined. A situation which will, of course, affect you and Georgiana. So, you see, there's nothing to be done about it."

Ravenna sighed. He was right in the particulars, but this situation was horribly wrong. "I've lost your father and your brother. I can't lose you, too, Harrison. Please, reconsider this."

A faint smile crossed his lips. "Sounds like you're assuming I'll lose the match. What if I win?"

"I'm being sincere. It's so dangerous, and if you're caught, you'll go to prison."

"We won't get caught. We're going to Battersea at dawn, and in a few moments' time, the matter will be settled, and we'll be on our way before anyone can catch us."

Ravenna drew deeply from her port. "If he kills you—"

"He won't. We're only firing two shots at twenty paces. It's not to the death."

"I know the intent is simply to shoot *toward* each other and prove your bravery. However, you know as well as I that the aim of these pistols isn't always to be trusted. What if one of you strikes the heart or the head accidentally?" Ravenna sighed.

"That is the risk one takes in a duel."

"I can't say or do anything to change your mind?"

"You cannot. A man must protect his honor and the honor of his family."

He stood. "But I thank you for your concern. If there's nothing else?"

She shook her head. He bowed. She stood, searched his face, tears pricking at her eyes. She embraced him, hugging that lanky, mop-headed sixteen-year-old she met five years ago. "Please, Harrison. I wish you would listen to reason." She closed her eyes, tears slipping out with her silent prayers for his safety.

He pulled away from her gently, kissed her forehead. Suddenly, he was completely grown. A man. She watched him walk from the room. When had his shoulders broadened? When had he grown so tall?

The door clicked shut, and the lid on her rage flew open. *Damn Emmett's eyes!* She clenched her fists, and her blood pulsed with heat. *I don't care if he's in The Unity or not. After this, I'll see him ruined. He'll never be accepted in this town again. I'll see him chased out of polite society like the scoundrel he is!* Ravenna downed her drink, slammed the glass on the table, and marched to Georgiana's room. She knocked on the door, but didn't wait for permission to enter.

Georgiana was curled up on the bed, wiping her eyes and blowing her nose. She sat up. "What's the matter?"

Ravenna stood by the bed with crossed arms. "I've just spoken with Harrison, and he explained the entire story. Seems there's much you didn't tell me."

Georgiana flushed, looked down, and scooted to sit on the edge of the bed. "I'm sorry I didn't tell you everything."

Ravenna shook her head. "How could you be so thoughtless, Georgiana? You've behaved in a disreputable manner with a man you barely know. Things could've gotten out of control and landed you in a great deal more trouble and heartache than you're currently suffering."

"I'm sorry." Georgiana's lip trembled. "I didn't know what to do. I like him. And when he kissed me, I didn't want to say no."

"Well." Ravenna sighed. "You should know Harrison will not call off the challenge because he believes Mr. Emmett's behavior has dishonored you and this family. While I don't like the dueling, he's not wrong in philosophy."

Georgiana clutched Ravenna's arm. "You must stop them!"

"I can't. I tried. Harrison won't hear of it. He's quite determined."

"But if one of them is killed, I won't be able to live with myself."

"I'm sorry, and my heart aches that you're in this position, but there's nothing to be done now. We must let it play out and hope for the best."

Georgiana broke into tears, hiding her face in her hands. "I'm so sorry. I didn't mean for any of this to happen."

Ravenna didn't know what to do. Part of her wanted to scoop the girl into her arms and comfort her. Another part of her wanted Georgiana to sit with her suffering in order to learn the hard way that her decisions had consequences, not just for herself but for others, too. She clenched her fist, her nails digging into her palm, while her heart twisted in its cage. She could no longer bear it. She sat on the bed beside Georgiana, wrapped her arm around the girl, and tried to console her.

Chapter Twenty-Nine

When Ravenna had calmed Georgiana—and left Keene to watch over her—she called for a footman to prepare the carriage. While she waited, she dashed off a note to Catherine.

Dearest Catherine,

Horrible news! Mr. Josiah Emmett, whom I had entrusted with Georgiana's education, has sought to impart a different sort of education to her. Fortunately, Harrison intervened. There is more I would tell you, but I will wait until I speak with you in person. Emmett's attempt to dishonor my niece must brand him as a scoundrel and guarantee he will never find refuge in this town again. You know what to do.

Ever yrs.

R.

That would settle much of the matter. Catherine stood at the center of the rumor mill. She would know how to spread the word about Emmett while protecting the reputations of Georgiana, Ravenna, Harrison, and Gordon House.

The carriage was announced. She jerked on her gloves and took up her fan. There was another matter to attend to now. The carriage rattled down Grosvenor, past Buckingham Palace, toward Westminster, turning left onto Barton Street before reaching the ancient abbey. The carriage stopped in front of an old Tudor-style tenement. The white building with brown beams striping the front stood, leaning and unshapely on the corner of the street.

Not waiting for the footman, she jumped from the carriage and knocked on the green door.

A dumpy, red-faced woman answered the door, wiping her hands on her apron.

Ravenna assumed this was his landlady. "I would like to speak with Mr. Emmett."

Her rheumy gray eyes took in Ravenna with surprise. "Yes, milady, right this way," she said, her missing teeth lisping her words.

The house smelled of onion and turnips. Ravenna followed the wobbly woman across creaking wood floors to a small, dusty room filled with a worn, lumpy sofa and chairs. "If 'ee wait here, milady, I'll get him for 'ee. Can I get 'ee some tea?"

"No, thank you. I shan't be long."

The woman nodded and disappeared.

Ravenna paced her anger into the worn rug, her fingertip tapping the gold medallion on her fan.

Mr. Emmett opened the door, his surprise breaking into a genial smile. "Lady—"

Jerking off her glove, she rushed toward him and slapped him across the face with a loud pop. "You blasted scoundrel!"

"Ah," he bowed his head and stepped into the room sheepishly. He pushed the door closed, holding the red blotch flaming across his cheek. He motioned to a nearby chair. "Please, sit. Let's—"

"No. I will not sit and discuss anything as if we are friends."

"Very well." He stiffened. "Then you won't mind if I sit."

"I don't care what you do."

"Why are you here?" He sat on the sofa and relaxed into the corner, crossing his legs and resting his hands on his knee.

"I've come to ask you to refuse to duel my stepson."

He lifted his chin and nodded. "I see." He sighed. "I wish I could honor your request, but I cannot. I have been challenged and must defend my honor."

"Honor?" She scoffed. "What *honor*? I trusted you to come into my home to tutor my niece and help her gain a useful education. Instead, you attempt to seduce her and ruin her." Her finger itched to release the blade from her fan.

"I'm sorry for what happened with Georgiana."

"Unfortunately, she's fond of you."

"I'm fond of her. Truly. She's beautiful, charming, and sweet. If I were in a position to ask for her hand—"

Ravenna spat. "I'd sooner die than allow you to have her hand after what you've done. Had you approached me with respect and asked to court her, had you pursued the matter like a gentleman, I might feel differently. Instead, you chose to approach the matter like a fox in a hen house."

"I do apologize for my...."

"Dissimulation? Deceit?"

"Very well. I didn't approach you because I thought you wouldn't agree to it. I didn't have steady employment and no money. I hoped, if things proceeded well in tutoring the princess, I might secure a future. I had planned to approach you at that time to make my intentions toward Georgiana known."

Ravenna shook her head. "If you could wait to approach me, then you might've waited to pounce on my niece, too. Yet, you did not. I want you to refuse to duel."

"I cannot."

"And there's nothing I can say or do to persuade you?"

"What sort of man would I be if I ran from my duty?"

She glowered at him. "Very well. So be it." She spun on her heel to leave. When she opened the door, the chubby woman stood on the other side. Caught, she blushed and skittered away. Ravenna turned and glared at him. "I'll tell you exactly what sort of man you'll be..."

Frowning, he stood.

"You'll be absolutely ruined. The reputation you hope to salvage will lay in tatters when I am finished with you. The wheels are already in motion."

Ravenna rose before dawn and dressed in a black dress and black pelisse. Harrison hadn't asked for her intervention in the duel, but she was going anyway—with her medicine chest—in the event her limited medical skills were needed.

She and Hart lingered in the foyer, waiting for the carriage, when Harrison came down the stairs, pale with dark circles under his eyes. He wore his greatcoat, black kid gloves, and hat. His tobacco pantaloons were tucked into shiny Hessian boots. He looked as though he was ready to attend a picnic rather than a duel—but for his father's pistol case tucked under his arm.

He paused on the stairs. "What are you two doing?"

Ravenna whispered, "Waiting for you. We're going with you."

"No, you're not. It could be dangerous."

Ravenna scoffed at the irony. She held up her medicine chest. "Our presence might be the difference between an injury and a death. We're not going to interfere with your fight. Though I will ask you one more time to reconsider."

"I'm determined to make the cad pay his debt of honor to this house and family."

Ravenna inhaled and released a cleansing breath. She said a silent prayer for the safety of both men. She wanted them both to go home to their families—even if Mr. Emmett attempted to seduce her niece and might be tied to a family of Irish rebels attempting to commit treason.

They all climbed into the carriage, sitting in anxious silence as they crawled by St.

James's Palace and Buckingham Palace toward the Thames. The sky grew lighter, changing from dark gray to a dusky purple as the sun approached the horizon. They crossed the river. The stench of fish and offal wafted up as they crossed the bridge. Sometimes, the highest heat of summer rendered the stench rising from the Thames unbearable since the populace emptied their sewage into the river. But, thankfully, the cooler air of dawn reduced the fetor.

The sun marched forward quickly. Already a gold sliver appeared on the horizon as the purple-gray sky morphed into pale blue streaked with pink. They trailed alongside the park, turning in toward the lake, where the fog rolled off of the water and blanketed the land around it. The silhouette of two horses tied to a tree and two men stood in the distance.

The carriage pulled down the lane and parked near the water. Harrison climbed out of the carriage, pulled off his great coat and his olive suit coat. He cut a dashing figure in his linen waistcoat and puffy shirt sleeves. He opened his pistol case and selected his pistol.

Horse's hooves sounded behind them.

"Who is that?" Ravenna peeked out the carriage window, hoping it wasn't a Bow Street Runner. She couldn't see him clearly. But soon, Lord Donovan emerged from the fog and slid from his saddle to speak with Harrison.

"Donovan!" Ravenna said. "What are you doing here?"

His shoulder-length blond hair was loose from its usual ponytail, and a light stubble darkened his square jaw. He had refrained from wearing an ascot, his collar open at the neck.

Surprised, he straightened and bowed. "Lady Birchfield, Miss Hart." He smiled warily. "Pardon me, but I'm far more concerned about your presence! This is hardly the place for ladies. I beg you to return home, madam."

"I will not. I brought my medicine chest. If someone gets hurt in this stupid enterprise, I hope to offer aid. Now I ask again: why are you here?"

He chuckled. "I'm Harrison's second. In the event something goes wrong after the first shot, it's my duty to replace him. And I'm going to count them off."

"Well, I'd be far more appreciative if you could stop this madness."

"I fear I cannot. As his second, I've already tried to negotiate a settlement. Both men refused. The matter can only go forward now."

A whistle sounded from across the field.

"It's time," Harrison said, grabbing the pistol kit and handing it to Donovan.

Ravenna grabbed Hart's hand and watched her stepson, the last of her husband's family, stride across the field with Donovan at his side. The light breeze rippled Harrison's linen shirt, which shone like a light against the fog. Donovan's great coat billowed with his steps. Mr. Emmett and his second met them on the field. There was a brief conversation, and then the duelers stood back-to-back. Lord Donovan and the other second stood to the side, and Donovan began counting the paces as the duelers took their steps. The men turned and took aim. A deep stillness fell over the land. It seemed even the birds held their breath. In unison, the men fired their pistols. Hart jumped and squeaked at the sudden blast. The sound echoed across the field. The horses neighed and snorted.

Ravenna froze, every muscle hard as marble, her hand over her heart. She searched the men for signs of a wound. No one doubled over or grasped a part of their body. No blood bloomed into clothing. *Thank heavens!* Just one more. She inhaled, closed her eyes, and said a silent prayer as she breathed out her fear.

The duelers and seconds separated to their starting point. The seconds handed fresh pistols to the primaries. Harrison and Emmett gathered back-to-back in the center of the dueling space. Again, Donovan counted off their paces.

However, as the men turned, someone ran from behind the tree. A woman. Ravenna squinted. "Georgiana!" she shouted, pounding the window. "Georgiana, no!" Ravenna climbed over Hart, jumped out of the carriage, and ran in the dew-laced grass toward Georgiana, shouting, "Georgiana! No!"

But it was too late. It all happened at once. The men fired as soon as they turned. And just as Georgiana crossed behind Mr. Emmett, she froze in shock and dropped to her knees, screaming and holding her upper arm.

The men all paused, stunned, as Ravenna rushed forward and dropped to her knees in the cold, dewy grass beside her niece. "Georgiana, lay back let me see."

The girl screamed and cried, blood dripping between her fingers. Ravenna pulled her hand away. The arm of her spencer had a hole in it, but it was in the way. The men gathered around them. "An ascot. Quick. Someone give me one."

Donovan pulled his from his pocket and handed it to her. She wadded it up and pushed it against the hole. She glanced over her shoulder. "Hart!"

Hart dropped beside her with the medicine chest.

Ravenna flipped the medallion on her fan and withdrew the dagger. "Georgiana, lay still." Ravenna put the dagger tip in the hole of the cloth and cut away at it until a much larger tear emerged. She dropped her dagger and, with both hands, ripped open the garment to reveal Georgiana's bare arm. A small hole oozing blood greeted her. Ravenna stared at it. She had a decision. She'd never extracted a bullet. She could cause further damage. Or she could leave the bullet and send for a surgeon. If she sent for a surgeon, what were the chances Georgiana would lose a large quantity of blood? Further, would the surgeon report Harrison for dueling? The bullet seemed to be lodged in muscle. Maybe her decision should depend on how deep the bullet rested.

"Hart, give me the laudanum."

She received the small bottle from Hart and lifted Georgiana's head. "Here, take a sip of this. Just a bit." Georgiana sipped and winced at the bitter taste. Ravenna lowered her head to the ground. "It's going to make you feel strange. Lightheaded, tired, and dreamy."

She took in a deep breath and exhaled. She picked up her dagger, rolled it in her hand nervously. Georgiana's eyes shone full of pain and fear. "I'm going to stick this blade in the wound to test the depth of the bullet. This will hurt, darling, but I need you to be brave and be very still."

Georgiana nodded, tears streaming from her eyes. Harrison dropped to his knees at Georgiana's other side. He took her hand. "Here. Squeeze my hand. You'll be well. Look at me."

Donovan removed a leather glove from his hand. "Here, bite down on this, so you don't cause further harm to yourself." He handed the glove to Harrison to put the glove between her teeth. Emmett stood at a distance, blanched and somber. His second had disappeared.

Ravenna stuck her dagger in the wound until it hit the small metal ball. Georgina winced and whimpered, biting down on her bottom lip. The ball was about a quarter of an inch deep, if that, and, thankfully, lodged in the muscle. When Ravenna removed her dagger, she wiped the spot to judge the flow of blood. It was oozing slowly. Another good sign. "I think it's best if I take it out now. I will be as gentle and quick as I can."

Georgiana nodded.

Ravenna wiped her forehead on the sleeve of her pelisse. She let out a huff of breath and took a moment to steady herself and her hand. She said a silent prayer and gently, slowly eased the dagger into the hole, slipping the tip along the side of the ball and scooping underneath.

Georgiana bit down on the leather glove, releasing a guttural squeal. Tears streamed along the side of her face.

"Hold still," Harrison said, rubbing her forehead. "You'll be well."

"I know," Ravenna whispered. "I know it hurts, dear." She pushed the tip of the dagger against the bullet, easing up, up, up, little by little, toward the opening. Until finally popping it out. It rolled off her arm, leaving a bloody trail until it dropped into the grass. Blood trickled from the wound.

Ravenna sighed in relief. "Hart. Give me the garlic chives tincture."

Hart handed it to her, and Ravenna poured the garlic-chive oil over the wound. Then she took the cut-off portion of Georgiana's spencer and folded it small, pressing it over the wound. "Hart, hold this."

Hart reached to hold the patch. Ravenna unfolded the bloody ascot, wound it tightly around the wound, and tied it off. "This will suffice until I can get you home and change the dressing. We should go. I need to wash my hands. Harrison put Georgiana in the carriage. I'll be there directly."

Ravenna knelt by the lake to wash the blood off her hands and dagger. When she rose, Mr. Emmett stood beside her. "What you did was incredible…"

Ravenna didn't want to hear from him. He was to blame for much of this horrid event. Unable to look at him, she wiped the blade of her dagger on her dress to dry it. She had hired him to tutor her young niece, and he took advantage of the girl's naivete and abused Ravenna's trust in him. Further, what Mr. Emmett did not know, she'd recently seen his brother colluding with a man who may or may not also be a member of The Irish Unity. She no longer had patience for this man. She jammed the dagger into her fan and locked it in place.

He was still speaking. "Thank you for saving Georgiana. I—"

"Enough." Ravenna held up her hand, stopping his speech. "I need to attend to my niece, so I'll be brief. I did what I had to do. It wasn't her fault that she'd been deceived by an adult man who should've known better than to abuse the trust of her and her family. I don't like dueling. I wish Lord Birchfield hadn't taken such irresponsible action, but it's been done. Know this, Mr. Emmett. You are no longer welcome at Gordon House, and should you come near any one of us again, you do so at your own peril. Do you understand?"

He blinked. "You certainly do not mince your words, madam. I understand you perfectly."

"Good." She spun on her heel and marched across the field, the dew gathering on her hemline and soaking her shoes.

Ravenna climbed into the carriage where Harrison held Georgiana, her head laid over on his shoulder as she slept off the laudanum.

He started to speak. And Ravenna said, "Harrison, it's best if you don't speak to me at the moment. I'm gravely disappointed in your insistence on proceeding with the duel. This injury to Georgiana is your fault."

"She's the one who ran onto the field."

"Yes, but had there been no duel, then she wouldn't have felt compelled to her rash actions. I'm so thankful you weren't hurt or killed. But both of you have behaved with supreme stupidity. All I want in this moment is silence."

Harrison glared at her, his jaw tensing in knots. Then he released a heavy sigh and turned to stare out the window.

Chapter Thirty

When the sullen party had returned to Gordon House, Harrison carried the sleeping Georgiana upstairs to her bedchamber. Ravenna asked a maid to send up vinegar water and fresh linen. Keene carried in the supplies. She gasped. "Cor', what happened to her?"

"She's been shot. We need to change the wound. Set the bowl on that table there. Get a fresh nightgown for her and help me get her undressed." They undressed Georgiana, and Ravenna removed the bloody bandages. The bleeding had stopped.

Ravenna cleaned Georgiana's arm with vinegar water, then mixed a poultice of marshmallow, honey, and tallow. She rubbed it over the wound and re-wrapped the site with fresh, clean linen. Then she and Keene dressed Georgiana's limp form in a clean nightgown. Georgiana slept through most of the procedure, her eyes fluttering, her head lolling. It was like tending a giant rag doll.

When they had tucked Georgiana into bed Ravenna said, "Please have tea and a few biscuits sent to this room. I'll watch over her."

Keene bobbed a curtsey and left to fulfill her mission. Ravenna went to her bedchamber to grab a book and the invitations that had been delivered earlier. She sat at a table by the window, sipping tea, nibbling ginger biscuits, and addressing the invitation cards. Occasionally, she glanced at Georgiana, who continued to sleep peacefully, or she stood to place a hand on the girl's forehead to check for a rising temperature.

When she had finished the invites, she brought a chair near the bed, opened her book, and settled in to read Catherine Seldon's *Serena*. She spent the rest of the afternoon watching over Georgiana until the laudanum had worn off, and she sat up in bed, blinking. She sucked in a breath and grabbed her arm. "Oh. That hurts."

"Yes, it will for a while." Ravenna stood and tugged the bellpull in the corner. "Now that you're awake I'll have tea and broth brought up to carry you to dinner. How are you feeling? Do you feel feverish?"

"No. Just weak."

"Yes. You lost some blood. So, you will feel a little weak for a few days. You need to eat and rest. You'll be better soon." Ravenna sat on the bed and brushed a hair out of Georgiana's face. "I do hate to chastise you while you're weak, but you should know your behavior today was beyond the pale. It was incredibly stupid and could've gotten you killed."

"I know. I'm sorry. I feared for Mr. Emmett. I didn't want him harmed."

"How did you know to find him there?"

"He had written me a letter last night and told me what was happening."

The cad. It was in the poorest taste and most dishonorable for him to reveal such information. He surely had expected that by revealing the location of the duel, Georgiana would somehow intervene. Coward. "But you should also know he is no longer welcome in this house, and he will be given the cut direct should we see him in public. I encourage you to do the same."

"But you are the one who has preached from the day I entered this house that I should look for a good man. I should secure a good husband and get married. Then, when I attempt it, I'm condemned."

"Lower your voice," Ravenna warned. "Yes. You are right. I once believed Mr. Emmett might be a good husband for you. He is handsome and educated. But he has displayed a horrible judgment and an utter lack of character in attempting to seduce you. I want better for you. A gentleman worthy of marriage would never take advantage of you in the manner in which he has done. He has used you most dishonorably and cannot be trusted."

Tears pooled in Georgiana's eyes. "No. Please. You can't do this. I love him."

Ravenna struggled to keep from rolling her eyes. "You cannot possibly love him. You hardly know him. And he has proven himself most unworthy of your love, to be sure. Further, he admitted to me yesterday that he has no living to provide for you, and he had no intention of applying for your hand until he secured such a future."

Georgiana frowned. "Shouldn't he have a future, if he's applying to marry me?"

"You don't understand. He was going to seduce you and then, maybe somewhere down the road, secure employment to provide for you. Which might never happen. The proper order is for him to have a living first, then ask for your hand. Otherwise, he will enjoy your charms and may never be in a position to marry. A situation that can cause a host of problems and lead you down a path that would destroy your reputation, all your prospects, and your future. Do you not see how dire the situation is?"

Georgiana rubbed her face. "I suppose."

"Besides, I thought you fancied Lord Donovan."

"Not any longer." Georgiana shrugged. "And you advised me against him as well. Am I to be advised against every man in London?"

Ravenna chuckled. "No, I promise." She held her niece's creamy, soft hand. "You needn't worry, Georgiana. You have many years before you die a spinster. Now…" She patted her hand. "Don't fret. Be still and think only of getting better. I didn't mean to upset you. When you are healed, we'll find you a proper suitor you will fall heels over head for. You are still so very young."

The servant entered with the tray, and Ravenna helped pour and prepare her tea. "I think you can manage the rest?"

"Yes, ma'am."

"Good. I'm going to have fencing lessons with Mr. Norris, then my own supper. I need to go out after supper, so I'll have Keene sit with you tonight. Stay in bed to rest, then we'll keep an eye on your dressing to ensure the bleeding doesn't resume and you don't come under a fever."

Georgiana nodded, biting into her buttered bread with ravenous delight.

Ravenna gathered the book and invites and returned to her bedchamber, pulled her fencing kit out of the wardrobe, and rang the bellpull for Hart. She pulled on her pants under her dress, and when Hart entered the room, she asked to have her dress unbuttoned. She slipped out of her dress and put on her fencing top. "I have a request. Please procure a pair of black pantaloons and a black shirt for tonight. I need it by midnight."

Hart lifted her brows. "So quickly? I'll see what I can do. I know it's not my place, but may I ask why you require such clothing?"

"To be honest, I need to do a bit of spying, and I can't risk wearing a dress where my legs might get tangled if I need to run or fight."

"I'm intrigued. Who are you spying on? Have you found a suspect for Lord Thornley's killer?"

"Possibly. Or it might be something much bigger—and more frightening." She pulled the coded poem out of her writing desk. "Read this."

After Hart read it, she said, "What a strange poem."

"Except I think it's a coded message from the Irish Unity, or at least a band of Irish rebels, who mean to stage another rebellion in Ireland."

Intense interest lit Hart's brown eyes. She looked at the poem again. "I can see that now." She handed Ravenna the letter. "I'll do my best to get the things you require."

"Thank you. I'd like to have them by ten, so I can leave by eleven and be at the churchyard before midnight. I'll also need you to arrange with the stable grooms to have a horse prepared for me. Ensure the groom is discreet above all things. I don't want to alert Mr. Banks or the rest of the staff."

"Understood."

A knock sounded on her bedchamber door, and a maid entered to inform her of Mr. Norris's arrival. Ravenna grabbed her épée and mask and jogged down the stairs to meet her fencing instructor in the ballroom. Memories of Braedon, fear of The Unity and a potential rebellion, concern for her family, and anxiety for Lord Thornley's murder ate at her and propelled her toward Mr. Norris with ferocity. Over and over, she lunged, whipping and thrusting her épée and forcing him back. It was as if each of her attacks, each parry, and riposte, could bring back Braedon, put a hedge of protection around her family, settle the matters about The Unity and Lord Thornley, and bring peace to her spirit.

"Very good, madam." He danced backward, shouting instructions. "Parry. Parry. Thrust. Yes!" He stopped, walked in a circle, and wiped his sweaty forehead with his sleeve. He slashed the air with his blade. "Return. *En Garde*. Attack! Lunge. Lunge. Parry. Riposte." Around and around, they went. With each of his attacks, Ravenna returned with more fire. At the end of the sparring match, he said, "Very good, Lady Birchfield. You have improved wonderfully. Shall we meet in a few days' time?"

"Yes," she panted, wiping the sweat from her face and the back of her neck. "I think that will do." Unfortunately, the peace she hoped for eluded her.

When her lesson had ended, she ran upstairs, bathed, dressed in a black muslin dress, and wrote letters. It was only six in the evening and time for supper; it was seemingly a lifetime until midnight. Harrison had left the house for the evening, and Georgiana was still recovering, so Ravenna ate a supper of ham, potatoes, cheese, bread, and apple tart alone in her bedchamber. The hollowness of the room expanded within her. She didn't usually feel lonely, but suddenly, she longed for Braedon's presence, his wit, his charm, his playfulness, and conversation. When she'd finished, she visited Georgiana, who was playing cards with Keene. Georgiana had eaten her supper already, the dirty dishes cast aside.

The girls chattered happily and giggled over the cards. Georgiana's spirits had returned, and she seemed little affected by the pain and limits of her arm. Ravenna interrupted their game to inspect the wound and test Georgiana's temperature. The dressing contained some blood, which was to be expected, but the bleeding had slowed dramatically—a wonderful sign. "Looks like you're healing well."

She sat in the corner reading her book, sipping coffee to keep herself alert for what she expected to be an eventful evening. She enjoyed the girls' buoyant spirits until the clock in the foyer chimed ten. She closed her book and stood. "Well, girls, I need to go out for a while. I expect to be home in a few hours. Keene, I'll need you to stay with Georgiana. Keep watching for signs of a fever."

"Yes, ma'am. Though I believe she's on the mend."

"It may seem so, but a fever can come on quite unexpectedly. We aren't in the clear for a couple days yet."

"Yes, ma'am."

"I'll be back home as soon as possible."

Ravenna returned to her room in time to find Hart dressed in black pantaloons, a black shirt, and ankle boots, laying out the black clothes Ravenna had requested.

Ravenna's eyebrows shot up. "What are you doing? Why are you dressed like that?"

"I thought you might need help this evening. In case something goes wrong."

"But I also need someone here to manage things."

"The house will be going to be soon." Hart clasped her hands and gazed at Ravenna steadily. "I'm going with you, milady."

Perhaps there was some wisdom in having assistance. "Very well." She changed into the shirt and pantaloons and sat at the vanity. "Please plait my hair and pin it into a very short coiffure so it won't get in my way."

Hart braided Ravenna's hair down each side, twisted the braids together, wound it into a chignon at the base of her neck, and pinned it into place.

Ravenna stood and tied a black cape at her neck. "Do you have protection?" she asked Hart.

Hart put on her own cape. "I do." She reached into her pantaloons pocket and extracted a small pistol.

"Good. Then we must go. I want to be at the churchyard in plenty of time to see who might arrive. Let's take the servants' stairs."

Ravenna and Hart jogged down the stairs, like shadows, their capes billowing behind them. They came out in the dark kitchen and took the door leading into the alley. They ran around the side of the house and climbed into the saddles of a pair of chestnuts. Fog snaked around their hooves as the horses pawed at the ground, eager for the adventure. They cantered down Curzon Street, past St. James Palace and Park, past Buckingham Palace into an ever-thickening fog and stench as they neared the Thames and London Bridge. The nearer Ravenna came to the bridge, the more her heart pounded in her chest. Though they were closing in on the dangerous rookeries, she was more familiar with this side of the Thames and could easily avoid running into grave trouble.

Once they crossed the bridge, she was less familiar with the streets and neighborhoods, so she didn't know where all the rookeries and gaming hells were. Which meant they might inadvertently stumble into a dire situation. At this moment, she was desperate for Braedon. He would likely be able to better navigate the territory she was about to enter. There were but few gas lamps around the river, and thieves and cutthroats lingered in the shadows in these parts.

She kicked the sides of her horse, prodding it into a faster pace as they crossed the bridge. On the right, the silhouette of Southwark Cathedral with its square tower and four sharp spires struck against the night sky.

They veered to the left and headed toward St. Thomas Street, a narrow, cobbled street lined with buildings. They came to a church of gray stone with an ogival arched front and a large stained-glass rose window at its apex. St. George's was a small church with a statue of the Virgin Mary at the door and arched stained-glass windows. Large, twisted oaks and limp willow trees guarded the small ancient cemetery at the back of the building. Across from the church, a row of businesses lined the street.

Ravenna pulled the horse to a stop; the horse snorted and bobbed his head. "We should secure the horses with the tavern down the street and walk to the church cemetery." She pointed across the way to the side street, where light spilled out onto the street. They guided their horses toward the light. "Whatever we find tonight, I don't plan on following them. I only want to see if my instincts are right. If the first part of the poem proves true, then I'll know how to act."

They stopped at the Red Turtle Inn and dismounted. Ravenna paid a few shillings to the adolescent boy outside the tavern. "You ensure the safety of my horses; there's more when we return."

He eyed Hart and Ravenna with curiosity and suspicion. After all, it was highly unusual to see two women dressed as men wandering the streets at this hour. He accepted the coin in his grubby hands and tucked it into his fob pocket. "Aye."

Hart paused. "There's more money if you've never seen us. Understand?"

He frowned. "Aye." He took the reins and wrapped them around the horse hitches near the water troughs.

Ravenna and Hart ran back to the churchyard to find a place to hide. A thick fog blanketed the ground. In the center of the churchyard stood a mausoleum surrounded by angel statues. Several feet away, a row of sepulchers occupied the ground shaded from the moonlight under the low-hanging boughs of the ancient oak trees. "Let's hide there."

They sat on the ground behind the sepulchers and waited. Ravenna's ears perked to locate the slightest noise. On the street adjacent to the church, a few carriages rolled by, the horses' tack jingling. Ravenna and Hart pulled their capes tighter around themselves as a light chill settled in the air.

Ravenna glanced at Hart, who had tucked her chin, her lips moving as if silently praying. Ravenna whispered, "Are you frightened, Hart? Do you want to return to the tavern and wait for me there?"

Hart gazed at her with wide eyes. She whispered, "I'm well. Kirkyards like this always bring bittersweet memories."

"I see." Ravenna didn't want to pry, so she didn't ask her any of the questions whirling through her mind. Hart was deeply protective of her privacy. So, she sat in shocked silence when Hart spoke.

She looked out across the shadowy churchyard. "I was a wee girl when it happened. So, my memory of it is in bits. But the first night I hid in a kirkyard, some men came to our home in the dead of night. My mother woke me and my sister. She kept her calm, but I could see the fright in her eyes. It's interesting how much the eyes give away, isn't it?" Hart's face and eyes fell blank. She had been transported to another time.

Hart continued, "My sister was older than me, so my mother whispered to her what to do and where to go. My only concern was my dolly. Eulie was her name. I have no idea where I came up with such a name." A faint smile flickered and faded. "Momma left the room, and my sister fluttered around to put on our capes. Then she pulled me down the back stairs,

250

practically dragging me, insisting I be very quiet. Then we slipped out the door." She hugged herself tighter. "I didn't understand why we were outside. I tried to ask, but my sister shushed me. It was winter. I'll never forget. We didn't have shoes on. Even now, my feet ache, remembering how cold the ground was as we ran up Candlemaker's Row toward Greyfriars Kirkyard. I remember hearing my father screaming and crying out. Not like he'd been hurt. This was different, like something injured his soul. It's an unusual sound, isn't it? That soul-wail."

Ravenna nodded. She knew what Hart meant. She'd often heard the soul-wailing of survivors who had lost their children in the Wexford massacre. It wasn't the same as the crying out accompanying physical injury. Soul-wailing cut to the marrow. Ravenna swallowed back her emotion and found her voice. "Yes. It's quite different."

Hart looked at her, haunted. "That sound still follows me, especially at night." She shook her head and stared into the darkness again.

She continued. "My sister pulled me into the kirkyard. Much like this one. It was terrifying. Ancient. Ghostly. We sat on the ground behind the largest stone we could find. My sister wrapped me in her arms with her cloak and sang 'Barbara Allen' to me." Hart pulled up her legs and wrapped her arms around them, rocking gently back and forth; she hummed a little of the old ballad. "I don't know how long we sat there. I just remember waking up again to see my mother's face in the lantern light. But her face was bruised and cut, her eyes brimming with love and tears. We'd never been so happy and relieved to see her. We clung to her neck, and she covered us with kisses." Hart swiped the tear sliding down her cheek. "She called us her good girls and praised us for doing exactly as she asked. She took us home and held us in her lap by the kitchen fire. Even now, I remember her holding us, stroking our hair, and saying, 'Any time there's trouble, lasses, hide in the kirkyard, and I'll come find you, my doves. I'll always come find you.'"

"Did she ever tell you what happened?"

Hart looked at Ravenna, her teary eyes full of hate and anguish. "She didn't have to. We eventually found out. And when we did..." She paused, licking her dry lips. Something vicious passed over her features. "We solved the problem."

Ravenna pulled back a little. She'd never seen this side of Hart.

Hart again turned her gaze to the darkness. "There were many times when we had to hide in the kirkyard. Every time Mamma came to find us there. Until…" Her voice cracked. She set her jaw. "Until one day she didn't." She sniffed and wiped her eyes on her shirt sleeve. "Nothing was ever the same."

Ravenna's heart ached for her friend. She knew how much it hurt to have your family, and then suddenly they're gone. She wished she could scrub the darkness out of Hart's mind. Instead, she rubbed soothing circles across Hart's back. "I'm so sorry, Charlotte. I'm so very sorry."

Hart nodded and looked down. After a moment of silence, she said, "You remind me of her sometimes, the way you're both strong and kind and protective of the people you love."

In the distance, Big Ben sounded the midnight bells.

Soon after, a cart rolled into the churchyard. Ravenna and Hart turned to kneel and peeked over the edges of the sepulchers. The back door of the church creaked open. A man in a robe crossed the cemetery and unlocked the mausoleum, where the cart pulled to a stop. Two men jumped out of the back of the cart. Though the moon shone full and bright in a cloudless sky, it was difficult to discern the identity of the men. They whispered among each other as they pulled barrels, guns, and other munitions out of the mausoleum and loaded them into the cart.

Ravenna whispered. "Just as I suspected. They're gathering munitions. I wager they're rebels."

"Do you think they're with The Unity? Or standard fare rebels?"

"It's difficult to say with certainty, but I'm inclined to believe they're with The Unity."

"Then we're witnessing something with the potential to be quite dangerous."

"Indeed. And now I know how to act."

Ravenna shifted, her knees beginning to hurt. A twig snapped.

The men stopped and listened. "What was that?" They looked at each other and all around them.

"Who goes there?" One of them shouted, sweeping around his lantern.

Ravenna and Hart ducked down. Ravenna closed her eyes, hoping they were hidden well enough.

Another man said, "It's probably an owl or a cat."

"Let's hurry and finish this," said a third man. "I don't like being in this cemetery. We'll be lucky if no ghosts follow us home."

"You're a ninny," laughed one man. Then they fell into a discussion of ghosts, and how one of them had a cousin haunted by ghosts, and others claiming ghosts didn't exist.

The men carried out at least six barrels of gunpowder, an indiscernible number of guns, and ten cases of what was probably bullets, or pistols, or even cannon balls. When the men had finished, the robed man locked the mausoleum and returned to the church. Was he actually clergy or posing as one? It wouldn't be surprising for a member of the Irish Catholic clergy to be embroiled in such a plot. Many of them in Ireland had unified against the English in the 1798 rebellions—especially since the English had adopted such a strong anti-Catholic stance. The men covered the weapons with oilcloth. One sat in the back of the cart; the others climbed onto the driver's bench. The cart eased out of the churchyard and disappeared into the night.

Ravenna nudged Hart. "Let's go this way." She pointed toward the back of the churchyard. They ducked into the treeline, ran through backyards, and came out further down the street. They crossed the street and ran back up toward the tavern, where the young man stood guard over their horses. Ravenna handed him a guinea, and his eyes popped open wide. Ravenna and Hart mounted their horses.

Hart threw him another shilling. "Remember. You never saw us."

He nodded. "I remember."

Holding her dancing horse, Hart said, "Where to now?"

Ravenna considered going to see Mr. Chadwick, but arriving at his home in the middle of the night, dressed in men's clothes, would alert him to ask questions—too many questions. It wasn't likely they could sail for Ireland tonight anyway. It would probably be at least a day or two before the tides would cooperate. She would write to Mr. Chadwick in the morning.

"For now, we'll go home."

Chapter Thirty-One

As soon as Ravenna woke, she dashed off a letter to Mr. Chadwick, requesting he visit her as soon as possible, and had a footman deliver the note. She then checked on Georgiana to ensure the girl had managed through the night without a fever. Feeling at ease about Georgiana's healing and health, she returned to her bedchamber for breakfast and settled in at the table by the window for a meal of buttered caraway buns, oranges, and tea as she read through the morning newspaper. There were no reports of the duel or shots being fired in the Battersea area, so that eased her mind.

After a knock at her door, Harrison entered, dressed for travel. "I've come to bid *adieu*." He looked ghastly, pale with dark circles under his eyes, as though he hadn't slept or eaten in days.

Ravenna frowned. "*Adieu*? Whatever for?" She wiped her mouth and hands on her napkin and stood. "So soon?"

He sighed. "It's best for me to retreat to Birchfield Manor until it's time for me to return to university."

"I don't understand." She approached him.

"I'm clearly not wanted here. At least one person wishes me far away. And, like you say, it was my fault that Georgiana—"

"Oh, Harrison." She rushed to him and took his hand. "I'm so sorry. Please don't go. I spoke too harshly to you. I was upset. Granted, if you hadn't challenged Mr. Emmett, then Georgiana wouldn't have been shot. But, if he hadn't taken advantage of her, then *none* of this would've happened. This is all at the feet of Mr. Emmett. Please don't blame yourself. And please

255

forgive me for speaking rashly."

"I forgive you, and I appreciate you trying to make me feel better, but I'm already packed. My things are being loaded in the hackney now. I've already alerted Wiggins of my arrival today. The decision is made."

Dejected, Ravenna touched his cheek. "I'm so sorry, Harrison. For the way this has all turned out."

He nodded. "Yes. Wise men ne'er sit and wail their loss but cheerily seek how to redress their harms."

"Shakespeare's *Richard II*?"

"*King Henry VI.*"

"Ah. Wise words." She paused. "Are you certain you won't reconsider? I do enjoy having you here and I'm sure Georgiana does, too. Especially as you are closer to her age."

"I'm certain."

"Have you spoken to Georgiana?"

He shook his head, sadness marking his features. "No. At the moment, I can't bear to see her. Perhaps, after some reflection, I will write to her to address this unfortunate situation. I think it would be best for me to simply go away and set us both free."

Ravenna bit down on her tongue to keep from reminding him that she had warned him of this. "Poor Harrison." She stood on tiptoes to kiss his forehead. "I am sorry for you. But, there are many young women in the world who would faint away to have your hand in life."

A trace of a smile touched his lips. He nodded. "In time, perhaps. Well..." He sighed. "I should go. Bye, Amma. I'll write to you when the cottage is ready at Birchfield Manor." He kissed her cheek.

"Bye, dear." She kissed his cheek and squeezed his hand as he slipped away from her and out the door.

Her shoulders slumped, and she rubbed her face. "Oh, dear Harrison." She didn't want him to leave. Guilt over her previous words to him clawed at mind. She'd never meant to hurt his feelings. Perhaps, by the time they retired to the countryside for the Great Twelfth, he would be sufficiently recovered to receive her and Georgiana at Birchfield.

Ravenna dressed in a black Swiss dot muslin with short puff sleeves and black slippers. She looked at the jet jewelry in her jewelry box, her fingers hovering over the coral necklace and earrings she once favored. In just a few weeks, she'd be one year a widow and three months a mourning stepmother.

She selected the coral necklace of orange beads and the matching dangle earrings. She also put on the matching bracelet and pinned a coral brooch to the center of the empire waist just below the short bodice. Checking her image in the mirror, the little splash of color from the coral brought her a bit of happiness.

A maid knocked on her door. "Milady, you have a visitor. A Mr. Chadwick."

He arrived much quicker than she'd expected and long before proper calling hours. Ravenna collected her black lace fan and the coded poem she'd extracted from Robert Emmett's pocket. She would keep the black wax seals, and the piece of torn rose taffeta secret for the time being.

She descended the stairs, panic rising inside her. Every time she conversed with Mr. Chadwick, it was as though she was entering a cage with a lion. She might accidentally say or do something to expose her past as a spy. Or she might reveal a bit of seemingly insignificant information that he would pull on like a loose thread, leading him to the truth about her past.

She entered the drawing room. Mr. Chadwick stood at the fireplace, staring up at the portrait of her late husband, Philip Gordon, Lord Birchfield in his red parliament robes. Chadwick turned when she entered the room. "Good morning, Lady Birchfield."

"Good morning."

"I apologize for the early hour, but I thought it best to come as soon as possible after receiving your note."

"I understand. Please, sit. Would you like some tea?"

"No, thank you. I just finished breakfast."

She sat in a chair by the dark fireplace and motioned to the empty seat across from her. The lilacs of the fireplace bough-pot drooped in their vase between them. He sat and crossed his legs, his hands resting on his knee.

"Thank you for coming to visit." She struggled to maintain an even voice.

"I have some valuable information for you." His steely blue gaze pierced her, delving into the darkest portions of her mind. "I believe there may be another Irish rebellion afoot, similar to the one attempted in 1798."

His brows shot up. "What makes you think so?"

"I will tell you on one condition."

He tipped his head, his eyes glittering with curiosity.

"I will not answer any questions about *how* I came upon the information."

He frowned. "An odd request. Unless you're attempting to protect someone connected to the rebellion, I can't imagine why you would want to keep such information to yourself."

"My reasons are my own."

"Very well..."

She offered him the poem. "I came by this poem, which I believe contains a secret message divulging some of the particulars about the rebellion. Specifically, how some munitions are being collected and transferred."

He read the poem. "A strange poem, but how do you know it's related to a rebellion? This could be some schoolboy nonsense."

"I wondered the same. So I went at midnight to St. George's of Clennam in Southwark last night. And witnessed for myself a group of men moving munitions from a mausoleum into a cart."

"*You* went to a cemetery at night and spied on a group of rebels and smugglers?"

"I did."

His eyes lit with humor. "I hadn't supposed you were of an adventurous nature, milady. You surprise me."

"Nevertheless, I wager, if you were to go to the Albishore docks and the Dancing Fiddler, you might find the men and the weaponry before they sail to Bray."

"Bloody Jacobins! They won't rest until this country is in shreds!" he hissed. "How did you come by this information?"

"I've already told you I won't answer such questions."

"That's unfortunate because I have no choice but to believe you may be in some way involved with this rebellion. Perhaps this is a ruse meant to throw me off the trail of a bigger plot?" He gazed at her with suspicion.

"You may think whatever you choose. I cannot prevent it. But I am acting in good faith."

He folded the paper and tapped the corner on his knee. "Why? Why are you sharing this with me?"

She didn't want to tell him that she'd hoped it would break up The Unity once and for all, guaranteeing safety for herself and her family. She lifted a shoulder. "Because it's the right thing to do. As a citizen loyal to The Crown." He nodded, studying her. "But there's more."

He shifted in his seat as if preparing himself for a greater shock.

"There is a man by the name of Mr. Robert Emmett. I believe he is one of the men involved. He has recently come here and is spending time among the nobility, including the royal family. He was recently at Prince George's birthday ball. I think his motives cannot be trusted. His brother, Josiah, is staying in Barton Street. You might question him about Robert's whereabouts. I do not know if Mr. Josiah Emmett is involved in his brother's treason."

He nodded, his eyes growing distant as his mind processed the information she'd given him. "I think you're right." He tucked the paper inside the breast of his coat. "Is there anything else I should know?"

"I have no more information at this time."

"Very well." They stood. He said, "If you should discover anything new, I'd appreciate you telling me."

"I will. I think you should look into this as soon as possible, sir. I'm sure they'll sail at first opportunity."

"Yes, of course." He bowed. "Thank you, Lady Birchfield." He crossed to the door and paused. He turned. "I was certain you and I were enemies of a sort."

"True, you and I have not been amicable. But I think enemies is a strong word. Besides, there is no enemy greater than an enemy to my nation where so many lives might be adversely affected."

"But aren't you Irish?"

"I am."

"You would betray your homeland to protect England?"

"We were Loyalists, so I do not see it as a betrayal. Further, the rebellious factions haven't exactly been helpful in bringing freedom to Ireland. In many ways, they have caused more problems than they've solved. They've left a great deal of violence and vigilantism in their wake and often rule with more tyranny than the kings they seek to overthrow as each faction vies for power among themselves."

"Do you think our king is a tyrant, Lady Birchfield?"

Ravenna didn't want to descend into a political debate that could drown her in the waters of treason. She quickly added, "Thank you for coming this morning, Mr. Chadwick. Should I hear of anything else, I will inform you immediately."

After he left, she climbed the stairs to Georgiana's room. She sat in the window, looking down at the street, humming.

"Georgiana, ring for Keene and get dressed. You're coming with me."

"Where are we going?" She jumped up.

"The Penitent House is hosting a dinner before everyone decamps for shooting season, and you and I are delivering the invitations. It will take us the better part of the day. So, do make haste."

Chapter Thirty-Two

Delivering invitations took most of the day. Fortunately, the weather was a boon: bright sun, cloudless skies, happy birds, and balmy air. After visiting their last home, Georgiana climbed into the carriage and flopped back against the seat. "Heaven help me, I'm tired!"

"I know. We have one more visit, then we'll go home. We need to stop by The Penitent House."

As they entered The Penitent House, a familiar man exited the building. He was tall, lanky, with greasy blond hair falling to his shoulders from under his hat. Stubble shadowed his long chin, and dark eyes stared out of a gaunt, haunted face.

Ravenna stopped on the stones. "Mr. Cossard?"

He paused and blinked at her. "Uh, Lady, uh…"

"Birchfield."

"Yes, yes. How do y'do?"

"Very well, thank you. I'm surprised to find you here."

"My sister is here. I'm hoping to get her home with us, but haven't been able to manage it yet."

"I do. Who is your sister?"

"Mrs. Mariah Vincent."

"Yes, I know Mariah. But you said, 'Mrs.' She's married?"

"Was. She's a widow. She and her husband worked in the family silk factory until it went out of business. Then, he was pressed into service to go fight against France in Holland in 1799. He died in service. I think you can guess the rest."

She did understand. Without work, without a husband to provide, Mariah would've been forced into prostitution to help feed the family. It was the curse war and economic crises often brought to the poorest families in the country. "Yes. I'm sorry for it."

He nodded. "At any rate. She'd like to come back to live with us, but refuses to until she can afford to get her children back. They've been farmed out since she couldn't afford to keep them. And she didn't want them to know how their mother made money."

"I see." Ravenna's heart ached for Mariah and her children. Farming children was a common practice for the poor. When a family had more children than they could feed, they would place them with a childless family and pay a small one-time fee. The fee would help with the upkeep of the children and often turned out to be less expensive than keeping them at home. Sometimes, the harboring family would eventually adopt the children, sometimes there was an understanding that the parents would return to claim their children once they had financially stabilized. Poor Mariah, to be so separated from everyone she loved and held dear. "How long have her children lived apart from her?"

"Since 1800. She fought to keep them for as long as she could, but in the end, Lady Fortune had her way."

"I'm sorry to hear it."

A wan smile tickled a corner of his mouth. "Ah, there's always hope, milady. And she has reason to believe she will soon be flush with enough money to return to the family and have her children brought home, too."

"Oh? How is that?"

"She hasn't told me the particulars, but I hope it's true."

Reverend Howarth burst through the door in his wide-brimmed hat and clergyman's garb, carrying a basket. "Lady Birchfield! What a pleasure to see you again."

Ravenna and Adam said a quick goodbye as Reverend Howarth swept her and Georgiana into The Penitent House.

"What brings you out today, Lady Birchfield?" Reverend Howarth asked, removing his hat.

"I wanted to discuss the dinner party with you and Mariah. I've delivered all the invitations, and everyone has already accepted. They are very much looking forward to the dinner and a tour of the property."

"Fantastic!" He bounced on his heels. "However, unfortunately, you've caught me on my way out." He stopped a young woman in the hall and asked her to fetch Mariah, then he turned back to Ravenna. "There is a young woman with a few children, including a newborn, in a nearby rookery who has come to my attention through the grapevine. Seems she's desperate for food and shelter. I've been trying to convince her to come to The Penitent House. God willing, today is the day we can provide refuge for her."

"Do you allow the children to come here, too?"

"We aren't able to take in the children yet, but we work with a few families just outside London who have farms. They take in the children on a temporary basis, and the women can visit weekly. Once the women can establish themselves, they can go retrieve their children."

"Why do you separate the children and mothers?"

"The women here are quite unstable and still in need of deep healing themselves. Many are enslaved to alcohol or opiates. We must help the mother before they can help their children. The farms can provide a steady foundation for the children while they wait for their mothers to return."

That was understandable. "Do you think they will ever get their children back?"

His cheer dipped a little. "We are a young organization, so it's difficult to predict the future. But it is my hope and my life's mission that all these young women will be thoroughly healed by the Holy Spirit and be strengthened enough to reclaim their children and put their lives and families back together. But it's difficult and unpredictable work. Humans are complicated creatures."

Ravenna searched his merry brown eyes and felt the weight of awe. She didn't understand how this man could do such heavy and complicated work and yet maintain persistent joy, optimism, gentleness, and kindness. "Perhaps an impossible task, some might say." In an instant, she, too, felt the weight of humility as she understood her own comparative smallness and ineffectiveness. Surely, she could do more.

He chuckled. "Perhaps, but nothing is impossible for the Good Lord." He opened the drawing-room door and guided Ravenna and Georgiana inside. "Though I must rush off, I trust Mariah's good judgment and yours. I have faith in the abilities of you ladies to make a wonderful dinner for our guests. Now, I must go. There is much work to do." He clapped his hat back on his head and rushed out the door.

Ravenna and Georgiana waited in the drawing room, the ticking clock filling the silence. Soon, Mariah entered the room in a pink batiste dress. "Good morning. I apologize for making you wait. We were at our lessons. Please, come into the library." They followed Mariah down the hall and sat at a long table. "Would you like some tea?"

"No, thank you. We won't keep you long. I wanted to discuss the seating for the dinner. Everyone has accepted. May I see the space where the dinner will be held?"

"Of course."

Mariah led them down a dim hall to a large room with long windows casting sunlight on a long wooden table in the center. "This seats twenty-seven to thirty people comfortably. This is where we all dine. We have fifteen women here now, with more likely on the way soon. There are so many women who need assistance."

"Granted." Ravenna took in the room, the stone walls bare of any decor. "We would need enough tables to fit at least twenty more."

"Yes," Mariah said, studying the room. "Of course, since our women will serve and cook, that will empty many of the seats for our guests."

"You're right." Ravenna thought then said, "This should suffice then, I think. If you need more space we can always bring the library tables in here."

Mariah smiled. "That's a grand idea!"

Ravenna added, "Between me and the other *Les Roses* ladies, we can provide all the clothes and table pieces you'll need. It will save us from renting them."

"That sounds lovely."

They returned to the library, and Ravenna turned to Georgiana with a pointed gaze. "Look at all those books. Perhaps you should see what titles they have." Georgiana noted the hint and moved away to inspect the bookshelves. Ravenna sat at the table and began drawing a seating chart. She said, "I met your brother earlier."

"Yes. He visits at least once a week if he can."

"That's good of him."

"We're hoping I can move back with the family soon. I think I'm very close to having enough money. Yet, I'll still need work, as will my brother. If you know of anyone…" Her voice trailed off.

Ravenna was torn. What if Mariah had been involved with Thornley's death? She studied Mariah's profile. Anything was possible, she supposed, but she liked Mariah and was invested in seeing her succeed. She simply needed to trust in Mariah's innocence. And she would do her best to remove Mariah from her list of suspects. "Absolutely. I'm happy to recommend you if I hear of an open position. But it will be difficult with your children."

Her blush grew deeper. "I know."

"There might be some situations where you might still find some employment. Don't give up hope."

"Yes, laundry and sewing." She rolled her eyes. "All of us here make our money with such jobs now. For most of us, the pay isn't enough to pay for rent and food to properly care for our children. I'm fortunate, but…" She stopped and shrugged a shoulder, looking at the list of dinner guest names.

"I know. However, many of us in *Les Roses* are dedicated to the education of women. We can all help you get your education so you can become a governess. They don't make a great deal of money, but they fare better than a scullery maid. And work in better conditions."

Mariah smiled. "What a generous offer. I thank you."

"Forgive me, but your brother seemed to indicate you might have already found something, and you should have your children back soon."

A look of guilt entwined with vexation etched her demeanor. "Did he? I think he's confused. I told him there was potential, but I never said it was certain."

"I see. Has someone offered you a job? May I know her name? I could provide a reference."

Mariah became agitated, wringing her hands and biting her lip. She spoke with sharpness. "Truly. There is no one yet. My brother misunderstood my meaning and then misspoke."

Ravenna blinked. "I apologize. I didn't mean to annoy you."

"No…" Mariah closed her eyes and rubbed her forehead. "I apologize. I didn't mean to speak to you so harshly. I appreciate all your efforts." She sighed, her lips tight and eyes glittering with heat. "I simply shall have to speak with my brother to correct his misconceptions."

Chapter Thirty-Three

A full week had passed, and Ravenna hadn't heard anything more about Lord Thornley's murder or the missing opal. Her own investigation was at an impasse. She didn't know where else to turn to get more answers. Catherine, Yarford, and Lady Thornley had all written to her, impatient to have answers. But she had nothing to tell them. As a result, she kept herself at home, unavailable for most social calls in order to avoid their disappointed looks when she told them she had no answers.

Just a few days before The Penitent House dinner, as she finished up her fencing lesson with Mr. Norris, she received a surprise visit from Mr. Chadwick.

"Good day, Lady Birchfield." He dipped his chin and touched the brim of his hat as she passed through the foyer on her way to change out of her fencing kit.

"I'm sorry, Mr. Chadwick, I'm in no condition to receive visitors."

Interest and amusement marked his features. "I do apologize for catching you at an inconvenient time, but I require only a moment of your time."

It was wildly inappropriate for her to receive Mr. Chadwick in breeches and with a sweaty, red face, but she wanted this over. Maybe he had some answers. She motioned to the left. "I believe you know the way to my drawing room?"

"I do." He removed his hat.

They stepped into the drawing room. She pulled a shawl from the chair and wrapped it around her as they sat facing each other in the chairs near the covered fireplace.

"May I offer you refreshment?"

"No. Thank you."

"To what do I owe this pleasure? Have you found Lord Thornley's killer?" She sat in anticipation of his next words, hoping he would have good news she could share with Catherine, Yarford, and Lady Thornley.

"Unfortunately, I haven't. His killer still eludes me."

She deflated.

"I thought you should know you provided sound information. As a result, we've arrested a few people down at the Albishore docks and uncovered a ship filled with munitions bound for Ireland."

Her eyes widened. "I see."

"I wanted to thank you. You could've decided to assist your fellow Irishmen in their endeavor, but instead, you stopped a rebellion before it began. You acted rightly."

Did she? She wasn't sure. Though her family was Loyalist, she wasn't entirely unsympathetic to the Irish cause. Even if their tactics were sometimes brutal or misguided. "I wish I could be happy, Mr. Chadwick, but I think you can understand I'm in a difficult position."

He pinched his lips together and nodded. "I do. It couldn't have been an easy decision. But I thank you, and I'm sure The Crown, when they are made aware, will also thank you."

Panic fluttered in her chest. She didn't want any attention drawn to her, attention that might cause people to ask questions, to pry, to uncover a past she'd rather keep secret. "Please, Mr. Chadwick, I would prefer you keep the praise and commendations for yourself. Since my retirement from the stage, I prefer to keep my hermit-like privacy. I beg you would not bring such attention to me."

He frowned and tipped his head. "You are a singular woman, milady. Quite the quiz to work out. Are you certain this is your wish? Our king is generous and likely to reward you with money, titles, land, and other riches."

"I understand. And I've never been more certain of anything in my life."

"Very well. You should also know Mr. Robert Emmett has escaped. We think he might be making his way back to Ireland as we speak. I've written to the magistrate in his county to scour the land for him. I expect he will be arrested soon and will likely hang for his treason."

Ravenna swallowed, her throat tightening. She touched the base of her neck, then folded her hands in her lap. She hadn't wanted anyone to die. She only wanted to stop the rebellion so the English wouldn't send troops to brutally suppress the rebels as they'd done before; they'd destroyed entire villages. Far more people would die in a rebellion than in conspiracy. It was unfortunate Robert and his compatriots were going to hang, but, seen in a prudential light, it was better than chaos reigning on Irish soil to destroy everything. She didn't have anything to say. She only nodded.

He continued. "It's my hope, if he's still in town and you happen to see him, that you will alert me?"

She lifted her gaze to search his hard blue eyes. "I doubt I will. I've only met him the one time. We don't run in the same social circles."

"Someone told me his brother, Mr. Josiah Emmett, tutored your niece."

The mention of the former tutor who had attempted to seduce her niece caused her to flush. "Not any longer." She didn't want to share Georgiana's embarrassment with Mr. Chadwick. It was none of his business. "He left my employ a little over a week ago."

He perked. "Why?"

"He didn't say. But I heard he might be working with Prince George's daughter to tutor her?"

He tensed. "The brother of a rebel is tutoring the princess?"

"I don't know if he is now or not."

"Why didn't you tell me that?"

She dithered. "I-I-I did tell you he and his brother were at the prince's ball, trying to get close to the royal family. Further, I had no proof Josiah Emmett was involved in the rebellion. I was hesitant to accuse him of *treason*."

He looked at her with disbelief. "It's likely they're working together, milady."

"Seems you don't understand the nature of things in Ireland, sir. There are many families divided over English rule. Even in my own family…" She stopped. *Stupid, stupid Ravenna. You've said too much!* This was exactly why she didn't like talking with Chadwick.

He perked. "Even in your own family?"

"The material point is that the brothers might not be in agreement in their politics."

"Yes, but you were going to say something." She could see his calculations in his eyes. "I think you were about to say your own family was divided between Loyalist and Anti-Loyalist sentiment. Meaning, someone in your family was involved in rebellion?"

Sweat broke between her breasts, and she drew on her former acting days to blank her face and calm her breathing. *Careful, Ravenna.* "Such division was the case among many families. But, my village, including nearly all of my family, were destroyed by the English troops."

He seemed to soften. "I'm sorry."

She wanted away from him. Now. She jumped to her feet. "I apologize, Mr. Chadwick, but I must get dressed. I thank you for your visit. I'll see you to the door." She strode across the room.

He stood. "I do apologize if I've upset you, Lady Birchfield."

"Never mind, sir." She opened the drawing-room door. "I thank you for visiting me and sharing the information about Mr. Robert Emmett."

He put on his hat and paused at the door. "If you happen to hear any more about rebellion or information about Lord Thornley, will you tell me?"

"Of course, sir. I wish you luck in catching Lord Thornley's killer. I hope the mystery is resolved soon."

Chapter Thirty-Four

The night of The Penitent House dinner had finally arrived. The women and Reverends Howarth and McKirk had dressed in their finest and welcomed guests in a receiving line. Extra candles brightened the house and the chatter and giggles of the women filled the air with cheer, utterly transforming the sanctuary, infusing it with a life Ravenna hadn't realized existed within its walls.

As expected, Mariah wore the rose-colored taffeta dress. Ravenna had tucked the scrap of cloth she'd found in the gate at Thornley Hall inside her bodice in hopes of comparing it to the dress. While Mariah was distracted in conversation, she pulled the cloth out of her bodice and, holding it in her palm, compared the swatch of cloth to the dress. It was, in fact, the same material and color.

So, why had Mariah been behind the Thornley house on the day of Lord Thornley's murder? Why would she have been around the garden gate? Was it an innocent turn in the garden? Or had she been involved in something more sinister? Did she let someone in who murdered Thornley? Or did she let the killer out? If Mariah had been involved, Ravenna knew Mariah didn't commit the murder simply because she hadn't been covered in blood. It would've been nearly impossible to get large amounts of blood out of the dress.

Maybe Mariah noticed the killer and chased him out of the garden? Which didn't seem likely because, if that were the case, why wouldn't she have said something to Mr. Chadwick or reported what she'd seen to Bow Street? This was most unsettling. She turned away and returned the cloth to her bodice. She sipped her lemon punch, looking around the room. Tonight would be a good opportunity to discover more about Mariah's involvement, if any, in Lord Thornley's death. Ravenna wanted nothing more than to clear her suspicions about Mariah and prove her innocence once and for all.

The dinner bell rang, and everyone filed into the dining hall, beautifully decorated with fresh flowers and candles in the center of the tables. The dinner consisted of lively chatter, goose, ham, vegetables, cheese, fruit, nuts, wine, and a variety of desserts. Of course, the evening wouldn't have been complete without a speech from Reverend Howarth, who complimented the women and their contributions. He then expressed the deepest gratitude to all the benefactors on behalf of himself and all the women. There was plenty of delight and joy to go around.

When dinner ended, Reverend Howarth offered to give a tour of the house while the borrowed servants cleaned up the dining area and set it up for the remainder of the evening's entertainments. Ravenna dropped to the back of the tour group, lingering near Mariah's room until she witnessed the last of the group disappear around the corner. She grabbed a candle from a nearby sconce, slipped inside, and locked the door. As the house mistress, Mariah had a private room separate from the shared dormitory of the other women.

The sparsely decorated room contained a bed, wardrobe, washstand, and a small table in the corner with a candle in the center. Sadly, the room had only one tiny window by the table. The room was more like a dungeon cell than a bedchamber. A single book, *St. Augustine's Confessions*, an inkstand, and a few sheets of foolscap paper lay on the table.

Ravenna thumbed the pages of the book. Nothing there. She opened the wardrobe. Mariah had few clothes, all folded or hung neatly within. There was only one drawer with a couple pairs of stockings, one pair of gloves, and a few other such essentials. On one side of the drawer was a small space for accessories like a fan or jewelry. Mariah didn't have much to nose through.

However, Ravenna did notice a gold locket—without a chain. Perhaps this was the locket that belonged to the chain she'd found in Mr. Gibson's home. She picked up the locket and turned it in her hands, holding it close to the candle. There was no way to know for certain. Except…She looked closer. There was a dark stain on the hinge of the locket. Was that blood? It didn't look like rust. She popped open the locket. A dark stain marred the painted image of a man and children inside. Was this Gibson's blood? It wasn't purple enough to be wine. It had the dark reddish-brown color of dried blood. Her stomach twisted.

Perhaps she should take the locket to Mr. Chadwick? But then, how would she explain how it came to be in her possession? No. Best to put it back and have it still in Mariah's belongings. Ravenna replaced the locket and closed up the wardrobe. She rushed to the door and bent to peek out the keyhole.

Heavens! There stood Mariah and Mr. McKirk.

The knob jiggled. Mariah said, "I must've locked my room during preparations."

In a panic, Ravenna glanced around, looking for a hiding spot. The bed. She blew out the candle and ran on tiptoes to the other side of the bed. She dropped to her knees on the cold stone floor, pulled up the edge of the blanket, and shimmied on her stomach to draw herself under the bed. She pulled the blanket down as the door popped open. She tried to peek out from under the blanket, but could only see shoes.

The bed sank down on top of Ravenna. Mr. McKirk said, "Come here."

Ravenna's mouth opened in silent surprise.

"There isn't time." Mariah laughed as her weight pressed on the bed as well. "The tour will be ending soon, and Reverend Howarth will be looking for us. Imagine what he'd say if he found us alone together in my bedchamber."

McKirk laughed. "He'd have apoplexy and tried to have me defrocked."

Mariah laughed. "Difficult to do when you're not even a real minister."

Ravenna screwed up her face. What a nasty man to take advantage of the good, kind, and trusting Reverend Haworth in such a way. Vile man.

McKirk continued to laugh among the kissing sounds. "Then he would insist we marry immediately."

"And I would refuse him as I've refused you."

"Why do you refuse to marry me? Have I not professed a thousand times I love you?"

"I love you, too. I never thought I would love again." The sound of kissing. Then Mariah spoke again. "But I'm not inclined to marry. Yet. I can't even think of marriage until I have my children with me, and I can be assured my family can get on without me."

"Your wish, my dear, shall soon be granted with this little delight right here."

Ravenna grimaced. She wished she could see what they were talking about.

"You have it with you?"

"Of course. I'm not taking any chances by letting it lay about in my room."

"Let me see it again. One last time." There was some silence, and then Mariah continued. "It's the most beautiful thing I've ever seen. It's as though God took this ugly lump of shiny coal and dropped a precious rainbow inside."

The opal! Ravenna clenched her fists and softly tapped her forehead against the stone floor. They have the opal, which means they either hired someone to kill Lord Thornley for the gem or they killed him for it themselves. But what did they hope to gain by having it? They couldn't take it to a pawnbroker. They'd be discovered for certain and would hang for their murder and thievery.

"Let's have it back now," he said. There was another stretch of silence. Then he added, "By my clock, we have but a few more hours to wait."

"You need to be there at midnight?" She added with a pout in her voice. "You'll have to leave the party early."

"Yes. I'm sorry, dear, but it's necessary. The men are leaving for France tonight. We must get this little beauty into Napoleon's hands and collect our money as soon as possible."

Shock rattled Ravenna. She fought to keep her place and not jump out and attack them both. They were going to sell the opal to Napoleon, the enemy of England? The legend of the opal dictated that whoever held the stone would not be conquered, but turn his enemies' wives into widows.

Why would they want to give such power to Napoleon?

"Will the men come back with you, or will they be sent separately."

The men?

"Some will come back with me. We'll land in England, travel up through Scotland, and go across to Ireland from there. The rest will be sent separately, in different boats at different times so as to not attract attention. They'll go straight to Ireland."

Ireland!

"How many has Napoleon promised?"

"Emmett tells me he negotiated five thousand men and their weapons."

Now Ravenna understood. This was yet another Franco-Irish rebellion. After the first one failed in 1798, The Unity went into hiding for a while to make the English believe the threat had abated, then later rallied to try again. McKirk was part of it. As was Emmett. But which Emmett? Or were both involved?

"I'm going to miss you terribly while you're gone," Mariah said. "Please do come back to me safe and in good health."

"Of course I will. I'll be healthy and wealthy. Then you'll not shirk to marry me."

She giggled. "Don't forget you promised me a portion of the money for the part I played. It's the only way I can get my children back from the farmer."

"Of course. Your part was crucial, dear. Had you not attended to that pesky Mr. Gibson, our little plan might've been cut down prematurely."

Ravenna squeezed her eyes shut. Mariah had killed Mr. Gibson! It explained the chain found at Mr. Gibson's and the stained locket in her wardrobe.

"I still have nightmares about it. Do they ever go away? The thoughts and bad dreams?"

"I suppose. I hardly think about Lord Thornley at all."

And the last piece of the puzzle clicked into place. Mr. McKirk and Mariah clearly had a past and an ongoing relationship. Mariah found out about the opal prior to the gala, probably through Reverend Howarth, who would've shared the information in his excitement. She then engaged Mr. McKirk to pose as a clergyman, not only be close to herself, but to get close to Lord Thornley and gain access to the opal. Mr. Gibson must have seen or heard something, so Mariah and McKirk believed it was necessary to kill him and silence him. They would then take the money to Napoleon in exchange for money and troops to aid The Unity and the rebellion and to get Mariah's children from the farmer. Nevertheless, she needed to give all this information to Chadwick as soon as possible so he could settle the matter of Thornley's murder once and for all and completely exonerate Yarford and Catherine.

Mariah and McKirk lingered a bit longer, then left the room. Ravenna waited, listening to be certain both had exited and that Reverend Howarth and the tour had passed by. She lay, her forehead on her hands, her mind in a whirl. She needed to get out of this house and find Mr. Chadwick. McKirk needed to be stopped immediately before the opal left English shores and fell into the hands of Napoleon. Even if the legend was nothing more than silly superstition, there remained the very real threat of another Irish uprising.

Chapter Thirty-Five

W hen Ravenna felt secure enough to leave Mariah's bedroom, she rolled out from under the bed and dusted off her dress. She cracked open the door and peeked out. All clear. She slipped out of the room and ran on tiptoes down the hall toward Reverend Howarth's booming voice.

She edged up behind the last person in the tour group and searched the crowd for Georgiana. She needed to leave this place immediately. The clock in the foyer struck nine-thirty.

The reverend said, "Well, I've kept you all long enough. I believe the women of The Penitent House have put together a little play for your enjoyment. Let's reconvene in the dining room, for this theatrical delight." The women nudged each other and giggled and ran off toward the dining room.

Ravenna grabbed Georgiana's arm. "I'm sorry, but we need to leave. I'm going to claim a headache and take you home."

Georgiana frowned. "But why? I want to see the play."

"Darling, I will take you to a dozen plays in a real theater. I can't explain at this moment, but it's very important for us to leave now."

Georgiana huffed. "Very well."

Holding Georgiana's hand, Ravenna approached Reverend Howarth. "Reverend..." He turned to her, his eyes lit with good cheer and a good heart. She hated lying to a man of the cloth, but it was necessary. *Please forgive me.* She put on a pained look. "I'm so sorry, Reverend. I would like nothing more than to enjoy the rest of the evening's festivities..." That part was not a lie. "But I've developed a horrible headache, so my niece and I need to leave."

Concern marked his features. "Oh, I am sorry to hear it, Lady Birchfield." He sandwiched her hand in his warm, soft hands. "But I will sing your praises for the rest of my days for the part you played in making this evening's festivities and this charity house possible. You cannot know how much happiness and joy your generous works have brought to this house and to the women here."

Guilt yawned inside her. "You're too kind, sir."

Within fifteen minutes, Ravenna and Georgiana climbed into their carriage and headed back to Gordon House. Miller assisted Georgiana to the stones.

Ravenna said to Miller, "Bring two oil lamps directly." Then she said to Georgiana, "Go inside. I will be home as soon as possible."

Georgiana turned, shocked. "You're not coming?"

"I have an important errand to run, which is why I had to leave."

"At this hour?"

"I know. It's highly unusual."

"But..."

"I apologize. I must go." Miller returned with the lamps turned low, and Ravenna hung them on the hooks in the corners.

Georgiana disappeared inside the house.

Ravenna said to Miller, "Take me to Mr. Chadwick's home. Bow Street." The carriage shifted as the footman climbed up beside the driver.

In a blink, the carriage door popped open. A man swept into the cab. Instinctively, Ravenna flipped the medallion on her fan and released her dagger as he closed the door.

The carriage jolted forward, heading toward Bow Street.

"Would you kill me after so long a separation? Is this punishment for not writing often enough?" He pushed back his hat to reveal his shocking blue eyes and the scar on his brow.

Her breath caught. *Braedon.* "What are you doing here? At this hour? And why did you frighten me half to death? Couldn't you have come at a better hour? Or, at the very least, you might've announced yourself."

He chuckled and pushed her blade away. "I would feel more at ease in this conversation if you would lower your weapon, my little raven."

"Sorry." She returned the blade to its home in the fan. "But you frightened me." She stared at him as if he might disappear like a ghost. "How...why... you..." She couldn't formulate a complete thought now. The shock of him suddenly being in her presence unraveled her. He was dressed in black pantaloons, a silver waistcoat, and a great coat. The spicy musk of his cologne reached out for her. The cab closed in on her, and the air inside grew thick and warm.

He laughed. "I think I'm witnessing a miracle. I've rendered you speechless. I will answer your questions eventually. However, it seems to me you're up to something far more pressing. And interesting. So, I must oblige you to tell me what you are doing."

Ravenna sighed. "Truth be told. I'm glad you're here. I hope you're armed?"

"Typically, I carry a pistol, especially when I travel; however, in my rush to see you, I have only the knife in my boot." He turned his foot outward to reveal the handle of a knife sticking out of the top of his boot. "Yet, my greatest question is why do you have need of a weapon?"

"A group of Irish rebels are meeting down at the Albishore dock in Southwark. I'm going now to notify Mr. Chadwick in hopes he can arrest them before they set sail."

His brows shot up. "My instincts were correct then." He grew serious. "How many rebels are there?"

"I don't know for certain."

He shook his head. "And how do you expect you won't get killed? Or worse?"

"I hadn't thought that far." They proceeded down Long Acre Street in Covent Garden. Loaded with coffee houses, theaters, taverns, and gaming hells, Covent buzzed with its usual nightlife of theater-goers, salep and pie vendors, pedestrians, prostitutes, ruffians, and pickpockets.

He moved to sit beside her. Cupping her face in his hands, he kissed her, hungrily. He pulled away and ran his eyes over her, his thumb stroking her cheek. "I can't tell you what a balm to my spirit it is to see you again."

She searched his face. "I'm glad you've returned." She grew warmer. Her nerves stuttered in fear at admitting the truth. "I've thought of you often. I've…" She grabbed his hands. "I've missed you. I'm so glad you're here." She leaned into another kiss, deep, probing.

When the carriage pulled to a stop in front of a red brick row house, Ravenna and Braedon broke their heated kiss and separated. Ravenna sent Miller to knock on Chadwick's door.

Eventually, the door opened. Mr. Chadwick looked in the direction of the carriage then approached. He opened the door and ran his eyes suspiciously over Braedon. "Lady Birchfield, this is most singular."

"Yes, I understand this is an unusual visit. I'm sorry to intrude on your evening, but I have something of great urgency to discuss with you. Please, come inside."

Braedon slid over to sit beside Ravenna. His closeness thrilled her. She longed to touch him, but refrained.

Chadwick glanced around, then stepped into the carriage and closed the door behind him. He was in his shirt sleeves, black ascot, green waistcoat, and black pantaloons. "Lord Braedon." The men nodded at each other and shook hands. Then he turned to Ravenna. "What brings you here at this hour, milady? You seem distressed."

She told him everything she'd heard in the conversation between McKirk and Mariah and how she'd heard the conversation. "McKirk is going to meet at the Albishore dock at midnight tonight. He stole the Widow's Fire opal when he killed Lord Thornley for it. I believe his lover, Mariah Vincent, is responsible for the death of Mr. Gibson." She told him what Mariah had said and about the blood-stained locket. She continued, "His plan is to carry the opal to France so he can sell it to Napoleon in exchange for money, arms, and troops. They're going to take the arms and troops to Ireland to start another rebellion. He's hoping to amass at least five thousand French troops in dribs and drabs." She clutched her folded fan. She could feel Braedon's intense, curious stare. She refused to look at him.

Chadwick sighed, licked his lips, and rubbed his gray stubbled chin. He hissed. "Demmed Jacobins. Why would Napoleon want this particular opal?"

She told him the legend of the opal. "Now, I'm not certain there's any truth to the claims of the stone's power. However, I've heard that Napoleon is a superstitious man and would pay an exorbitant price for a stone rumored to have powers to conquer nations and turn his enemies' wives into widows. That price will fund a rebellion against England to divide her forces and cause a distraction, thereby weakening her and making it easier for Napoleon to defeat England or invade her shores."

"Yes. I can see that." He nodded, thinking. "And where is this Mariah Vincent?"

"She's still at The Penitent House. She isn't aware I know anything, so she is resting in the assumption the plan will go forward uninterrupted."

He nodded again and glanced out the window. "Then I will gather reinforcements and go directly to Albishore to arrest this McKirk fellow to recover the opal." He faced her. "Do you know how many men I can expect to encounter?"

"I'm sorry, I don't."

He bit his lip. "Very well. I will round up as many men as I can find." He opened the carriage door and jumped to the stones. He turned. "Thank you, Lady Birchfield." He paused. "I must say, you've proven to be quite different than I at first expected." He closed the door and rushed inside his house.

How long would it take for him to round up assistance? Big Ben announced eleven o'clock, the strikes echoing through the still night air. Chadwick might not be able to gather enough men in so short a time. McKirk might need to be stalled—to buy time for Chadwick to arrive. She let out a nervous sigh. It fell to her and Braedon. She said to Miller, "Take us to Albishore dock. Make haste."

As the carriage rushed toward the Albishore dock, Braedon said, "I'm astonished at what you've encountered in my absence. I'm sorry I left you in such an entanglement. I'd like to hear more about this opal. Someday. But for the moment, what are we doing? Why are we going to Albishore docks?"

"We need to create a distraction and a delay so Mr. Chadwick has enough time to round up his men to make it to the docks and arrest the rebels."

"What sort of distraction and delay? What's your plan?"

"I don't have one yet. I'm hoping an idea will come to me."

As the carriage approached the Dancing Fiddler tavern, Ravenna beat on the roof, and the carriage rolled to a stop. Ravenna grabbed both lanterns, jumped out of the carriage, and handed a lantern to Braedon. "Keep the light turned low and come with me."

They ducked into the shadows near the opening of an alley.

"Perhaps this is too dangerous for you to be involved in," he said. "Why don't you let me handle this on my own?"

"I'm sure you're right, but I will not let you go in alone." She looked up and down the streets.

They slipped through the streets like shadows. As they neared the water, the air grew heavier with moisture, the scent of brine mingled with offal and coal. Large brick and wood structures rose up around them, blotting out the moon at various turns. They came out at the bank of the Thames near the West India docks at Blackwall Point, where the Albishore Mill docks stood. This was primarily an area where exports were loaded and sent to various colonies and countries. The water gurgled and lapped the walls of the embankment.

Ravenna pressed close to the brick wall and peeked around the corner. Ships, barques, schooners, and brigs of every type were tied along the docks, their naked masts pointing like needles against the night sky.

Braedon stood behind her and whispered, "What ship are we looking for?"

"I'm not certain, but I suspect they will not want to attract much attention."

"So probably a sloop and maybe a two-mast schooner. That's what I would opt for if I were a rebel trying to avoid attention. Nothing very big, but big enough to carry munitions."

They shielded their lights from potential onlookers and scurried like mice along the buildings at the edge of the dock. The buildings soon disappeared, replaced with scaffolds indicating new construction. That, too, soon disappeared, and they were faced with open land descending toward the banks of the river.

In the distance, Ravenna noticed a still light and a bobbing light. "That could be them," she whispered, pointing toward the lights.

"What do we do now?"

"I don't know. Perhaps if we created a distraction of some sort. Then, one of us could push the boat away from shore. At least it would delay them long enough for the Bow Street Runners to arrive."

An idea came to her. "Here's what we will do. I'll cause the distraction and try to lead the men away. While I'm doing that, you cut the boat loose and push it into the water."

"I can't allow you to do this. To pretend you're a prostitute? Perhaps you should stay here, and I'll try to lead the men away."

"I'd never get the boat into the water. I'm not strong enough." She worked at pinning up the front of her dress with a brooch to reveal her shins. "Can you think of anything better?"

He sighed and looked away, biting his lip. He shook his head. "No."

"Then this is what we'll do. Both tasks have their perils, but I think you'll have the better ability to manage the boat." She pinched her cheeks to make them appear rouged and tugged her bodice down to reveal more of her bosom.

"I don't like this," Braedon hissed, sneaking off toward the shoreline.

Swaggering, she approached the men walking back and forth between the cart and the boat. She turned up the light on her lamp. "Hey-ho, gents." She smiled and ran the tip of her folded fan along the top of her low-set bodice. Then, men stopped in their tracks. She counted four men. They looked at each other, then looked around.

"Who're you?" One of the men said.

"Who I am isn't important," she said in seductive tones. "What is important is I have a bevy of women younger and prettier than me in a house just up there. They're quite lonely and looking for attention from powerful men like yourselves."

A couple of the men smiled.

A voice from the water shouted. "What're ye doin'?"

One of the men shouted over his shoulder. "There's a bit o'skirt here offering her charms."

Ravenna giggled. "No, poppet. Not *my* charms. The madam never involves herself in the trade. Besides, when you see my beautiful girls, you won't want me anyway."

One of the men snorted. "Girls wot all got the pox, I wager."

A shadow emerged from the shore as Braedon's shadow slipped near the sloop. As the shadowy man came closer, the light revealed Mr. McKirk. He was dressed like an impoverished fisherman instead of his clergyman's clothes. For fear of being recognized, she popped open her fan and hid her face behind it. She struggled to keep her voice steady. "Oh no, poppet. *My* girls don't have the pox. They're new to the trade. And you'll get all the wine and claret you desire. For a price."

McKirk narrowed his eyes. "Go ply your flesh trade elsewhere, strumpet. We have work here." He was all seriousness. Then he said to the men, "Get back to work."

One of the men said, "It's been weeks since we've had any diversion. Maybe we can visit this fine lady's establishment for a while and then finish our work."

"There'll be plenty of women and pleasure when our work is done." McKirk glowered at the men. "Time is of the essence. We have important work to do. The tides won't favor us much longer."

The men grumbled and returned to pulling munitions out of the cart as McKirk said to Ravenna. "Woman, be gone. We don't have time for your distractions."

"Are you certain? I have—"

Before she could finish her thought, he picked up a river rock and threw it at her, striking her in the hip.

"Ouch!"

He bent to gather up another stone. Behind the men, a flare of light and the scent of burning wood filled the air. McKirk, poised to throw the rock, stopped. He sniffed the air, turned, dropped the rock, and ran toward the water where all the men stood, awestruck, staring at the sloop that had drifted away from the bank, its bow streaked with flames.

Ravenna searched the shoreline. Where was Braedon? At last, she spotted a low shadow slinking away toward the buildings.

"How...What?" McKirk shouted. "Get the boat! Get it! Put out the flames!"

She hadn't planned for the boat to be set aflame, but it was a nice touch. Lamp in hand, Ravenna rushed toward Braedon's shadow. They ran toward the docks. She wished she'd taken the time to change into her black pants. Though the skirt of her dress was pinned up away from her shins, the material still snaked around and between her legs. Further, having her skirts pulled up made her feel naked and exposed.

McKirk shouted. "You!"

Ravenna glanced over her shoulder. McKirk ran toward them as his men piled into the water to capture the boat. He ran inhumanly fast. He launched himself on Braedon and knocked him to the ground. Ravenna put down the lamp and threw herself on top of McKirk, clinging to his back, her fingers knotted in his hair as though she were trying to break a stubborn horse. Her weight seemed meaningless to him as he pounded Braedon's face bloody. She was surprised at the amount of power his lean form contained, although he was smaller than Braedon. She shouted between gasps of air, "Leave him alone! Stop it now!"

She flicked the medallion on her fan and released the blade. She lifted her arm and stabbed him in the shoulder.

McKirk bellowed and bucked up. He reached around, grabbed her by the hair and shoulder, and tossed her to the ground as though she weighed no more than a sack of flour. The wind knocked out of her, Ravenna gasped for air and, coughing, rolled to push herself up to her hands and knees.

McKirk paused to grab the blade and ripped it from his shoulder. Braedon rose up and slammed McKirk to the ground. He forced Ravenna's dagger from McKirk's hand, then set upon him with ferocity, delivering blows to his face and ribs. McKirk grabbed a stone and whacked Braedon in the side of the head.

Braedon grunted, grabbed his head, and fell to the side, rolling back and forth.

McKirk scrambled backwards, coughing, groaning, and spitting out blood. He stood, stone still in hand, and wiped his face with the back of his hand. He glared at Ravenna. "You've ruined everything."

Braedon eased to his feet, swaying and shaking his head. He pulled the knife from his boot.

McKirk rushed Ravenna.

Braedon jumped between them, slashing the air.

A shot sounded, and McKirk stopped in his tracks and lifted his hands.

A voice behind Ravenna said, "Back away. Slowly."

Ravenna spun away and ran to grab her dagger. Chadwick. He aimed his flintlock pistol right at McKirk, and behind him stood at least five other men, all with their pistols drawn. Relief rushed over her. *Thank heavens!* She rolled her eyes upward to look at the stars.

Holding McKirk at gunpoint, Chadwick said, "You two should go home now." He pushed between Ravenna and Braedon, instructed McKirk to turn around and walk toward the scene where mayhem had broken out between the rebels and the pack of Bow Street Runners that had set upon them.

Chapter Thirty-Six

Ravenna and Braedon dragged their beaten bodies back to the carriage. They stood under the gas lamp on the street corner as she inspected the side of his head where McKirk had struck him with a stone. She dabbed at his temple with a handkerchief as he winced. "There's no blood at least. But I suspect you'll be well-bruised. Your face, unfortunately…" She let her voice trail off as she looked at his swollen, bloody mouth and the cut under his eye. "He must've been wearing a ring to cut you so." She pressed the handkerchief to his eye. "I'll dress your wounds when we get back to Gordon House."

They returned to Gordon House. She led him to the drawing-room, lit a few candles, and poured two glasses of port. "Wait here. I need to change and get my medicine chest. I won't be long." She handed him a glass and set hers on the tea table.

Ravenna ran upstairs to her bedchamber. She quickly inspected her face and body and fortunately had no open wounds, but her dress was torn. She washed the dirt from her hands and face and changed into a nightdress and lilac dressing gown. She retrieved her medicine chest and returned to the drawing room, where Braedon sat on the sofa. He had removed his coats and ascot and lounged in his shirt sleeves and waistcoat as if he were lord of the house.

Her stomach fluttered. She sat beside him and opened her medicine chest. She washed his wounds with vinegar water and applied chamomile ointment to his injuries. He sipped his wine. "Thank you. I'm so glad to see you've not changed. You're still as beautiful as when I left for Italy."

"There have been a few changes here, though." She told him all about Georgiana and Harrison and some of the drama visited upon Gordon House in the last few weeks.

He shook his head. "Sounds like quite the melodrama. I look forward to meeting your niece." He kissed the back of her hand. He continued holding her hand, running his thumb over her fingers. "I have missed you terribly, painfully."

She squeezed his hand. "I missed you, too. But I must ask, why are you here so soon? Why didn't you tell me you were coming home?"

He sighed, touched the corner of his mouth where it was swelling. "Well, had I known that I'd be beaten on my first night back, I might've stayed away longer." He drank from his wine, then tried to smile. He sucked in his breath and touched his swollen mouth.

"Sincerely. I want an honest answer. I expected you to be gone much longer."

"Lucky for me, Lady Fortune and Dianthe's erratic fancies freed me from my obligations. You see, said lady absconded with an Italian count. They are currently, who knows where and, there are rumors, she might be with child." He shrugged. "All I know is I am free of her. Her uncle arrived in Italy to console her addled mother and to search for her."

Ravenna sat back in the corner of the sofa with her wine. "Your relationship with Dianthe confuses me. On the one hand, you seem obligated to her. On the other you seem to almost detest her. I don't understand it." She narrowed her eyes. "I get the distinct feeling there's something you're not telling me."

He sighed and stared into his glass, swirling his wine. "I confess, there is something I haven't told you. Something I have wished to keep private, but I fear I won't be able to for much longer. Further, where you are concerned, I don't want to keep secrets from you."

Ravenna frowned and steeled herself for what he would say next.

"It's true, Dianthe and I have a...*special* sort of bond."

"Oh," she said, dejected. "I see."

"Not like you might think. You see..." He rubbed his forehead and ran his fingers through his unruly hair. "Dianthe and I have a child together."

Her stomach dropped as though the floor fell out from under her, and she was set afloat in mid-air. "I-I-had no idea. I don't know what to say."

He nodded. "She and I had an *affaire de coeur*. It was heated, but short-lived. As such, things generally are. But, she bore the fruit of our passions."

"How old is the child?"

"About a year. A little girl, pretty and spirited."

"Where is she? As often as I've seen Dianthe and her family, I've never seen a child."

"Dianthe's family placed the child in a nunnery. As often happens in these situations where one is unprepared to care for a child and the other is incapable."

Ravenna lifted a brow. "Which are you?"

"I'm the thoroughly unprepared one. For now. My estate is an ancient abbey, full of structural problems in need of repair, and the work goes slowly. However, as soon as the repairs are completed, it's my greatest wish to move her Rushingwood and be a perfect father for her. Dianthe, for her part, is absolutely incapable in spirit, body, and mind to care for a child. Her attachment to laudanum makes it impossible. Further, her parents seek to protect her reputation by keeping the child a secret as long as possible."

"Incredible. What's your daughter's name?"

"Constantina Rose."

"Pretty name. Do you see her often?"

"About once a week. I would like it to be more."

"Doesn't Dianthe ever see her?"

"To my knowledge, Dianthe hasn't seen the child since a few weeks after she was born. Dianthe is a selfish creature, thinking only of herself and her own desires."

"How sad."

"It is. Yet, the nuns have been very good to Constantina. She seems happy."

"That's a blessing, but regardless of how good and kind the nuns are, they are not the same as the child's mother."

He nodded. "That's true." He sighed and reached for Ravenna's hand,

and slid his fingers between hers. "So, you see, that is why I have remained entangled with Dianthe and her interests. That is why I felt obliged to take her to Italy to help her eradicate the hold the laudanum has on her. I have failed over and over. Now that she's run off with another man, I can officially wash my hands of her. I will do my best to help Constantina grow up protected and loved." He kissed the back of Ravenna's hand. "And I make you the same promise. If you'll have me."

It all made sense now. His secrecy, his unexplained attachment to Dianthe, his entanglement with her long after their affair was over. Of everything Ravenna had witnessed of late, it was clear Dianthe was trying her best to win him back into her arms, to resume their affair, and perhaps snare him into a marriage. Ravenna couldn't fault Dianthe. In fact, she almost felt sorry for her. Dianthe must feel desperate: her lover gone, her child in a nunnery, and her reputation only a word away from complete devastation, hurting forever any chances she might have of making a good match and future for herself.

"Why did you never marry Dianthe and give your child a complete home?"

He scoffed. "At first, I tried. And her parents tried to force the match. We became engaged. But Dianthe is half-lunatic. She caused scenes. Imagined affairs where I had none and, in a jealous fit, would sleep with other men to provoke my jealousy. The first couple of times, it worked. But I grew tired of fighting unwitting men ensnared in her games. I grew tired of her games. So, I tried to break it off. But Dianthe continues to pursue and provoke."

"What a trying ordeal."

He chuckled. "I hope you understand now my actions? And my frustrations? And my desperation to completely break from Dianthe?"

"I do. I understand it all." But could she disregard it? What sort of complications would she invite into her life if she dared entangle herself with Braedon. Would Dianthe be content with her new life with her Italian count? Or would Dianthe find a reason to torment her and Braedon?

Braedon pulled her close, wrapping his free arm around her. "I don't want to talk about her anymore. Never again, if I can help it. I want to talk only of you, me. Us. Give me one sign, something to allow me to hope for a future with *us*."

Ravenna studied him, searched his poor bruised face, his blue eyes. She marked only sincerity. She squeezed his hand. With a faint smile, she leaned forward and lightly kissed his cheek.

Chapter Thirty-Seven

The next morning, during breakfast, Ravenna sat at her desk, the gray light of a misty morning lighting her way. In spite of trying to focus on writing letters, she found her mind returning again and again to Braedon: the shock of his return and his confession, the relief of having him back in London. She sipped her tea and nibbled at her pound cake with fresh strawberries.

As she finished off her breakfast, a knock sounded at her door. A maid entered and announced, "Mr. Chadwick to see you, milady. He's in the drawing room."

He was particularly early and well out of the acceptable hours for visiting. "Tell him I'll be down directly." She had already dressed but hadn't finished her toilette, so she splashed a bit of rose water on her face and neck and knotted her hair in a loose chignon. She jogged down the stairs and entered the drawing room.

Chadwick stood at the window, looking down at the street. When she entered, he turned. "Good morning, milady." He removed his hat. He was dressed in his dark blue suit with a red waistcoat and black ascot. He bowed.

"Good morning. I'm surprised by your early visit, sir. You must rise with the roosters." She smiled.

He smiled as he sat in the chair across from her. "Quite. The wicked never rest, so I suppose I shan't be allowed to either."

"May I offer you refreshment?"

He shook his head. "No, I've just finished breakfast, and I shan't keep you long."

"I trust all the rebels were rounded up?"

"Indeed, they were. Which was why I wanted to visit. To thank you and Lord Braedon for the role you played. I trust he is not too badly injured?"

"He's a little beaten, a cut below the eye, a bruised temple, and a bruised and swollen mouth. But otherwise, he's well."

"I'm glad to hear it." He shifted to cross one leg over the other. "We have also arrested the woman, Mariah Vincent."

Ravenna deflated a little. She had liked Mariah and had entertained high hopes for her reformation. She'd seemingly been a good role model and influence for the other women at The Penitent House.

He tipped his head, studying her. "You don't seem happy to hear that news."

She sighed. "I'm sad to have been fooled by her. She had, in many ways, been a good leader and example for the other women. And many of the women looked up to her. Now I worry for them. Who will lead them and guide them to a better life?"

He nodded. "I understand. It must be a hardship for them."

She didn't want to talk about Mariah any longer. "Were you able to recover the Widow's Fire opal?"

"Yes. McKirk had it on him."

"What will happen to it?"

"I will take it to the king today. It wouldn't surprise me if it eventually lands in the British Museum with so many other archaeological discoveries."

"At least it won't be in Napoleon's hands. Why can't it be returned to its homeland."

"That would be far too expensive, and then we run the risk of losing it forever should the ship sink. Perhaps it's not ideal that it should've ended up on our shores, but it will be well preserved for posterity."

"That's a kindness of a sort, I suppose."

"We've also arrested Robert Emmett. I received word this morning. He was taken into custody last night and is currently sitting in prison in Dublin."

"I imagine he'll be hanged."

He frowned. "He'll stand trial first. If he's found guilty of treason, which is highly likely, he will, indeed, hang. They all will hang for the role they played in the attempted rebellion."

"Mariah, too?"

He nodded. "It's likely."

Ravenna's throat constricted as if the ghost of a noose slipped around her own neck. Another time, in different circumstances, it might've been herself to step on the scaffold. Her stomach twisted. It weighed heavy on her to think she had a hand in these people, her own countrymen, in going to the scaffold.

Chadwick said, "I think King George will be thrilled with your and Lord Braedon's bravery and courage in catching the rebels and recovering the opal. I'm sure you will be richly rewarded."

"No!" She cringed. She'd said sharper than she'd intended. And it grabbed his attention. He narrowed his eyes. She didn't want any attention—especially from government officials who might dig into her past and discover her own treason. She backed up. "I'm sorry. I didn't mean to speak harshly. As I've told you before, I'd rather not have any such attention. I would much rather you and your men take the credit for the arrest and the recovery of the opal."

"If you wish, madam. Though, I must say I find it singular."

"Yes. I'm finding that is the prevailing opinion of me lately."

He stood with a sigh. "Then let me say on behalf of the king, England, and The Crown are grateful to you for your service. Even though I do not understand why you would turn away fortune and accolades and posterity." He held out his hand.

She accepted it. He shook her hand. "It's an honor and a pleasure to know you, Lady Birchfield. You are braver than many men I've known. If lady-Runners were allowed at Bow Street, I might consider hiring you."

She laughed. "Sir, I think I would make a poor Bow Street Runner, but I understand your sentiment, and thank you for the compliment."

"Should you need anything, milady, do not hesitate to reach out to me."

"All I wish at the moment is for you to deliver the good news to Adair House and Thornley Manor to put their minds at ease."

CHAPTER THIRTY-SEVEN

"I will indeed."

She stood at the window, looking down at the street, watching Mr. Chadwick walk away. Hopefully, for the last time. Yet, uneasiness rippled over her. Though he had caught the rebels, how many of The Unity were still free? How many were still hunting her and her brother, Niall? When would they strike again?

Only moments after Mr. Chadwick left Gordon House, Lord Braedon arrived.

"You look frightful," Ravenna said, touching his swollen cheek gently.

"It looks worse than it feels." His lip was still red and swollen, the skin around his eye had purpled some, the cut was healing nicely. "I thought you might want to take a ride in the park."

She glanced out the window. The mist had cleared, but the dull skies remained. "It looks like rain."

He smiled, an impish gleam in his eyes. "Yes, but isn't that the stuff of novels where a woman is caught in the rain with the man who has caught her interest? And he must sweep her away to an abandoned cottage nearby where any number of things might happen to her reputation."

She smiled. "The presumption!" She laughed. "To think *you* are the man who has caught my interest. I'd sooner take shelter in said cottage and lock the door, leaving you out to soak."

He stepped closer and touched a dark, glossy tendril. "I know you jest." He ran his fingers around the side of her neck, cupping her cheek.

Goosebumps covered her skin as a thrill shot through her, but she continued to smile up at him. The moment was becoming too serious, his gaze too intense. She was in danger. "You might think I jest, but—"

The door popped open, and Ravenna jumped away from Braedon. Keene rushed into the room, pink-faced, breathing heavily. "Milady," she panted. "Milady." She began rattling off a slurry of words Ravenna could hardly comprehend with Keene's thick accent.

Ravenna held up her hand. "Keene. Stop. I can't understand you. What's the matter?"

Keene took a deep breath. She tried to speak slower, but her voice shook under the strain. The longer she spoke, the faster her words poured out. "I've just found this note. I thought Miss Georgiana was sleeping too late, so I became worried. I carried up her breakfast. I was going to wake her and help her dress. But she weren't there."

"What do you mean she wasn't there?" Ravenna tried to shove down the panic bubbling up inside. "Maybe she went shopping or for a ride in the park?"

"No'm. That weren't it at all." She shoved a note at Ravenna. "She's run away."

"Run away?" Ravenna snatched the paper from Keene's hand.

Dear Auntie,

I'm leaving. I can no longer stay in a house where the man I love is not welcome. So he and I are eloping. By the time you read this, I will likely be styled ...

Mrs. Josiah Emmett

Ravenna clapped her hand over her forehead. "Stupid girl. I can't believe this! Mr. Emmett of all people!"

"What's the matter?" Braedon said, taking the note and reading it. "I haven't had the pleasure of meeting either of these people, but I see it certainly distresses you. For that, I'm sorry. What can I do?"

"I told you the story last night. My niece, Georgiana, is convinced she loves him."

"Young people have often eloped—"

"No, you don't understand. First, I want something better for her than an elopement with a scoundrel. Second, his brother, Robert, was just arrested for collaborating with France to foment another rebellion in Ireland. Josiah may well be a rebel, too."

Braedon grew serious. "I see. Terrible news, indeed."

"They must've gone to Gretna Green. It's the only place they can get married without reading the banns."

"Of course."

"Then I must go. I must find her. I cannot allow this marriage to take place. If he's discovered to be a rebel, I won't have her implicated in his crimes. Nor will I have her become a young widow." She started for the door. "I'm sorry, but I must go. I can't ride with you in the park."

"Correction, dear. *We* must go. I'm going with you." He followed behind her. "I'll go this instant to prepare my bags, and I'll return directly. I don't need much."

"Please. There's no need to involve yourself in this."

"There are all manner of miscreants, bandits, and ruffians on the road between here and Scotland. You will need protection. You may be well-suited to poke people with your little dagger on occasion, but it will not be enough."

"Braedon—"

He grabbed her arm. "Ravenna, how could I live with myself if anything happened to you when I might've been there to prevent it? Now that I'm home, I refuse to be separated from you again. I'm going with you."

In one fell swoop part of her hope for her future was swept away as another entered, like an ocean wave receding as another crashed ashore. Searching Braedon's face, the determination in his eyes, she could not deny him and, what's more, she didn't want to. She welcomed his assistance. She was tired of bearing the burden alone. She was going to find Georgiana and rebuild her family. And, if all went well, Braedon would be a part of her rebuilding efforts. His presence brought her relief and buoyed her spirits, carrying her forward to a new hope, and a new life.

A Note from the Author

As with the first book, *Widow's Blush,* this book was inspired by actual history.

The Irish Unity written about in this series is entirely a creation of my own. Though inspired by the many factions fighting the British Crown in the late Georgian Era, it is *not* based on the real United Irish organization of history.

Ireland has a complicated history where some have wanted unity with Great Britain and some have not. Some of the factions were Protestant, some were Catholic, and some were a combination of faiths. Some were loosely organized, barely more than a street gang, while some were highly organized.

Naturally, these varying alliances divided communities and families. While the British government did violently suppress the 1798 rebellion, homegrown violence was not unusual. Some of the rebel factions committed regular attacks against each other as they fought for supremacy, and innocent people were often caught in the middle. I touched on this complicated system through Ravenna and her family and will likely expound on it in the next book.

One figure in this book is loosely based on a real-life Irish rebel by the name of Robert Emmet. (I spelled the character's name Emmett, in the book).

The real Emmet was born in 1778 and, though he was 20 years old when the Irish colluded with the French to overthrow Britain, he did not participate in the 1798 uprising. After the rebellion was suppressed by British troops with extreme violence, Emmet was instrumental in helping to re-establish the United Irish organization. As a Catholic republican, he wanted to overthrow the British Crown and the Protestants, who were often Loyalists, in hopes of building an independent Irish Republic modeled on the United States' constitutional republic. The innerworkings of his revolutionary enterprise are too complicated to discuss here, but, in short, his attempts to bring an uprising in Dublin in 1803 fell apart. He was captured on August 25, 1803 and executed for treason.

I took authorly license with Emmet's life and timeline to better fit the story in *Widow's Fire.* In my book, he was caught earlier in August. Further, his real brother's name was Thomas. Since Thomas is the name of Ravenna's stepson, I had to opt for another name. So, in this story, Emmet's brother became Josiah.

Finally, a word on the giant black opal recovered by Lord Franklin Thornley. In the book, the giant opal hails from New South Wales, which is what we now know as Australia. The giant opal in the story is based on the Aurora Australis, a precious black opal only slightly smaller than a goose egg at about 180 carats and 3 inches by 1.8 inches (a goose egg approximates 3.3 inches by 2.2 inches). The Aurora was discovered in 1938, not 1802, in Lightning Ridge, Australia by Charlie Dunstan. The Aurora is not the largest opal in the world; that title goes to Olympic Australis, which goes down in the *Guinness Book of World Records* as the largest and most valuable precious opal discovered to date.

The Aurora is currently valued at around one million dollars, and, as far as I know, does not carry a powerful curse.

I chose a giant opal because these gems are by their nature beautiful and mysterious. Could there be any gem better suited to hold a curse? And I wanted to use such a relic to highlight Napoleon's very real superstitious character. For instance, he believed his first wife, Josephine, brought him good luck, so he always carried a miniature portrait of her. If he dropped the portrait or damaged it, he believed bad luck would beset him. He also had a particular "lucky star," which he would seek out in the sky.

1803 was a time when people believed in ghosts, fairies, witches, and vampires, so Napoleon wouldn't have been considered unusually superstitious for his time. However, viewed through our modern lens, his beliefs might seem a tad eccentric and I wanted to play with that a little.

For me, the thought of having a beautiful opal imbued with supernatural powers was too much to resist. Even if a bit fantastical, it is my greatest hope that you will enjoy the little tale I spun around some real history. And, as always, Happy Reading!

Acknowledgements

I thank God in everything, always. I could do nothing without Him.

I'm thankful to a few key people who make my books possible:

Dawn Dowdle, who is, unfortunately, no longer with us. I really miss your guidance and support. You opened the door for me and I'll always be thankful for that.

Shawn Simmons and the wonderful team at Level Best for all your hard work and patience.

Carmen Erickson, the absolute best writing buddy who's always there for the good, the bad, and the ugly.

Hallie Lee, I'm so thankful you're in my life. I look forward to many more brunch dates, book fairs, and helping each other navigate the writing life.

The continued love and support from my husband, family, friends, and readers is everything to me. I could do none of this without you. You know who you are by now, but I want to remind you of how precious you are to me.

About the Author

Born and raised in the beautiful Bluegrass state of Kentucky, Michelle Bennington developed a passion for books early on that has since progressed into a mild hoarding situation and an ever-growing to-read pile. She delights in transporting readers into worlds of mystery, both contemporary and historical.

In rare moments of spare time, she can be found engaging in a wide array of arts and crafts, reading, traveling, and attending tours involving ghosts, historical homes, or distilleries.

AUTHOR WEBSITE:
www.michellebennington.com

SOCIAL MEDIA HANDLES:
https://x.com/MichelleAuthor
https://www.facebook.com/michelle.bennington.7
https://www.instagram.com/michelle.bennington.author/

Also by Michelle Bennington

Contemporary mystery series

Small Batch Mysteries:
  Devil's Kiss
  Mermaid Cove
  Unbridled Spirits

Hazardous Hoarding series
  Dumpster Dying

Historical mystery series

Widows & Shadows Mysteries
  Widow's Blush

www.ingramcontent.com/pod-product-compliance
Lightning Source LLC
Chambersburg PA
CBHW020353110726
47899CB00006B/1705